Praise for *Behind the Locked Door*

"David Jones is one of the great thinkers and writers of northern California. He pours his intellect and life experience into *Behind the Locked Door*. Run, don't walk, to devour it, and be ready to be consumed."

—Gary Evans, former World Bank economist and
financial advisor to the Republic of Poland

"It requires exceptional skill to twist a thought to express a sensation, a tender emotion. David has that skill... to create a mood, a reality, a truth made from illusions."

—James Maxwell, painter, sculptor, graphic designer,
and author of *My Ghosts*

"Jones has delighted us for years with his blog www.thinkinthemorning. com. Now, in his engaging first work of fiction, he takes readers to Mexico as a young man searches for the gift of healing."

—Katy M. Tahja, author of *An Eclectic History of
Mendocino County, 1852–2002*

"What a treat! I've followed David's blog and travels, and now am delighted to be able to fully immerse myself in the richness of his imagination, truth telling, and talent. Hurray—and more, please!"

—Susan B. Wood, artist and "teller" of the
secrets of an amazing, aging, single, woman artist

"David Jones has chosen a difficult subject: the story of a desperate 'everyman' grasping at any straw (Laetrile, in this case) in hopes of surviving his incurable cancer. Set in Mexico, the novel is liberally sprinkled with indigenous mysticism and surreal interludes, enhancing the story and helping make *Behind the Locked Door* a wonderful read."

—Gil Gevins, author of *1967: The Autumn of Post-Coital Despair*

"In this genre-bending ode to his much-loved older brother, who died of cancer at a young age, David Jones has imagined an inner and outer life for a dying man. Imagine a gritty tale of intrigue, international crime and corruption and the harshest, cruelest, most savage details of high-tech medical reality merged with the slippery, elusive, shimmering world of shamans, visions, totems, and magical realism, a tale populated with a full cast of characters, some of whom—gangsters, hucksters, crooked politicians—resemble walking, talking cancer cells, while others—a native healer, an obsessively principled eccentric scientist, a sweet, beautiful love interest, an enlightened Catholic priest—put us in mind of powerful immune cells channeling the primal forces of life. The reader ponders the age-old philosophical question: Do we dream that we are awake, or are we awake when we are dreaming? And is there a difference?"
—Eleanor Cooney, author of *Death in Slow Motion*
and *Midnight in Samarra*

"From a dying brother's letter of despair and hope, David Jones creates a harrowing mix of humanity and inhumanity; love and terror; medical madness and mirages of miracles. The searing journey the author imagines for his brother compels readers to confront profound questions of how life is best lived and death best met.
—Jeffrey Amestoy, Former Chief Justice, Vermont Supreme Court
and author, *Slavish Shore: The Odyssey of Richard Henry Dana Jr.*

Behind the Locked Door

David Herstle Jones

Think in the Morning

Behind the Locked Door

Think in the Morning
www.thinkinthemorning.com

Cover design by Cypress House/ Charles Hathaway
Book design by Cypress House

With thanks to Cypress House for their help
in bringing this book to fruition.

Lyrics to *Moonshadow* by Cat Stevens used
by permission of Hal Leonard.

Lyrics to *Crazy* by Willie Nelson used by
permission of Hal Leonard.

Excerpt from *The Evil Garden* is reprinted courtesy
of the Edward Gorey Charitable Trust.

ISBN: 978-0-578-58955-8
E-book ISBN: 978-0-578-58956-5

Library of Congress Control Number: 2019917037

Printed in the United States of America

2 4 6 8 9 7 5 3 1

First edition

I dedicate this book to my brother, Errol Miller,
my rock in life and death, that his memory will never die.

Living is only a dream and experience teaches me that a man who is living dreams what he is until he awakens.
—Calderon de la Barca, *Life is a Dream*

Recordar es vivir.
—Antonio Reyes

Acknowledgments

This book had a long gestation period. The idea first occurred to me in 1972, and I began to research in earnest in December of 2010. I first put pen to paper in Zihuatanejo, Mexico, in January 2011. Much of the book was written in Oaxaca, Mexico, over several years while I stayed at the beautiful Casa de las Bugambilias, where the friendly and attentive staff went out of their way to create an atmosphere conducive to my work. Parts of the book were completed in Puerto Vallarta, Mexico, and in Mendocino, California.

I had some professional assistance with the book, but the final product represents my work, errors and all. I won't mention names so as not to ruin reputations. What I will say is, without the generous help of many other writers this book would lack whatever merits it possesses. I have been influenced by a number of authors, especially Ambrose Bierce (*The Incident at Owl Creek Bridge*), Jorge Borges (*The Secret Miracle*), David Dephy (*Before the End*), Tobias Wolff (*Bullet in the Brain*), Abram Tertz (aka Andrei Sinyavsky, *Fantastic Tales*), D. H. Lawrence (*Mornings in Mexico*), Ken Kesey (*One Flew Over the Cuckoo's Nest*), and Oliver Sacks (*Hallucinations*). Obviously none of them is responsible for anything I put in print.

Along the way I trusted the manuscript to many friends—especially John Porter, Terry Johnson, Marlene Hall, and Mitchell Zucker—whose substantive comments made this book better than it would otherwise have been.

Cathy, my wife, offered patience, understanding, and encouragement, especially during the bleak times when the inevitable writer's block darkened my mood. I can only imagine how difficult it was to live with me then. I'm lucky to have had Cathy's generous love throughout the many years I've been consumed with this all too personal and selfish project, and I am grateful to have it still.

Part I

1.

Somewhere in Tijuana

1972

After the accident, Louie Frieze could hardly walk from the kitchen to his workshop. He started working later and had to stop earlier. His house was always dark. Any casual observer would assume it was vacant. The garden was overgrown, the paint was peeling off the walls, there was no dog on the front porch, and the birdcage that hung from the beam by the front door was empty and rusting. The Mexicans left Frieze alone, though if asked, people would say that "the Frenchman" lived in the cheerless house at the end of the winding street.

Marcos, the idiot boy who roamed the neighborhood, believed Frieze was *El Diablo* because you could sometimes see fires burning through his windows. Everyone just laughed when Marcos told them. Mrs. Martinez, always curious, noticed the trucks coming and going and the boxes being loaded and unloaded, but she threw her hands up if anyone asked what she saw—she had a strict rule of never letting anyone know what she knew.

Frieze was in a fine mood despite the lingering pain from his burns. There is no pleasure without pain. That is a great truth. He had a box packed and ready, expecting Ana Luisa to arrive with her Indian driver. She worked with the local *curanderas,* the ones who

1

had received *el don,* the gift of healing. They served the poor Indians living in the hills and mountain villages. They helped the migrant Mexicans who arrived from the southern states in search of a better life. Even foreigners who were desperate for something exotic to cure the incurable would sometimes seek out their services.

Frieze was taking a box of apricot pits to the grinder when he heard the knock. He put the box on a table, walked silently to the door, and bent down to look through the small eyehole he had installed. It was Ana Luisa.

"Ah, *bonjour,* come in," he said as he unlatched and opened the door.

"*¿Cómo está, Señor* Frieze?"

"Speak *Anglais,* Ana. You know I cannot understand *Espagnol.*" He spoke with a sour disposition.

"Not even something as simple as 'How are you?' Everyone knows that."

"Not even that, Ana. Did anyone follow you?"

"No one, Louie. I always take every precaution."

Ana brought some warmth into the cold world of Louie Frieze. They were nearly the same age, but Ana looked much younger, with her chestnut-colored hair clipped short and large brown eyes in the shape of almonds. She kept her skin guarded from the sun. It was unwrinkled, soft and smooth. A simple gray skirt encircled her slender waist. Her ample bosom was wrapped in a blue cotton blouse splashed with pink and purple flowers and green leaves. These details did not go unnoticed by Louie Frieze. She kept the collar open around her neck. Tiny fluted gold earrings hung down on long stems like honeysuckle flowers and bobbled about her head. Black patent-leather pumps added an inch to her height, but she still had to look up at Frieze, who noted the splash of pink on her eyelids.

Ana's presence softened Frieze's stern countenance; his chiseled, expressionless, stone-like features came alive. The deep creases about his eyes, forehead, and jaw began to move in ways that highlighted the intricate connections between muscle, flesh, and bone—connections normally hidden in a man whose entire life was a riddle.

Ana stepped aside as the gangly chemist rushed out the door. Lanky, but with an emerging paunch and the wide flat feet of a duck, Frieze lumbered awkwardly onto the porch. He cocked his head and smelled the air like a wild deer prancing here and there, searching for any danger that might lurk in the shadows. He didn't speak until he was satisfied and had stepped back inside.

"Ze box is ghready to go. Have your Indian driver come in and carry it to ze Jeep."

His thick French accent made Ana smile. She quietly observed the peculiar mess that enveloped Frieze's workshop. She knew the rest of his house was no better. A foul chemical odor hovered over beakers and vials strewn haphazardly on the shelves; metal pots large and small sat on Bunsen burners, and the ugly old gas stovetop waited to be ignited into action. Boxes, seemingly in no particular order, packed and unpacked, hid in the corners with the dust and the spider webs. There were jumbled heaps of apricot pits that Frieze used to make his serum.

It was for this secret potion that Ana had come, a magic elixir that offered an escape from the grasping tentacles of the demon first named *karkinos* by the ancient Greeks; the black crab with its fearsome claws and crushing pincers—the disease we now call cancer, that brought terrifying visions of mutant rats scurrying through the blood in deadly hordes. After years of experiments, Frieze had perfected a serum that chased the rats away like Heracles with his club, eradicating them with crushing blows.

"You really need a housekeeper, Louie."

Frieze's face turned grim. Myriad hopes and sorrows had etched their way permanently into his skin. Disappointments and tragedies lay deep. He scowled at Ana Luisa as he spoke.

"Euh? What? No, I don't."

"I know a fine Mexican woman who would love to have the job. I could send her by this afternoon. She would make your life so much easier."

The vicissitudes of time had taken their toll on Frieze and left him worn and frayed like his faded blue boiler suit.

3

"Ah haw! Woman? Easier? Hire her to clean your own house if she need a job. I am getting on just fine."

Frieze had met Ana Luisa through Father Jordan. Frieze didn't bother with the unanswerable questions. He didn't dwell on his eternal inadequacies or try to explain life. He didn't go to church. He'd met Jordan at the time he delivered his serum to the clinics—before being cheated by "the American swindlers"—and they became instant friends. They got on well with the simple people who worked the fields and mined the hills and fished the seas at the top of this little finger of Mexico hanging precariously from the foot of a giant and guarded by the city of sin—"Tee-ah-wanna" to the Americans. Jordan called Frieze "my mangy parrot," and exhorted him to repent like Pedro Sarmiento in that ancient novel by Lizardi. Frieze called Father Jordan "Tartuffe," the impostor, because of his double life.

"If my house looked like this, I would have to hire a *bruja* first to scare away all the ghosts and evil spirits, but the woman I have in mind, she could tackle both jobs."

Frieze scrunched up his eyes, which caused his nose to wrinkle and enlarge and his mouth to fall open so he looked both disgusted and perplexed.

"Euh? If she is such a good worker, she should 'ave a job alghready."

"She's between jobs. Her previous employer, Señor Velasquez, died a week ago."

"Ah haw, haw! You see what I mean! Your fine woman, she is the murderess. She stings that poor man. She was after his money if he has some. *Les femmes,* they can be such a nuisance around the house. I know exactly where everything is. She would just mess things up, how do you say, like crazy. No, she is not for me."

"Oh, Louie, the maid is not a killer. You really need someone to keep things organized around here. You could be much more productive, and it would be safer, too, in case you have another accident."

"Pro-duc-tif? Why? Why must I be pro-duc-tif?"

"The work you do, Louie, it saves lives. You could save so many more if you were just better organized."

Frieze threw his hands into the air, nearly toppling the water bottle on the table by the grinder.

"Organized? That is about money and fame. The most organized are the least effective at saving lives."

Louie Frieze wandered about, aloof from reality, hidden away from the rest of the world. He spoke with an irritating nasal tone and his face was often fixed in a stupid smile. He didn't care that his discovery of a serum to combat cancer was disputed by so-called established medicine. Those baritone voices and noble faces that confront the world's complexity with naïve confidence, they only made him laugh.

Ana Luisa threw up her arms. "Be careful! *¡Eres imposible, imposible!*"

"Speak *Anglais!* Now, go get your driver. The serum is ghready."

Frieze preferred his disorganized life and living alone. He hated the brainless, heartless mob. He observed that most people could live side by side with genius or tragedy as innocent as babes. He had no feeling for them, no patience for those who saw life differently or didn't see it at all.

Ana turned toward the door and yelled: "*¡Ven aca, ven aca. Hay trabajo por hacer!*"

An Indian—short, dark-skinned, eyes of obsidian—hovered about the door like a shadow. Frieze motioned toward a giant box. The Indian rocked backward on his heels. His eyes came alive with flashes of white. Ponderously, deliberately, he walked around the box. He looked at the box. He looked at Frieze. He looked back at the box. Frieze and Ana Luisa stood quietly, watching. The Indian dropped his head and looked sideways under his black lashes. He touched the box cautiously. He pulled his hand back hastily as if he feared getting burned. He looked first at Frieze, then at Ana Luisa, but he said nothing, did nothing. He stood like a frozen image on a single frame in an ancient movie.

The suspense was building. For a brief moment, the three stood silent, the only sound a faucet dripping into the sink. Suddenly, Frieze bellowed an emphatic "*Sacré bleu!*" Ana burst out laughing. The impassivity disappeared from the Indian's face, and a shy smile graced his thick lips. Frieze pushed the large box into a corner and brought out a much smaller one. It was an old joke, loved by all, especially the Indian who, like a little boy, knew what was coming but pretended to be surprised.

"Get on with it then."

Not once did the Indian speak. He soon had the smaller box tied expertly into the back of the Jeep. He returned to the driver's seat and sat fixed—outside of time—like a statue carved of stone. In the overgrown garden surrounding the car, the leaves rustled and shook. An obnoxious, musty smell, the smell of despair, filled the wide nostrils of the Indian's flat nose. Something tickled deep in his lungs. He coughed. He raised his head but saw only a thick, still surf of weed and bush, dark, green, impenetrable. He sensed something hiding there, something wild and evil, but he said nothing, did nothing.

"Who gets this shipment?" asked Frieze.

"It's for Itandehui in the mountain village," answered Ana Luisa. "She needs the serum more than any of the others right now. Two in her village are very sick, and she said something about a *gringo*."

"Euh? Gringo?" The nasal voice rose to a higher pitch. "No Americans! I will not provide my serum to Americans. They can afford to go to one of the clinics."

"Oh, Frieze! You know that the quality of the serum at the clinics is inferior. The young man is Jordan's friend. Please, Louie. Not all the Americans are scoundrels."

"The Americans are pigs and thieves and whoremongers. They do anything for a piece of slop. Let them have their slop."

"Americans are not the only scoundrels, Louie. Those partners who tried to steal your formula—Krump, he's a German, and Napier is Canadian. Don't throw your ire like sand in the wind, and don't malign my good friend."

"Friend? Pfft! Jordan is your lover. I don't care if you hide it. That is your own business. Irish American. German American. Canadian American. The stupid Americans not even have their own race. They are a stubborn mishmash, a bunch of mules."

Frieze reached out and steadied himself, putting his hand on the table. The pain surged through his body like an electric jolt. His mind went blank. Sparks flew in the air in random colors like a rainbow gone berserk.

"Enough! Enough of that, Frieze. Tell me, how is the salve working?"

"Euh?" He was breathing hard. "Salve? Oh... I suppose it's doing me no harm."

"You're an old dry shoe, Louie, nothing but an old dry shoe."

A stranger looking at Frieze's fire-disfigured face would think he was a monster, especially when he ranted and raved, as he was prone to do at the least provocation, but Ana Luisa had known him long before the workshop explosion that crippled his legs and scarred his face. She knew him before the disastrous events with his partners, Krump and Napier, now enemies, who had tried to steal his formula. She knew that Louie was a kind man behind the mask, knew that he would agree to her request.

The pain subsided. Frieze took a container of ground apricot pits and dumped them into a large cauldron on the stove.

"Better an old dry shoe than a fool or a thief. Go. Take the serum to Itandehui. Remind her: Just one tablespoon in a cup of tea, just one. A higher dose would be toxic, and a smaller dose would not be effective. I don't even know if it works on Americans. They resist everything."

At first, Frieze had hated the scars on his face. He'd argue with that monster he saw in the mirror. He'd made faces and the monster made faces back. When he opened his mouth to speak, the monster did the same. He put his hands up to his ears and the monster mimicked him again. "You are not me," he yelled at the apparition in the mirror. He... he was surely someone else. Under the scars, separate and unchanged, was the young boy he remembered. It was true he'd never been attractive, but after the explosion, he became grotesque.

When he finally adopted the scars, a kind of relief followed. He learned to enjoy the effect he had on people, especially those who considered themselves superior. Ordinary people accepted him well enough after the initial shock, but those who put themselves on a pedestal, "*les parvenus*," as he called them, avoided him as if the scars were contagious. Frieze could imagine nothing worse than these ill-equipped social climbers. He laughed when he saw them turn away from him in disgust.

"Itandehui knows exactly what to do. You must not worry."

"*Bon*. Go on then."

"You're a saint, Frieze. Your serum is a miracle."

"There are no miracles. Not even life itself is a miracle, not even love. There is evil, there is good, there is knowledge, there is ignorance. None of it means a thing."

The pain was coming again. Outside the door a cat meowed and a pig grunted. Frieze put his hand on the table. On the stove, the cauldron began to boil.

"It's wrong to say that life has no meaning, Frieze. We cannot say such a thing even if we do not know what the meaning is. I'll say a prayer to the Blessed Virgin for you."

"Bosh!"

Ana Luisa shook her head. There was sadness in her large brown eyes, but she managed a sympathetic smile as she left.

Frieze closed the door to be alone with his thoughts, alone with his pain.

Where is she? Gone? Damn this pain, damn this hour and this day! What? Is someone out there? Hello?

Prayers! What good are prayers? Prayers are mothers' balm for helpless children. The instinct for worship occurs on a natural cycle. When depressed or euphoric, I look up at the sky like anyone else, but... the idea that someone is listening? Bah! Praying for something we can get for ourselves... what folly. There is nothing beyond the curve of the days. Anyone can see we come from nothing and return to nothing. We must make of our lives what we can with the time we have. Pfft! I get lost in such musings. Ah, well! Let Ana Luisa pray if it make her feel better. Perhaps it help after all.

Marcos heard a piercing voice ring out in a mixture of flutes and trumpets. Perched in his tree outside Frieze's house, he searched for the source through the thick foliage, but saw nothing.

Ana Luisa sped away in the Jeep with her Indian driver and her precious cargo. Through the window, she saw Frieze watching them leave.

When they were out of sight, the dark house at the end of the winding street sat once again forlorn amidst the weeds and thistles, and Frieze resumed his wretched solitary existence. The pain throbbed on and on. It beat and pounded like an alien heart, demanding his attention like an unwelcome guest. On the stove, the cauldron made little popping sounds as it began to bubble.

2.

Informal Examination

Eric's Sacramento Apartment

May 1972

A small bird tapped at the window. Eric awoke to cramps in his lower abdomen. The pain, sharp, excruciating, pounding to the rhythm of his pulse, took his breath away. His intestines twisted and bulged like tied-off sausage casings. A weakening dam held back a raging river. The pressure built until it could no longer be contained. Eric ran to the bathroom. An explosion rocked his body. Rhythmic cramps, salt in his mouth, an ocean of saliva, afraid to swallow with nowhere to spit, he spat on the floor. Another blast followed, then another. Fearing he might vomit, he slowly breathed in and out. Mouth half open, salt and saliva flowing continuously, he spat again. There was no letup from the demon's thrust. It ripped through his stomach like a corkscrew.

He climbed off the toilet, cleaned the floor with a towel, and threw it into the hamper. On the way to the kitchen, he looked at himself in the mirror. What if he were to die? Would anyone care? The ability to completely detach from who you are is either impossible or deadly. Vanity, straight or inverse, is the Heisenberg factor in all examination of the self.

Eric dropped two slices of bread into the toaster and sat at the table. He watched the steam rise from the slots and curl into the cool air above. By the time the bread popped up, everything had returned to normal. He buttered the toast. There was an empty feeling in the pit of his stomach. He walked to the front door and picked up the newspaper from the step. It was warm outside, the air thick and heavy. Summer had arrived early. He heard a lone owl hoot from its perch high in the tree across the way.

HOOVER DIES, NIXON APPOINTS L. PATRICK GRAY
FBI DIRECTOR
NORTH VIETNAMESE ARMY CAPTURES QUANG TRI CITY

The heat lulled Eric into an idyll. Happy summer memories of the Sacramento Valley brought forth the pleasant odor of freshly harvested barley, yellow and ripe, and the weedy aroma of green alfalfa cooked by the sun. The sticky humidity of the rice paddies, the pungent odor of the sugar beets swelling silently in their dark tombs—an infinity of smells came back to him. He floated through time like a seed, floating inside a great womb, primal, amniotic.

He was jolted from his reverie when an enormous black cat jumped onto his lap. Eric was a fan of low-budget gimmicky horror films like those by William Castle—*House on Haunted Hill, Mr. Sardonicus*. A friend with a quirky sense of humor had given Leon to Eric as a housewarming present. A note with a line from *The Tingler* hung from Leon's neck: "Have you two met, in the same alley perhaps?" In spite of the joke, or because of it, Leon became Eric's best friend.

Leon was the only creature Eric allowed in his apartment on a Sunday. The peace and quiet of a morning alone was not to be spoiled by letting another human being enter his space. Eric didn't answer the phone or respond to a knock on the door until he'd finished the Sunday paper together with his usual breakfast—fried eggs with potatoes, bacon, and toast, the one meal he could prepare on his own. He let Leon out through the backdoor before doing the dishes. Bob Dylan's *New Morning* album was on the stereo.

Eric's apartment was too small. After passing the bar and handling an important case, he was on his way to becoming a full partner at Noakes Martin Noakes, the law firm started by his father. When Eric's father died, Thomas Noakes said there was a need for a Martin to fill the gap. Eric's stepmother, Karen, was an excellent attorney, but she didn't want the partnership. She had her eyes set on a judgeship. Her political connections were with the Democrats. She'd have to wait until Reagan's term as governor ran out. She was certain to be appointed a judge if the Democrats won in the next round. In the meantime, she was too busy with her own life to put in the energy to make senior partner at the firm.

Eric, the obvious successor, would need a larger apartment. He dreaded the thought of entertaining, but he knew what the job of partner entailed. The law, like medicine or finance, was an intricate game in which success depended on maintaining a proper distance from the hoi polloi. This meant, among other things, participating in and hosting the arcane social gatherings of the cognoscenti. He learned early to control the passions and emotions that got so many young men in trouble. He was determined to succeed. Growing up poor, he'd seen poverty, experienced the thin line between success and failure, and knew the disappointment failure brought. He'd watched his father walk out the door and never return. His mother and grandparents had done their best. Eric didn't want for love, but from that day forward he was on his own.

The Noakes brothers, Ralph and Thomas, were flashy and bold. Eric's father had partnered with them because of their flamboyant style. The rumors of seedy connections in their past hadn't prevented the law firm from building a prestigious clientele of the rich and famous. There's something about the wealthy that impels them toward expensive legal maneuvers. The most lucrative clients can be selected from a laundry list of nefarious characters. Over the years, Noakes Martin Noakes had built an impressive reputation for having the uncanny ability to successfully defend wealthy clients and notorious criminals—kidnappers, murderers, rapists. It was nasty work, but it paid well. The Noakes brothers' courtroom antics rattled even the best criminal prosecutors. In the civil cases the opposing attorneys nearly always settled out of court. Most were too intimidated to argue against the Noakeses in public. When they did go to court, the press was there to watch. Thomas Noakes was short and stocky. He looked and often acted like a bulldog. Ralph was tall and attractive, a pretty boy who appealed to female jurors. The brothers were not well organized in the office or in their personal lives, but in the courtroom they performed an intricate dance that could have been choreographed by Bob Fosse.

In stark contrast to his father and his partners, Eric was quiet, even shy. He kept his apartment scrupulously clean. Not a speck of dust marred the pristine countertops. Neither a crumb nor a pebble could be found, nothing that didn't belong, with the possible exception of a few of Leon's stray hairs. Eric's laundry was folded and dispatched into drawers and closets, the dishes were cleaned and methodically stacked in the cupboards. He made his bed neatly, the bedspread pulled so tightly across the top that a quarter dropped onto the bed bounced a foot into the air, something he'd learned in the Army Reserves. His books were arranged according to his tastes. Mexican and Latin authors like Borges, Fuentes, and Rulfo became passions after he'd worked on a legal case in Mexico involving the Bracero program. His albums were expertly catalogued beneath the stereo. His musical tastes ranged from Buddy Holly to Shostakovich. He especially liked story music—country by Patsy Cline, and folk from musicians like Bob Dylan and Cat Stevens. He organized his own life, but he did have a maid to tidy up and cook his dinners.

Mathilda was fastidious in her application of the *Hausordnung*—the German rules of the house. These she applied diligently to Eric's apartment and to Eric himself.

"A young man's blood runs faster through der organs than it does through der brain, Eric. Don't let some young girl get her hooks into you before you've made your vay in life."

Mathilda spoke with a wry little smile. She was a small woman with wrinkled skin, wiry legs, and gray hair that she kept neatly bundled in concentric braids.

"I take care of you like a son. I buy for you der very best cleaning agents, powders, and soaps at der cheapest prices. You see me do this. You must be attentive and careful, Eric. Do not let der old men, der *schmocks* like Nixon with his Pinocchio nose, make you der fool. Old men suck new blood from der young, like vampires. Vatch out for der dreams zey plant in zat young brain, Eric. Stay away from der evil escapades zey dream up for you."

There was no use arguing with Mathilda. She was old and wise and as full of advice as a teapot was full of steam. Eric knew she meant well. He marveled at her unbounded confidence, the confidence of someone who knew she possessed true wisdom.

"I cook for you der sauerbraten. I do not cook for you der French sauces zat ruin der meat and turn young men into *das Spatzenhirn*."

Eric laughed at the strange word. Mathilda's eyes brightened.

"Spatzenhirn—birdbrain, foo-foo head."

Eric always did his best to follow her advice. When he failed, Mathilda pounced on every little mistake, insisting that his life would end in disaster. She shook her head at the colorful suits and ties from Cable Car Clothiers that hung in his closet.

"An attorney must be professional, must vear only brown or black or gray. Der vild colors and styles make you look like *das Spatzenhirn*. What vill your clients zink?"

Eric was no doubt more influenced by Mathilda than he realized. He lived an austere life according to a precise plan. The colorful suits and ties were one of the few luxuries he afforded himself.

The pain struck again. It doubled him over. The world informed him with clear intent: it was going to be less friendly on this Sunday morning.

What to do with this problem that arrived when least expected? A retired doctor named Emanuel Marx lived in the apartment next door. In his time, he had treated some of the most prominent people in Sacramento. He and Eric had become good friends. Eric once discussed his bowel problems with Doctor Marx, who had given him advice that Eric unwisely ignored. In spite of Mathilda, in spite of his passion for an orderly life, Eric had a bad habit of ignoring embarrassing problems, but this time the pain was impossible to ignore. He'd been working on a will for Doctor Marx. He would deliver it and tactfully bring up his health problem. At one o'clock, Eric walked over to Marx's apartment and rang the bell.

"Oh, it's you, Eric. Come in."

Doctor Marx's apartment was nearly identical to Eric's, though the doctor had a more eclectic approach to housekeeping. Books lay around together with the odds and ends of a long and successful career, but nothing objectionable. Marx and Eric got on quite well. The doctor wore sweats and an old T-shirt. His hair was uncombed. He hadn't shaved. He looked as if he'd been working out. The American chess phenomenon, Bobby Fischer, was being interviewed on TV:

When I beat Spassky, then Americans will take a greater interest in chess. Americans like winners. The U.S. is not a cultural country. The people here want to be entertained. They don't want any mental strain, and chess is a high intellectual form. Americans want to plunk in front of a TV and not have to open a book.

Doctor Marx was an avid reader. A book of short stories by Ambrose Bierce, *Tales of Soldiers and Civilians,* lay on the table. Manny switched off the TV.

"You think Fischer will beat Spassky?"

"I think he could," said Eric still looking at the coffee table. He was trying to remember a short story by Bierce, something about a man jumping off a bridge. "Ambrose Bierce. Didn't he disappear in Mexico?"

"That's right," said Manny. "He vanished across the border into Chihuahua. In his last communication he was on his way to visit Pancho Villa's troops during the Mexican Civil War. Carlos Fuentes wrote about it in *The Old Gringo.*"

"Oh, yeah. And the facts of Bierce's death, they're still a mystery, isn't that so?"

"Yes, still a mystery. Bierce was preoccupied with death, but there are no facts known about how he died. He didn't get the recognition he deserved as a writer until after his disappearance. He went to Mexico looking for an adventure. He must have found it, or it found him. He became famous after he died, more so than he'd ever been during his life."

To Doctor Marx, Eric did not look well. His eyes were missing the usual sparkle. His face was pale and haggard.

"I see you brought the will. I hope you honored my request."

"You're the client, Manny. I disagree with what you're doing, especially the part about leaving out your kids, but don't worry, everything's exactly as you specified."

"Unchallengeable, right?"

"Not a chance in hell anyone could break this will, Manny."

"I don't give a jot about hell. I just want to be sure that no one can break it in the Superior Court of Sacramento. I've supported my family all my life. I'm entitled now to do as I wish, don't you think?"

"It's your family, Manny."

Doctor Marx was a wiry seventy-year-old, nearly bald, with a penchant for chewing on toothpicks. He soaked them in water flavored with cinnamon and sugar. He had small round eyes and a subdued smile that never quite formed successfully.

Eric was looking through the large living-room window. The girl across the street walked out to wash her car. She had on short shorts and a tight shirt.

"It's okay to look, but take my word for it, Eric: women are nothing but trouble."

"Gosh, Manny, you sound like Mathilda. She's afraid I'm going to run off to Reno with some young thing before I've sown my wild oats."

"That woman sometimes displays a bit of common sense, but I find the Germans heartless and tedious. She's right, though, about the girls. Stay away until you've made your way in life. It's the best advice I can give. Besides, that one's taken."

A little boy came running out the door and ran to his mother.

"I thought her husband died."

"He did, but she's dating a guy who lives in the apartment next door. Roger Penalt. Have you met him?"

"No. I thought that apartment was empty."

"Roger works a lot. He's a chemist. He's taking some time off from his job to travel to Mexico to learn about alternative medical cures.

I can't imagine why he's interested in something like that, given his scientific background. Maybe he just needs a break from the stress of the job. Women will hold you back, Eric. Young years are for young things. If you give up on that too early, something in your soul dies. Love's a full-time job. You have to play by the rules if you want it to work. Take it from me. I've learned the hard way."

"You're old, Manny. You've been soured by a bad marriage. Besides, you probably can't get it up anymore."

Eric laughed. Manny's small eyes lit up.

"Hey, watch your mouth! Come with me to the racket-ball court. Let's see what you have to say after that."

Eric and Manny played every Sunday afternoon and sometimes in the evenings if they could find the time. Manny relied on Eric to keep him young. Eric relied on Manny to keep him healthy. They trusted each other as casual friends can do. Best friends are too close to trust completely.

"Not today, Manny. I'm not feeling so well."

"What's going on? Got the flu or something?"

"Something."

Manny saw the distraction in Eric's eyes. Something was on his mind that he was holding back.

"Are you having those bowel problems again?"

"I had a terrible bout with diarrhea this morning."

"Was there blood?"

"Yes, dark red blood. Last night I woke up with a terrible pain in my lower abdomen, worse than before. I thought I was going to die. Thankfully, it didn't last long. I went back to sleep, but the pain returned again this morning. That's when I had the diarrhea."

Doctor Marx walked over to his bookcase. He turned and walked toward Eric with a serious look. Eric noticed he was still in his socks. They looked as if they hadn't been washed in a while.

"Eric, we've talked about this before. Did you follow my advice and discuss this with the doctor?"

"Well... actually... no. It went away. I didn't think it was important. Now it's come back."

"Damn it! The young can be so stupid at times. Admit it, you were too embarrassed. Your health is important, Eric. Ignore it and you'll regret it. Has your doctor ever given you a rectal exam?"

"You mean...?"

"Yes, Eric. Has your doctor ever stuck his finger up your ass? Don't beat around the bush with me."

"No."

"Look, Eric." Manny grew very serious. "I'll do the examination right now. Obviously, you can't be trusted to get it done on your own. It'll only take a couple of minutes, no big deal. This is no time to procrastinate. Later you can speak with your doctor."

"I've had these symptoms all my life, Manny. It's nothing. I'm sorry I even brought it up. Really, I'm just fine." He didn't feel fine. He knew Manny was right, but he dreaded any kind of test, especially what Manny proposed.

"For God's sake, Eric, don't be blind. Your body is talking to you. The discomfort you experienced last night could be a sign of something that requires treatment."

Doctor Marx left and returned with a rubber glove.

"Turn around. Pull down your pants, bend over, and put your hands on the table."

"I think we should pull the shades first, Manny."

"Oh, sure, of course."

As Eric pulled the curtain shut, something flew past the window. He yanked open the curtains to get a look. It was gone, whatever it was.

"Close the curtains, Eric. Don't play peek-a-boo. The girl outside will wait."

Doctor Marx took over. Eric did as instructed.

"This won't hurt. Relax." Manny sensed Eric's embarrassment. He tried to be reassuring, compassionate, and most of all professional.

Just as Doctor Marx inserted his finger into Eric's rectum, Eric thought he saw a tiny opening in the curtain. He jerked to the side. He sensed something looking in, something that frightened him.

"Christ, Eric! Are you trying to break my finger? Hold still."

Doctor Marx completed the exam and went into the bathroom to wash up. Eric pulled up his pants. His face was red when Manny came back into the room.

"Don't worry, Eric. I've done hundreds of those."

"Okay, what's the deal? What did you find?"

"I can't say for sure."

"Jesus! I pull my pants down, you stick your finger up my ass, and you're not sure!"

Manny wasn't smiling.

"Look Eric, it's probably nothing. I felt a small polyp, most likely a benign growth. I want you to make an appointment for a thorough exam next week. Don't put it off this time. This is important."

Eric was stunned.

"What do you mean, a small polyp? What if it's not benign? What if it's something... something worse? Cancer?"

"Don't jump to conclusions. You need a thorough exam, that's all."

"Okay." Eric moved toward the door. "All right." This was not something he'd expected. As an attorney, he knew never to ask a question unless he was prepared for the answer. He should never have brought it up. Doctor Marx's revelation was upsetting. Instinctively, Eric knew something was wrong, but he was loath to admit it. Now he worried about how bad things might be and how it might affect his life.

"Look, a rectal exam is an imprecise test. You've got to explain everything to your doctor. I'll write up a note for you to take to him. I'll bring it over later today."

Eric was shocked.

"Listen Eric, an informal exam like that doesn't tell us much. That's why I'm insisting you see your doctor. Don't get yourself all worked up about it. You're a strong young man, but you need to understand your limitations. You can't do everything. It's okay to rely on others once in a while. Doctors are there to help you. Use them."

Relying on others was exactly what Eric didn't want to do. He left feeling worse than when he'd arrived. His heart was pumping. The girl outside smiled at him. He didn't notice. Back in his apartment, he lay down on the couch to think. Leon jumped onto his chest, purring. He was face to face with the cat. Eric stroked Leon's sleek black fur and looked into his green-gold eyes. The ancient Egyptians believed that cats could divine the future, but Eric saw nothing in Leon's eyes that gave him any clues.

Leon stretched out his arms, baring his claws momentarily. Eric put his finger into the cat's mouth and let Leon nibble on it gently. According to legend, King Charles I of England attributed his good luck to his black cat. Shortly after the black cat died, Charles was arrested and assassinated.

"Stay healthy," mumbled Eric before he drifted off to sleep.

Leon lay heavily on Eric's chest, his eyes, with their slitted black pupils, focused languidly but steadily on Eric while Eric's eyelids flitted and fluttered. The cat was oblivious to whatever thoughts resided there. A second sense kept him poised. A secret animal wisdom circulated under the thick black fur. It was in his blood, a primeval spirit force connecting him to an ancient past. Leon sensed a malign presence outside the apartment. He leaped from Eric's chest and disappeared into the darkness.

3.

Itandehui

A Remote Mountain Village Outside Tijuana

A tiny creek trickles along a canyon, winding its way down through the thick jungle that nearly blocks the narrow trail. Small but determined, an old woman treads upward, against the creek's flow, collecting obscure flowers and herbs that others might discard as weeds. Occasionally she stops to rest and listen. She approaches a small farm, a muddy enclave of sticks and tin and rags sitting near the mouth of the canyon. The road here shrinks to a rough trail heading up the mountain. As she draws near the farm, she smells the pigs long before she sees them playing in the mud with two young brown-skinned children, completely naked. No adults are in sight. The mother is in the back, cooking and washing. The father is out collecting sticks for fuel and dragging back the small trees he'll add to the pile next to the hovel they call a home.

The old woman trudges on, past the gaping dark holes that once marked the openings to the now-abandoned silver mines, up to a shallow pool where the butterflies come to collect nectar from the flowers that grow there. The butterflies are everywhere after an early morning summer thunderstorm. Stopping by the pool, she surveys the bank on her side of the stream and spots the tailfeather of a red-tailed hawk. The spirit God, Maayhaay, often leaves her special gifts by the pool.

As a little girl she found the severed limb of a black jackrabbit. It was a sign from Maayhaay that she was to be a healer. He sent this amulet to her from the desert island in the south because it contained the power of the shamans who lived there long ago. From that day her knowledge grew with her curiosity. She learned about the wild plants on the mountain. The rabbit's energy propelled her on her walks. The rabbit's spirit taught her to freeze when danger was near.

She approaches the hawk's feather carefully and with respect. It embodies the spirit of the hawk. She grasps the feather and gently raises it to her lips, her eyes, and above her head. Then, into the basket it goes with the rest. As she touches the feather, a shimmering light appears in her mind's eye, dazzlingly bright, and grows instantly into a massive arch that contains the entire heavens. A hawk circles under the arch in brilliant waves of color.

The woman sits on the bank to catch her breath. The vision subsides. She's not surprised by the visions. She accepts them as they come, and learns what she can while they're with her.

Sometimes she collects the Indian foods she knew as a young girl. The last time she was here, she discovered a bee's nest in the tree by the pool. It was full of the little white worms her grandmother showed her how to prepare. They're filled with grease from the wax they eat, and taste just like nuts when they're roasted. She likes these familiar foods of her childhood better than the food at the stores in town. She watches the broad bands of yellow sunlight filter through the tall trees and dance around the pool chasing the Jesus bugs that skip across the surface. She sits quietly. Under the colorful designs on the cotton *huipil* that covers her shrunken breasts, she feels a familiar energy. The spirit guides have messages, but she is not ready to receive them.

The trail becomes steep ahead as it weaves back and forth toward the sky. It is seldom used this time of year. There is no time to make the long journey up to the top of the mountain. Ana Luisa is arriving in the Jeep today with supplies and medicines. The old woman must turn back even though her basket is not yet full. Few in her village were bold enough to walk alone all the way to the top of the mountain. They believed it was haunted with the lives it had taken. Some who lived in the village said that when the wind blew down from the mountain, they could hear the wailing of those who had died. Bad things can happen on the mountain. It's alive and powerful and can read thoughts. The mountain watches all life unfold. If you climb the mountain with bad intentions, you will be harmed. It depends on the purpose of your visit. If you go for a good reason, there will be no trouble. If you pray sincerely, something positive will happen. That's how the spirit of the mountain manifests itself. Itandehui had heard about the power of the mountain from her grandmother when she was a little girl, soon after she'd discovered that Maayhaay had given her the gift of healing.

Back down she trudges, retracing her steps, thinking of who will replace her when Maayhaay calls her home. So far there were none in the village who showed the signs. She was old, and her time was short, but she knew one would arise for her to train before it was too late. Even if the people angered Maayhaay, he wouldn't leave them without a healer. They were his people, after all.

Walking down the mountain along the stream, Itandehui hears a scream. Kee-eee-arr! Kee-eee-arr! The red-tailed hawk is telling her that a man will arrive, someone she must teach to be a healer. Kee-eee-arr! Kee-eee-arr! Kee-eee-arr! He will not be a man from the village but from far away. His ways will be strange to her, but his heart will be pure. She will know when she sees him.

She freezes in her tracks, sensing the presence of an animal. She cannot see it, but she knows it's in the bush close by. She closes her eyes. A shape moves forward through the mist patiently, silently. The vision finds its way through the chaos of the jungle and brings a surprise, a rare black jaguar, the keeper of circular time. The fierce cat stares at her, eyes gleaming green and gold. She stands firm, undaunted. The jaguar idly stretches its lean forelegs with its sharp claws exposed. Its downturned mouth opens slightly, revealing a row of fearsome teeth. Itandehui stands completely still as if in a deep sleep. She understands the jaguar's thoughts. The gatekeeper to the unknowable has a message.

The jaguar's eyes burn brightly in the shadows. Itandehui communicates through an ancient thought language that all living creatures understand. Spears of sunlight pierce the thick green foliage hanging high off the trees. The jaguar brings an urgent plea from yet another stranger, a young man who needs her help, someone who speaks to her from far away. She will wait for him to come to the village, but she can reach out to him in a dream through the jaguar. She sets the plan in motion. Agile as air, the jaguar leaps upward and is gone. Itandehui turns and walks slowly down, down, down. She'll wait. She'll be ready when the stranger comes.

The only time people in the village ever go up the mountain is late in the summer at the time of the pine-nut harvest. Itandehui never goes with them. She goes alone to the mountain to protect the secret and magical places where she receives her gifts. The people of the village pay little attention to Itandehui until they get sick. Then they appear at her door to ask her help.

It was long before Itandehui's time when the silver mines flourished and the mule trains tore through the jungle and the forests. The great wealth of the mines ended up in the hands of the Spaniards. The local Indians, Itandehui's people, worked deep inside the earth, squeezed into narrow holes carrying heavy buckets up and down ladders and across little passageways, sometimes in stifling heat and sometimes in bitter cold. The wealthy built the beautiful stone buildings with the tile roofs and the cobblestone streets. Even now the beauty of the village, though worn and faded, takes away the breath of the few visitors who come. The Indians who did the work lived on beans and corn and hard tortillas that were almost impossible to chew with the few teeth they could keep in their heads over their short lives.

On and on Itandehui walks, past the caves where she goes to capture bats to help those who are going blind or bald, past a wide spot in the creek where the men from town pulled out Father Jordan's truck last year after he got it stuck. Sometimes she sees her grandmother smiling her toothless smile up in the trees along this creek. It makes her feel safe as it did when she first came here and learned from her grandmother how to use her special powers. Grandmother had had tattoos all over her face. In those days they believed that the tattoos helped the women from getting wrinkled and gray and to have good health and happy babies. Her grandmother had two husbands and nine children. None of them lived except Itandehui's mother. She too died at childbirth.

The power of the tattoos was not weak. Her grandmother told her that the power of death is sometimes too strong. The bad things happened to their family because her grandmother's first husband went up the mountain before being properly initiated as a shaman. He mistreated the mountain and brought back things without Maayhaay's permission. In its wrath, the mountain killed everyone in the family except Itandehui. She was spared because Maayhaay had chosen her to become the next healer. When Itandehui was young, the women no longer put girls through the fasting ceremony or gave them the tattoos. She would have gone through with it if they'd asked her. She believed in it, but they didn't ask.

Smoke comes from a fire at the crude farm where Itandehui picks up the road back to town. The man is burning trash, and the smoke wisps around in the air like dirty ghosts rising above the mud; it spreads out among the trees and gives everything a horrible smell. Itandehui shakes her finger at the man. He keeps on feeding the fire, and she keeps on walking.

She arrives back at her small hut outside of town just as Ana Luisa and Carlos pull up with the supplies. Carlos coughs and coughs as he unloads Frieze's serum and the other medicines. Itandehui tells him he needs some tea. He says there isn't time because there are many more deliveries of food and supplies around the village, plus the long journey home. Itandehui gives him some *yerba santa* leaves and tells him to chew on them and swallow the saliva to get rid of his cough. Chewing the leaves, he walks to the Jeep and drives away with Ana Luisa.

After they leave, Itandehui stores the jugs of serum under a shelf along one wall. Later she will pack the serum up the mountain to be stored by the sacred pool where she keeps many of her remedies. When she handles the jugs of serum she notices a peculiar moldy smell like wet fur. She looks outside and sees only the sunflowers waving in the garden. The sound of flutes fills the air. Vision and time become distorted. She looks through a sheer curtain blowing in the wind. Through the curtain she sees a young man, his face hideously distorted, going up the trail. She sees a monster, its face multiplied millions of times, reflecting off the jugs of serum stored along the wall. This terrifies her. Reeling with fear, she turns away. She has a vision of Frieze in his shop where the serum is prepared. The monster together with Frieze is an ominous sign. Itandehui turns back to the sunflowers until things return to normal.

She carefully separates and places all the cuttings she has collected into fruit jars and places the jars on top of the shelves. She sets aside a few wild cherries, Manzanita seeds, and edible flowers and roots. She stores them in dried gourds and little bags made of agave fiber.

A mother and young girl appear at her door. There is a tick inside the girl's ear, which is painful and swollen. Itandehui pounds and boils a bunch of sage leaves until the liquid is strong and thick. She puts a drop in the girl's ear. The warm syrupy liquid deadens the pain. It tickles the girl and makes her laugh. A few minutes later Itandehui puts in another drop. The girl feels the tick crawling out, and there it is, big and ugly. The mother is pleased. She gives Itandehui some dried fish and some sea snails her husband brought from the coast. Itandehui tells them the story of the olivella shells. They are babies that fall from the stars. When the Big Dipper gets too full, it dumps them out. The small shells fall all around near the ocean. The girl and her mother laugh at the story and leave.

Itandehui puts the fish and snails into a reed basket and covers it tightly to keep them fresh. Tired from her walk and satisfied with her treatment of the girl, she lies down on a reed mat in the corner. Sleep comes quickly. Her tiny body, withered and wrinkled, twitches imperceptibly as the spirits navigate in the darkness. Each plant has its own spirit form that does the healing, just like the animals have their own spirit guides. They enter her dreams and tell her what she must do—how to remove the evil spirits and the bad spells of the witches, the right incantations and singing to encourage the healing process. Her body shakes but she sleeps soundly. The spirits surround and enter her body. They cleanse her and open her mind and renew her healing powers.

The tailfeather of the hawk sits on the shelf over her bed. The hawk's spirit circles above as the black jaguar glides through the jungle. Itandehui's body stops shaking and the dream abruptly ends. A short time passes while nothing happens. She is awake, rested and refreshed.

Without spirits there can be no magic. She has seen the spirits in the herbs and flowers she collects. She has heard the souls of the animals. In Frieze's serum, Laetrile, there are no spirits. She wonders how the serum can work without spirits to guide it.

The play of the shadows in the afternoon light calls forth a presence. She recognizes the familiar healing power of nature. She submits to its positive energy, absorbs it, and gives her own strength in return.

She walks into the garden to urinate. She feels danger all around. The face of the monster emerges from a patch of weeds. It isn't animal or human, or insect, bird, or reptile. It's an improbable combination of all these life forms. When she was young, she saw such a chimera in the sacred rock paintings on the mountain. She has seen it also in the dreamworld and just now lurking around Frieze. It is the harbinger of sickness and bad luck. Once, long ago, an ancient medicine woman visited her grandmother and showed her how to fashion the dreamcatcher from the willow hoop to chase away this evil spirit, but the monster is powerful, and the dreamcatcher cannot always stop it. She spits at the face. It shrinks away. This time she is lucky.

She goes inside and makes a cup of tea with chia seeds. Everything is very quiet. The sun has begun to sink behind the terracotta tiles on the rooftops of the white-plastered buildings in town. A dog barks in the distance. When Itandehui closes her eyes she sees the three men of her visions, men she does not know. She will do what Maayhaay tells her to do, but she fears it will be useless. Everything she teaches the young fades with the bliss of youth. Tears form in her eyes. It's always the same. Grief follows wisdom and the wise die as fools. Far from the village, high up on the mountain, the black jaguar walks slowly, silently on its journey, and fades into the fog.

4.

Conversation Between Doctor Rice and Doctor Marx

May 1972

"Doctor Marx? Hello. Doctor Gerald Rice here, Stanford Oncology. Eric Martin asked me to phone you."

"Yes. Hello, Doctor Rice. I'm glad to hear from you. Or maybe I'm not."

"You and I both know about delivering bad news. They don't teach you how in medical school, but they ought to."

"But we learn, because we must. No need to spare my tender feelings, though, Doctor. Give it to me from the hip."

"Thank you, Doctor. Our tests show the tumor has metastasized throughout the peritoneum. It's worse than we suspected when he first presented with a lesion in the ascending colon. We were hoping surgery would be possible, but it would be unwise given the nonresectable metastatic disease in his liver."

"What about hepatic intra-arterial chemotherapy?"

"I don't think that approach would be any better than the normal intravenous chemotherapy we recommend for asymptomatic patients like Mr. Martin."

"No debilitating symptoms then?"

"Not at this time. Should he become symptomatic, the usual options such as extirpative resection, diversion, endorectal stenting, and other therapies are available."

"Well, this is certainly dreadful news for Eric, but thanks for your forthright explanations."

"Doctor Marx, I'm sorry for the news I must give you about your friend. Our tests show that the cancer is probably all over the stomach and liver. The spores have come pouring through from the tumor in his rectum. Based on his odd behavior and the visions he's having, we think it's spreading to the brain. However, it may not be entirely hopeless. We've been working on an experimental treatment we think could alter the course of events for patients like Mr. Martin, those who are otherwise young and healthy. I must tell you, the side effects are horrendous, similar to but far worse than what most patients experience from chemotherapy and radiation. We believe this treatment could give him a little more time. Some even think there's a chance of a complete cure, but we're skeptical about that. We must take care not to encourage false hopes. It is not yet an approved therapy. I might be able to pull some strings and get him into a trial program."

"That sounds intriguing. What exactly do you mean by odd behavior and visions?"

"On occasion, Eric speaks about strange people and places. The senior nurse on the ward tells me he's become stubborn and difficult."

"Eric's an emotional wreck right now as he tries to process all this. I think it's wise we don't inform him quite yet. I've learned it's best to leave him alone when he's in a mood. I'll come for a visit and feel him out. After that, he may be amenable to something radical like the experimental treatment you mention."

"As I say, the odds of complete remission are extremely low. It's a long shot. He would be confined to the hospital throughout the treatment period. It could be very uncomfortable for him. Honestly, I fear he has a life expectancy of just a few months at most."

"It's his decision, of course. I'll try to put him into a frame of mind such that he can give it fair consideration. I think I know what your response will be to my next question, but I must ask on his behalf. His stepmother is a brilliant attorney. He trusts her—"

Doctor Marx hears a laugh on the other end.

"I can't imagine anyone trusting an attorney, even another attorney."

"I know what you mean. I've had my share of run-ins with them. His stepmother suggested that he go to Mexico for treatment with Laetrile. She has done quite a lot of research on it. Sloan Kettering ran some tests and concluded that it's ineffective; however, one of their researchers did find some benefits. Eric's stepmother maintains the Sloan Kettering tests were presented in a biased fashion. The researcher who found the positive results is a well-respected scientist who has discovered other unusual cures in the past. He stood by his studies at a recent press conference. What do you think about it?"

"I'm surprised you would even ask, Doctor Marx. What do you expect me to say? Do you expect me to condone the exploitation of severely ill patients by quacks and opportunists? Some of those Laetrile clinics are operated by known criminals. I can give you no encouragement at all. Patients are better off in their own surroundings administered to by trained professionals. You should know that."

"Of course. Of course. Thank you, Doctor Rice. I appreciate your time. I'll be in to see Eric sometime soon."

Manny hung up the phone. He looked down at the newspaper on his desk.

GOVERNOR GEORGE WALLACE SHOT BY 21-YEAR-OLD ARTHUR BREMER

May is shaping up to be a bad month, he thought. Poor Eric. As for Wallace, too bad the kid didn't kill the son of a bitch.

5.

Stanford Medical Center

May 1972

A scream comes from the sky. Kee-eee-arr! Kee-eee-arr! He looks up. A bird attacks, scratching his face with its claws. Blood flows from the wounds. He tries to recover the past, imaginatively reconstructing events, running through every permutation in hopes of finding answers.

The dreams came first. They started before the diagnosis, even before Manny discovered the polyp growing inside his body. And they didn't stop. It wasn't like imagining or hallucinating. What he dreamt felt actual, true. Pictures flashed in front of him. He was shocked at how strongly he could hear, see, and smell things that he knew weren't there, everything in great detail. Sometimes he was merely a spectator, watching the show unfold before his eyes. Other times he was a participant in a series of continuous episodes so real that he lost the ability to distinguish dream from reality.

He heard the snap in the darkness of the night like a mousetrap being triggered. Caught between the wire hammer and the wood, a drop of blood, a bit of flesh, the remnants of a life. This time it was not a mouse; the hammer had snapped down on him. He would have to make a sacrifice, his hair, his skin, an organ, a limb, whatever the escape required. He would surrender whatever was asked. The odds of escape were poor, but odds are just statistics. He could be at the tail end of the curve.

When Eric called to tell his younger brother that he had cancer, Devon was unequivocal: Stanford University Medical Center (SUMC) was the only place to go. Eric wasn't surprised. Devon had spent his undergraduate years at Stanford, and thought Stanford had the best of everything. He insisted Eric get a second opinion from the "Rolls Royce" of hospitals.

Eric's stepmother thought otherwise. Karen knew Devon's concerns. She believed in science too, but she had seen that a human approach to healing was best. She watched with horror as her friends died surrounded by cold rationality. She looked into all the medical treatments for cancer, even the ones that seemed crazy at first glance. What she saw inclined her toward a more holistic approach using alternative methods that modern medicine didn't always accept.

Eric couldn't do both. Conventional medicine is scientific, but Karen argued that conventional medicine was controlled by Big Pharma and dependent on government grants. Doctors have good intentions, of course, but they're constrained by the law. Conventional medicine doesn't have a cure for cancer. Even the doctors admit this. They're still experimenting. The patients bear the costs of these experiments, and the benefits are uncertain. Karen had been looking into Laetrile, a treatment illegal in the States. She knew friends who'd had fantastic results. She insisted Eric not let any doctor touch him with drugs or radiation until he'd given Laetrile a chance.

Eric was wary of those kinds of alternatives. The advocates spoke like religious zealots blinded by their faith. The claims seemed too good to be true. Eric believed in science. The scientific method provided proven results verified by evidence. Of course, science could be abused. Pseudoscientific theories abounded, with just enough real science to give them an air of respectability. The benefit of the scientific method is that bad theories are eventually eliminated. Economic incentives can sustain bad science longer than it deserves, but the good guys ultimately win. The problem is that it takes time, something he didn't have. An alternative approach that might work faster was attractive, but he was loath to give up on a scientific approach now that he was sick. With something as important as his health and his life, he was fearful of abandoning the traditional, rational path.

Karen didn't back down. She understood his reservations but assured him there was good science behind Laetrile. She showed him documentation. She insisted doctors were biased against it because of financial incentives and pressure by the drug companies.

Eric reluctantly told her about the dreams. Fear and guilt, personal insecurities—things he hid during his conscious moments—took center stage in the dreams. Karen thought the dreams were fantasies he was acting out during sleep that told him something important, to take a chance, to go outside the ordinary. Eric said they were more like warnings; warnings that he should stick with modern scientific medicine. He was afraid of what he saw in the dreams. He was terrified to think he might lose the ability to think rationally. He'd never gone in for the eccentric. The treatments Karen proposed used vitamins, minerals, enzymes, enemas, and diet together with Laetrile—methods consistent with nature. Natural might be okay, but it was naïve to think natural was synonymous with good or helpful. Botulism was "natural," wasn't it? So was rabies. There were plenty of dangers lurking behind nature's veil, dangers van Leeuwenhoek discovered when he turned his microscope onto a simple drop of water. It was tempting to consider that something could cure him without the cruel theology of lasers, poisonous cocktails, and other atomic wonders, but his life was on the line. This was no time to experiment.

Devon lost patience with Karen. The cure she was pushing seemed to him foolish and dangerous. He pleaded with Eric not to go down that road.

Karen kept at him. Eric was torn between his brother and his stepmother, between science and something he couldn't understand but couldn't entirely dismiss. Karen told Eric his dreams were like letters from hidden parts of his mind. They were telling him to step outside the box. Cancer is an epidemic, and the doctors here keep going back to the same-old pot because it's all they've got.

That approach is brutal, heartless, and hopeless. She knew people who'd been cured in Mexico without the debilitating effects of chemotherapy and radiation. She wanted him to have that chance.

The decision was complicated at every step. Eric plunged into the world of cancer armed with all the knowledge he could absorb. He read technical books and articles. He spoke with friends and friends of friends who knew something or had some experience with his disease. He read all the articles about the alternative cures Karen proposed. The research was overwhelming. Eric soon realized that little was known, even by the best doctors, about how to proceed in his case. Life was a series of random events over which he had far less control than he imagined. With cancer the spread could be erratic and unpredictable, like some madman beating him into submission with a club. Whichever way he turned, a new blow arrived to throw him off balance. He was the victim of a cold and uncaring and unjust universe. In the end, he stuck with Devon's advice because he'd been inoculated with the optimism of science. It was the one solid thing he had to hold on to. He could hope for some Borges-like secret miracle. He could dream of one brave roll of the dice to buy him the time to accomplish everything he'd failed to accomplish up till now. He could hope, he could dream, but he wasn't going to count on a miracle cure. He wasn't going to risk his life on that.

The National Cancer Act of 1971, signed by President Nixon just the year before, was a rallying call to the medical establishment and to all Americans. Nixon was obsessed with the war on cancer because he thought it was more winnable than the war in Vietnam. Americans are great believers in the shining city on a hill; confident they can do anything once they set their goals. Nixon compared conquering cancer with splitting the atom and walking on the moon—two specific goals America had set and achieved. Even Ann Landers climbed onto the bandwagon in her column. There would be mistakes, but we would learn from our mistakes. Our knowledge would accumulate sequentially until cancer was eradicated. Patients should think of themselves as the foot soldiers. Some would be tragically lost—after all, war is hell—but the key was to push forward.

With cancer spreading through the population like Poe's Red Death, we were all called upon to do our part.

Because of a stellar reputation in research and treatment, the doctors at SUMC attracted an unlimited supply of infantry to march into battle. Eric was in one of the first units to arrive. The receptionist rattled off instructions to the patients as they reached the small square window like moviegoers buying tickets for a show. She drank her coffee casually while she twirled a pen between two fingers. There was a precise system for admitting patients, and it was her job to see that this system was followed. Periodically she gazed out from a pair of thick eyeglass frames bejeweled with sparkly rhinestones. When Eric's his turn came, this happened: "Complete all of the forms before stepping back into line. Don't overlook the backside on pages 2 and 3. That will only delay things for you. Remember to provide your insurance card and identification. When you're ready, you can step back in at the end of the line. We will move you along to admissions once all the forms are in order."

After doing as he was told, Eric stood in line a second time. When his turn came again, he handed her the forms. She studied them.

"Which Doctor Rice will you be seeing, Mr. Martin? Would that be Doctor Lawrence Rice, Doctor John Rice, or Doctor Gerald Rice?"

"Doctor Gerald Rice." *No wonder,* he thought, *they call Stanford The Farm.*

She looked up, as if noticing Eric for the first time. The name Gerald Rice caused her to exhale through her nose, "Hmm." She gave Eric a sad look.

She paused over the paperwork and shuffled the forms back and forth as she arranged them in the desired order. Her eyes peered over the rhinestone frames, looking at him as if she were sizing him up like a farmer at an auction. She reached out through the window and handed him a slip of paper.

"You're a handsome young man, Mr. Martin. Admissions... down the hall to your right."

She waved her hand in that direction. A little smile formed on her face, one small drop of kindness in an ocean of ennui.

"Next."

As Eric walked toward Admissions, he passed a black custodian handing out leaflets. The doctors and nurses did their best to ignore the man, but it was obvious they were unhappy about what was going on. Eric took a leaflet and stuffed it in his back pocket. Later, while he waited to be processed, he pulled it out to see what it said. It was propaganda for a group called Blacks and Browns United. There was a claim of discrimination, and a list of demands calling for the formation of a union. This was the wrong time to explore the politics of the hospital. If he wasn't sick, he might have considered offering legal advice to the group; now, he just wanted to get on with the business at hand and return to his life. He crumpled up the leaflet and threw it in the trash.

It was half an hour before he met with the admissions clerk, but things went smoothly after that. It seems they were happy to admit him because he had insurance and could pay, something highly prized, especially in research hospitals. SUMC worked hard to perpetuate the myth that it was some sort of benevolent and philanthropic institution. In reality, few poor people could afford the care, so few were admitted. A battery of pricey tests and treatments awaited him. They would be giving him the full workup and collecting the toll at every gate.

He stood in a holding pen with the other cattle. The new arrivals wandered in with fear in their eyes. Some bruised, some crippled, some moaning—they all had the same knowledge or lack of knowledge of something bad to come. It was crowded, and the bumping caused problems. The room echoed with thuds that came from next door. He became lost in the chaos of the moment. There were more arrivals until it was nearly impossible to breathe. Those whose names were called bellowed loudly. They kicked and struggled as they were led away, prodded up the ramp out of the dust and manure that covered the dirt floor. Through the blurred window he could barely make out the heads in the adjoining room, heads without skin to cover the flesh, and with eyes dangling from a thin cord. The bodies hung on hooks. The eyes, or what he could see of them, were looking away toward some other place outside his line of vision. From that hidden place, he could hear the sound of saws cutting and bones cracking. He looked up and was blinded by the light.

A man sat next to him. He wore a loose olive-colored shirt that hung below his knees. White pants protruded from under the shirt, and further down a pair of brown shoes, scuffed and worn, dangled as if from the feet of a scarecrow. The man's dark skin identified him as a foreigner. When he saw Eric looking, he opened his mouth to reveal a set of perfect white teeth that worked in tandem with a pink tongue to form words.

"I see you are curious, sir. My sister-cousin insisted I come here." He spoke loudly, each word chopped like an onion on a cutting board. "It is the long-cut to health, you know? I will be easily cured by the ZamZam water I am soon to be drinking, but don't tell this to my sister-cousin or her meter will turn high."

Eric, still in shock, not yet quite back into the actual moment, gave the man a puzzled look. The sun peeked through the windows like a voyeur looking in from a place where everything was still right in the world. Some of the new recruits traded stories and jokes with slapdash nonchalance. It was how they tamed the approaching terror. Beneath the veneer, no one doubted they were leaving this world for one far less friendly and benign.

They took the Pakistani man away. As he left, he turned toward Eric. "Suffering is not good for the soul, sir, in spite of what the Christians say. There is no redemptive value in it."

Had Eric known of the events that were to come, he would have asked the man more about the ZamZam water. In the corner across the way an odd couple traded opinions.

"I want the truth, see, the good news and the bad news," said the man, who looked to be in his seventies and wore his thinning gray hair in a ponytail.

"I've heard all the truth there is, honey, and let me tell you, it's all bad." The woman, about the same age, was lean, her tanned skin wrinkled and rough. "Hope springs eternal for these doctors. They've always got something new to try."

"Yeah, but what are the odds that any of it works?"

"Well, when your time comes, honey, it comes. There isn't anything anyone can do about it."

"You don't really believe that." He cocked his head like a chicken scratching the grass as if he heard a worm in the dark earth below.

"Sure, I do."

"Then why are you here? Why not go to the quacks in Mexico?"

"I stay away from snake oil salesmen."

"Yeah, but what if one of them is right?"

"You're damned if you do and damned if you don't."

"Ain't that the truth."

Eric was escorted to the inner sanctum, where a rigorous atmosphere prevailed. The doctors and nurses had their specific parts in a complicated hospital ballet. They danced, mixed, separated, and recombined like components in a human cell. Their knowledge was great but insufficient. Eric presented with a disease that evaded all the cures. They tried every available means, but the treatments inflicted had horrific side effects and inconclusive results. The battle went on. The patient's bodies were the battleground; the doctors were the generals. Those in the infantry, like Eric, were necessary but expendable. He arrived wounded, dying, and none of the usual tricks seemed to help. The nurses' accusatory looks made him feel responsible for his own lack of progress. He was an object of study, to be carefully scrutinized by the young men in white suits. Whether or not he could be cured, his purpose was to aid the doctors in their search for a cure. In this he was expected to play a positive role and keep his complaints to himself.

Life soon became gruesome. In every room there were implements of torture. Torquemada would have been envious. There were the inevitable screwups. A young Hispanic nurse, new to the job, tried to draw blood. She hit a nerve instead of a vein, setting his arm afire. The head nurse, a woman with a face that looked as if it had been assembled from mismatched parts, raged at the girl's mistake: "You're only here because we we're forced to hire you. Do you understand what I'm saying?"

She threw the used needle into the trash.

"Get another kit. Do it right this time. We don't want to destroy Mr. Martin on his first day."

The young nurse reddened with embarrassment. "You want me to try again?"

"For God's sake, do I have to tell you twice? Nothing is right around here. Nothing is good anymore since... well... with all these new people here!" The old nurse stomped out of the room.

Instead of being angry, Eric felt his heart beat a little faster when the young nurse drew close. She was different from the rest. Large brown eyes, gleaming white teeth, soft, chocolate skin—he forgot all about his illness.

"It's okay, she's gone. Don't worry about it. No harm done. You'll do better this time. Lao Tzu says new beginnings are often disguised as painful endings. Here, take my arm. Try it again."

"Lao Tzu?"

"Oh, sorry. He was an ancient Chinese philosopher."

"Well, I hope he's right."

The nurse focused and went on with her work. Eric's face warmed. She held his arm and this time the blood draw worked perfectly. He looked into her eyes. She smiled. The mistake and subsequent success formed a bond between them.

"Thank you for your understanding," she said as she left.

"Will I see you again?"

"Probably, if they don't fire me." She disappeared into the hallway.

Eric wanted to see her again, but there was no time to dwell on wants. How stupid, he thought, to bring up Lao Tzu. Of course she'd never heard of him. President Nixon probably hadn't either, even though he'd visited China a couple of months ago. "The week that changed the world," Nixon called it. Well, Eric needed someone to change his world, and soon. The war resumed. He was quickly moved back to the battlefield.

He developed a bowel obstruction that caused painful contractions. For the second time he met Nurse Marta, the one who'd snarled at the young nurse during the blood draw. He'd been told the other nurses called her the maneater. She drifted into his room out of the hallway lights like the planet Mars falling away from the moon with a reddish glow. Eric was told no one escaped her poison. He would soon see the truth of that.

"Good morning, Mr. Martin. The doctor is going to thread a little tube through your nose, down your throat, and into your stomach. I know you'll cooperate, won't you?" She didn't wait for his answer. "Yes, you will. This will just take a few seconds."

Her steely blue eyes locked onto him. Her creepy, mannish face frightened him. He prepared himself for a period of pure misery. Nurse Marta handed him a cup of water and looked on as if waiting to be entertained. The doctor inserted a tube into his left nostril.

Nurse Marta prodded: "Drink, drink, drink!"

Eric gagged and choked. Disgust and impatience distorted Nurse Marta's features. She looked ferocious, larger than life because of the thick blonde hair that surrounded her face like a lion's mane.

"Drink faster! Come on, come on! Do it!"

Her noisome breath, so close to his face, left him hot and sick. He forgot what he was doing and, choking and spitting, dropped the glass on the floor.

Nurse Marta stepped forward immediately with another glass of water. It was torture by drowning. The shock created a lasting image. Eric saw it as the beginning of the end. She smirked as she attached the tube to a canister behind the bed. She was in full control now and she knew it. Those cold blue eyes stared into space as she savored her power over him.

Some on Eric's ward swore that Nurse Marta infected patients with a mysterious sickness, something that didn't kill them but tormented them for days. She carried the antidote in her pocket. Later, when the time was right, she made them well again, and with this trick gained the attention and praise of the doctors.

Bile and muck from Eric's stomach slowly flowed along the tube into the canister. Eric gagged every time he swallowed. The tube irritated his throat. Thankfully, it was removed the next day, and miraculously, it worked. His stomach felt as empty as a basketball.

The blockage was gone. He became as regular as a clock. They track your bowel movements in the hospital with the zeal of astronomers looking for new stars.

One night the young Hispanic nurse returned to his room again. He perked up when he saw her.

"I'll be extra careful this time, Mr. Martin." She looked pleased to see him again. He tingled all over when she touched him. He felt a slight sting as the needle penetrated his arm. He watched his blood flow into the clear plastic tube, which turned red as it filled. Everything was over in a few seconds. She was gone before he could think of anything to say. Events moved along like clockwork throughout the day.

The next morning brought Nurse Marta again. Eric wondered if she ever took a day off. He tried to imagine what was under her starched white uniform, but couldn't picture her with the body of a woman. He reasoned she was held together with wire and tin. She'd come to force down the chalky milkshake he was required to drink before his upper GI X-ray. At the first taste, he balked. He tried to sip it slowly.

"Hurry it up, Mr. Martin. The faster it goes, the easier it goes. You mustn't *try* to do what the doctor says, you must *do it!*"

She'd been known to sedate patients and strap them to the bed to force medications into them when they wouldn't or couldn't do it themselves. Just the threat of being bound like an animal was enough to encourage Eric to follow her instructions.

Cancer is the great equalizer: It strikes the poor, the rich, the old, the young, the famous, and the unknown without preference or reason, silently creating a hell on earth for its victims. For many, the pain of treatment surpassed the pain of the disease. Some even begged to die, but they weren't allowed to. When Nurse Marta shrieked, death ran and hid in the corner like a frightened child. Nurse Marta preferred her patients to linger. Those who suffered had to endure day after day while the agony went on. Whenever a doctor or a visitor came by, Nurse Marta could sing as melodiously as the softest flute, hiding her natural brutishness behind a mask of feigned compassion.

The nurses wore buttons with smiley faces, and the maintenance crew did its best to paint the walls in happy colors, but it was all a lie, a conscious, ugly lie. The food was inedible. Eric's appetite quickly disappeared. Rotten smells pervaded the wards, poorly masked by all-purpose industrial cleaner. The humiliating gown, the sick and dying who hung on in the adjoining rooms—everything around him contributed to an obstinate depression that made him limp and languid.

A skeletal man attached to his IV stand roamed the hallways, his eyes perpetually focused on some invisible speck on a distant wall. His wife followed behind him with her straw-blonde hair and flowing red skirt. As she passed by Eric's door, she looked in curiously.

"How is he?" asked Eric, unsure what to say.

"Not good. It's in his liver. I don't think he'll make it."

When she saw the look on Eric's face, she quickly changed her tune. "Believe me, though, there is hope here. There *is* hope."

"Is hope enough?"

"God only knows."

Eric didn't want to get into *that* discussion. He didn't say any more. The woman left to follow her husband down the hall.

Trailing behind, a black spider the size of a man, invisible to all but the sharpest eyes, wove its web around the crimson folds of the woman's dress. She was doomed like her husband. Hope was no protection for her or for him. As they disappeared into the darkness beyond, the spider blew up into a giant disc, then exploded into bits that circulated like dust throughout the ward.

Many die young. Jesus and Alexander the Great were thirty-three, the same age as Eric. Shelley and Keats, Mozart, Anne Frank, James Dean, Janis Joplin, Patsy Cline, Marilyn Monroe, and Martin Luther King were just a few that came to mind. These were just the famous, but there were the many babies who died at birth, and the countless casualties in all the wars.

Eric closed his mind to this worthless knowledge. Such thoughts provided no relief, no perspective. What he suffered was real. It was his pain. He didn't care about anyone from the past. He was the one scheduled to die, to die now without justification.

Detailed daydreams, like the strange dreams he had at night, began to plague him. He understood that the stimulus for these fantasies lay in the real events of each day, but the dreams tortured him with their surreal transformations. In some curious way, his dreaming brain did a better job of sorting things out. Knowledge that these visions were dreams did nothing to dispel the illusion that through them he lived another life in another world. He wished he could control the dreams or summon them on demand, but it wasn't possible.

The pain was constant, sometimes manageable, sometimes not. The daily prick of a needle, the itching from the little scraps of tape that were applied, the discomfort of an IV, even the annoyance of being awakened every night by nurses with blood cuffs and thermometers—these were manageable. Stomach blockages, nausea, dry cough, shortness of breath—these were endurable. The occasional insertion of the nasogastric tube was miserable but soon over. How quickly he had grown accustomed to the loss of privileges, to following someone else's instructions, to depending on others, to losing his dignity, but the probing and prying and pressuring in his most sensitive areas soon became unbearable. The pain and indignities accumulated. He felt his will to carry on erode the way a cliff crumbles from the incessant pounding of the ocean.

One night his bowels delivered a nasty surprise. The stench and slime of his own waste spewed forth, and he was quickly lying in a pool of liquid shit. Locked in place by the IV, he had no choice but to ring for the nurse. Some of the nurses were saints. He hoped for one of those. His gut sank when Nurse Marta materialized.

"God damn it! What a mess you've made. It's all over the place! Why didn't you ring the bell sooner, before you lost control? Last night you rang the bell every five minutes. Just look at this mess! I'll have to change all the sheets and give you a bath! What a disaster. There are other patients. Don't you know that, Mr. Martin? My world doesn't revolve around you. The time I have to spend here to clean up your mess is time taken away from the others."

As she lifted him out of bed, their two faces came close. He could see the pores on her nose and the little dark hairs growing on her upper lip. Her asymmetrical face skewed to the right while her mouth pulled in the opposite direction. The whites of her eyes were enlarged and the pupils looked wild, distant and near at the same time. She bared her teeth like a hyena as she growled at him. Her body lurched and lunged like a top losing momentum. There was something odd about her teeth. They looked like a set of ill-fitting braces. There were layered rows as if the baby teeth had simply moved aside when the permanent teeth came in. When she reached over his chest, he saw the reddish hair on her arms rising up to the armpits where it bushed up thick as a man's. He caught a whiff of a distinctive gamey animal smell emanating from her rough skin. Nausea prickled his salivary glands. He wondered if she knew she was ugly and fearsome. Of course she knew.

"I'm the way and the truth and the law around here, Mr. Martin. No one gets anywhere except through me. Call me earlier next time. Otherwise, I'll rub your face in it!"

Eric wasn't a fierce person. He'd never been in a physical fight in his life. Still, he wanted to punch her in the face, to attack that smug smile and knock out those barracuda teeth. He imagined grabbing onto her neck with both hands and choking her until those blue eyes turned dull and lifeless. He knew better. In his condition, she would have knocked him over like one of those weighted punching bags with pictures of clowns, and he wouldn't have bounced back up.

"I'll wash myself, thank you. Just help me to the bathroom."

She ripped out the IV and steered him along. Eric used a towel to maintain a bit of dignity. He shut the door and cleaned himself as best he could. He didn't want her vile hands to touch him. He sat in a chair covered by his towel while she changed the bed and cleaned everything using a green foam cleanser, all the while whispering aloud about the idiocy of her patients and the crosses she had to bear. She gave him a clean gown that he put on by himself. Afterward she pushed him onto the bed like a sack of dirty laundry, hooked up the IV, and gave him a sleeping pill. Set free of the immense burden of his care, like an arrow finally let loose to fly, she vanished instantly.

He noticed after she left that his watch was gone. He decided not to pursue the notion that she'd taken it.

The drug put him into a deep sleep. Dream faces swirled by in the air, some normal, some distorted in various ways, flickering on and off like lights. Sometimes one face multiplied into hundreds, or millions, of identical copies. At first they were unrecognizable, but occasionally the face of someone he knew appeared. Some he knew well: Devon, Manny, Karen; others were people he'd just seen—the receptionist, the Hispanic nurse, Nurse Marta, the doctor. Other faces he didn't recognize at all. It was very disturbing.

As Eric relived all the embarrassment and pain experienced at the hospital, his body twitched as if he were being attacked with hot pokers. Unbeknownst to him, Nurse Marta watched from the door like a fiend in a cloud, her lips curled in a sadistic smile. Wild winds swept through Eric's brain, and he shivered with cold. He knew in his deepest thoughts he was in the clutches of a monster, and there was no escape.

The next day he went through a battery of new and painful procedures. In one test they shot air up his rear end into his intestine. He passed out from the pain.

That was when everything changed.

Eric could no longer be sure of himself, or of anything. The world around him shrank to the size of an acorn. He lost all hope and confidence. He feared he would never gain them back. The white walls of the room seethed with images of wild beasts that charged him while he lay powerless to do anything in his defense. Exhausted and sweating, he awakened outside the room on a gurney. Those blue eyes were staring at him.

Then something happened to remind him how the lowest and most invisible of people can provide the greatest comfort. An orderly pushed his cart down the hall, bent down and whispered into his ear, "Don't you worry none, sir. I gonna get you right back to your room directly. Don't you worry 'bout that ole nurse. She ain't been here more'n a minute. She ain't heard none of your sorrow. You with *me* now, and I gonna take care of you."

Eric looked up into the man's smiling black face as the gurney rolled along the hall. His despair shrank and his confidence returned.

"Thank you. What's your name?"

"Nelson, sir. My name's Nelson."

"Well, Nelson, you're the first person around here who I believe actually has a heart."

Nelson's laugh echoed in the blank spaces of the hallway. He leaned down to whisper into Eric's ear so the others couldn't hear him. "There's some mean honkies out there, man, that's no jive. I seen things, scary things. Gotta be on your guard round here."

"Didn't I see you handing out flyers earlier?

"Shh!"

Nelson stood up. The nurse down the hall looked at him suspiciously.

"They all got hearts, sir. Some just made of stone. Made of stone, sir, hee-hee! That's right, made of stone."

Nelson pushed Eric down the hall to his room, mouthing the lyrics from the Rolling Stones song *Heart of Stone*.

Nurse Marta watched from the nurses' station. She gave Nelson a sharp look and made a note in her log.

"Bitch is out to get ya, boy," whispered Nelson to himself. "You gotta be chill to get along round here."

He stopped with the lyrics and smiled broadly as he rolled the gurney past the nurse's station.

"How you doin', you sweet woman?" He was speaking to a nurse Eric hadn't seen before. "Got some time for ole Nelson tonight?"

Nurse Marta gave him a sharper look and made another note in the logbook.

Damn, thought Nelson, *she got me twice. They'll be on my ass now.*

The nurses and doctors became apparitions that haunted the doorways. The patients wandered around zombie-like in suspended animation. A spectrum of eerie lights emanated from the rooms along the hallway.

In the end we all become pathetic. The utopian ideas of progress are useless thoughts. We're all spirits that melt into the air and become the stuff of dreams.

The man who shared a room with Eric complained constantly about the food. Elderly, white-haired, he had no visitors.

"Look here, they give us chicken, friend. Every day they give us chicken. They must've bought a whole damn load of chickens. It's the same damn chicken breast they gave me for lunch, friend."

The man shoved his tray in front of Eric's face. "Take a look, friend. I put my mark on it. You see? I know what they're doing. I'd better get rid of it or I'll get it back again for breakfast. Everyone round this place has an edge, even the cooks."

The man stuffed the chicken into the flower vase next to his bed. He winked at Eric, then his head fell back on the pillow and he drifted off.

Eric slept restlessly during the night. He sensed people coming and going.

His roommate sat on the bench grinning as the nurses discovered the chicken in the flower vase. The clock on the wall struck one. Everything took on a blue tint. Lines dropped from the ceiling and shot out of the walls. They divided the room into a three-dimensional checkerboard, each cube taking on a different color. The old man rose up from the bench and passed through the colored cubes on a specific path—purple, blue, red, green, and orange. A dazzling white light floated in the middle of the room. The clock struck 3:00. In the blue-tinted background, the nurses made up the old man's bed with clean sheets. They pulled a curtain between the beds. The clock struck 5:00. Eric looked up just in time to see the old man merge into a cluster of black cubes in the space beyond.

The next morning, the other bed was empty and neatly made up. Eric asked about his roommate. The nurse, a new one on the ward, frowned. She refused tell him anything. Nurse Marta rushed to his room.

"We have rules here, Mr. Martin. No one gets to break the rules. We can't discuss the other patients' conditions. I'm sure you can understand *that.*" She shook her head and left.

Well, she had certainly discussed *his* condition. He'd heard her out in the hall with the other nurses. She berated and humiliated him. There didn't seem to be a rule against *that.*

He heard Nurse Marta in the hallway. "Nelson! You know you're not supposed to pass those out around here. I told you what I'd do. Now give those pamphlets to me and get back to work. Your job is to help the patients, you hear me? There will be none of your political activities on my ward. The administration has made it clear that such activities are not to be allowed here."

A few minutes later, Nelson walked into Eric's room.

"Anything you need, sir?"

"What was that all about, Nelson?"

"Nothing, sir. Here, let me fix that gown of yours. It's all tangled up."

Nelson smiled, showing one solid gold tooth, slightly off center. He leaned over Eric and whispered softly into his ear.

"We organizin' a union round here. They do everything to keep us in our place, but when you ain't got no money you gotta get an attitude. Shit, I take home less than two bills a week, man. I gotta pay for the lights, gas, clothes, food... every fuckin' thing. I got a wife, and a kid on the way."

Nelson straightened Eric's gown while he spoke. "Hey, don't let 'em know I told ya 'bout this, okay? They give the doctors and nurses everything they want, paid vacations, sick leave, big wages, everything. Workin' man don't get a goddamn thing."

"I won't say anything, Nelson. By the way, what happened to my roommate?"

"He cut out, man. You know, went off to his reward and to meet his maker. They don't like us to say it around the patients, but I don't give a shit what they say. You might as well know it. We all get there in our own time, right?"

Eric looked at Nelson with the haunted look of a child who knows that something awful is about to happen that he can't do anything about.

"Hey, you ain't done livin' yet, Jack. Perk up. You ain't gonna have no bad trip. Nothing like that while Nelson's here. No, sir. You been slammed around with the stuff God hits your ass with when he wants to shake ya up, teach ya a lesson. Okay? God don't wanna kill ya, just slow ya down."

Nelson rose from the bed and assumed the mien of a humble hospital attendant. He wasn't handsome, but his face had the bright, cheerful, attentive look of someone who really wanted to help those he cared for.

"You want some Jell-O, sir? I seen some on the cart outside with bananas and marshmellers."

The tenseness left Eric's body. His face relaxed into a smile. He was grateful for some real human contact.

"Thanks, Nelson. I'll see what they bring me. They have me on a restricted diet."

"Them folks, they got more rules round here than Moses. You take care, Mr. Martin. I'm always here to help if you need me, sir."

Nelson winked at Eric and left. Eric pictured the hospital workers he'd seen going about their unglamorous daily routines—mopping the floors and scrubbing the walls and delivering the trays to his room. He tried to imagine what it was like in the kitchen. He'd been so consumed with his own burden that he'd never really considered what their lives must be like. He wondered what people like Nelson did when they got sick. They couldn't afford the expensive care at SUMC. Were they only supposed to work at the hospital? Were they not to be treated there? The system stinks and there didn't seem to be any way out of it. He hoped they got their union. They deserved some improvement in their lives. People like Nelson had important jobs. They worked hard.

Eric upgraded to a private room. He didn't want another roommate. He felt guilty about the expense, but told himself that the peace and quiet were essential if he was going to get well. He couldn't bear another roommate dying right next to him.

A month ago he was a gazelle bounding over the wide-open plains. Now he was trapped in the jaws of a carnivorous monster, stronger and meaner than anything he'd ever known. His whole body was one massive sore. The pressure in his chest plagued him, the pain in his back. His dry cough grew worse. He couldn't breathe. His whole world had turned into the chalky mud that he drank before the endless enemas. He couldn't read, couldn't write, couldn't think. He'd never known real pain or real passion in his life up to this point. He had no words to describe how he felt.

> A bright light appeared outside the window. It expanded until it encompassed everything in his view. Sharp zigzagging borders surrounded it in brilliant colors. A scene appeared: A monkey tried to escape a band of hunters. Poisonous arrows flew in the air. One arrow nearly crashed through the glass before veering off toward the parking lot. An animal-control vehicle sped onto the grass and stopped abruptly, sending chunks of grass and mud flying. Everything swirled about outside, but inside all was calm, as if he were in the eye of a cyclone.

Cancer is the diagnosis most often kept from the patient to prevent thoughts of suicide. Love, work, even sanity could be jeopardized. A federal law, the 1966 Freedom of Information Act, cites "treatment for cancer" in a clause that exempts it from disclosure as "an unwarranted invasion of personal privacy." Cancer is the only disease mentioned.

Turmoil and ineptitude surrounded him. Whenever the doctor arrived, Eric forgot the questions he wanted to ask. As soon as the doctor left, questions raced through his mind like electronic bits along telephone wires. He was a tiny speck in a universe that bounded along, buffeted by cause and effect, subject to a probability that had no regard for him or for any living thing.

When he saw Doctor Rice's face, Eric knew the news was bad.

"You have a malignant growth, Mr. Martin. You're seriously ill."

"Can it be removed?"

"There's a slim chance we can operate, but the odds are not good."

"How long do I have?"

"If we can operate successfully, you may have two to three years. If not, two to three months."

"That's not enough time, Doctor."

"It spreads very quickly in young people, especially those otherwise healthy."

"Well, let's go for the operation then. I need time to put my affairs in order."

"We have some additional test results to analyze before we can make that decision. I'll let you know as soon as we have the information. How do you feel?"

The question sounded automatic, devoid of any real feeling or compassion.

"How are *you* feeling, Doctor?"

Doctor Rice left without answering. Eric was alone. He tried to compress everything he wanted to do into two or three years, then two or three months. It wasn't much time. He grabbed a notebook and pen from the nightstand. He started to write but couldn't concentrate. A vision of Mexico entered his mind. Karen had kept on him about going to Tijuana for Laetrile treatments. His first reaction was to reject it as quackery. Now he dreamed about it nearly every night. Her arguments took on a new life. Why not enjoy whatever time he had left, see something new, escape the pain and suffering inflicted on him at the hospital, all the endless tests and ordeals leading to a dead end? The question ate away at him.

The day proceeded with little drama. Eric felt stronger, but there were times when he didn't know how he felt, times he didn't feel anything. Manny called. He wanted to come for a visit.

Doctor Rice returned later in the day. It wasn't his habit to visit patients so late in the afternoon.

"We've had a change in plans, Mr. Martin. In consultation with the other doctors, it's been decided that we will start you directly on chemotherapy and radiation."

"What about the operation? Shouldn't we proceed with that first?"

"The consensus is that an operation would not be successful in your case."

Two or three years quickly shrank to two or three months.

"I need to think about this. My friend, Doctor Marx, will be here tomorrow. After that, I'll make my decision."

"I understand. We should start the treatment soon to get the best results. I'll be back after Doctor Marx's visit."

Doctor Rice left. Eric turned on the TV. Karen had called earlier to tell him about a special report on the Laetrile clinics in Mexico. It was about to air. On the screen, a reporter spoke about cancer cures while an invisible camera silently recorded and transmitted.

Narrator: Last year President Nixon declared a war on cancer, but it seems that at least one desired weapon is off limits. Laetrile, a purported cancer drug, is illegal in the United States, but a state-by-state movement for legalization is gathering steam. Laetrile is manufactured in Mexico by BioPharm, a company owned by Canadian businessman Russell Napier and the man who discovered Laetrile, Elvin Krump, a San Francisco chemist. We recently journeyed to Mexico to interview Mr. Napier.

A map of northern Baja appeared on the screen. The camera zoomed in on a view of a clinic high on a hill above the *Playas de Tijuana*. Eric thought the place looked pleasant enough. The camera's view entered through a window into an office. Eric noticed a phone, a calendar, a clock, and a framed photo of Russell Napier with Fidel Castro on the wall behind Napier, who sat at his desk.

"Isn't it true, Mr. Napier, that what you are doing is illegal?"

Napier wore a yellow shirt, a thick gold necklace visible through the open collar. Eric could see the braided leather belt on Napier's tan slacks as he stood to face the camera. He barely made out the large bronze crab with small legs that adorned the buckle, the giant pincers with black tips that stuck out of a circular shell attached to a square metal clasp. As the camera zoomed in for a close-up, the scene etched on the buckle became clear: Heracles was crushing a giant crab with his foot, one of the twelve labors assigned to him, according to the Greek myth.

"In your country, yes, it's illegal, but not in Mexico. The diversion of Laetrile from Mexico to the United States—that would be an offense against the American food and drug regulations. Conventional medicine has no cure for cancer. Those who suffer from this horrible disease want to explore every possible solution. We think they should be allowed to do so. The policies of the American government, well-intentioned though they may be, are causing people to die needlessly."

The camera moved to the picture of Napier with Castro.

"Apparently you have engaged in illegal activities before."

"That depends, I suppose, on how you define illegal. It's true. I did help divert arms shipments from the United States meant for Batista to Castro's rebels. Batista was a curse on the Cuban people. The Americans were using Cuba as a playground for activities illegal in their own country. What I did was follow my conscience. I have no regrets about what I did then and no concerns about what I am doing now."

"Do you think Laetrile will be legalized in the United States?"

"I certainly hope so. We have filed with the Food and Drug authorities in Canada, the U.S.A., and here in Mexico all of the information that normally is adequate for the release of a new drug for clinical testing in humans. This information includes extensive animal efficacy studies in accordance with the protocols of the National Cancer Institute as well as toxicity studies for the various routes of administration recommended for this drug. In Mexico an independent preliminary evaluation of Laetrile in terminal cancer patients has been carried out under government auspices with most encouraging results. In a few months I will travel to the United States with a group of doctors and scientists to make a presentation to Congress that I hope will encourage them to change the law. We have a very strong case.

The camera swung around the office. It was filled with books and newspapers. Various awards and mementos were visible on the walls and shelves. The camera focused on a picture of an obese man.

"Tell me about Elvin Krump, the man in this picture."

"Laetrile was discovered by Elvin Krump. Mr. Krump lives in San Francisco. He is prohibited from distributing his cancer medication in his own country. The campaign to legalize Laetrile in the United States is led by the group Americans for Cancer Freedom headed by California physician Jonathan Blackstone. A number of legislative bills have been introduced across the country. Many of the bills' sponsors are cancer sufferers or relatives of patients who fervently believe in Laetrile. The arguments are often strengthened by the testimony of cancer victims who claim they have been helped by the substance. The opposition disagrees vehemently, of course. That is their right but it is worth taking into account the financial incentives behind their opposition."

Narrator: There have been reports that criminal elements are involved in the marketing of Laetrile. Joseph Zacco of New Jersey, the reputed Mafia boss, and the Dos Negros brothers, powerful Tijuana businessmen, have been implicated in the smuggling of illegal drugs, including Laetrile, into the United States but no charges have been filed as yet.

A different scene appeared on the screen. Two FDA scientists, one male, one female, in immaculate white lab coats, were working diligently with vials and beakers and scales in a scrupulously antiseptic environment.

Narrator: The opposition to Laetrile comes from the FDA and the National Cancer Institute and the majority of mainstream doctors who are horrified at the prospect of their patients demanding Laetrile. We asked the President of the Memorial Sloan Kettering Cancer Center what he thinks about such alternative cures for serious illnesses.

"These are bad times for reason, all around. Suddenly all the major ills are being coped with by pseudoscience approaches like acupuncture. If not acupuncture, it's apricot pits."

Narrator: Laetrile is derived from the pits of apricots and other fruit seeds. We asked Doctor Ainsley Parker, the leader of a team of investigators at four cancer research hospitals, about his recent findings.

"Laetrile has been tested. It is not effective. It did not relieve the symptoms of cancer patients or extend their life span. In only one case was there a reduction in tumor size and it proved temporary. Indeed, patients died rapidly. Oral doses of amygdalin produced some evidence of cyanide toxicity. In sum, Laetrile failed to meet the FDA's safety and efficacy standards."

Narrator: Doctor Jonathan Blackstone disputes the findings of the investigation.

"The whole thing is a put-up deal to discredit Laetrile. It was a phony test. It is common knowledge that the best and most experienced researcher testing Laetrile at Sloan Kettering obtained positive results. They were ignored. 'The Americans who come here, many of them feel a little more free than they do in their own country,' says Jesus Cabral Peron Estrada, the Mayor of Tijuana, the city where many Americans go to obtain their Laetrile treatment."

The camera moved out through the window of the FDA lab room until the entire building, a modern cement colossus, became visible.

Narrator: We will continue to follow this important issue as further events develop.

I'm sure they will, thought Eric, *but that could be too late for me.*
Lights blinked on and off in Eric's head. Everything had changed for him. Weeks, months, minutes—each took on increased urgency. If surgery was not the answer, what was? Patients who received radiation and chemotherapy found the side effects hideous: baldness, nausea and vomiting, diarrhea, clogged veins, loss of libido, loss of self-esteem, horrible weight loss—and there was no assurance that the pain and suffering wasn't for naught. The case for Laetrile was quickly building.

Storm, and what dreams, ye holy Gods, what dreams!
For thrice I waken'd after dreams. Perchance
We do but recollect the dreams that come
Just ere the waking. Terrible: for it seem'd
A void was made in Nature, all her bonds
Crack'd; and I saw the flaring atom-streams
And torrents of her myriad universe,
Ruining along the illimitable inane,
Fly on to clash together again, and make
Another and another frame of things
For ever. That was mine, my dream, I knew it."
—Tennyson, *Lucretius*

Eric tossed and turned all night. He was often awake.
My God, I'm going out of my mind with confusion!
The cure that once seemed possible ultimately became ridiculous, like trying to prevent earthquakes and hurricanes. His own body produced the cancer, a hyperactive copy of the original. Like Pogo, he'd met the enemy. But now what?

He lay on the beach in Mexico. It was warm, quiet, peaceful. A little boy ran by, stopped, and looked down at him. The boy's mother followed. She said something in Spanish. They went on.

Eric looked down. He looked up and saw a woman with leathered skin, missing teeth, piercing eyes. The ocean had disappeared. A pungent, smoky haze surrounded him. It soon cleared to reveal a jungle. He coughed when he tried to speak. Stinging tears filled his eyes. He blinked away the tears. The old woman was gone. The little boy ran to Eric and put a sea snail in his palm. The boy squealed in laughter, then ran back to his mother and circled around her. Eric held the snail to his nose to smell and the snail turned to a powder that he inhaled. A powerful spiral circulated through him. It was the dream. The dream was the way. He gave himself over to the dream.

The light of a new day slowly filtered into Eric's room. The morning sounds of the hospital arrived as usual—nurses taking the patients' vital signs, doctors making their rounds in teams, breakfast carts rolling up and down the hall. His mood picked up when his favorite nurse arrived. He thought about that first blood draw, the one she'd botched. His heart began to race. He felt anxious and confused. She took his blood pressure, heart rate, temperature, oxygen levels, and drew some blood for yet another test. She did it all expertly. He was reading Borges when she entered his room. She moved around him slowly, impersonally, like a planet. He looked into her brown eyes as she drew the blood. Her eyes sparkled when she saw him stare at her. She and Nelson were the only two at the hospital that made him happy.

And God made him die during the course of a hundred years and then He revived him and said: "How long have you been here?"
"A day, or part of a day," he replied.
—The Koran, II 261

"Do you remember when I first saw you?"
She blushed. White teeth shone as her lips parted.
"I'm so sorry I bungled that first blood test, but you helped me gain the confidence to try again. Thank you! I must be on my way. Good day, Mr. Martin."

Manny arrived around ten o'clock.

"How do you feel, Eric?"

"Horrible. I didn't sleep well at all. The gruesome tests and all that. I think I'm a goner, Manny."

Manny didn't smother him with the ritualized optimism so common to hospital visits. The worst is when everyone knows, but no one talks about it, veiling the truth with false smiles.

"Things don't look good, that's true. But it's not over yet."

"Doctor Rice wants to move ahead with radiation and chemotherapy. He says they can't operate."

"That's what I hear. What do you think?"

"Look, I don't know. What I *do* know is that I'm not going to be the guinea pig for more of these experiments."

Manny winced at the words. He didn't know what to say.

"Doctor Rice mentioned an experimental treatment on the phone. It sounds promising. I understand you might not be up for it, Eric, but what if it works?"

"Short of genius, there's no way for a healthy person to imagine what it's like to be sick, Manny. Real illness, serious illness, is impossible to describe. Your faculties diminish as the illness progresses. You might think, being healthy yourself, that illness focuses the mind. It doesn't, not for the truly sick, not for me. It makes everything foggy and muddled. At night I die a million imaginary deaths, each worse than the last. Doctor Rice isn't very convincing. The whole thing is a crapshoot, a toss of the dice. Admit it: They don't know what to do. No one does. I don't feel compelled to present some kind of heroic image to the world, to be a martyr in the name of science. I just want to live what life I have left comfortably, maybe accomplish a few things that I missed along the way."

"What things?"

"Everything. I don't know. I haven't traveled much. I've missed out on a lot, working all the time. I haven't had a decent relationship outside of work. I suppose what I really want is to take the time I have left to find out who I really am."

"I know what you're going through, Eric. I've had many patients—"

"Manny, with all due respect, you don't know. I've thought it through. It's time I took responsibility for my life. I'll listen to Doctor Rice. I promise I'll give his ideas my full attention. What else can I do? I don't really have many options, do I?"

"Well, Eric, do what you think is best. I wish I had a better answer, but I think it's okay to follow your heart on this."

Manny left. The illness had progressed more quickly than he'd expected. Eric's eyes had that hollow look as if the candle were flickering out.

In Eric's dreams there was a private place where no one could disturb him unless he willed it. He grew to love these deep sleeps. He learned to relish the new life he found there. When bits and pieces of his old identity, his hopes and fears, leaked through, he fought them off and tried to hold onto the dream world. Unlike what he'd read about near-death survivors, he found no blissful sense of a divine presence, no mission to be accomplished, no inkling of immortality. What he found was a new life, a better life, a more complete life than he'd known before.

He drifted off to sleep. He heard music. Patsy Cline, singing *Crazy.*

A conversation was going on around him.

A bright light blinded his eyes.

"The dreams of men belong to God. The time you need has been granted."

"Crazy... for thinking that my love could hold you."

He was running furiously, pumping his legs and arms, sucking in air through his mouth, trying to find his stride.

"I'm crazy for trying... crazy for crying..."

He choked, his head pounded, but there was no letting up. He was alone near the front of a pack of runners. He came around the last turn and saw the final straightaway. He saw the white tape spread out in front of him. The music grew louder.

"And I'm crazy ...for loving ..."

He fought with his legs and his arms. He struggled against time. He reached out. There was nothing but air. The scratching sound of a needle carelessly jerked from a record in the middle of the song was the last thing he heard. Then everything went black.

"The words of a dream are divine when they are all separate and clear and spoken by someone invisible."

When Manny was gone, Eric sat and looked at the phone for several minutes. He finally picked it up and called Karen. When dinner arrived, he tried to eat but the food turned to lumps in his mouth. He was too excited to eat. He slept jaggedly, awake then asleep then awake again.

In the middle of the night, a man frantically screams. "Light gone! Light gone!"

It's the man he met that first day who told him about the ZamZam water.

"Light gone! Light gone! Are you on parade out there? I get no lift."

Others on the ward join in. "Light gone! Light gone! Light gone! Light gone!"

An eruption of sounds fills his room.

A nurse adjusts the monitor.

It's quiet again.

Part II

6.

Departure

Eric opened his eyes. The sun leaped into the sky.

Devon stood in the doorway.

Eric sat up, his packed suitcase alongside him.

"Eric, what are you doing?"

"We're leaving, Devon. Carry my things and help me out to the car."

"You can't just walk out. You have to be discharged."

"They can't stop me. Let's go."

Nelson entered the room. He looked askance at the suitcase on Eric's bed.

"How you doin', Mr. Martin? You leavin'?"

"Hello, Nelson. Yes, I'm walking out of here. My brother, Devon, says I can't, but I'm going to do it."

"You messin' with me?"

"No, Nelson. You're the only friend I've got here. I'm sorry to leave you, but I won't miss the rest."

"Hey, man, wait a minute. What about that little nurse? You gonna miss her too, right?"

A playful smile exposed Nelson's gold tooth.

"Have you been spying on me, Nelson?"

"No, man. I ain't done no spyin', but it ain't hard to see how you feel about that little sweetie. You gonna get her too, cause you talk cool, man. I heard her tellin' the other nurses how you talk about philosophy and shit. She gonna follow you right on outta here. You wanna leave? Go on. Get out. Ain't no one gonna stop ya. I'll see to that."

In the hall there was only skeleton man. Two nurses laughed and talked by the nurse's station. Nurse Marta had her back to them. Eric and Devon headed toward the door at the opposite end, which led to the parking lot where Devon had parked. Eric saw the blue sky through a window.

They were nearly outside when Nurse Marta spotted them. She charged down the hall shouting furiously through the black corridor.

"Where do you think you're going, Mr. Martin? You cannot leave like this. Come back. Come back immediately!"

Her face was bright red. Her hair, usually tied conservatively in a bun, was coming unwound. She started to gain on them. She flew above the floor like a giant bird. When he glanced back, Eric spotted Nelson, who pushed a gurney along the side of the hallway. Nelson looked up and gave Eric a high-five. He let the gurney ease out into the hallway to block Nurse Marta's path.

"Where the hell did that gurney come from?"

She stopped to push it out of her way, which slowed her just enough to give them time to reach the door. Nurse Marta arrived simultaneously. She flashed her clipboard in Eric's face, would have broken his nose if he hadn't ducked.

"We must fill out the exit papers and get the doctor's approval. Don't you move, not one inch, or I'll have security after you!"

A doctor raced down the hall.

"We're not finished with your tests, Mr. Martin. Your thoracentesis is scheduled for this afternoon."

The doctor and Nurse Marta stood alone in the dim light at the end of the hallway, bewildered and confused. Silence and a cold indigo sky were all that greeted them as they looked out the door.

7.

Arrival

The plane bounced through the air like a giant whale. There was none of the magic Eric felt when he read Antoine de Saint-Exupéry. From his small plane, Saint-Exupéry saw the "true face of the earth unveiled." Inside the whale—the recycled air, the dangerous food, the boring conversations with randomly chosen seatmates—there was nothing to celebrate. Eric chewed at the hair on the back of his hand. He didn't even know he did it until he saw the stewardess looking at him strangely. When they brought the tray for lunch, the man in the seat next to him coughed on it. Eric had no intention of eating after that.

Oh, that I had wings like a dove! For then I would fly away, and be at rest.

The hostess looked at him again. He wasn't doing anything odd. He thought maybe she wondered why he didn't eat. The next time he looked up, he saw her help another passenger. He smiled when she returned to take his tray. She smiled back.

The flight was punctuated by interstices between soft white clouds and a brutal blue sky pierced by violent sunlight that blinded Eric when it came through the window. He tried to read. He had a book of short stories, *Fantastic Tales,* by the Russian Abram Tertz, real name Andrei Sinyavsky, imprisoned by the Russians for anti-Soviet writings. It was hard to concentrate in the close atmosphere of the plane, but Sinyavsky's stories fascinated him. The bizarre visions and odd characters reminded him of some of the Mexican authors he'd read. On the back of the receipt for the book, he made notes. He had a habit of writing down words he couldn't immediately understand and thoughts he wanted to remember. At home he had notebooks full of these scribblings. They sometimes took on a life of their own. He'd wake up in the morning and see sentences floating around in the air.

One of the stories, "The Icicle," was of particular interest given Eric's illness. It seemed to offer a way out. Sinyavsky wrote, "there is no single "I," we are many "I's" in the past and the future. There are no endings in life. Death is inevitable and senseless, yes, but the worries and dreams, the flotsam and jetsam of life, they don't disappear. They turn into memories. Memories of the past return in the future, conjured up by others willingly or not. And these memories are another kind of life.

Eric slipped the receipt between two pages of the book to mark his place, and put the book back into his bag. He was in a prison quite different from Sinyavsky's but just as terrifying. Mexico was his way out.

Eric lived alone yet could never find time for the things that interested him. He wondered how Devon got anything done with his two young girls and his overbearing wife, but he hadn't done much better himself. He had piles of books and articles he'd clipped, boxes full of pictures, letters, and other things he felt compelled to save. They sat gathering dust while he became a slave to the nonsensical idiocy of the ordinary. The person he wished to be, that person deep inside, the one who spoke while he lay awake at night, derived some small comfort simply knowing those things were still there—waiting to be brought to life.

"Will you ever get to them?"

"It all depends on whether I survive."

"You should speed up the time frame. Your disease is inoperable."

"I'm going to find a cure in Mexico."

"A tiny thread of hope."

"When you're in my shoes, you'll grab at anything that's been known to work."

Worry gripped him with long, thin fingers, sharp nails, and utter disdain for his privacy. It poked into the dark corners of his brain, ferreting out any happiness he might have stored there, tearing it away layer by layer.

There was an alteration in the space around him. Something approached from behind. He turned and saw a green haze in the back of the plane. An intricate pattern formed around him that distorted everything to conform to a new and peculiar geometry. Passengers grew large or small as they expanded into huge spaces or squeezed into tiny ones. Shimmering bars of colored light intersected where corners had formed. Like the ripples in a pond into which a stone is thrown, the pattern moved in waves toward him.

A familiar form inside the green cloud negotiated its way forward, pausing at each row of seats to scrutinize the passengers. My God, Nurse Marta! He concealed himself using the airline blanket on his seat. She moved on until she reached the front of the plane.

Outside the window, torrents of rain cascaded down accompanied by violent thunder. The deafening sounds of giant copper cymbals; burning tubas flying haphazardly; mangled drums and cornets limping off in revolt; a living gramophone disguised as a cactus; melting clocks; musical notes murdering each other in a random flurry of meaningless pitch and tone.

The usual reassurances blared out of the PA system: "We apologize for the unexpected turbulence. The coast looks clear ahead. We should be landing shortly."
One grain planted differently in your brain and you'd be a lunatic.

Eric checked his ticket and passport and the paperwork from the clinic. He arranged them neatly in his carry-on bag. Once happiness had been more than the silent charade it had become. He'd failed at life. At the fork, he took a wrong turn. *Prudence is a rich ugly old maid courted by incapacity.* He ended on the edge of a dried-up stream filled with dead rocks. All his life he sought the endless horizon, yet here he was behind a locked door.

The plane began its descent. An abrupt change in acceleration made real the reason for Eric's journey. He could not have handled the luggage. Karen, who'd arranged his reservation at the clinic and who put him up at her house until it was time to go, had wisely suggested shipping everything except his carry-on directly to the clinic. It turned out to be a damned good idea. By the time he arrived in San Diego, he could barely lift his small bag off the plane. A suitcase would have been impossible. He'd have held up everyone behind him. Karen was right about Mexico. What kept him away until now was a ridiculous assiduousness related to his work as an attorney. His worship of diligence and penchant for the safe way out gulped up every minute of his life like a giant whale swallowing plankton.

No more excuses!

He thought the stewardess winked at him as he left the plane. After further consideration, he decided there was probably just something in her eye that made her blink.

The taxi driver met him at the gate and carried his bag. He was tall for a Mexican. He guided Eric through the crowd with a hawk's vision. His hair was thick, the color of onyx. His name was Solomon.

Eric and Solomon left the familiar United States for the land of sun and superstition, insanity and torment, witchery and healing. Mexico was a place where a man could die alone like Ambrose Bierce, a place for lost souls like Malcolm Lowry. Was it a place to be healed? Eric pushed against the mass of humanity heading north. The sign at the border greeted those leaving Mexico with the words of a mother: VETE, PERO NO ME OLVIDES (Go, but don't forget me).

The young boys and girls flying kites along the border were oblivious of the fact that they straddled two worlds. Eric was skirting the outer limits of survival. He was headed away from science and reason, the rule of law, toward a strange and controversial miracle cure that only a few brave renegades (or idiots) dared seek. He hesitated. Solomon gently pushed him across the line to the taxi waiting in the dusty lot.

"No can split life in two, señor. Must choose."

Eric asked to explore Tijuana before going to the clinic. In the rear view mirror, Solomon's teeth flashed white as a piano keyboard when he spoke. "Si, La Revo," he grinned. Eric didn't respond. He sat mute as a stone. Worry had discovered fear in a corner of his brain and used it to badger him. He realized that any peace of mind from having arrived safely was an illusion. There was no peace. The clock ticked on.

Solomon drove slowly along the famous Avenida Revolución. The avenue was flat and straight, bracketed by two-story shops, colonial-style streetlamps, and little green trees. In the distance you could see the hills that surrounded the city. Eric spotted a bench and asked Solomon to stop. He wanted to see if it would calm his nerves to sit and watch the sights.

To anyone who failed to look closely, Eric didn't look seriously ill. He was thin but not emaciated. His brown hair and emerging mustache had not a bit of gray. His slightly tan skin gave no indication of what he'd been through over the past few weeks. One might or might not notice the patchy spots on the backs of his hands where he'd chewed the hair away. At first sight his brown eyes were clear and inquisitive and perfectly normal, but a closer look showed a conflict inside, a conflict between order and disorder, harmony and discord.

The visions were preceded by a sudden unexpected blindness. What happened next was new and unexpected. This time a swamp formed in the darkness. In the rank mud a silent chthonic battle unfolded. Up from the poisonous fumes a hydra rose from its cave. A giant crab attacked with venomous pincers. It bit and burrowed through the byzantine darkness. A body struggled, twisted and turned. The scene decomposed into an intricate array of lines. A woman in a red dress stepped forward in the frame.

"How is he?"

"Not good. I don't think he'll make it."

An Indian woman approached Eric. The first thing he noticed was how small she was. She stood beside him in her faded dress and embroidered apron. The older women he saw wore aprons, the younger ones didn't. Her gray hair was parted in the middle, pulled tightly over her head, braided and coiled into a bun in the back. She smelled of cigar smoke. Eric thought maybe that was what had ruined her teeth. Her eyes were deep and dark as if they'd been burned into her head. Her hand was withered and brown. She shook a tarnished metal cup. The coins rattled inside. He reached into his pocket and pulled out a coin. It fell into the cup with a solid clank. He wondered if the Indians here believed in karma, if this, in some way, might help him.

At the clank, the locals swarmed like insects. A mob of Indian children, all boys, with coal-black hair, bright teeth, and penetrating dark eyes, surrounded him. They wanted to sell him Chiclets. He waved them away. A street photographer pulled a donkey with spray-painted zebra stripes that added to the carnival scene that formed around him. He shook his head, "No!"

It was the first time Eric remembered sitting on a bench since his trip to Paris. He arrived late at night without a hotel reservation, and slept on a park bench with only his overcoat to stay warm. It didn't go well. He practically froze. Here in Tijuana there was no danger of freezing.

At the corner, the sign from a pharmacy—PEQUEÑA AYUDA DE MAMA (Mother's Little Helper)—made it clear to Eric that the Americans came here to buy what was illegal or expensive or impossible to get back home.

DISCOUNT DRUGS, NO PRESCRIPTION NEEDED—VALIUM, DARVON, NEMBUTAL, MDA.

Out front, a family—a man and woman with two small children and a baby wrapped in a dark blue rebozo—sold textiles and leather goods. The man danced across to Eric between the cars with a small table runner.

"More cheaper here. You like?" He had a broad smile. "I give special price. *Primera venga.*"

Eric shook his head.

Death was in the air. It circled the bench. Eric stood quickly and reached out to push it away. There was nothing but the savory smoke from the taco stands.

"What else you want? We have more stuff."

"Nothing. I want nothing, thank you." Eric turned from the man and looked farther down the street. The little man appeared on Eric's other side like a sparrow hopping from one limb to another. He pulled leather wallets out of a sack.

"Very fine leather, señor. You smell." He handed Eric a wallet.

Eric recalled a tale by D. H. Lawrence about the Aztecs using human excrement to tan leather. According to Lawrence, when, in Montezuma's day, Bernal Diaz came with Cortés to the great marketplace of Mexico City, he saw the little pots of human excrement in rows for sale, the leather makers going round sniffing to see which was best before they paid for it.

He gave the man an American dollar. A boy with a bent leg walked by using a guitar as a crutch.

"I give you five, five wallets, four dollars, a deal?"

"No."

Eric turned away. He was dizzy from the heat. He sat back down on the bench. A steady stream passed by: Mangy dogs, a mule weighted down with large packs led along by a Mexican in worn boots and a hat, Indians wrapped in their blankets silent as ghosts. A drunk hobbled along in a cloud of filth and muck, followed by a beggar who looked dangerous as a feral cat. Americans, his people, they were there too, vigilant predators, suspicious shoppers. People looked at him as he sat on the bench. He didn't look back. He closed his eyes. He could hear noises, car horns, coins jingling, boots clomping along the sidewalk. Most of the voices he heard were Americans on holiday. Random bits and pieces of the conversations bounced around in his ears.

"Gladys, look at this cute little piñata for the grandkids."

"Since when have you been interested in the grandkids, Fred? They'll just break it apart."

"Hurry it up, Maisie. We haven't got all day."

"I'm doing the best I can, Henry. Come over here and look at the..."

"You! Get away from that car! What's the matter with you folks anyway?"

"He just wants to wash the windows."

"He wants my money."

"What'd you find, Maisie?"

"Perfume, at a great discount, Henry. I'll bet—"

"Let me do this. Hey, buster, I'll give you a quarter for the perfume."

"Henry, it's only a dollar. At home I pay—"

"Shut up! Everybody bargains down here."

"No es posible, señor. Nobody sell for quarter here."

"Listen, pal, fifty cents, that's it."

"No, señor. Dollar is very cheap."

"Come on, Maisie. Let's get out of here."

"But Henry, look at the poor man; he's starving and he's practically giving it away."

"What do you expect? This is Tijuana."

"Oh, my!"

"What is it, Millie?"

"That man on the bench. He looks as if he's about to keel over."

"Young man, are you all right? Can we help you?"

There were eyes at different levels. There was a siren several blocks away. Music competed with other music. Eric was locked in a vapor of sound and heat with no way out.

"No, no, I'm fine, really. Thank you." He tried to relax. He felt foolish. He stood up to shake their hands hoping to assure them he was okay.

He collapsed as they walked away. The woman glanced back, turned, and went on ahead. She spoke incessantly until Eric could no longer hear her. Her husband followed behind like a giant ship escorted by a tiny barge, very old, very frail, very delicate, but still serviceable, a barge that must have guided endless ships through tricky harbors. She was from a time when people still paid attention and cared. She lived in a world that Eric faintly remembered, a world of grandparents and grandchildren, old homes with verandas and rocking chairs, vegetables and fruits from the garden, neighbors you actually spoke to. She was in Mexico on an adventure. Adventures can't happen to people who stay at home. You have to travel abroad. Eric was on his own quest, exciting as the dream of landing on the moon and just as frightening.

His luck was sure to change in Mexico. Devon had told him that Laetrile was a fraud, a big money-making swindle run by con artists posing as cancer therapists. Well, the casinos in Vegas are a scam, but some people win. The doctors at Stanford had said he was a goner, had given him up for dead. They gave him no hope. He couldn't believe it. He knew there was a cure. This was a first step in his awakening, like Didion's *Slouching Toward Bethlehem*, learning to walk anew like a baby, seeking an ancient alchemy that would get him back in the game, or not.

He felt happy and strong. Was it a sign? Devon doubted Eric would have the energy to fly to Mexico. Even Karen, who wanted him to travel there, worried that he wasn't physically able to make the trip. Eric didn't have the time to wait. He had to take his life back. Being in control provided an unexpected boost. It was as if the cancer had suddenly gone into remission. Sure, it was an illusion, but illusions can turn out to be true for those who dare to dream. He had to avoid second-guessing his decision, allowing for the possibility that he'd made a mistake. Yes, that worry hounded him, hung around like a bad coin. Doctor Rice's experimental cure might have saved him, but thinking about that only weakened his resolve. He wouldn't allow it. He'd made his choice, and had to stick with it.

A shiny red Thunderbird pulled up next to the taxi. *Black Magic Woman* blared on the radio. A girl in a sleeveless T-shirt jumped out and disappeared into one of the small shops. The driver turned toward Eric. He wore a tan Super Fly big hat and a black silk shirt, a Mr. Sardonicus smile frozen on his face. Eric looked down. A cockroach ran under the bench.

Mexico was real, alive. Eric stood and shouted, "Alive! Alive!" People quickened their pace near his bench. He knew he was acting peculiar, but it was magnificent to have such euphoric feelings when misery pulled at your collar. If he failed to grasp life, it would elude him. It might elude him anyway, but why should he worry about death? For Christ's sake, life was everywhere. He just needed to *pay attention.*

Across the street a young boy played the accordion. He worked it back and forth and stared cross-eyed into the crowd. He abandoned himself to the music, alternating between his blank stare and an innocent smile. The driver of the T-Bird went over to listen. The crowd parted and let him through. He dropped some coins into the boy's cup, and stood transfixed. The boy went on playing, totally absorbed in the moment. The girl strutted out of the shop. The man walked back to the car and they drove off.

A foreigner dressed in oversized red shorts offered Eric an American dollar for one Mexican peso. His legs stuck out like the legs of a stork. The guy had no clue about the exchange rate. He was going to lose money on the deal. He looked sad, lost. Eric didn't have any pesos. He told the man to ask for more Mexican money from the next gringo. The man disappeared into the crowd.

Light gone! Light gone! Light gone! Light gone! I get no lift.

Solomon came to check on him.

"¿Cómo está, señor?"

Eric looked up. He couldn't see Solomon's face in the bright light. He thought of Kubler-Ross. People really do get along better with illusions. Explicability, even when false, is acceptable in a way that utter inexplicability is not. Yes, he was afraid to die, but at the same time, he wondered what it was like on the other side.

"I'm sitting here like a valetudinarian among the imbeciles, invalids, and children. Let's go. It's time to get to the clinic."

A swarm of flying beetles emerged from a hidden nest in the nearby foliage. They fanned out like policemen surrounding a crime scene. People on the walkway flapped and swatted, dodged and ducked. A minor panic ensued. Eric heard loud crunching noises as people squashed the giant bugs with their shoes.

> Bang, bang, bang! A man lives on and on, but suddenly bang, he's dead; then other people walk around in his place until they too are destroyed. All you get is: bang, bang, bang! No explanation.

He followed Solomon across the street, avoiding the beetles the same way he'd avoided cracks in the sidewalk when he was a child.

The music stopped. There was a crowd next to the boy with the accordion. People spoke all at once as if they'd just arrived at a party and wanted to impress the host. They had faces like rats: protruding noses, ravenous eyes, and ears set high on the sides of their heads. The scene brought to mind a Diego Rivera mural.

"*Pesos de oro,*" they were saying. "Pesos de oro."

Solomon stood with his arm on the roof of the cab and watched.

"What's all the excitement?" asked Eric.

"That man with red car, he put gold pesos in boy's cup."

The accordion started again. The boy lived in a private world all his own. His eyes closed softly. His lips parted into a little smile while he played. The notes from the accordion travelled through the heavy warm air. The music caressed each moment that passed by.

> The cocks did crow to-whoo, to-whoo,
> And the sun did shine so cold!

"Why would he do that? Why would he give away gold pesos?"

"Everyone know that story, señor. Him name Hector Hernandez. Him rich. Him have accident with little brother Marcos long time ago. Marcos no get well, *nunca*. Them father start drinking. Him drink and drink. Lose job. Hector so sad him try kill self. Drink poison. But God no let Hector die. God put curse on face. Hector run way. Him give up on life. *La vida no vale nada, no vale nada la vida.* Him now with bad men*, mucho malo. Dinero de sangre.* Him have bad end, señor. *Pobre* Hector, he lose God. *Está perdido, señor. Está perdido.*"

Solomon crossed himself. He opened the door of the taxi and Eric climbed in. Eric pulled the notepad out of his bag and wrote, "pesos de oro—gold pesos." Farther down the avenue they came to the clubs and strip joints in the *zona de tolerancia*. Lonely men walked along in a daze, their hungry eyes paralyzed by the women in the doorways. A chubby dancer emerged from one of the clubs dressed in shorts and a tight shirt. The club's logo read SEÑOR SUERTE. She looked at Eric and rolled her tongue, fondled her breasts, and shook her hips. She laughed and lit a cigarette. Lying in the corner by the door, a man covered in filth slept, oblivious to the flies buzzing around him. The girl ignored the man and waved to Eric as Solomon drove along.

Outside a bar on the next block there was a drunk who danced with a chair like a bullfighter with his cape. He moved slowly and deliberately but convinced no one. He had a toothpick in his mouth. His eyes were closed. He had a scruffy beard. He suddenly made a few giant leaps, spun around, dropped the chair, and walked into an alleyway so narrow that his hands could touch the buildings on either side at the same time. Arms outstretched in a faded black sports coat, the man looked like a giant bat searching for prey.

"Who is he, Solomon?"

"Gringo poet." Eric saw the look of disgust on Solomon's face. "Him gamble dog races, *muy loco, este hombre, mucho* crazy."

Yes, thought Eric, sometimes you go a bit crazy.

The wild and tawdry scenes morphed into a row of opulent hotels. To turn around, Solomon pulled into a massive circular driveway leading to the entrance of El Azteca. There a bust of Cuauhtémoc, the Aztec emperor tortured and killed by Cortés, jutted out from the large golden awning. Elegant palms and perfectly manicured gardens surrounded the complex. Young men in khaki pants and starched white shirts scurried about trying to look busy. Eric noticed a black limousine with tinted windows. The red Thunderbird was parked alongside.

Two men in fashionable silk suits stood by the limo and spoke with Hector Hernandez. Two women, sleek and sophisticated, spoke with the girlfriend. She wore the wraparound dark glasses she'd bought at the store. One of the women laughed. The shorter of the two men laughed along with her. The sun's rays reflected off his gold teeth. The man looked like an Egyptian statue, immobile and proud, but with a sinister animal head that reminded Eric of Don Corleone in *The Godfather,* a movie he'd seen twice. Brando was a favorite. Hector and the other man were deeply involved in a discussion. They paid no attention to the others. All were decked out with jewelry, which dangled from every visible appendage, a meeting of the ostriches and the peacocks. The limo driver opened the door, and the two stylish women slid into the darkness followed by the silk suits. Hector and the girl went into the hotel. Eric detected the faint smell of sewage. He closed the taxi window.

The ride to the clinic was along a road more or less parallel to the border that rose up through the hills on the western side of town. Eric saw a tangle of crooked streets and alleyways. There were arroyos and tiny tin shacks, some layered precariously on the hillsides terraced with old tires packed with dirt to protect against the torrents of rain that sometimes ravaged the area. They passed a dead cow floating in a shallow river in a circle of glutinous red blood. Cardboard dwellings were scattered across dirty bare mesas where clouds of suffocating dust rose up to engulf much of the city. The rutted streets looked impassable. The people he saw seemed desperately poor and unhappy, as if they were living in vast temporary camps.

The streets, crude paths through the dirt and muck, rose and fell in all directions. Tiny soundless figures marched along synchronously like the intricate wheels of a clock mechanism. They were everywhere, as far as the eye could see, baskets balanced on heads or held in arms or carried in wooden carts that they pulled along behind them. Blighted vines surrounded the worn pathways harboring an army of evil messengers—insects, lizards, snakes, and spiders. Periodically one of these fiends of nature would rise up in an angry fury and attack, forcing one of the clock's wheels to fall off its track, sending everything into disarray and causing great distress. The wind blew hot. A flock of crows swept across the empty sky shrilling, "Caw! Caw! Caw!"

Who knew how the people on these roads really felt? The vagaries of human life were indecipherable. The brain tricks stories out of us, and most of them aren't true. Life is not a continuous function of time, it's a patchwork of discontinuities that we stitch together one by one.

As they approached the clinic, everything changed. They were close to the ocean. Foamy whitecaps crested in the distance. The neighborhoods looked rural and friendly. Occasionally, down an alleyway, Eric glimpsed immense houses built of tile and stucco, stone and wood. Men in tan shirts and pants and black boots carrying machetes tended to the landscaping. One man, sturdy and thick like a boxer, looked like Eric's father, who'd died before Eric passed the bar. The law was the only thing they shared. Passing the bar might have made a difference in their troubled relationship, but his father would never know.

The clinic was larger than Eric expected. There were white plaster buildings with red tile roofs. A barbed-wire fence surrounded the complex. Outside, a few struggling cacti were staggered throughout a parched field littered with trash. One lonely ocote tree towered over a wasteland. Inside there were luscious plants and a kaleidoscope of flowers. Heaven and hell separated by the fence. A religious mural that dominated the front entrance told the story of a Mexican doctor as Christ. The doctor's eyes were blank, white marble orbs like those of ancient Greek statues. Peasants and animals received benediction from his outstretched hands.

"Believe and you will be healed."

"I cannot believe, but I wish to be healed."

"It isn't possible."

In front of the mural, a woman knelt in prayer for a patient, for herself. Eric tried to recall the words to *Amazing Grace,* but he was never good with lyrics. He paused for a moment to take everything in. Here he was at last, like Ambrose Bierce at that moment he crossed the Rio Grande. Did Bierce find what he'd searched for? Eric's pulse quickened as he crossed the threshold into the office. He was greeted by a Bible phrase displayed on the wall:

And God said, Let the earth bring forth grass, the herb
yielding seed, and the fruit tree yielding fruit after his kind,
whose seed is in itself, upon the earth: and it was so.
And the earth brought forth grass, and herb yielding seed
after his kind, and the tree yielding fruit, whose seed
was in itself, after his kind: and God saw that it was good
(Genesis 1:11-12).

As an altar boy Eric used to hide in the vestments closet and
jump out to scare the priest. Given access to the priest's quarters,
he stole the sacramental wine once. That was before he decided he
was an atheist. He looked up at the ceiling. There was no sign. God
doesn't tell you what he's thinking.

When Eric joined the Army Reserves, a priest was assigned to his
unit, a clumsy man who could never keep his butt down when they
crawled under the barbed wire. Eric always had to pry him loose. The
drill sergeant screamed at the poor priest with words that made him
blush. The sergeant, a swarthy Italian with a shaved head and a hard
body, had the penetrating eyes of a religious zealot, like a fanatical
member of Opus Dei. No doubt he believed in mortification of the
flesh. The priest responded with a silly grin, then whispered to Eric:
"That poor sergeant, stuck with his pope's nose. Say a prayer for him,
my son."

Life was simple and straightforward then; now things were
harder to figure out. The answers to life's questions were folded inside
an intricate origami. Life was a maze in which the pathways ran off
in all directions, with doors opening unexpectedly, leading back to
the beginning or to some random spot where a new journey started.
Some physicists believe time and the three dimensions of space are
set in permanent relationship like a giant fruitcake. Everything exists
simultaneously, past, present, and future. Maneuvering inside such
a bog is tricky. A wrong turn and out you go through a wormhole,
like Alice.

A buxom Mexican woman sat at a desk piled high with files. She
failed to notice Eric, who approached quietly as if he were afraid to
make himself visible. He looked at her white uniform. It was tight.

It fit her like a second skin. The two top buttons were undone and exposed her ample décolletage, the color of coffee and cream. She had brown hair with streaks of crimson, and wore thick makeup. Her eyebrows were plucked clean and penciled back to resemble sharp black claws. Behind her on the wall was another inscription.

And God said, Behold, I have given you every herb-bearing seed which is upon the face of all the earth, and every tree in which is the fruit of a tree-yielding seed; to you it shall be for meat (Genesis 1:29).

"Hello. I'm Eric Martin. I'm here to see Doctor Milagro." He didn't want to stare or be impolite, but his eyes were disobedient. They veered off into places that embarrassed him. The woman rolled her eyes upward from the desk. Her face hung in the air like a mask thickly painted with reds and blacks and purples. Eric was surprised by the unexpected comfort he felt just being around her.

"*Bienvenidos. Me llamo Mida.* At your service. You have deposit?"
Eric was frozen by her smile.
"Oh, yes... of course." From his bag, he pulled out the envelope with the cashier's check and handed it to Mida. Twenty-five hundred dollars US. It was the custom at the clinic to pay in advance, something Devon said proved the clinic was nothing but a fraud.
"*Gracias.* Come please."
The red lips, the auburn hair against the pure white uniform—the palette of colors on her face—she was a mix of Madame Matisse and Aline Gauguin. She seemed the archetypal woman—wholesome, sexual, nurturing, and wise. Eric was amazed at the effect she had on him.
The body demands attention at the most inopportune times. He had a sudden need for the toilet.
"Is there a bathroom near?"
She pointed to a door ahead.
"Thank you."
Four walls, gleaming white—a bright light overhead, a yellowish tint. Eric assumed she could hear him. He winced at the thought.

His whole life he had been plagued by constipation. Why now did his bowels choose to race headstrong to the finish? Diarrhea, vomit, blood—the Black Death—he was afflicted by all the miseries. What would come next? Not, he hoped, the unbearable pain he'd experienced at Stanford. He hurled Job's curse at the four walls, but like Job, all he got back was gibberish.

He ran cold water over his face, then walked meekly back into the hall. Mida was already out of her chair. He followed as she led him down a wide hallway, her body shifting around like jelly as she escorted him to an empty office. He was tempted to hug her, and wondered how she would smell if he did.

Eric found himself inside a room with high ceilings, clean white walls, and rectangular clerestory windows offering views of the spindly pines around the courtyard. There was a glass door through which he saw a gardener trimming the grass.

"Wait, please. Doctor to come."

She looked into his eyes as she left. He knew what she saw. He'd seen it himself when he looked into the mirror in the bathroom. It pulsed through him. She must have seen it in every patient who walked through the doors. It was impossible to hide the fear in the mind, the pitiful state of an afflicted body, the worry of the unknown yet to come. She offered a pleasant smile. It had the strength and intimacy of a tender hug, and it made him comfortable.

"Every bad comes with a good," she said, then turned and walked quickly out of the room.

8.

Penalt

Sacramento, California

May 1972

At the very moment he achieved the pinnacle of scientific success and recognition, Roger Penalt discovered that he wasn't cut out to be a scientist. He worked in a sterile lab housed in a cement building located in a city like every other city. It was as if he woke up in a bowl of mush and discovered he was the lone nut on which a mouthful of giant teeth was about to crunch. He was brilliant. He knew he was brilliant. With that confidence, he was certain he could find a better gig.

One of his cohorts, someone he'd stayed in contact with since their wild days together as undergraduates, had become director of research at Yawnix Pharmaceuticals, a company that five years ago had been a not-too-promising startup. After a series of remarkable new drugs brought to market, Yawnix became the biggest and most powerful player in the exotic world of botanical pharmacology.

Over lunch with his friend, Penalt expressed his fear of spending thirty years in a room with four walls, no windows, and nothing around him but dead animals. "Research is so damned frustrating! It's impossible to study anything as it is. First you change it in a way that defeats the whole purpose. Think about it. To figure out how a cat works you take it apart. What do you have then but a dead cat?"

Penalt's friend raised his eyebrows. He was a giant of a man, the kind that could slap your back and send you across the room.

"You've been inside the lab too long, Roger. What you need is a job in the field."

"What does that mean, a job in the field?" asked Penalt, who began to have vague recollections of the famous Smith Herbarium and visions of himself as a protégé of Richard Schultes, whom he had met briefly at Harvard when he'd first developed an interest in hallucinogenic plants.

His friend wore impeccable gray slacks, a light blue shirt, one of those flashy wide ties in the new '70s style, and wide black suspenders. He pulled the suspenders out with his thumbs and let them snap back onto his chest sadistically. Penalt doubted his friend had been reading Sacher-Masoch's *Venus in Furs*, but he'd have fit right in.

"Most of our best drugs have come from the plants and herbs and animal compounds indigenous healers have been using for centuries. We've been working in Central and South America. Now we want to focus on the healers in Northern Baja. We could send you down there as our man on the ground. You'd send back whatever you can gather. It would be like a scientific holiday. We'll have our chemists look at your finds to see if they can be replicated in the lab. We're looking for profitable drugs. There's millions to be made, buddy. You'll be paid handsomely for your efforts. You'll also have the enjoyment of working outside in a natural environment. No dead cats. If it works out, we'll send you off on one expedition after another. You'll live the life of Riley."

Mephistopheles couldn't have composed a better speech.

"Is that legal?"

"Of course it's legal. Everything we do has to be according to the rules, buddy. No way around that. Don't sit on this offer, we need to move fast. Our competition is circling like vultures. First come first served."

It wasn't a huge leap for Penalt. He had no family, plenty of money in the bank. He was hungry for a real challenge, and decided on impulse to go for it.

"I'm in!"

"I knew it! This is the perfect solution to your problem, Roger. We'll get the papers in order. I'll contact a local guide. You should be ready to leave in a few days. Pull your affairs together. Do you need an advance in pay?"

"No. I'm fine. I want all my pay deposited in my bank account here in the States." Penalt was abstemious and careful with his money.

"Done!" As his friend raised an arm to slap him on the back, Penalt maneuvered out of the way and made for the door. He didn't want to start his new job with a fractured spine.

"Thanks! This is going to be fun."

For the first time in years, Penalt felt real excitement. He had nothing to lose and much to gain. On the way back to his studio apartment he bought a book and some tapes to brush up on his Spanish. He'd studied the language in grade school and had a basic foundation in vocabulary and grammar. Even his pet fish sensed that something was up and swam around the tank with unusual alacrity. Penalt wondered what the fish would think about his plans. He'd need someone to care for it while he was gone; probably best to give it away. Alex, the boy next door, was the perfect age. His dad had died of a defective heart not long after Alex was born. Penalt and Alex's mom had been spending time together. Penalt would miss that, but he could still help her out financially while he was gone. He would make that clear before leaving.

A week later he met with his friend one last time to sign the contract and get his last-minute instructions.

"The people in the hills are independent and naïve to the ways of the world. They're happy to share their knowledge once they trust you. Establishing trust is the key. Dress simply, nothing new or fancy. Don't say anything about money or Yawnix or Western drugs. They have no respect for capitalism down there. Be inconspicuous, try to blend in. Use the same buses the local people use. Pretend you have a personal interest in the ancient methods of healing. Hell, maybe tell them you want to be a healer yourself—you know, become one of them. You've got to act the part so they'll accept you. They have a natural distrust of outsiders, but you have a way with people, buddy. I remember how you were in college. Christ, you got me out of one jam after another with your sweet talk. Have you ever thought about politics?

"Are you kidding? I would hate a political career."

"Oh, well, you know what I mean. We've hired a guide to help you with language and logistics. The ball's in your court now, buddy. Any questions?"

"I'm not as confident as you about my communication skills. What if I can't gain the trust of the locals? I've heard some of these healers can see into a spirit world. Of course, I don't believe that, but I'm sure they're very good at figuring people out. They'll know right away if I'm not being honest with them. But I don't have to lie—I do have an interest in the methods of these healers."

Penalt had paid dearly for a life of deception, mostly deceiving himself. He wanted no more of it. If he was expected to gain someone's trust, whoever they were, he wanted to gain it sincerely.

"Come on, Roger," said his friend with a smirk. "You don't really believe all that mumbo-jumbo, do you? These healers know which plants are good for which illnesses. They've experimented and tested just like the rest of us, and killed quite a few of their people along the way. The spirit stuff is strictly a show. It fits in with the kooky ideas of the New Age spiritualists who flock down there in search of gurus. Get on with it, buddy—do what you think is best, but don't lose sight of why you're there. Finding the right plants is where the money's at."

The black suspenders whacked away indiscriminately. Penalt pictured purple bruises on his friend's chest.

Penalt didn't like such a cold attitude. Despite some reservations, he did have respect for the healers he'd read about. The so-called spirit world wasn't so far from science, was it? Science has its oddball theories that seem ridiculous until they're tested. Had anyone actually tested these alternative methods? He'd studied all about plants. This whole thing excited him. To be out in nature in a new culture and to have the opportunity to learn, maybe even to discover, some new and wonderful medicines was something he looked forward to. Who knows? He might learn something truly fascinating—something beyond the mundane world of Western drugs. He'd do what he wanted once he got down there; satisfy his curiosity and let Yawnix pay for it. He didn't tell this to his pal, who was big and stupid but very adept at shoving people around. Penalt had no intention of being shoved around.

As Penalt ruminated on these thoughts, his friend leaned forward with an earnest look. He put his hands on the table and his feet beneath his broad shoulders. He looked like Leo "The Lion" Nomellini, the retired tackle of the San Francisco 49ers. His mouth was slightly open, his teeth crooked, his eyes crossed. Looking into those eyes, dark and deep in their sockets, Penalt felt like a sparrow trying to face down a cobra.

"There's a small village up in the mountains, Roger. That's where we want you to go."

His friend spoke almost in a whisper as if he wanted to make sure no one could hear but Roger even though no one else was there. "It will be tricky getting there, but we've arranged it. It's the home of a famous healer, an Indian woman who's known throughout the mountain villages as the oldest and wisest of, I don't know, I think they're called *cure a deras*. If anyone knows about this healing shit, she does. We think she may be the clue to what we're looking for down there."

Penalt's friend raised his hands off the table and snapped his suspenders twice.

"This is the real deal, the reason we're sending you down, but it's strictly hush-hush, top secret. You gotta keep this to yourself, okay? Nobody gets the details, especially if you get interrogated by the authorities."

"What do you mean, interrogated?"

Penalt felt a little squeamish, like he was being dragged into something not quite kosher.

"Well, the locals don't exactly welcome us poking around in their business but, as I've said, you've got the skills. And then, you might run into our competitors. Mum's the word. Got it?"

Penalt's unease gnawed at him. He knew there were risks, but he hadn't thought about how serious they might be until now.

"Rumor has it this healer lady has a renegade strain of Laetrile, you know, the purported anti-cancer compound made from apricot pits. The stuff is currently illegal in the States. We think Laetrile is just another quack remedy, but it's very popular with cancer patients because everything else has failed them. The clamor for Laetrile is one thing that's united the crazies on the right and on the left. The John Birchers and the New Age hippie-types are both fighting the government on this. The tests to date have been negative; however, we heard that one of the researchers over at Sloan Kettering got hold of an oddball sample that produced good results. This drove our competitors nuts. They buried the report. No respectable drug company wants to touch it. It's all about money: the expensive drugs on the market are very profitable, and Laetrile could change that."

Penalt's friend stood up. He paced nervously as he spoke.

"We don't have an anti-cancer drug on the market, so we have nothing to lose. We want a stake in the game. It's a real competitive business. We think the initial results justify further testing, but we don't want to look like a bunch of crackpots. That's why we're keeping a lid on our efforts until we have a chance to check it out. It's a long shot, but if it proves out we could have a blockbuster on our hands, a once-in-a-lifetime opportunity. We'd piss off a lot of our competition, which would be just fine with us, buddy. A proven cancer cure would be worth a fortune. Put a lot of our competitors out of business. A reliable source told us this oddball serum might be available at this remote mountain village. We're putting all our faith in you. Do whatever you need to do. Find a way, but get us a sample. We'll fund you. There's a big bonus if it all comes together. But remember, this is off the record. We can't tarnish the Yawnix reputation."

9.

Russell Napier

Clinica Buena Salud, Tijuana

The titles were filled with medical and scientific terms. *The Laetriles—Nitrilosides in the Prevention and Control of Cancer, Chemotherapy of Inoperable Cancer: Preliminary Report of 10 Cases Treated With Laetrile, Laetrile Therapy in Cancer.* Eric thumbed through a brochure about the foundation Russell Napier had set up to fund Laetrile research.

The Napier Foundation specializes in sponsoring independent research; it is particularly interested in scientists who are unable to get backing from orthodox research organizations either because their ideas are too far off the normal thought of the day or because the individual himself, because of his personality, is unable to get along with organizations.

The door to the office opened. Eric recognized the man he'd seen on the news report at the hospital. In person he was quite impressive.

"Hello, Mr. Martin. My name is Russell Napier. Doctor Milagro is on his way. I'd like to speak with you first, if that's okay with you. My firm manufactures the Laetrile used here at the clinic."

...the individual himself, because of his personality, is unable to get along with organizations...

Napier's presence filled the room like a strong aroma. Sunlight coming through the window reflected off his large diamond ring and projected tiny rainbows onto the walls of the office as Napier moved his hand. Blue, green, yellow, and red—a ribbon of color danced around the white background.

"I know who you are." Eric's words echoed in the large room.

Napier had come to test him. It made sense. Powerful forces conspired against Laetrile. The companies that pushed drugs on cancer victims and the doctors who performed those expensive operations had a lot riding on the idea that Laetrile was just bunk. Here was a man who claimed to have a cure for cancer without drugs or surgery. If he turned out to be right, the people who called themselves experts would look foolish. The large pharmaceutical companies would lose a lot of money.

"I've read your file, Mr. Martin. You're an attorney from Sacramento. You were treated at Stanford. You present a difficult case. I'll be honest: We're a small company, but we have large goals. I believe Laetrile could be for cancer what insulin is to diabetes. We cannot speak of a cure, not yet. It would be premature to do so, but we're very optimistic."

Napier paused. He walked into the cone of sunlight coming through the window like Captain Kirk climbing into the transporter on *Star Trek*.

"Life cannot always be a peaceful day at the swimming hole, Mr. Martin. Sometimes it's a torrent with a multitude of forces that are difficult to subdue."

Eric knew how easy it was to be deceived. Those innocent-looking Indian boys selling Chiclets downtown would sell you their sister in the alleyway for the right price. The words "not so easy to subdue" hung in the air. Eric needed a special geometry where parallel lines could cross and straight lines could curve. He wasn't interested in experimental treatments. He wanted results.

"Look," he said irritably, "I know the odds are against me."

Big black ants crawled along the windowsill. They moved
in two directions. Eric watched them grow to the size of
people. He saw their faces—the oversized eyes, the sharp
mandibles, the short, pointy teeth. They were hunters. They
bumped into each other but tried to stay on course. When
order broke down there were collisions.

"The odds are better than you think," said Napier. We've had
more success than I imagined. Laetrile has made a difference for so
many. I think it can make a difference for you too, Mr. Martin. Your
condition is very serious, but it is far from hopeless."

A dark shadow entered the room. A large bird flew down
from the ceiling and pecked at the ants. Terrified, they
scattered in all directions.

"Are you okay, Eric? Do you mind if I call you Eric? You seem
distracted."

Eric had a blank stare. His mind made the connection. *The Naked
Jungle, Leiningen Versus the Ants*—he'd seen the movie when he was
in high school. Thoughts flew loose like the scattered pages of a book
unbound. Arbitrary scenes from his past and the present.

For Christ's sake, just pay attention.

"I'm not going to let them use the chemo or the radiation." He
spoke the words with no feeling, without thinking. The movie reel in
his head continued to unravel.

There... the fat girl in the Señor Suerte T-shirt. There... a
mangy dog chewing at a bone, the stringy sinews shredding
apart and flying up, bits of dead meat. There... a lost
poet guiding a young boy's hands along the keys of an
accordion. There... lips drawn back in a perpetual mocking
grin... a curse not from the God above or the fiend below
but from the man himself—the man in the red car. There...
hope or despair, cure or poison, sanity or madness....

Eric paid attention to his health. He monitored his body with the
same discipline he brought to all aspects of his life. He lived cleanly,
didn't smoke, didn't drink, ate wisely, exercised. He knew the seven

warning signs of cancer. Still, his body had been under attack for years and he hadn't known. How could that be? The cancer grew right before his eyes all that time. The familiar becomes invisible in the same way that any idiosyncrasy does. Like a Trojan horse it hides in plain sight.

Eric's symptoms were visible to Napier. At first he thought Eric might be a spy sent to sabotage the clinic. Eric was an attorney, but he didn't disguise it. All the signs pointed to a real sickness. At first glance, Eric looked healthy, but a faint wheezing accompanied each breath, a sign of the fluid on Eric's lungs. He was anemic, tired, debilitated. He spoke with a peculiar *staccato obbligato* like a robot. It was as if he were in a trance. He was easily distracted, a fault Napier attributed to brain malfunction from the cancer. Like all the rest, Eric had undoubtedly come to the clinic for the usual reasons. He was no spy. He was, however, the kind of patient whose treatment posed risks for the clinic. Napier had to guard against taking on a difficult and potentially dangerous challenge.

Eric had grown up in awe of his father, the consummate showman attorney with a giant ego. His very name, Vayne, said it all. His reputation was made during the famous Crenshaw case. It was during that case that Vayne Martin pulled a severed limb out of a bag in the courtroom to shock the jury. It worked. Criminal cases were never the same after that. Eric would have loved to pull out his tumor and throw it on the floor, to stomp on it, spit on it, yell, and curse, but he was not his father, and cancer was more complicated than a court case.

Napier watched as Eric stood frozen and mute, lost in thought. He had to take control of the conversation or they would never get to the point. "Don't give up, Eric. We haven't even begun. In the end, we all die, but we can give you a longer and better life than conventional medicine. Don't withdraw into yourself. No one needs to die like a rat in a hole. You have to do the necessary work, but we'll meet you more than halfway if you take the first steps on your own."

The ant people and the giant bird disappeared. The black ants returned to normal size. Eric watched them push and pull the carcass of a dead bee up the wall to their nest.

He knew he was going to die. The uncertainty about when or where was maddening, yet it was this that in some odd way made life interesting, gave it a new intensity.

"I won't give up. I'm a realist. I know I have a date with death, but there's been a mix-up in the paperwork. I'm still alive, you see? I'm here. I've been granted a little more time. With your help I want even more."

On the back wall of the office there was a counter with a sink. On it, doctor things were laid out—knives, probing tools, a stethoscope. Eric shuddered as he thought of Stanford. There could be nothing worse than going through that debacle again with a different set of characters. He'd gambled everything on the hope that Napier and the doctors in Mexico could cure him without all the pain and suffering. There was no going back now.

"What do you mean, a mix-up?"

"Well, I didn't die did I? That's all I meant. I'm not going to worry about how that happened."

One moment he languished in the hospital at Stanford, the next he was in Mexico. Life is full of baffling events. He didn't believe in fate, but sometimes you have to make allowances.

"Well, you've come to the right place, Eric. We believe that cancer is a metabolic disease. The tumor is a symptom. You've heard that tale about the operation being called a success even when the patient dies? We do things differently here. Our treatment with Laetrile and diet challenges the very foundation of medicine. A metabolic disease results from a lack of vitamins or minerals. Think how scurvy was cured with vitamin C, and how pernicious anemia was cured with vitamin B12 and folic acid. No operations were necessary, no poisonous drugs—the only things needed were proper vitamins and a good diet."

As the bird by wandering, as the swallow by flying, so the curse causeless shall not come (Proverbs 26:2).

His cancer was not the hand of random fate. It was the result of a cause, and causes could be corrected. Right here in Mexico, with Laetrile and vitamins and diet. Maybe he was a raving madman, a fool in search of harmony in a world turned upside down. Sometimes, however, magnificent thoughts could creep into the head of anyone, even a perfect fool.

He heard a choir. Confusing voices, discordant sounds, garbled words. *Ignore it!* The choir was a trap, a reflex of his auditory senses, like the voices one hears after someone he knows well dies.

"Eric? Are you sure you're all right?"
"I'm fine. Tell me about Doctor Milagro. Is he a minister or a doctor? What's the deal with these biblical quotes all over the walls?"

And he shewed me a pure river of water of life, clear as crystal, proceeding out of the throne of God and of the Lamb. In the midst of the street of it, and on either side of the river, was there the tree of life, which bare twelve manner of fruits, and yielded her fruit every month: and the leaves of the tree were for the healing of the nations (Revelation 22: 1-2).

"Milagro's an excellent doctor. He's also a very religious man. Dealing with the mysteries of the body can make anyone wonder what life's all about. There is no reason a good Christian can't be a fine healer. Christians preach compassion and optimism. Many of Doctor Milagro's patients share his religious views, but religious belief is not a requirement for recovery. I myself am not religious. The treatments work regardless."
Eric was rattled by the religious fervor. He wanted to make that clear.
"You see, Napier, Christianity is an extreme form of romanticism, something to be avoided, particularly now that I'm sick. Religion

confuses the wish with the reality. I was raised Catholic, but I gave all that up a long time ago. I choose to face life straight on, even now in the hard times. Many Christians think what matters most of all is faith—an enchanted orange tree, a font of holy water, a magic Askalon. Some need faith if they are to give their all, their best. I'm quite capable of doing without it, and I prefer it that way."

"Faith can help some people who might otherwise be stuck in their gloom. Don't worry about it, Eric. Doctor Milagro sees things in a religious context. If that puts you off, just ignore it. He has thirty years of medical experience. He was a military doctor during the war, and a good one. He's saved hundreds of lives, and he can save yours. He provides the patients at the clinic with the most modern scientific treatments available. He's one of the most competent and compassionate doctors I know. If I were in your position, I'd trust him with my life. That's the truth. If I didn't believe it, I wouldn't waste your time or mine."

"I get it. Just one more thing, because I want to be clear: The idea of paradise doesn't work for me, you see? Life is about what we do now, while we're alive, how far we go, how far we reach with our little bit of consciousness. I don't believe my life's over yet. I refuse to believe it. I want more, more of everything. There are things I have to do before I die. I don't know if the Laetrile works. The only way for me to find out is to try it. I can't get on my high horse now. I don't have any choices left. If it does work, if I survive this, I will be your best advocate in my country. If it doesn't work, well, you won't have to worry about me then. I suspect you think I have a hidden agenda, that maybe I'm in cahoots with your enemies up north. I give you my word that the only reason I'm here is to get well. I'm counting on you and the clinic to see me through this."

"Thanks, Eric. I hear you. It's true that monied interests have lined up against us, against their own people. Thousands die needlessly because of a misguided attempt by your government to protect people from themselves. Your laws sentence them unnecessarily to hopelessness and despair. But... first things first. We must get you well."

Eric was a sick man struggling to survive. Napier was impressed with Eric's clear view of his situation, clearer than most. Of course he was angry and afraid, but he wasn't in denial. Many patients never progress beyond that—most retain elements of it right to the end, and it makes treating them more difficult. When the chips are down and medical science has failed them, everyone comes in search of miracles, the realists and the dreamers. Eric was no different. He was here because conventional medicine had failed him. He knew that death was around the corner, but he wanted to fight. It was time to proceed with the treatment.

"Look, Mr. Napier, you don't need to worry—I understand and accept that there are no guarantees. Like anyone under these circumstances, I want to beat the cancer. I may ultimately die, but I won't go down without a fight. I'm not a whiner, nor do I pretend to be some kind of martyr. I have a lot to accomplish. I'll need my physical strength to do that. That's where you and the clinic come in. Give me a few more weeks, a few more months. Don't put me into a drugged-up stupor. If you can do that much, my trip down here will have been worthwhile."

It was a good speech. Napier was a businessman. Every patient is different. Philosophy was really just a grab bag from which people picked out and used what worked best for them. Napier knew most successful people didn't waste time on such foolishness as philosophy. Philosophers think too much, talk too much. Truly successful people don't spin philosophical arguments. Eric talked himself out of the pain and fear—good. This would make Napier's job easier. His strategy was to get Eric to focus on the treatment. Eric was an attorney, a practical man. He would respond best to a specific plan of care designed and carried out step by step. This made him an ideal patient.

"The most important consideration in your case, Eric, is to get the maximum amount of Laetrile into your body in the shortest period of time. We provide important supportive measures here at the clinic, measures we believe are essential for recovery. Doctor Milagro will discuss each of them with you and answer your questions. We use a comprehensive approach. It's a slow process, but it's possible you could recover completely."

"Completely?"

"I've seen it in cases like yours, believe me. Of course, no one can promise a complete cure in every case. Each individual is different. If you undergo the full metabolic approach together with Laetrile you'll maximize your chances of recovery."

Eric made up his mind to forge ahead and follow the plan. There were no other options. The worst thing was to second-guess every move. It was time to stop worrying, take things as they come. It was time to trust his instincts and get on with it.

Napier, approaching sixty, looked no older than forty—tall, trim but sturdy, with a neatly groomed dark beard and mustache, a golden tan, sharp features, hair sandy but still dark, a man at the top of his game. His green-and-hazel eyes followed Eric around the office. Eric, a fan of Shakespeare, knew about the green-eyed monster, jealousy. Were those eyes of Napier's a warning, or did the hazel in his eyes indicate steadfast and dependable friendship like Shakespeare's Benvolio? How could Eric know? What he did know was that those blue eyes of Nurse Marta were pitiless and cold. Thank God blue eyes aren't always in season; hazel eyes, like hazelnuts, have their season also.

"Have you ever faced death, Napier?"

"A few times. There's a difference between facing death in war or wild adventure, and the quiet, vicious self-destruction your body is going through. Cancer is not like battling some outside force. Your own body is fighting against itself. Adventures come to an end, and sometimes you get a boost from the adrenaline that runs through your veins, but cancer goes on. There's no release. It debilitates. Laetrile works with your natural will to survive. It doesn't battle your body like chemotherapy and radiation. At Buena Salud we treat the body that has the disease, not the disease that has the body. No matter what, keep up your spirits, Eric. We'll work together on the cure."

A black limousine entered the clinic compound. Eric saw two Mexican men in suits emerge and walk into a room on the other side of the clinic. He recognized them as the same men he'd seen outside El Azteca when he was with Solomon. Seeing them here brought on his unease.

"Who are those men? I saw them earlier when I was in the taxi."

Napier looked anxious. His eyes locked onto the two characters as they entered his office.

"Their names are Tomás and Rafael Negros. They are called the *Dos Negros* here in Tijuana. The two brothers are investors in the manufacturing plant. They've invested in all of Doctor Milagro's clinics. The fact is, doing business in Mexico requires the right contacts. We couldn't function here without their support. I see it in your eyes that you think they might look a little treacherous. The point is, we need them and they let us do our business without interference. I can assure you of that."

Necessary maybe, thought Eric, *but not welcome.*

Napier's magnetic personality and stunning résumé made him an easy sort of man to like and admire; a strong man who played god, guide, and judge with the clinic and its patients. Eric didn't want to become a pawn in someone else's game. He'd been told the Laetrile business was sketchy, but at this point he had no other choice. Those Dos Negros gangsters rattled his nerves. He didn't like it. He was trying to make the most important decision of his life, but what he needed to know was sealed in a box like Schrödinger's cat. Eric didn't like complications. His stomach cramped up, and he started to sweat.

"I suppose I'm just one more statistic in your pile of data."

"No, Eric. Let me tell you, my life has been up and down the keyboard. I've been to the top and to the bottom, happy and miserable. I don't dwell on the difficulties life throws at us. That's just life. Working through life's problems has its therapeutic side. Fairytales are fun, but I choose to face the messy facts. A rosy picture of life may be a coping mechanism for some as you yourself have said. Not for me. The world is complicated, but the reality is always better than an illusion. One thing you must understand, you will never be a mere statistic to us. We're here to help you, to help all of our patients as individuals. We work hard to make a difference. We use every minute of every day to make you well. You can find me in my office whenever you need me. Right now I must leave to meet with the Dos Negros. We're planning a new line of Laetrile-based products to bring to market. Some day we will eliminate the plague of cancer for good. Thank you for your candor. We understand each other. You will be happy at the clinic. Your decision to come is the first step in a journey that will make all the difference in your life. Doctor Milagro will be on his way shortly."

They shook hands. The meeting was over. Eric wouldn't allow things to flip backward. He'd made up his mind: he was moving ahead.

"Jesus, this whole thing is so maddening. I'm right at the end of my rope."

"Whoa. Slow down, man. That mind of yours is playing tricks. Try a spoonful of this. It'll put things right."

"Huh? I don't need to slow down, Nelson. I need to think straight. I need to figure out what I should do."

"Hey, come on, just one sip. That ole nurse is busy and I sneaked in here to calm you down. You got plenty of time to figure it all out... there... that's it... yeah! Put that head back down on the pillow."

10.

Doctor Milagro

T he doctor's grip was firm but soft. The bones in his hand were as delicate as a small bird's.

Feathers fluttered behind the curtain. A tiny beating heart pulsated. A frightened bird navigated in the darkness with anxious red eyes. A sharp beak pushed forward and tore jagged holes in the fabric. Fingers emerged, each one a record of lives broken and saved. Five slender fingers, a smooth, cupped palm, an entire hand.

Doctor Milagro (*did that last name really mean "miracle"?*) arrived with a jovial smile, but Eric sensed a quiet sadness behind the bushy black eyebrows and thick mustache. Hidden away in the inscrutable interior of this gentle man was a deep sorrow, the result of a constant stream of horrors that fanned the fires inside the doctor's brain.

"You have a malignant growth, Mr. Martin. You are seriously ill, but you have come to the right place. We have a way to slow the cancer. There is a chance that we can stop it altogether. Yes, I believe there is a good chance, God willing, a good chance."

Doctor Milagro exuded confidence, yet all around him there was chaos.

Outside the door in the hall, a woman shuffled along like an apparition. She wore a loose red dress.

A loud screech came from the shadows.

The woman stopped and turned, then walked on, looking confused and unsettled. Pale, drab hair, unkempt like a windswept pile of straw hung in scattered ringlets from her head. A skeletal man stumbled alongside her, squinted his eyes to read the inscriptions on the wall. Mida arrived. Without a word she took the lady's hand and guided her back to her room.

> A shadow followed, rising, falling, hovering anxiously, weaving a web with the skill of Arachne. It was visible only as a black mass. The strange group was quickly out of sight. Nothing remained except a pale yellow light that reflected ominously like the eerie glow of a submarine trapped at the bottom of the ocean where lives slowly suffocated away.

Eric took a deep breath. The acrid smell of a disinfectant interrupted his thoughts. Doctor Milagro saw Eric looking at the photo of a young Mexican woman on the desk. She was dressed in a vibrantly colored off-the-shoulder Second Empire gown.

"My wife, when she was on the stage," said the doctor. Milagro's soft brown eyes brightened with pride as he spoke of his wife. "As you can see, she has Napoleonic and Indian blood." Milagro's head was bald on top but had patches of black hair slicked down on both sides. His warm attitude and folksy manner was in sharp contrast to Napier's businesslike efficiency.

"I've reviewed your file from Stanford, Mr. Martin. I have great hope, thanks to God, that we can cure you. I cannot make promises, but your case is similar to those where Laetrile has had optimal impact."

Eric liked the words "optimal impact."

"Doctor Rice told me my cancer is inoperable and recommended chemotherapy and radiation. I looked into that, the side effects and the results. It wasn't something I wanted to pursue."

A tiny yellow-green iguana scurried halfway up the wall and stopped.

> The iguana lunged about in a series of random movements—up, down, left, right, like the keys of a typewriter. A pattern appeared. The marks left by the

iguana's feet as they dug into the wall looked like some kind of message.

"Your cancer has metastasized, Mr. Martin. It has moved from the original tumor to other areas in your body. It's in your bloodstream and lymph nodes. I do not recommend the operation, nor do I like the idea of drugs or radiation. To cut, to burn, to poison—that is not God's way. The poisons invade and debilitate your body, which is left weak and in need of repair. Our treatments with Laetrile and other metabolic therapies work in a way that is natural and holistic. A strict diet is an essential part of the cure. You may not be familiar with the dietary rules in the Bible, Leviticus 11 and Deuteronomy 14. At the clinic we take these rules seriously. Our patients do much better with our approach."

I guess this means my Sunday mornings with bacon and eggs are over, Eric thought. He'd never considered going vegetarian. Even Stanford hadn't forced that on him. Was meat the problem then? Could he have prevented the cancer by eating differently?

Doctor Milagro paged through Eric's file. The doctor wore a white coat over a white shirt with a lime-colored paisley tie. Polished snakeskin boots protruded from beneath his dark pants. His face grew flushed as he spoke. Eric wondered if the tie was too tight.

"Like all our cells, cancer cells are part of our bodies. There is no victory for cancer. If it kills the victim, it kills itself. God created life in all its forms. This includes cancer. God made the malignant cell for a purpose. We may not know that purpose, but here at the clinic we do not argue with God. Our approach is to control your cancer, not to destroy it. Sometimes the tumors shrink, sometimes they disappear. That is not necessarily our goal, but sometimes God wills it. We encourage the body to heal itself. We teach you how to live a healthy life together with your cancer."

Something twisted inside Eric's stomach. He didn't want to live with his cancer. He wanted to be rid of it. He glanced back at the wall. The iguana had reached the top and was slowly making its way into the corner. The strange marks were gone.

"I understand. When can I start the treatments?"

"Before the treatment comes the examination. I think we can move forward as soon as possible, assuming you feel strong enough. We could start this afternoon if you wish."

"Yes, I'd like that."

Outside the window Eric saw the Dos Negros leaving.

Doctor Milagro pulled down the window shades. He washed his hands thoroughly in the sink. When he approached Eric with a thermometer and a stethoscope, the smell of soap was still on his hands. "May I ask you please to remove your shirt?" Milagro took Eric's temperature and listened to his lungs and heart. He tapped around on Eric's body, inspected Eric's ears and throat, then took his pulse. He felt around Eric's neck and below his ears, then massaged Eric's chest, stomach, and his armpits.

"Your vital signs are good. Are you tired? Do you want to wait until tomorrow? You've had a long and exhausting trip. Maybe you need a rest?" Doctor Milagro raised the shades. The courtyard was visible again.

An old man sat on the bench outside.

"I've seen that man before."

"What?" Doctor Milagro looked out the window into an empty courtyard.

Had it come to this, seeing things that weren't there? The cancer slurred the stops between illusion and reality, hallucination and perception. Dislocations occurred.

"I sometimes have these visions. I see things that may not be there. I suppose it's my illness."

"Perhaps it's best if you rest for the remainder of the day, Mr. Martin. We can start your treatment tomorrow."

The disorientation threatened and overwhelmed. Eric had no time to rest. He had to get started. "No. I'm fine. I just need to learn my way around in this new world, that's all. Let's begin as soon as possible. How long will I be here?"

Eric's behavior was not unusual for a patient who'd just made the long trip from the States to the clinic. Physically he looked better than most. The majority of the patients were elderly, in rough shape, near the end of their lives. Doctor Milagro did what he could. With Eric, there was a real chance of success. It wasn't often the doctor had such a welcome prospect.

"The daily Laetrile injections take about three weeks. We ask you to stay here at the clinic during that time. We keep you on a strict diet of juices and organic vegetables, and insist you eat all your meals at our cafeteria. We are quite proud of the food here. Your meals will be prepared according to our exacting standards. We provide supplements designed to enhance the treatments. Coffee enemas are also part of the program. They remove the carcinogenic toxins from your digestive system, a prime cause of many internal disorders. The road to a cure is not personal. It is the same for everyone. It includes proper food, proper exercise, a clean physical environment free of pollution, and a pleasant emotional environment free of stress. Unhealthy foods, you see, cause the malignancy to grow. Healthy foods allow the body's natural defenses to work and absorb the malignancy."

First, no bacon and eggs, now enemas! This was going to be a trial. It sounded logical. Unconventional, yes, but logical. Outside the door, a man in a black shirt and red shorts ambled by. He had a gray ponytail, and moved across the courtyard at a slow, steady pace.

"Based on your experience, what are my chances?"

Doctor Milagro looked at the ceiling and his jowls stretched upward. Whatever he had used to slick down his hair had worn off.

"We've seen spectacular results, but it's all in the hands of the man upstairs."

"I'm more interested in what we do here on the Earth, Doctor. I should tell you, I'm not a religious person. I hope that doesn't prevent me from being treated here, that it won't interfere with your ability to heal me. Do you really think there's a chance I can be healed? Completely healed? I've heard Laetrile contains cyanide and is toxic. My brother mentioned this to me. Is that something I should be worried about?"

A rationalist, thought Doctor Milagro. *Here come the questions.*

"We treat everyone regardless of their religious beliefs. I'm sorry if anything I've said disturbed you. The success does not depend on your views of God. You will soon see the results for yourself. Laetrile is a natural substance. It's true that it contains cyanide, but the cyanide is inert unless unlocked by a particular enzyme. It's a common misunderstanding that the cyanide in Laetrile is dangerous. The medical establishment in your country misrepresents the facts. I'm sorry to say this, but the FDA, the doctors, and the drug companies discredit us to protect their profits. Laetrile works against cancer through a very simple process based on its unique connection with cyanide. The research is there for anyone to see. The enzyme that unlocks the cyanide in the Laetrile is present only in the cancer cells. It isn't present in the normal cells. The cyanide kills the cancer cells but has little impact on the other cells. For someone without cancer, Laetrile is as harmless as sugar water. We are so confident of its safety that we are working on using Laetrile as a preventative measure for healthy people so that they will never get cancer."

Clinica Buena Salud was an odd place. No doubt about it. There was much that made Eric uncomfortable, but would Stanford have been any better?

"I haven't any time to lose. According to the doctors at Stanford, the cancer is moving through my body quickly. They told me it's an unfortunate side effect of contracting cancer at a young age when my body is more vigorous. What do you think, Doctor? Can you slow it down?"

"I think, with God's help, you and I together will bring the cure."

"I want to be informed about everything. I want the whole truth, none of this 'the patient can't handle it' sort of thing they do in American hospitals. Honestly, I don't have much hope. If things start moving in the wrong direction, I'd probably want to go home to tie up some loose ends."

Outside Milagro's office patients walked aimlessly in the courtyard. Illness was all around. A sweet, foul odor permeated the hallways. Being at the clinic was like being at a big dance where cancer was everyone's partner.

A fantastic zoo of strange colors, people, animals, and
objects flew in the space around him. A thorny bush
clawed its way along the walls of the courtyard. A tree with
enormous green leaves pushed its way upward toward
the sky. A monkey sat on one of the limbs and fidgeted
nervously. The monkey looked sad. Its eyes were closed.
The monkey's lips parted as if it were about to speak. This
bizarre scene vanished to the sound of garbled words.

"If you *are* healed, Eric, you will heal yourself. The Creator designed your body to heal and repair itself. All the physician can do
is cooperate with God. Cancer is not a monolithic disease. It varies
from one patient to the next. Treatment of the disease must reflect
each individual's distinct metabolic profile."

A frenzied woman danced in the air. Her words were the
words of truth but undecipherable. A cat's whiskers brushed
against his arm. They foreshadowed the future but only the
cat understood. A snake's tongue hissed a prediction too
quietly to be heard. A ragged figure ran from tree to tree.
The fool sees not the same tree as the wise man sees.

"I'm ready, doctor. Let's get started. Once I get the hang of things,
I'm pretty good at keeping up a regimen, even if it's difficult."

Under a framed picture of an apricot tree Eric sees another
biblical phrase.

And I will raise up for them a plant of renown, and they shall
be no more consumed with hunger in the land, neither bear
the shame of the heathen any more (Ezekiel 34:29).

"Healing is built into nature, Eric. Plants, animals, and human
beings normally heal automatically. In case of illness or injury, the
brain tells every organ in the body just what to do to bring about the
needed repair. You know I'm a religious man. In this hospital, the
medical director is Jesus Christ. *That* makes all the difference! We
can control your cancer if you let us, if you will work with us."

The God stuff crept in at every turn. Eric had to admit to himself
that it bothered him. Doctor Milagro saw his doubt.

"You don't have to be a Christian or share my religious beliefs. I sometimes have a hard time separating them from my doctoring, but I will do my best to minimize that as we move forward. It is part of the cure to *wish* to be cured. When the body is sorrowful, the heart languishes. Healing requires a positive attitude above all. Mida will take you to your room and administer your first injection. As you requested, I'll keep you informed and will hold nothing back. We are here to help you, Eric. We are here to make you well."

They shook hands. Doctor Milagro's grip was solid and firm, not the delicate birdlike touch Eric felt when they first met. There was nothing tentative or unsure about it. He had a look of cheerful confidence. Eric couldn't decide if Doctor Milagro was a quack or a pioneer breaking new ground like Galileo or Columbus. This morning Eric had awoken in the familiar surroundings of his regular life. This afternoon he was in a strange border town where he listened to a doctor in cowboy boots give a lecture on health and nutrition, quote from the Bible, and promise to cure him with seed kernels and diet and juices and enemas.

Mida rifled through the files on her desk.

"Excuse me? Doctor Milagro says you'll show me to my room."

"*Ay, si, señor, momento, por favor. ¡Ay, caramba!* These files all wrong. *¡Dios mio, estos me estan volviendo loco!*"

Eric stood outside the office waiting for Mida. Three weeks ago he was healthy with a bright future. Now he was trapped in a nightmare. He had plunged out of the sky and crashed to earth. Like Saint-Exupery's little prince, he found himself in a vast desert. Nothing was clear except the snake at his foot, ready to strike. His only defense was a miracle cure based on obscure biblical phrases and a science that was dismissed as quackery in his own country. Blood rushed from his heart into his stomach. He felt sick, and walked off in a panic, in despair, as the optimism he'd felt moments ago evaporated.

"Señor, señor! *Espera, que voy.*"

Mida ran after him, but his mind raced ahead. What role did the Dos Negros really play at the clinic? Was the place a scam like Devon said? He wasn't about to let those crooks manhandle him. His stomach churned. It was all so strange, so peculiar. He almost retched at the thought of what he had done.

11.

Tomás

Napier walked into his office. Tomás sat on Napier's desk, legs outstretched, smoking a cigar. Rafael paced back and forth in front of the window.

"Hello, Tomás. Rafael."

"How is the research going, Napier? Have you cracked Frieze's formula yet?" An unpleasant smile surrounded the cigar between Tomás' teeth.

"Not yet, but we've made progress. I'll be visiting Elvin Krump in a few days. After that, Joey Zacco comes to discuss the strategy moving forward."

Zacco was a New Jersey mobster. His sister, Rose, was being treated with Laetrile in the States. Napier's company provided the Laetrile. It was illegal, but easy to smuggle across the border. Zacco was an early investor in BioPharm. He'd introduced Napier to Dos Negros. The three strongmen helped get Napier established in Tijuana. The relationship was tense. Napier knew his position was fragile and perilous, but he had experience with dangerous situations.

"Has Zacco got that congressman on board?"

While Tomás asked the questions, Rafael stared out the window at the light filtering through the trees. Sunbeams shone into the office and reflected off the picture of Napier and Fidel Castro that hung on the wall.

"Yes. I had Congressman Shipley set up the appointments with the Veterans Administration, the FDA, HEW, and the doctors at Walter Reed. We've managed to swing a few to our side. The Senate hearing has been scheduled. Everything should be in place by then."

Willard E. ("Will") Shipley was a congressman of influence and importance both inside the U.S. and abroad. A Democrat from New Jersey, he was a key member of the prestigious House Committee on Foreign Affairs, and was prominent in his party and fluent in the government bureaucracy. He'd been among a handful seriously considered by Lyndon B. Johnson as a running mate in 1964. Shipley had good looks, charm, and intelligence. He also had an impressive record in World War II and Korea, wounded three times, won eight decorations. He was just the sort of man Joey Zacco cultivated behind the scenes when the U.S. government went on one of its periodic rampages against organized crime.

Congressmen typically do their constituents favors. They help them get hearings in the halls of the capital. Shipley had helped Zacco behind the scenes when Zacco's businesses had been under investigation. With BioPharm, Zacco was asking Shipley to put his reputation on the line. There were bigger risks involved, so Zacco had to sweeten the pot. Shipley's attorney and law partner, Ed Dwyer, was a board member and major owner of the First National Bank of Bayonne in New Jersey. Zacco sold Dwyer a pile of options on BioPharm stock at a ridiculously low price. He thought this would be sufficient incentive for Shipley to cooperate.

"We were on the news in California, Napier. 'Criminal elements,' that's what the reporter called us. He connected Rafael and me to Joey's mob friends. I don't like that. Someone has a loose tongue. Find it. Cut it out."

"I'm sorry, Tomás. I don't know where that information came from. I'm sure it wasn't anyone here at the clinic."

"We have a problem with Velasquez." Tomás adjusted his legs on the desk and knocked a few papers onto the floor. He didn't bother to pick them up. "There's no time to wait for the old man to die. The Velasquez property is the last remaining hurdle before we can build our Laetrile products factory. We own all the surrounding properties.

Manuel Velasquez is an old man and very stubborn. He won't part with his property. He needs to disappear."

Rafael stood quietly hypnotized by the reflections of the flowers on the glass window. He was oblivious of the conversation. Napier knew what Tomás was suggesting. It was how things got done in Mexico. As long as they gave him a free hand in the manufacturing plant and the clinic, the rest was their business. Still, he worried about being drawn into the criminal activities Tomás and his brother pursued.

"I don't want to hear about it. Do what you must, but don't do it in a way that implicates the clinic or our Laetrile business. I have enough problems without getting caught up in one of your evil schemes."

Tomás sneered. His cigar rolled to one side of his mouth. A large gray ash dropped onto Napier's desk.

"The reporter quoted the mayor, Napier. He's a little man, but he can cause trouble. I keep him on our side. Stay away from reporters. They're up to no good. I won't upset your little fairytale world, *amigo,* but it's time to move ahead. You do your job. I'll do mine."

Tomás threw an annoyed look at his brother. "Stop prancing around like one of your fancy racehorses, Rafael. Time to go back to the car. *Nuestro negocio aquí está hecho.*"

Every day Manuel Velasquez opened the door to his small repair shop where he fixed everything—sewing machines, typewriters, clocks, sometimes even televisions, but they were hard to figure out and most of the time he couldn't get the parts. Years ago he'd repaired a mechanical doll for Doña Maria's daughter. Her granddaughter played with that same doll today. So many memories! Velasquez closed his eyes and the recollections arrived like a cool wind to bring him joy on a hot day.

His shop had stood for more than fifty years. It had been blessed with joy and plagued with sorrow. Manuel thought of his wife, blessed himself, and kissed his fingers.

He remembered making a toy train for Juan, the cook's son, out of odds and ends most people would throw away. When Jorge's father died, Jorge needed a job to support his family. Manuel converted an old bicycle into a sharpening tool for knives. Jorge first worked on the streets. He did well. He eventually opened his own shop. It was just a little cubbyhole next to the market downtown where the window washers drank their coffee, but it belonged to him. People came from all around to have him sharpen their knives and scissors. Manuel would never sell his little repair shop. It had been good to him and his neighbors. He hoped someday his son would carry on the business. There had been hard times for his son, Juan, after his mother died, but Velasquez was sure Juan would pull out of it and find his way in life. The thought of how the world had changed angered Velasquez. He stood and pounded his fists on the table.

Who are these Dos Negros brothers to threaten me, to try to force me out of my home and my shop? Money! I don't want their money. I'm not afraid of them. Come what may, I will leave it all in the hands of God. Not even the Dos Negros can interfere with God's plans. There is no family in this town I haven't helped. All my neighbors will stand up for me when the time comes. The Dos Negros are not men, they are brute animals. The decent people here know about their crimes, about the drug smuggling and the prostitution of young girls. The Bible says there is a time for everything. This is my time to draw a line in the sand. I will not be run out of my shop unless God wills it! *¡Dios ayúdame!*

Tomás had a unique ability to develop plans. Sometimes his plans upset his *hermano*.

"Don't search the vest for sleeves," complained Rafael, who avoided conflict.

Tomás sneered. For him, every problem was an opportunity. When he'd been an interrogator in Mexico City, one of his jobs was to question the government prisoners. Everyone knew about the torture that went on behind closed doors. He once told a wide-eyed rookie reporter who questioned his techniques: "Before the assassinations come the investigations, young man." Amused by the shock on the young reporter's face, he smiled diabolically and added as an afterthought: "*¡Es broma!*" But it was no joke. Tomás walked away, laughing, in his impeccable $1,400 suit that rustled with $100 bills, his cuffs twinkling with diamonds. Left alone, the reporter choked into the camera.

As an investigator, Tomás sometimes crossed the line. The screams of agony were so enjoyable. Oh, yes, even a saint could lose control and be moved to rapture. As the interrogation went on, everything got easier. You went into a rage and there was no stopping. It's just a normal human quality, yes? Reasonable when you look at it like that. You must do everything slowly. That's the trick. A little push, a little punch, and then a wire ignited like a thin trickle of fire, a series of little burns spaced to provide false comfort. Hah! Just the thought of it raised the hair on the back of his neck. Sadly for Tomás, he could not use these finely tuned investigation skills in this situation. He wasn't dealing with a prisoner—Manuel Velasquez was a crazy old man who acted like a stupid woman, a *suata,* who hadn't changed with the times. He didn't want money. Who doesn't want money? He couldn't be bribed with women. The silly *viejo* still loved his wife, though she'd been dead for years. An imbecile! Tomás had some of his thugs threaten Manuel with physical torture. The old man laughed at them. Laughed with his rotten teeth and his stinking breath. Napier didn't want to create suspicion. Tomás would not create suspicion. He gloated at his plan. It was perfect. It was brilliant.

If I didn't know I was a genius, I would die. If I was afraid, I would die. Why live like that? Humility, morality—they are for la panocha, *those with needs and desires so small they can be thwarted. Those who hold back their natural brutality are not real men. La panocha is a girl in a man's body, like Doctor Milagro. How revolting! Napier too is weak. He doesn't have the killer instinct. A weak man might be able to run a business, but you can't trust a man like that.*

Manuel Velasquez could not believe there was evil in the heart of his son. Many parents have this weakness. Tomás was thankful he had only bastards. Manuel's son might love his father, but his love for money was stronger. Tomás was an expert at exploiting the greed of the weak and stupid. The son was a perfect tool to carry out the plan Tomás had crafted. He reveled in his ability to pull the strings of the puppets around him.

Riding along La Coahuila Street in his limousine, Tomás knew his hermano could never think of such a plan. Rafael was cautious. He lacked the gusto to get things done, but he always accepted the results. Rafael and Tomás shared the same goals, if not the same methods. Rafael cultivated the business tycoons and the effeminate patrons of the arts. He enjoyed mingling with the showy *políticos*. He worked by manipulating the rich. He was offended by Tomás's crude ways. Rafael fancied himself a gentleman, but he refused to participate in the sordid world that makes the gentleman. Tomás had to do that for him. Rafael liked his fancy clothes, his toys, his women, and his connections with the rich and famous. The connections were useful, true, but it fell to Tomás to work in the other world, that shady underworld where the real deals got done. There are times when the art of persuasion works well. This was not such a time. Velasquez was a large root in their path. The solution with roots is to cut them out. Rafael didn't like to admit such realities, but he would accept the rewards they brought. Tomás was sure of that.

Tomás laughed at Rafael's uppity ways. "They say if you're born to be a *charro*, Rafael, your hat will drop down on you from the sky. Hah! I don't see no hats falling down on your head, hermano."

When Tomás looked up at the sun and squinted, his sinister smile chilled everyone, even Rafael, to the bone. Tomás drew pleasure from ridiculing the ways of the rich. He cavorted about and recited silly tunes. He mocked and heckled anyone who thought they were superior, even his brother. People laughed, but those who knew Tomás knew what lay behind his entertaining antics. Tomás was a monster never to be tested. His plan was to use Manuel's son. Like Rumpelstiltskin in the fairytale, Tomás would use the son to achieve his nefarious objective. Despite their differences, Tomás and Rafael were of the same blood. They had the same purpose in life. Most men have no goals any more than the hawks in the air. No course to run any more than the clouds. Tomás was different. He knew exactly what he wanted and how to get it. He used fear and greed and worked behind the scenes. Tomás thrived on raw power. Life without extremes was void of value. The monotonous pursuit of a daily vocation, never living, only working, never thinking, hypnotizing yourself by the routine and punctuality of your life—this turns a man into a mechanical toy, wound up tightly and fated to go on only for so long, then to stop when death takes him. Tomás never understood why so many men spent their precious days slaving for food and clothing, working for the bare necessities of life. These things are all there for the taking. Most men are small and pitiful, men like Manuel Velasquez. They're born to be servants. Only the favored few, like Tomás, were bold enough to take what they deserved.

The Golden Horseshoe was nearly empty at this time of day except for Juan Ysidro Velasquez. He was always there, drinking *cerveza* in his dark corner.

"*Que pasa,* Juan?"

As Juan looked up from his beer, Tomás gazed down at the pathetic face, thinking how easy it would be to smash it into an unrecognizable piece of meat, but he needed Juan to carry out his plan.

"Ah, Tomás. *Nada,* Tomás, nada. Sit down. Would you like a beer?"

"No. I just want, ah, to ask a question, hey?"

"*Ah, si, a sus ordenes,* Tomás."

"We both know, Juan, your father, ah, he will not live forever, God protect his soul. I been thinkin' we might strike a deal. You are a little short on money, si?"

"Ah si, si. *Es terrible.* I am so sad with debt and no work."

Tomás could hardly bring himself to speak with someone so wretched and useless. Juan had slipped down the ladder of life, and was now little more than an animal. Tomás doubted if Juan could reason or think on his own. He would have to make things very clear.

"I've known your honorable father for many years, Juan. You are a son to me. I want to help you. When your father dies, not soon, I hope, but one never knows," as Tomás spoke he worked to hide the twinkle in his eye, "you will have that property on Reforma Street, that run-down worthless shop."

"Ah, si, si, Tomás. I will have that shop, but it will be of no use to me. I know my father loves it, but I have no desire to carry it on."

"Just as I thought, Juan. Look here. I have this little piece of paper for you to sign. It says you agree to transfer the property as soon as it's in your name. If you sign today I'll give you 5,000 pesos, right now." Tomás took the cash out of his pocket and placed it on the table. "As soon as the property is in my name, I will give you 100,000 more. What do you think?"

"Where do I sign?"

Tomás pointed to the blank line. A few clear capsules fell from his hand.

"What are these, Tomás?"

"Oh, I'm sorry, they just slipped out. These capsules are very poisonous. Two or three dissolved in a cup of coffee would kill a giant. I carry them around in case, ah, in case I run into a giant that, ah, you know, might try to hurt me."

Tomás's smile turned Juan's stomach upside down, and his hand shook as he signed the paper. Tomás left the capsules on the table next to the pesos. He knew that even Juan would understand what to do with them. There was one problem: If the old man didn't pass out quickly, he might regurgitate the drugs, a special mix of Nembutal and an anti-nausea medication that a pharmacist had created for Tomás. The pharmacist had assured him that two or three capsules should suffice for the job.

"This is a good deal for you, Juan, a very good deal. Money solves all problems, hey? You will make a good businessman someday. I can see that your future is bright, bright like a meteor. There is a problem, though, if property values fall. Things have not been going well in that neighborhood around the shop. I would make an adjustment in the price if that happened."

Juan was afraid to stare too long into Tomás' cavernous eyes. He glanced down at the table before he softly asked a question: "What adjustment do you mean, Tomás? How large could it be?"

"Ah, that depends on the market doesn't it? I've heard that a more modern shopping area is opening a few blocks away. If that happens, I would have to offer much less. But today, today the price is good."

Tomás excused himself and walked out into the blinding sunlight. He was short and stocky like a little bull, his dark face always in a scowl. Scars on his left cheek and forehead told the story of a violent life. The bright sun made him squint. His mouth fell open, exposing his shiny gold teeth. He could almost hear the wheels turning in that worthless head of Juan's.

There will always be a dead beast for a hungry vulture.

Tomás was pleased as he climbed into the limousine. He looked at the gold watch on his wrist. He had time to spare. He instructed his driver to take him to a posh brothel on the outside of town. Tomás and Rafael set up this special whorehouse for their friends. It was outside the *zonas de tolerencia* where sailors and such could partake of charms illegal in the U.S. No *turistas* could enter this exclusive club. It was private and secure. Only the prominent and powerful were allowed. Wealthy and important patrons could indulge their fantasies without worry.

A young girl in a micro-mini and pigtails latched onto Tomás as soon as he walked into the cool, dark bar. The bar's backdrop was simulated tropical—a plastic rainforest of sparkling ferns and exotic flowers artistically planted in the cracks of rust-colored boulders. The girl hugged Tomás, sighed, and held both his hands.

"Oh, baby! Come on, baby, let's go to bed. I show you everything!"

Only the best new girls worked at this club. They were strategically deployed to light up the room with the sheer candlepower of their flashing teeth and eyes. They sat and vibrated with sweet promise. The chief of police was having lunch with some associates in a booth across the way. Tomás laughed at the girl and walked over to the bar, where he quizzed his manager, Aurelio. As they spoke, Tomás carefully watched Aurelio, whom he suspected of skimming the profits.

"The *Departamento de Sanidad* was here yesterday for the monthly health inspections, boss. As usual, the inspectors want larger bribes. And the cab drivers in town, they're asking for higher commissions." Aurelio looked nervous under Tomás's cold stare.

"We have a big problem with those cab drivers, a terrible problem," answered Tomás. "They're not as bad as they used to be, but they think they're the owners of this city. I told the mayor, they do whatever they like here. They want no controls. They are scaring off the tourists with their intimidations. This is very difficult for us. The mayor knows, the tourist department knows, but it's not our jurisdiction. It belongs to the federal government. We have to pay. We'll pass it on to the customers by raising cleaning fees, room rentals, the fee for the nurse's inspection, and the price of the contraceptives. Tell the girls downtown we're raising the quota. They'll have to speed things up. This is business. Tell them if they can't work at a faster pace, they'll be moved out to the cheap cribs in the barrios."

"Okay, boss."

"One more thing, Aurelio. I've been studying the receipts. They seem a little low this month."

Tomás watched Aurelio's reaction closely. He focused on the veins in Aurelio's neck to detect the pulse rate. He listened to the sound of Aurelio's voice to see if it was weak or strong. He observed whether Aurelio was too friendly or too repentant. All the signs pointed in one direction: Tomás was being played.

An Amazon in a blond wig strolled by and diverted Tomás's attention. She winked at him and walked upstairs. He followed.

When he left later, Tomás bumped into the mayor coming through the front door with his friends. Despite the hot sun, the mayor looked as if he'd just walked out of the tailor's shop.

"*Ah, mucho gusto, Tomás.* How... eh, well nice day, huh? Just thought I'd drop by for a look-see. It's been awhile. I like to keep tabs on things."

The mayor was wearing horn-rimmed spectacles and a white shirt. A thin dark tie poked through the opening in his expensive suit. When they shook hands, Tomás felt the large diamond on the mayor's finger.

¡Cabron! thought Tomás. *My hard-earned money is paying for these extravagances.*

"I heard your interview with the American reporter on the news the other night. Sometimes you talk too much, Mr. Mayor. We like to keep everything among friends here, you know?"

"The Americans would rather break our laws than their own," said the mayor with a smile. "I simply reminded them of that, no harm done, Tomás."

"Of course," scowled Tomás. "We do everything according to the law in our clubs. I'm sure you understand that, Mr. Mayor." Tomás and the mayor needed each other. They were careful to maintain a good relationship.

"Some of the cheaper places, they abuse the girls, Tomás. I don't like that. I hear they recruit young women from central Mexico under false pretenses, then force them into prostitution."

The mayor knew where Tomás got his girls. Tomás knew the mayor knew. All the clubs used the same tricks to lure poor young women away from their families and their homes. A little money and the hope of migrating north were irresistible draws for any young girl who had seen nothing but the brutal poverty of the Mexican interior. Their lives were better in Tijuana—at least they had a job. The mayor was happy to turn a blind eye as long as the bribes kept coming. He knew the facts. The business was good for his city. The conversation between the mayor and Tomás was carefully scripted. Words can get you into trouble. Deciphering the proper meaning at the right time was a game at which they both excelled. Their very lives depended on it.

"In our clubs all of the girls are prostitutes by choice, Mr. Mayor. I don't know about the other clubs, but here we arrange a better environment for everyone. We make sure our girls are clean. This is for their benefit and the benefit of our customers." Tomás and the mayor stood face to face. Neither gave ground. "Without us, these girls would be out on the street."

A minute passed in silence.

"I know," said the mayor, a sardonic smile on his face. "You run a clean shop, Tomás. You have no worries from us."

Tomás slipped an envelope into the Mayor's hand. The mayor raised his eyebrows and, followed by his friends, walked into the bar.

As he left, Tomás yelled to the manager.

"Aurelio, fix up the mayor's party with drinks. Everything's on the house for my friends."

Life is cheap, but living it is expensive. In Mexico, you always need the right people to operate anything. It annoyed Tomás, but it was the way it was.

As he drove away, Tomás played a recording he'd made of the mayor's statement from the interview on American TV. He paid to have all the mayor's important statements recorded. He wanted to hear exactly what was said whenever it concerned him.

Our laws are different from yours. According to our constitution, a woman can be a prostitute and it is no crime. It is a crime to have prostitutes work for you, you understand—to exploit them, that is a crime. Some criminal elements do exploit the girls, but we are rooting them out. If a woman chooses to be a prostitute, you cannot put her in jail. It is true that there are houses with pimps and all that, but they work that way because otherwise we would have a much bigger problem. You see, we are more advanced than the United States in this respect, more sophisticated, you might say. We allow prisoners to receive what you call the conjugal visit, and you see that stops all this homosexual business you have in your prisons. Our principles are different, beginning in our homes with our families. We are not as free as you are, we might say, with your women, but we allow prostitution, and it is according to our law, and you don't. You have higher sex crimes than we do, maybe a thousand to one. When we figured that out, we decided we would rather have prostitution than that kind of crime. You are the other way around. You would rather have those crimes and try to stop prostitution.

Later that night, Tomás paid the brothel another visit. This time he brought along Hector. They found Aurelio in the back room counting the money.

"Stand up, amigo," said Tomás. Aurelio looked terrified.

"Check his pockets, Hector." Hector found Aurelio's pockets stuffed with cash.

"I was about to add these bills to the others, Tomás. They're from my last rounds with the girls."

"You're a liar, Aurelio." Tomás's eyes flashed red like a demon. "Sit down. Put your hands on the table."

Aurelio shook in his boots. Hector noticed that Aurelio had peed his pants. In a split second, Tomás pulled out the meat cleaver he'd tucked behind in his belt and chopped off the tops of the three middle fingers of Aurelio's right hand. Blood gushed onto the table. Aurelio squealed like a pig.

"Give him a rag. We don't want a bloody mess in the office. Now, get out Aurelio, and don't come back. If I see you again, I'll finish the chopping."

Aurelio ran out of the room, tears streaming down his face, the rag on his hand soaked with blood.

A week later, Manuel Velasquez was sitting at the breakfast table having his cup of coffee as usual. He felt happy because Juan Ysidro had stopped by for a chat.

"I know that I've not been the son you wanted, Father."

Juan looked lonely and afraid. He spoke the truth, but Manuel was a father, and his father's heart was large and forgiving. He let his heart do the talking.

"How do boys grow into men? That is such a great mystery, Juan. We all begin our journey as animals, but God shines his light on us and gives us the wisdom to become whole human beings. His light is shining on you now."

Juan fidgeted in his chair. He wiped his face with his hands. Manuel could see his son holding back tears.

"I'm not worthy to be your son, Father. There's no God's light for me."

"Do not say such a thing, my son. Men will do what they must do. Life destroys the pureness God gives, that is true, but God's mercy is infinite, and he gives it back again and again. I love you, *hijo*. I know that things will be better for you soon."

Manuel had never seen his son so disturbed, so sad.

"Has something happened, my son? Do you have something you must tell your father?"

"No father. Only that... I love you."

"Please, Juan, bring your father another cup of coffee."

Juan rose and went to his father and gave him a long and heavy hug. He took his father's cup and went to the stove to pour the coffee. His hand shook as he slipped in the capsules and stirred everything together with sugar until the capsules were all mixed in. He went to his father and handed him the cup.

"I must go now. There is a man I must see about a job."

"A job?"

"Si, I think I have a job as a mechanic. Rest in peace, father. I love you."

As Juan left, the words rolled around inside Manuel's head.

My son, a mechanic? Hmm. Well, maybe things will get better after all.

Manuel drank his coffee quickly as always. It nauseated him, but he'd always had a strong stomach. He wondered if the water had gone bad again. Outside he watched two boys playing in the field across the way.

Where will they play when Dos Negros builds the factory? Does no one care anymore about the neighborhood? I will never sell, never! Whatever they offer, no matter their threats, I will never sell.

Manuel's hand began to shake. His heart beat rapidly like the old oil rigs he had seen as a child in the fields outside Tijuana. He felt pressure rising in his chest. His head fell forward onto the table. It did not rise again.

The maid found him dead at the table, the empty coffee cup broken on the floor. Manuel had often spoken of his desire to join his wife in Heaven. Old people who are alone sometimes look at death as a blessing. There were those who thought Juan Ysidro might have had something to do with his father's death, but no one really believed he would do such a horrible thing. A few weeks later, Juan went missing. Some said he'd made it over the line to East L.A. Others feared that bandits had attacked him after he sold his father's property.

12.

Mary

Mida waved an enormous needle through the air to mix the solution. Eric cowered at the sight.

"Señor, no close eyes. You no look to me? I not pretty to you? You want skinny gringo girl?" She laughed through full red lips—the kind that stain cocktail glasses. She played the Sancho Panza to Eric's Don Quixote.

Eric took off his shirt. He stiffened his arm by making a fist with his left hand. Mida doused his arm with alcohol and plunged the needle in. Her fingernails were long and sharp. They reminded him of the talons on the red-tailed hawks he'd trained with his grandfather as a young boy.

An electric field of pulsing sine waves, a football-shaped pocket of dazzling light, darkness. Slowly the scene became familiar, a scene from his past.

He walked with his grandfather into a meadow next to his house in Sugarvale. He carried a young hawk on his gloved hand. Grandfather helped him fly the hawk back and forth across the field. After each flight, the hawk landed smoothly on the glove and took the little treat waiting for it. The bird's large brown eyes moved curiously from side to side as it studied Eric. It had mottled brown wings, a reddish tail, a dappled white chest, and sharp claws. It clung to the glove on Eric's hand as if it were an old lost friend.

"All finish, señor."

He hadn't felt a thing. When Mida drew close, he recognized the perfume. One of the girls in his office at home used it. She came on to him once. He might have asked her out if it hadn't been against company policy. He was awful with women, awkward and nervous. He always thought of what to say after it was too late. Whenever there was an opportunity, he panicked and put it off. Sometimes this worked to his advantage. Women love the men who are hardest to get.

"*Al mal paso darle priso,*" said Mida.

"What?"

"In English, how you say, to a bad step, rush, yes?"

"Oh, you mean hurry up and get it over with?"

"*¡Si, es bueno!*"

Piercing blue eyes, starched white uniform, the chalky taste of the milkshake forced down his throat...

"Hurry it up, Mr. Martin. The faster it goes, the easier it goes."

"Sometimes. Sometimes that's true."

"Hey, you been talkin' in your sleep. Be cool, else that mean bitch gonna come in and shake you around."

"Nelson?"

"Who you think I am, a ghost?"

Eric opened his eyes.

"Why are things so much easier with Mida, Nelson?"

"Huh? Who? You talkin' bout your mama?"

"Mida." Eric's voice was very weak.

"Mida? Is that your magic lady, make you feel real good, make you forget all the shit round here? The bosses been leanin' on me. They been sayin' I'm not following the bitch's instructions. Threatenin' my job. They'll do anything to keep us brothers in our place. Maybe you could help me. You're an attorney right? Hey! You asleep again already?"

"You okay, señor? You no look okay."

"I'm fine, Mida. I just..."

Mida cleaned up the mess, ignoring him. She put the dirty cotton and other disposables into a plastic bag. Eric watched her methodical movements.

"Cleanliness is next to godliness," he said.

"*¡Si! Es verdad.*"

She watched him fiddle with his shirt. She cocked her head to one side.

"Okay, señor. No more today. No use looking for three feet on a cat." She laughed. Her large happy eyes shone with satisfaction under the heavy makeup. Mida had a sure touch for agreeable commonplaces.

"*Mañana* I see you again, okay?"

"Sure, what time?"

"*A las nueve, comprende?*"

"Yes, nine o'clock tomorrow."

"You espeak Spanish?"

"A little."

He sat at the kitchen table at his friend's home with a few other friends from sixth grade. Everything appeared in miniature. Cookies were on the table, and hot chocolate. His friend's mother, Lilia, was teaching them Spanish. She was Puerto Rican. Outside the large glass window the swimming pool shimmered. Across from the pool, the grandmother pulled weeds in the garden by her little cottage. *Uno, dos, tres... ocho, nueve, diez.* They spoke the words together. *Rojo, verde, negro....*

"¡Bueno! You, I, good friends, *buenos amigos,* verdad?"

"Si, buenos amigos, Mida." Eric remembered. "Buenos amigos, verdad!"

"Don't put too much cream on your tacos!"

Her playful mood turned his attention away from the worries—the fear of the needle, the injection, the premonitions of death, everything that weighed him down. He felt at ease, relaxed. How did it happen? It pays to have someone who really cares about you when you're sick. To have someone laugh, to treat you like a normal person. Mida had the touch. His stomach growled.

"What time is dinner?"

"Dinner estart at five, estop at eight, *cinco a las ocho.* Here is eskedule." Mida handed him a calendar marked with all his appointments.

His first appointment was with Doctor Milagro at six in the morning.

"Things certainly start early here."

"*Si. Es más fresco que. Temprano es mejor.*"

"You have all your ducks lined up, Mida."

"Ducks?" Her nose and forehead scrunched up. One black-penciled eyebrow rose above the other. It happened when she was puzzled.

"You know, you have everything so well organized."

Mida's mouth opened wide as she laughed. She had silver caps on two of her teeth.

"We talk, if it okay."

"Talk about what?"

"What you do here."

"Sure, go ahead."

Eric discovered early that simple people have all the secrets. It pays to listen. Mida was a talker. Like most talkers, she relished each opportunity. For a talker, telling a story is irresistible. Most people are flustered if they see someone unexpectedly at the post office or at the park. A talker gets that gleam in the eye and starts up wherever they left off the last time you saw them. Most people ignore talkers. Some are bothered or uncomfortable with wordy types. Eric learned to listen. You never know.

"The weather is like always. Here is a little crazy. Summer, *verano,* comprende?"

"Si."

"Hope you like I set up kitchen. You want cool? More cool up hill in park. *Mira.*" Mida pointed to a small grassy area filled with trees up the hill by the chapel.

"Shade there, and breeze." She cocked her head to one side as she had done before and put her hand on her hip. She had a captive and she continued making small talk. Normally, Eric wouldn't have cared, but the long day had sapped his energy.

"Thanks, Mida. I think I'll rest now. I might take a walk later and explore the grounds."

Eric was not in his office. He didn't have his secretary to guide Mida out of the room. She stayed and continued.

"You want me show you around?"

"No. Thank you Mida. I'm a little tired. I want to take a rest first."

"Is there bad problem? Hope not."

"No problem. I'm fine. Just a little tired, that's all."

"Okay. Breakfast mañana, six to nine. We have date after. It says on eskedule." Mida started to leave the room. She stopped and looked back. "I really like you here. I looking forward... see again. I—"

"Mida, thank you. I like you too. I'm tired. You can go now. I'm sure you have lots to do in the office. All those files to be organized."

"*¡Ay, Dios! ¡Ay, caramba!* The files. *¡Estos me estan volviendo loco!*" Mida left Eric's room shaking her head and hurried back to the office, wiggling in her tight uniform in a way that caught Eric's attention.

He sat on the bed. Scenes from the day raced by. They played again and again until he lost track of time and place.

"Nelson, are you there?"

No answer. A menacing presence pulled at his blanket. It jarred and unsettled his sleep. He twisted and turned. There was no getting away.

Time froze. A depressive chill came over him. The world turned dirty gray. A stupid trance took over. He lay dazed, half conscious, disassociated. What once was important shrunk, and what was insignificant was suddenly charged with intense emotion.

Time resumed. Eric looked out the window. There was the blond in a red dress he'd seen outside Doctor Milagro's office. Needing to speak with someone, a real human being, he opened the door and walked nervously in her direction, half expecting her to disappear.

"Hi, I'm Eric. I saw you when I first arrived."

Startled, the woman jumped back. Her eyes blinked as if waking from a deep sleep. "Oh... yes. I... I was somewhat out of it then, my... my medication. Hello. I'm Mary."

She was charming, but Eric saw right away that she was quite sick. Her ankles were swollen. Her hair was a haystack in a fit. Up close he saw it was a wig. She managed a cheery attitude and smile. A positive attitude meant a lot. They were battling the same enemy. He was fresh from the back lines. She'd been at the front and understood the full horror of their position. Maybe there's nothing more when everything is falling to pieces than togetherness with another human being. Or was that too a sweet deception? When someone really needs you, that's when relationships fail.

"I didn't mean to frighten you."

"Frighten me? Oh, no, that's all right. My nerves are shot. I saw a brown pelican flying alone over the ocean this morning. I broke out in tears. Self-pity, I guess."

Eric knew that grip on his stomach. He awoke every night into the soundless dark, the total emptiness. This process of disintegration terrified him. He wondered if he had the same frightened look he saw on Mary's face.

"We're both dying."

"Shh! Be quiet, man, she's out there looking for me. I didn't say I was dyin'. What I said was I'm gettin' kicked out of my house. This place ain't no farm, it's a fuckin' plantation's what it is. They're tearin' down our homes to build more space for the military industrial complex. Where's folks like us gonna live, anyway? Hey, you listenin'? Okay, go ahead. Go back to sleep. Now I can sneak outta here."

Eric's throat was full of lumps.

"So, how have things been going, Mary?"

Mida would have warned him that curiosity killed the cat.

"For me? I'm feeling pretty useless. I collapsed almost immediately when I got here, couldn't leave my room for three days. I rallied a bit. We went into Tijuana on a shopping trip, but it exhausted me. All I could do after that was take rides in friend's cars. On a good day I might have the strength to visit the health food restaurant on the beach."

Doctor Rice came walking through the garden.

"I'm sorry, Mr. Martin. You don't qualify."

Thunder crashed down. He heard the thud of raindrops then the crackle of flames.

"What's happening, Nelson?"

"You doing fine, man. Those visions you havin', they part of the drugs. You all drugged up now because of the pain."

"I'm sinking... falling... Nelson?"

"Excuse me?" said Mary.

"Forgive me. I'm a little distracted. What I meant to say, what I wanted to ask... I mean, have you noticed any positive effects from the Laetrile?"

"According to my husband, the whole thing's a scam. He thinks Napier and Milagro are after our money. You know, I came down here because my church friends insisted. My husband, he's not religious at all. He doesn't understand. He was skeptical from the get-go. There are at least a dozen in my church who were given a death sentence with conventional medicine. After Laetrile, they're out playing golf and tennis. It's expensive, yes, but how much is a life worth?"

"My brother thinks it's a con, too. What do you think, Mary? You've been here. You've had the Laetrile. Does it work?"

"I'll admit, I was afraid to come down here. The idea of going to Mexico scared me out of my wits. I met with my pastor to ask his advice. He quoted from Luke 9:1-2, the part where Luke says that

God gave his disciples power and authority over all devils and the power to cure diseases. 'I don't recall,' he said to me, 'that Doctor Luke belonged to any medical associations or that he was licensed by the Roman government to help the sick back to better health.' Well, that gave me the confidence to come. I have to believe in the clinic. What else do I have? Doctor Milagro sees some improvement, or so he says. He says one of my metastases is gone, and there's less fluid on my lungs. I *so* want to believe him. I was sure I was feeling better, but two days ago everything started to go downhill. I don't know why, but the Laetrile stopped working. The last two nights have been filled with terror. I sleep in a chair—my legs must be propped up because of the swelling. I don't know what's going on. Maybe it's me."

"What do you mean? Why would you blame yourself?"

"Doctor Milagro says the treatment at home upset my body's balance. Before I came down I had a mastectomy, but the cancer came back. My doctor suggested removing my ovaries to cut the flow of estrogen. He said it would improve my chances of recovery to one in three, but that didn't work either. Doctor Milagro told me the operations sapped the strength I need to fight back. He's started me on supplements to correct this and has increased the dose of Laetrile."

"That's horrible, Mary. I'm very sorry."

"Oh, well, struggle and survive. It's all we can do. My husband can't understand it, but when you're sick like this, you cling to the tiniest life raft to wrest yourself from despair. I tried a faith healer on the advice of my friend. I didn't tell my husband. He already thinks I'm nuts. The faith healer said he could transfer the illness away from me. I wanted to believe him, but it didn't work. Everyone back home at church prays for my health and recovery. I try to be optimistic. If I'm honest, though, I don't really feel that much better."

The afternoon slipped away. Eric had planned to climb the small hill up to the chapel where he'd have a view of the sunset over the ocean, where it was cooler, where it was dark. He didn't have the energy.

"I hope you get better, Eric. You have youth on your side. Several times I've gone to bed and hoped I wouldn't wake up. Life grows more impossible every day. I could never have believed such great misery to be compatible with sanity, yet I'm quite sane. I've got all my wits about me. I remember everything from the moment I found out I was sick. It's hard to live with that, but the ones who forget, they suffer later. How long I or anyone can remain sane in this condition, only God knows."

"Is there a God, a God that cares?" Eric had lost his belief long ago, but this illness made the question more relevant than ever.

"God doesn't always answer me, but I won't doubt God. Often a desire to do it seizes possession of me, but I'm very quickly punished. Life is an ugly thing, Eric, but it's what we have. We must make the best of it. That's what I think. I still have hope, there's hope here."

Mary went back to her room. She weaved back and forth in an unsteady gait, her legs barely able to support her. The well-manicured courtyard was easy on the eyes. Eric tried to imagine an oasis, but a different vision destroyed his peace.

That dead cow in the half-dry riverbed he'd seen on the way to the clinic—balloon-like swollen stomach, insect-infested carcass, unbearable stench, soaking in its own putrid blood. No wonder we live in denial until the death rattle gurgles in our throat. We build towers to the sky. We climb the mountain. On the other side we find nothing but the way back down. To conjure death we must compare two things: the idea of a person alive and the idea of that person dead. When someone we know well dies, that's the first shock. As the years roll on, we get used to the man with the scythe. An acquaintance's death is nothing more than a bit of gossip. Then the time comes when we must contemplate our own death—the end of everything that we know or have ever known.

"Settle down, man. What's all this shit about towers and mountains? Don't dream about the bad shit. Dream about what you want and you'll get it. Ask that God you been talkin' 'bout. He's cool. Maybe he can fix it. Yea, he's the fix-it man!"

Nelson started dancing around in the room snapping his fingers. "The fix-it man, the fix-it man, go an' ask the fix-it man."

"I wish I knew what I wanted, Nelson. I'd like a little more time."

"Dude, you sound like you dropped a dime and can't find it. Stop woo-wooing. Don't let this shit get you down. Ask the fix-it man. Put a little faith in that Dude. You know what, maybe he's black." Nelson smiled as he pictured a black God. "Goddamn right he's black! He knows what you goin' through cause he's been through it hisself like all us niggers. Hey! What if he's a chick? Holy shit, a black chick. Lucy in the Sky with Diamonds, man. Whoa! That's... that's... shit, God a black chick... give them honkies a heart attack."

Nelson danced around to the music, then fell on his knees and raised his hands to the sky.

"Hey, Lucy! Give us some peace down here. Give it up, baby. Don't keep it all to yourself like some white honky bitch. You hear me? Give it up. Hee, hee, hee."

Outside, Nurse Marta had her ear to the door. She wrote down everything Nelson said in her notebook.

"I've got him now," she muttered as a twisted half-smile slid across her face.

"If there is a God, she's cursed me, Nelson. She's cursed me."

13.

Dinner and Father Jordan

Clinica Buena Salud

Eric awoke to strange sounds outside. Frogs croaked in crescendos and diminuendos. He feared he'd slept so long he'd missed dinner. A glance at the bedside alarm clock assured him there was still time. It was only around seven. Rustling dead leaves of thoughts stirred and fluttered in his brain. How humiliating it was to die—to die before leaving a clear mark on your friends, on your enemies. Death might be inevitable, but he would rebel, dispute death all the way.

He ran warm water into the old enamel sink that stood proudly on its pedestal, then washed his face and wiped the bleary sleep from his eyes. He walked cautiously but expectantly out the door of his room to the cafeteria. He wasn't hungry, but had been told to eat every meal. It would help him gain back some strength. He'd try. Food was laid out buffet style on a large table. Stainless steel pans and pots kept warm by chafing dishes held an impressive array of soups and stews. All his life, Eric had avoided restaurants. You never really knew what was in the food. How could you trust people you didn't know who worked behind the scenes in hidden rooms? Buffets were especially dangerous. People breathed and coughed on every dish. They stuck their dirty fingers into the food. Confounded by the choices, worrying about germs everywhere, he stood, paralyzed, and smiled like the Cheshire cat.

He spotted Mary at one of the tables. She waved him over.

"Hello, Eric. This is my husband Bob. Come join us."

Bob stood and reached out to shake Eric's hand. His arm was large and hairy. Eric knew what was coming. He prepared himself for an iron grip, one of those enthusiastic handshakes that can pull your shoulder out of the socket.

"Go ahead, load up on the food, young man. You paid plenty for it," said Bob as he worked Eric's arm up and down like the handle of a water pump. It was obvious from the snide look on his face and his condescending tone of voice that Bob hated the clinic. He and Mary were so different. Eric wondered what kept them together. Bob was feisty, argumentative, all about business, all about himself. He reminded Eric of Jimmy Hoffa, the powerful Teamster boss whom Nixon pardoned in December. His beady eyes looked like bullets shot into his head. His teeth barely showed through his tortured smile. His face was rectangular and full of determination. A receding splatter of pomaded hair gave the top of his head the appearance of a wheat field flattened by a strong wind. Mary was quiet, unassuming, and compassionate. She maintained her pride and dignity despite the debilitating cancer. They say opposites attract. Maybe people were like atomic particles with negative and positive charges.

Mary looked worse than she had in the courtyard.

"Tijuana's nothing, you know, just another Goddamned border town. All they want around here is the buck."

Eric was trapped. Bob's negative attitude annoyed him. Mary's decline foreshadowed his own. The two of them together depressed him.

"I'll get my plate and come back in a minute."

He couldn't move to a different table without offending them. He'd try to make the best of it. He didn't want to alienate anyone he might need later. When he returned there were two others to confront him. They looked at him like two chickens eyeing the same worm. Mary introduced them.

"Ira's from New Jersey. Cat's from L.A. Ira has a construction business at home. His son's running it for him, isn't that right, Ira?"

"It's just temporary, see." Ira looked at Eric as if deciding whether he could trust any younger man. "I'll have to straighten everything out when I get back. My kid, see, he's got everything *fahcacked*. These young kids today... well, you know what I'm talking about. No brains." Ira tapped his forefinger on his head. "You gotta exercise these noggins to make 'em work, right? My kid, he thinks money grows on trees, see. I guess I spoiled him, but what the hell. I shoulda shown him more about the business. What difference does it make now? He's gonna get it all anyway. I just hope he doesn't ruin it before I kick the old bucket."

Around the equator of his head, Ira had a fringe of gray hair just long enough to form a ponytail in the back. He combed it sideways to disguise his baldness. He was the man in the black shirt and red shorts Eric had seen struggle across the courtyard earlier. Cat was about Ira's age, but very thin and with the eyes and skin of a lizard.

"So far he's made a mess of it," continued Ira. "You know the worst? That crew of mine, those guys can run the whole damn thing without any help from Mr. Smart Guy. He changed everything. It takes a real idiot to screw up a business like that. You know what I mean?"

Eric knew all about men like Ira, self-confident, controlling men who tried to dominate and ruin the lives of those around them. He knew what a son-of-a-bitch his own father had been while he grew up. Eric sometimes thought he'd become an attorney just to prove to his father that he could. Men like Ira worshipped the ordinary and practical as if they were the only things of importance. Get a job. Make a buck. Do it like this. Do it like that. Don't let an opportunity pass you by. They had no patience for art or music, emotions and intuitions, the things that make people whole. Like atomic elements, they live little half-lives and slowly decay away over time.

Ira had round, white eyes with brown irises. His eyes bulged out of his head like big glass balls. He stopped talking and squirted something out of a small tube into each eye. He was about to go on at an even higher pitch when Cat lurched forward and grasped Eric's hand.

"It's okay, honey. Ira lets himself go to the dramatic with his kvetching."

Ira's mouth went into contortions. He couldn't believe Cat would interrupt him just as he was catching his stride. He stood with his mouth open and stared at Cat.

"There's a tipping point, honey," said Cat, "when the soul elevates over everything. It forgets the insignificant setbacks of the past. The soul goes on to fulfill its destiny, and—"

Ira held up his hand. They were like two little kids vying for attention.

"You don't get it, Cat. Nobody seems to get it. This world's going to hell, see. No one gives a damn anymore. When I grew up you did a job the right way because that was the way to do it. You know what I mean? People now have everything backwards, like these lazy Mexicans that run this circus down here."

Ira spoke loudly and waved his arms around to make his point. People in the cafeteria watched and listened, some in agreement, some horrified.

Mary turned pale. Bob nodded his head in a tacit pact with Ira. Eric glanced at Cat. She laughed nervously. There are things you can learn about a stranger from the way she laughs, the sound of it and the expression on her face. Eric saw the embarrassment and shame on Cat's face. He was embarrassed and ashamed too. He was tired of listening, of nodding his head, of trying to remain composed. He suddenly stepped forward to speak.

"I think the Mexican people are charming. They've been good enough to welcome us into their country and to put up with our quirks. It *is* their country, Ira. Take my taxi driver, Solomon. He showed me around town, answered my stupid questions, and watched over me. He explained things I didn't understand. What about Mida? She's lovely and friendly, kind of funny, too, a beautiful person. She's very good at what she does. She makes a difficult job seem easy."

Ira frowned and then broke into a big smile. "Ah, yes, Mida! Those beautiful *shadayim*," he said, cupping his hands in front of his chest. "You gotta love that Mida."

Cat smiled. She admired Ira's spontaneity despite his obvious faults.

"Cancer's all about diet and environment, see?" said Ira.

Oh, God, thought Eric, *here comes the lecture.*

"The sickle cell anemia of the dark races attacks just like cancer. It's the result of the whites taking the blacks out of their natural environment, away from their natural food source. Same thing happens to gorillas and monkeys when they're moved into zoos. You know what I mean?"

My God, thought Eric. *The man's a bigot. Out of control.*

"In the wild where they ate nuts and fruits, they were free of sickness, see, but here they all get sick. Bad diet. Their natural diet was chock full of Laetrile. We've all got the same problem, you and me and everyone down here. We eat nothing but dreck these days. Our natural diet's gone out the window. It's processed this, processed that. The doc told me all about this. He's right, too. I know he's right."

Bob rolled his eyes. He couldn't understand how any sane person could believe such nonsense. Cancer resulted from a mix-up in the genes, random bad luck, or a bad attitude. The key was to think positive thoughts so cancer couldn't get a hold on you. He wasn't going let Ira's baloney pass without putting in his two cents.

"We read all the books on Laetrile before we came here. Mary told me she couldn't just sit home and die. She begged me to bring her. Well, here we are, and whaddya know? Just like I said, it's one big scam. We got donations from friends and relatives so we could afford to come. I felt bad about it, but we couldn't do it on our own. Mary's church group encouraged us, but now that we've been here, it's obvious this whole damn place is just one big swindle. They force all these expensive drugs down your throat. They sell all the junk they manufacture here. None of it really works. It's a palliative, that's what they told me, what Napier told me, when I asked. It's a trick to make you feel better. It doesn't cure anything. The cancer cells are wily and adaptable, way smarter than a bunch of ground-up apricot pits. All that stuff about diet, Ira, it's a tall tale the doctor uses to bamboozle the gullible. I'd like to punch that smooth-talking Napier in the nose and just walk out of here. I stay against my better judgment because I haven't got the heart to go against Mary's wishes."

Mary squirmed and frowned at her husband's remarks. Eric was afraid she was about to cry.

"What you say simply isn't true," said Eric. "Just like you, I read all about it before I came here, Bob. My stepmother, who is a very smart attorney, checked everything out carefully. I came with my eyes open. Sure, there've been failures, but what about the doctors back in California? They didn't give me any hope at all. None. What they gave me was plenty of pain. I think they enjoyed it. You talk about cost, the treatment there is way more expensive than it is here. The doctors in those hospitals tear your body apart while the big pharmaceutical companies make a fortune on their drugs. It's a wonder that the people here at the clinic can do anything for you at all after that."

Eric wasn't as confident as he pretended. His doubts increased the more he saw, but he wasn't going to let a bastard like Bob talk down to him. He wasn't going to let Bob destroy Mary's hope, make her cry.

Mary waved her head in agreement with Eric. He felt stronger now that he'd expressed his opinion. He wondered if Mary was getting worse because of Bob's attitude.

"I'll bet you didn't know that the John Birch Society has taken up Laetrile as a cause." Bob stood up. He was on a roll. Eric could hear little clinks as Bob played with the coins in his pocket.

Mary spoke up. "Leave out the politics, Bob. You just don't understand any of this. You've never been sick a day in your life."

"Russell Napier told me," said Bob, ignoring his wife. "They don't give a damn whether the stuff works or not. They're against the government's role in medicine. For them it's all politics and money. I asked Napier how he could make common cause with a right-wing group like the John Birch Society. Do you know what he said?"

Eric didn't answer. He was angry enough that he had to suffer Bob's unending tirade. At least Ira and Cat amused him. They swooned and held hands like teenagers in love. It broke his heart to see Mary bite her tongue as her husband spoke. Eric just wanted to get away from all of them.

"He said he would work with anyone to advance Laetrile, his sole cause. Anyone! You hear that? I guess that includes the devil. They're in it for the money, Eric, and to validate their naive political views. They ask for cashier's checks or cash. They want full payment in advance. You're locked in. They sell all this stuff to increase the profits. They'd like to market the same crap in the States, but they can't get approval. We're the guinea pigs. Do you really believe there's a conspiracy against the proponents of Laetrile? Open your eyes. Our government is right to be skeptical. *We* should be skeptical. The stuff doesn't work!"

"That's all just your opinion. You haven't said anything that proves Laetrile is ineffective. Tell me, Bob," Eric asked with growing impatience, "if it was your life on the line, what would you do, huh?" Eric knew he should let it go, but Bob's cowboy mentality goaded him.

"I can tell you one thing: I wouldn't let myself be taken advantage of by a bunch of quacks, I know that much. A group of ill-informed extremists have whipped up this frenzy against the National Cancer Institute, the American Cancer Society, the Food and Drug Administration, virtually anyone with any real medical expertise. Why would our government sink millions into cancer research and then deny the public access to a drug or substance that might slow down or cause remission of cancer? Why? Something's rotten here in Tijuana."

"I'll tell you why, Bob," said Eric loudly, losing his composure. "Experts oppose anything different because it threatens their feelings of superiority. There are plenty of incentives for the drug companies and doctors in the States to oppose Laetrile. They make loads of money on their chemo and radiation. That's where you should look if you want to find something rotten."

Ira stood up. "I don't think anybody knows how to stop this damn disease. I could write a book on the doctors I've known and the blunders they've made about me. I don't trust any of the bastards. A man comes from the dust and in the dust he will end. Along the way it's a good thing to take a sip of vodka." Ira headed for the juice bar, his gray ponytail bouncing along behind him.

"He carries a flask in his back pocket," laughed Cat. She relaxed the tension in her face. "It's against all the rules, but Ira's not much for rules."

Things quieted down. Everyone focused on dinner. Cat ate little bird-bites of her salad while Bob had sloppy spoonfuls of his stew and looked disappointed at the lack of meat. Mary fiddled with her juice. Eric chose a pot of fresh vegetable stew and found it surprisingly good. When Ira returned, he had a smile on his face. He sat close to Cat and put one arm around her. With his other hand, he picked out some of the vegetables from her salad.

"Umm, good. What kind of meat is this, anyway?" he laughed as he kissed Cat on her forehead.

Bob and Mary left early. On their way out, Bob whispered into Eric's ear, "One more thing, Eric. You should know this: The Laetrile at this clinic, it's not the right formula, the real stuff. At least that's what I've heard. I'm not sure if there's any truth to that or if *any* formula works, but if I were you, I'd be on my guard. I don't trust any of these people down here."

Eric left shortly after Bob and Mary. As he walked back to his room, he watched an aberrant wind dart back and forth like a lunatic snake over the long grasses up on the hill. He wished the wind would scoop him up and blow him away to someplace free of his worries, all of them.

He squeezed into a small underground passageway. He carried a bucket heavy with silver ore. He climbed the ladder up, up, up but there was no way out. He heard a voice.

"It's time."

"I'm not ready."

"Your body is ready."

"Wait a minute."

"You all say that."

"Isn't there some kind of surprise, some fluke to save me like Borges or Sartre wrote about?"

"That only happens in books."

"It's all a random accident, then? No one knows what's going to happen?"

"What's going to happen is what always happens."

Eric sat outside his room. He meditated, dozed. It was a clear night, quite warm. A few yucca moths worked over a yucca plant outside his door. He felt full as a tick. A distant train whistle reminded him that Tijuana is a place where people come and go. Not every visitor dies here. The pure light of the stars and the sounds of nocturnal insects awakened his senses. A large brown-spotted frog croaked in the shadows. It sounded lonely and anxious, like a prince who waited patiently to be kissed back into human form.

Some of Laetrile's supporters were overzealous. Patients could respond differently even when their cases were similar. That was true with any kind of treatment, even chemo and radiation. Bob's concerns were real. Even if Eric disliked the man he could not ignore him. He'd put all his chips on the table. His head spun. The doubts Bob raised about Napier and Milagro were like seeds planted in fertile soil; they grew against his will.

Eric flinched when a yellow kitten ran off in fright as a man emerged from the cafeteria. The man walked in his direction. He wore a flowery Hawaiian shirt and khaki shorts.

"Good evening, Mr. Martin. I'm Father Jordan, the resident Catholic priest." He spoke in a mild Irish brogue familiar to Eric from priests he'd known when he was growing up.

"You don't look like a priest. You look like an aging surfer."

When Jordan laughed his big belly bounced about, bringing the Hawaiian scene on his shirt to life.

"Well, now, I suppose I might, but things aren't always as they appear, lad."

"I'm not in the mood for confession, Father." Eric's tone sounded thin and brittle like the ice on a puddle in winter. He didn't want to be rude but he'd had enough of God for one day. The quotes on the walls of the clinic, the mural of Christ at the entrance, Doctor Milagro's comment that Christ was the director of the clinic, Mida with her Bible phrases—all this religion put him off. He began to rethink his decision to come to the clinic. He feared he'd made a mistake. His confidence shriveled.

"I'm hoping we might talk for a wee bit. I don't want to interrupt anything, but I saw you sitting alone. I'm only asking for a few minutes." Father Jordan pulled up a chair.

"I thought Doctor Milagro was a Protestant. I'm surprised he allows his competitors inside the compound. Is this place a religious retreat or a medical clinic?"

"Ha. Grand! It's a medical clinic for certain, lad. Indeed, Milagro is a Protestant, and he takes his religion seriously, but he's wanting to provide for the spiritual health of all the patients."

Except for the way he was dressed, Father Jordan, big-bellied with twinkling blue eyes, could have been a medieval friar lifted right out of *The Canterbury Tales*. He had a jolly air that attracted, but Eric was in no mood to talk.

"It's been a long day, and I'm tired and sick. This isn't a good time."

"My understanding is that you're a Catholic, Eric. When's the last time you went to Mass?"

"Do you find the sick and dying to be lucrative clients, Father? Are you selling indulgences?"

The comment induced a chuckle.

"Well, now, I give them away, actually. Would you like one?"

"Where I'm going they aren't necessary, but thanks for the thought."

"You're a pessimist, then?"

"I wouldn't go that far, but I must say in all seriousness that if one looks closely at the essence of life, it's clear that everything ends in death."

They sat in silence. Father Jordan thought himself a good judge of character. Under the patina of irritation caused by the illness, Jordan detected the gentle nature at Eric's core. He saw fragility beneath that hard protective shell. Nobility and tragedy shone through Eric's eyes. After a few minutes' silence, Jordan spoke. "I'm sorry for your illness, Eric. You look like a worthy young man, just down on your luck, that's all. You can call me Jordan. We can dispense with the priestly business if it's making you uncomfortable. I am a priest, but lots o' my friends just call me Jordan. I'm a bit of a renegade within the church."

"I'd say it's a little worse than bad luck. What do you think about the Laetrile, Jordan? Do you think I'm a fool for coming here?"

"I wish to heaven you weren't going through this trial, Eric. I wish not one human soul had to go through it. Cancer is a terrible disease. Now mind my words, Laetrile has helped some o' the patients here. No, I don't think you're a fool for coming, not at all. You tried the hospitals up north, right? You know what they're offering, but you came here. Why? So you can make your own informed decision. That's sounding like a sensible approach to me, and I can tell you this: I've witnessed some grand recoveries here, Eric, I assure you, some grand recoveries."

"I heard tonight that something's not right with the Laetrile at the clinic. Do you know anything about this?"

Eric's question put Jordan in a quandary.

"Where'd you hear that?"

"From the husband of one of the other patients."

Father Jordan had to be careful with his response. "Mind you, Laetrile is a bit of an unorthodox treatment. There are different formulas, but they're all based on the same idea. Napier uses a formula developed by Elvin Krump, whose father was the first to discover Laetrile's anti-cancer benefits."

What Jordan could not say was that he knew the rumor Eric heard was true. His friend Frieze's serum was better, but Frieze stubbornly kept it away from the general public and especially from Napier's clinic. Elvin Krump's recipe was the only one available.

"I'm tired, Jordan. It's been quite a busy day, and I'd prefer to be left alone."

Jordan rose and folded his chair. As he started to leave, Eric stood and took a hesitant step in his direction. Something was going on that Eric didn't understand. He couldn't explain it, but he felt it, like some kind of conviction that tried to form, as if he were about to embark on a voyage of self-discovery, but lacked the courage to follow through. He felt an odd comfort with Jordan; strange as it was, he trusted this jolly priest.

"Look, I'm sorry. I know you're just doing your job. Honestly, I can't tell you my views on death, the next world, or God. The ultimate questions are too maddeningly unanswerable. I simply don't know. To have views, faith, belief, one needs a backbone. I'm bowled over by the universe. Just look at the stars. Look how many worlds like ours there are out there. I feel small amidst such immensity. My little life plods along. I feel stunned like a newt when someone lifts the stone."

Jordan stepped forward and shook Eric's hand.

"Come see me. Bring your troubles. That's what I'm here for. Right now, the best thing is to get some rest and get started with the treatments. It's grand to listen to someone who speaks his mind."

Jordan walked away singing a little Irish tune. Eric's question about the Laetrile weighed heavily on his mind. He'd have to work harder on Louie Frieze. There were so many people out there, people like Eric, who deserved better.

Eric was left alone to ponder the peculiar events of his first day at Buena Salud. He felt like a fish. The mind starts out blank, one thought grabs it, then another; eventually one of them hooks it and everything comes to an end.

"Tell me a riddle."

"I don't know any riddles."

"But isn't that the way out?"

"For Oedipus, yes, but not for you."

145

"I thought all miracles started in a riddle."

"Why do you always think you should have a miracle?"

"I don't want to die."

"Miracles are for those who die."

"What do you mean?"

"You'll see."

Like Tolstoy's Ivan Ilych, Eric's life up to now had been simple, ordinary, and terrible. The gap between the person he wanted to be and the person he was embarrassed him. If anything could be done about that, it would have to be soon. The sharp spines of cancer ripped through him like some vengeful cactus.

What a strange place the clinic was, with a doctor who acted like a priest and a priest like a doctor. It was impossible to know if Laetrile was a miracle or a sham. He had only his instincts to rely on. He wasn't sure if they were enough, but what else did he have to get him through this horrible time in his life?

Believe me, there is hope here. There is hope.

At night he noticed the symptoms. Breathing was easier when he was on his back, but his mind wandered when he stared at the ceiling. A healthy body is like a beehive: If you destroy one cell, everything else survives. A body that's sick is a sack tied with a knot. Once a hole appears anywhere, everything falls out.

A swarm of luminescent insects flitted around the room.
The shadows reflected off one wall, then the other.

Outside, a full moon, orange and bright, perfectly round, played with the leaves of a tree blowing in the wind.

Moon shadow, moon shadow... Leapin' and hoppin' on a moon shadow...
Did it take long to find me? I asked the faithful light, Oh, did it take long to find me, and are you gonna stay the night?

...many years of waiting... waiting... vanished... across the border... mystery to this day... stay away from girls... that one's taken... a guy named Roger... a guy named Roger... off to Mexico... to Mexico... to Mexico.

14.

Questions and Answers

El Azteca, Tijuana

He sat at a round table sipping a beer and making notes on a yellow pad with a Bic pen. He was alone after spending most of the day immersed in the crowd along First Street at *El Mercado Principal*. Immersed? That was the wrong word. Something peculiar had happened: He'd been lifted out of one life and plunged into another. He met people from the ranches and mountain pueblos— goat farmers and fishermen, railroad workers, weavers, stockmen, truckdrivers, beekeepers. He had arrived in Mexico believing he was in control of his life, but soon discovered life is a random churning of events. Nothing is pinned down. He was an open space, a field whose boundaries extended outward without end. He viewed his past with disdain, repelled by what he had been. Like his friend at Yawnix, he'd been too full of himself. To worship your own genius is as bad as worshiping the idols in the Mexican churches. For the first time, Penalt understood the meaning of humility—ordinary people are the least ordinary and the most extraordinary of all. A slow-burning fire of excitement ignited at his core. He had to be careful not to extinguish the flame. It was easy to slip back into the swamp, the swamp of personality that could pull him back down and drown him. He was Roger Penalt with a Bic pen and a yellow pad of paper, no more, no less, but he dreamed... he dreamed.

He wrote:

Garumbullo—sliced and boiled for hours, makes a tea useful for stomach ailments; pounded into warm poultices in a stone *metate,* it makes a paste that can be applied to the swollen joints of those suffering from arthritis.
Both the dried bark of the copal tree and the sticky juice from the lumboy tree are useful for healing wounds.

Penalt looked up from the notepad. An attractive Mexican girl was seated at the bar—copper skin, red lips, hair the color of dark chocolate, long, slender legs and all the rest to match.

Why now? He struggled with the distraction, tried to ignore it.

Melon tea—he'd seen it dripped from a tripod apparatus set up over a man's leg to heal a gunshot wound.
Chuchupate—the root is ground on a metate and the paste is placed on the bites of scorpions, bees, and spiders to stop the pain and heal the wound. When made into a tea, it can reduce swelling in the throat caused by some insect bites or stings.

Penalt saw the girl's alluring face reflecting back from the mirror behind the bar. Dark glasses hid her eyes. He couldn't tell if she was looking at him. He wondered what she was thinking.

Yerba de la vibora is ground on a metate, then placed on a rattlesnake bite after it has been bled and the poison sucked out.
Yerba Colorado tea—the roots make a tea for colds or coughs and can be made into a cough syrup by adding sugar.

He looked up again. A strange scene unfolded before him. A man walked into the bar and sat next to the girl, a huge man with a hideous face. The man reminded Penalt of a character he'd seen in a horror movie. It was impossible to work now: his concentration of a few moments ago was shattered. The ghoulish grin, the prominent teeth, the flared nostrils—made the man look like a wild animal. His massive arms and strong hands could have easily crushed a rock. The girl, unfazed, treated him like a harmless young boy. She ran her fingers through his hair, rubbed the back of his neck, softly stroked his shoulders, and kissed his repulsive lips. They spoke in Spanish. Penalt listened, but couldn't understand most of what they said.

Penalt's heart pounded. He kept one eye and both ears locked onto the couple while he jotted down a few more observations from earlier in the day.

A dark-skinned, auburn-haired, blue-eyed Mayo Indian woman sat stoically, her baskets woven of pine needles spread out in a circle around her. She had a baffling display of leaves and barks and roots. Thick stalks of a green cactus stuck out prominently, with star-shaped clusters of spines that grew on the crests of the ridges that encased the valuable pulp—garumbullo.

The Indian woman gave him a taste of the tea. She said it would sooth his stomach and it did.

He wrote:

These people use plants and barks and roots just like they use tortillas and beans. Some are healers and some collect medicinal plants and herbs that they bring to the market to earn a little extra cash.

The real reason he'd been sent to Mexico wasn't for the simple cures he'd seen at the market, but they were the ones that excited him. They were tested remedies even if they'd never be profitable for a company like Yawnix. Most of the names eluded him. There were several different names for the same plant—numerous Indian dialects as well as Mexican and English names.

The two at the bar became animated and spoke louder. Penalt thought he heard them say something about Laetrile. He listened carefully now. It frustrated him that he couldn't fully comprehend the Spanish. He finally got up the nerve to walk over to the bar.

"Excuse me, do you understand English?" he asked boldly.

The man turned toward Penalt. The face frightened him, yet Penalt felt unexpectedly at ease in the presence of this wild man. He was surprised at how soft-spoken and relaxed the man could be, and the girl was even more gorgeous up close—the beauty and the beast.

"Si, a little," said the man.

"I thought I heard you talking about Laetrile. Do you know anything about it?"

With the word *Laetrile*, the friendly vibes vanished.

"You spy on us?"

"No, no. I just heard something about Laetrile. I'm hoping to find some."

"Go the clinics. They help you there."

"That's just it. I've heard there is a better kind, a more potent kind outside the clinics. That's what I'm looking for."

Now the man's manner matched his face. His look was intimidating.

"Just go the clinics, gringo. *Yo no soy médico.*" The man turned away from Penalt. The discussion was over.

The couple continued to speak rapidly in Spanish. He stood by them for a moment hoping to resume the conversation, but he knew better than to push his luck. His hopes fully deflated, he went back to his table to finish his beer. He put away the notepad and started to read the newspaper.

He was startled by a tap on his shoulder. He thought it might be the man at the bar coming after him. Penalt lowered the paper and was confronted by an impish monkey of a man with eyes slightly out of focus. The little man rocked back and forth nervously.

"Excuse me, Meester, you want to know about the Laetrile?"

He spoke with a crackly voice while his head jerked from side to side.

"Yes. That man at the bar told me to go to the clinics, but I've heard there is something better. Do you know anything about that?"

"Pleeze, Meester. Who told you?"

Penalt quickly improvised a story.

"My uncle has cancer. A friend told him about it. He asked me to come here to see what I could find out."

"Wherr!" The little man made a strange whistling sound through his teeth.

"What did you say?"

"Wherr! Wherr!"

"Do you have something to tell me?" Penalt was put off by the man's antics but curious about what he had to say.

"Meester's uncle knows something big." At this point the man leaned over and whispered into Penalt's ear, "I got some special Laetrile, just a little, for my friend in California. I got it from a curandera in San Kuuchamaa, a little village way up in the mountains. It's all hush-hush, Meester. No one is supposed to know, but I know, believe me. She don't have any left when I go back. Maybe she have more now. I don't know."

"Where did the curandera get it?" asked Penalt.

"Who knows? Maybe she make it herself. All I know is that it worked. It cured my friend."

The man at the bar stared at them. To Penalt, the scowl on his face looked like a threat. The man climbed off his stool, grabbed the girl, and the two of them rushed toward Penalt. He nearly panicked.

"Go the clinics, gringo. They fix you up. Magic formula is lie. Why you listen that man? He make you gringo fool, take all you money."

The couple stormed out of the bar.

Penalt looked at the odd little man by his side.

"Why should I believe you?"

"Believe anything you want, Meester, but the Laetrile I got from that healer in San Kuuchamaa work better than anything at the clinics. I have nothing to sell you. I don't want your money."

Penalt believed him. San Kuuchamaa was the village Yawnix wanted him to visit. He had no idea why the man at the bar was so upset by the little man's story. There was clearly something going on with Laetrile he wasn't aware of.

"Thanks for the information. I might go to San Kuuchamaa and take a look for myself."

"If you find some of that Laetrile, Meester, you let me know, pleeze. Here is my card."

The man left. Penalt walked to the bar and put down a few pesos, then he left in the same direction as the others without even saying goodbye. Penalt glanced at the card. It was worn. The man must have been carrying it around for quite a long time. AT LARGE, was all it said, and there was a phone number. Scribbled on the back was the name of the village, San Kuuchamaa. Penalt put the card in his pocket. He was disappointed about the girl, but there were plenty of others. There was no way he was going to tangle with the monster beside her. He wondered how long it had been since the little monkey man had visited San Kuuchamaa. Maybe the curandera had more Laetrile by now. He'd been told to do whatever was necessary to get a sample. He knew now that it really existed—he would find a way to get a sample.

15.

Elvin Krump

At Krump's Residence, San Francisco

Russell Napier had first met Elvin Krump at a Walgreen's outside the airport in Miami. Krump's massive bulk captured Napier's attention as they waited in the checkout line. The attractive woman speaking with Krump also caught Napier's attention; he always had an eye for a pretty woman. He overheard her and Krump discussing an unorthodox cancer cure called Laetrile. Napier was intrigued by what they said. Napier and Krump had tickets to San Francisco on the same flight. While they waited to board, Napier engaged Krump in conversation.

Napier had just sold his Latin American businesses and wanted a new adventure. Krump told him he'd been working on a cancer cure. It sounded just like the sort of business venture Napier enjoyed. Krump had improved a formula developed by his father, and needed capital and expertise to manufacture, market, and distribute his cancer remedy. Napier grew more enthusiastic when he heard the details. He suggested they form a company and work together to push the product forward. Krump agreed. When it was up and running, Napier directed the operation. Krump, who was older, became the public spokesman and chief chemist. He spent his time pontificating on the Krump family cure to groups of cancer victims who were unhappy with conventional treatments. The two of them pocketed loads of cash all along the way; that is, until Laetrile was banned in the States as a dangerous and ineffective hoax.

The fog had burned off by the time Napier arrived at Elvin Krump's lavish San Francisco home. Krump lived alone, and spent most of his time in an elaborate foyer where doors led to seldom-used spaces and stairways. He ate most of his meals in restaurants or had them delivered. After escorting Napier into the foyer, Krump maneuvered his bulk onto a sofa and began to expound on his favorite subject.

"You know, Russell, the field of cancer chemotherapy is a world unto itself. This jungle offers the greatest opportunity anywhere in commerce today, but there are snakes in every bush. It's best to push hard, sell, and not be backward about disaffecting a few. Establish Laetrile right from the start as something precious that not even hospitals get for free. One can usually buy even the top medical investigators as one does sirloin steak… and at about the same price."

As Krump laughed his double chin quivered. "Laetrile is the first and last final hope in the prophylaxis in therapy of cancer in man and animals. I just don't understand why we can't convince the authorities to put it back on the approved list."

Krump's tiresome meanderings sometimes threw Napier off his game, but today Napier was focused. "We're moving forward at a rapid pace, Doctor. Rafael and Tomás are ready to begin construction on the new manufacturing plant for the amygdalin bars, shakes, and juices. In a few months we'll start production. Zacco is onboard. You're right about the federal agencies here in the States: They're difficult; they've turned us down twice. This may be awkward for you, Elvin, but I must speak the truth. Louis Frieze is back to producing his more effective serum with all the enzymes. We need to replicate his recipe. I'm sure we could get the approval we need from the authorities if we had Frieze's serum. I'm sorry to say it, but his is better than ours. I've seen the results. If Frieze goes to the authorities on his own he could knock us out of the game."

Napier had arrived from Tijuana and was adjusting to the cool weather. As much as he liked San Francisco, it was always cold and windy. He noticed Krump had put on even more weight since their last meeting. It was hard to tell where the sofa ended and Krump began.

Krump frowned. "Could he really do that? I thought Frieze was dead or at least too badly injured to work."

"He's out there somewhere, manufacturing on a small scale."

Krump's pride, his whole life, depended on the success of his Laetrile. His father had discovered its curative powers. Krump was unwavering in his belief that Laetrile was the ultimate cancer cure. He had worked for years to convince the public and the authorities. He wasn't going to let some upstart from below the border knock him out of the game. He had no medical degree, though he'd earned an honorary degree from an obscure Christian college in the Midwest. He called himself Doctor Krump and preferred that others do the same. He believed he was destined to be a great healer like Jonas Salk. He even thought he might someday win a Nobel Prize for his years of effort. Napier knew better than to offend Krump.

"How much is he producing?"

"We don't know. He's not selling to the general public or the clinics. I've heard he gives away most of his Laetrile to the poor. We haven't been able to locate him or any of his serum."

"The man's a fool. I'm sure I can replicate that formula. He stole his ideas from me, you know. I need a little more time, that's all. I'm almost there. How much of his Laetrile do we have left?"

"It's nearly gone. There's barely enough left for the most important patients. At the clinic we've gone back to your formula, Elvin. To be perfectly honest, it's not working as well as we'd like. We've had some successes, don't get me wrong, but there are too many failures. We need stronger results if we're going to convince the FDA. I'm worried all our efforts will be wasted if we can't get that formula before the hearings."

"I thought Zacco had that congressman on the payroll. What's his name? Why can't he get the job done?"

"It's a tricky business, Elvin. Sloan Kettering is working against us. The big pharmaceutical companies have the research hospitals in their pockets. They've got lots of lobbyists. Sloan Kettering sabotaged the one test that came out on our side. It's appalling what they did to appease those big drug companies. What's worse for us, the Feds are looking into organized crime again. That neutralizes Zacco and puts Congressman Shipley on the defensive. The patients at Buena Salud—well, Doctor, they just keep dying. I'm worried the word will get out."

Krump grew restless. His left eye started to twitch, his nose and mouth jerked erratically.

The doorbell rang. When Krump opened the door, his face quickly changed. It was Nicoleta Bugiardini. Nicoleta was tall and slender, and had straight black hair that shone magically in the light coming from Krump's stained-glass window. Her skin was white and silky. An alluring figure was visible under her dress, illuminated by the bright sunlight coming from behind. She innocently removed the cigarette from her deep red lips, which curled into a smile as she greeted Krump.

"*Buongiorno,* Elvin. I got a little present for you and Russell."

"Ah, listen to that, Russell. We have a present from this lovely young woman! I wonder what she has. It could be *something...* hmm... very interesting, don't you think?"

Shivers of sexual excitement lightened Krump's mood as he gazed at Nicoleta. Seeing her made him feel young and full of energy. She took his mind off the problems Frieze could cause. He smacked his lips when he spoke. With his straw-colored hair, luminous blue eyes, and pale, jowly flesh, he was a cross between W. C. Fields and William Jennings Bryan.

"Oh, you boys, Elvin, you always have your minds in the gutter. It's just a check... from my uncle Joey."

"A check?"

"Oh, yah, a large one."

Krump's eyes undressed her.

"Hey! Don't be a naughty boy, Elvin. Don't stare at me like that."

Nicoleta stepped away from the door and out of the sunlight. Krump enjoyed it when Nicoleta called him by his first name instead of the more formal title of Doctor. She conspicuously removed the cigarette that hung menacingly in her hand and delivered the check to Krump. Napier watched in amusement.

"Come in, come in, by all means, Nicoleta. Would you like some coffee? How about a drink?"

Beads of perspiration were forming on Krump's forehead. His eyes widened when he looked at the check.

"My, that's quite a significant investment."

"Uncle Joey wants ya to succeed, ya know."

There was a threat attached to the check. Like a wild and dangerous apparition, this menace scurried into a dark corner of the room. Both Napier and Krump felt its presence. A man like Zacco didn't *hope* for success, he demanded it. Anything less would have disastrous results. Whenever he doled out his money there were always strings attached.

"We'll do our best, Nicoleta. Now sit with me on the sofa. I'll get you a drink."

Nicoleta thought about the heat that would be generated by Krump's enormous bulk. She pictured herself melting like white chocolate onto an over-roasted marshmallow. She had no desire to sit next to Krump or to spend any more time in his presence than necessary to accomplish her mission. She thought he was creepy. As he turned toward the liquor cabinet, she slipped a note into Napier's hand and winked.

"I'm kinda in a hurry, Elvin. Hey, I'd just bore you two business tycoons anyways."

With the grace of a thoroughbred, she sauntered out the front door, Krump's eyes on her hips. She turned and fluttered down the stairs with charming little bounces and twists, after which she escaped in a cream-puff Cadillac that resembled a giant cumulus cloud racing toward the sunset. After she was gone, Krump sighed.

"Ah, what a stunning young woman, don't you agree?"

"Oh, yes, stunning, *absolutely* stunning!"

Napier felt the excitement rising inside, but his face remained stoic. He had glanced at the note. It was an invitation to join Nicoleta in her apartment. Krump was too preoccupied with his own thoughts of Nicoleta and with Napier's concerns about the Laetrile to notice the irony in Napier's voice.

The menace attached to the check glowed like a live coal in a corner of the room. Krump unfolded himself back onto the sofa and tried to put all these new worries out of his mind. He glanced at the copy of *The New York Times* on his table.

PRESIDENT NIXON LEAVES ON TRIP TO CHINA: STOPS IN HAWAII

"Nixon signed the National Cancer Act last year. You think he'd be on our side. What do you think Zacco will do if we fail? The FDA and I speak a different language, Russell. They speak legal jargon. I speak from the human point of view. If they understood the disservice they are doing humanity, there would be no problem. Laetrile is the crown jewel in a diadem of treatment. I agree that Laetrile cannot be put into just anybody's hands. It must be reserved for the cancer specialist who understands the full concept of the disease. Banning it, however, is wrong. It's criminal the way the government lets thousands die to protect the interests of a few."

Napier's chameleon personality enabled him to navigate both pirate ships and ocean liners. Long ago he'd learned the skills that made him indispensable to all sorts of people. He discovered that the departments of government, wealthy businessmen, even ordinary people, were all corruptible. With enough money and pressure, anyone could be coopted, cornered, and coerced.

"I know, I know. I'll take care of the legal issues, Doctor. Failure is not an option when you're working with Zacco. We both know that. Put the check into our private account—we don't want it showing up on the books."

"Let me tell you something, Napier: I've never deviated one micromilligram from the original formula my father and I perfected. That thief Frieze is an imposter!"

Krump spoke with the confidence of a man unaware of his own inadequacies. Like a child, he was blind to everything other than himself. He was a pudgy old goat, full of bombast, and dangerously secure in the fictional world he had constructed by altering the unpleasant realities around him. Napier wished he could enjoy the peace such illusions provided, but in his world you had to look reality straight in the face.

"The issue with Frieze is complicated, Doctor. I'll handle it."

Napier knew that the toughest and wiliest thugs ultimately emerge the winners in every game. It was the animal cunning every dog knows. He knew when to stare down the Dos Negros and the Zaccos and when to allow them a victory. He saw their threats as minor irritations, skin deep. Still, he had to be careful to see things didn't get out of hand. He kept his fingers on the controls.

"Keep your eye on the prize, Doctor. We're in a confidence game, a political game. Frieze is just another property on the Monopoly board. We must get that formula. I respect the quality of your work, but we need every weapon at our disposal if we're to win over the authorities. The real money will come after Laetrile is legalized and we take the company public. Then we can pay Zacco back and our worries will be over."

Napier left. Krump leaned back onto the sofa thinking of Nicoleta. He dialed a massage service and arranged for a girl to come. A goatish little laugh rolled out of his throat. The laugh echoed strangely, with a Doppler-like effect, around the large, well-appointed room.

Nicoleta sat in a soft leather chair in front of the large window overlooking Washington Square. She liked living in San Francisco. It was more diverse than Jersey. There wasn't much history out here, and fewer families had roots that went way back. You didn't have New York, but overall things were better. There was less stress. It was easier to make friends. Besides, New York was falling apart just like it said in that song *American City Suite*. Time to move on.

Her buzzer went off. She pushed the button to unlock the door. Thirty seconds later, Russell Napier had his arms around her.

"Hey, what took you so long? Did you and the doctor have a party?"

"You should have seen the way he looked at you. You're *so* beautiful!"

"Yea, I *did* see him looking. He's a silly old man, kinda harmless, I guess, but he gives me the creeps. Is he really so smart?"

"The man who cures cancer will stalk the earth like a colossus. Right now Krump has the terminal true believers, but he's poised to get much more than that. He says Laetrile is not just the best treatment for cancer but for an entire range of degenerative diseases. Think what a market *that* would be."

Russell was kissing her all over, on her lips, her neck, her breasts. He carried her to the bedroom, and she didn't resist. She got a kick out of it. Her Uncle Joey had sent her out to keep an eye on Napier. She'd met him a few times and knew he fancied her. They spent a little time together, but it had never amounted to anything. This time was going to be different, very different. Nicoleta loved men and knew just what to do with them. Russell Napier was a fine specimen. Older men had more patience with their lovemaking, and they were more satisfying.

Later, Napier sat at the window and watched Nicoleta comb her long black hair.

"Krump's a great partner, not perfect, but very useful. There is no perfect partner, Nicoleta. The important point is that he has total confidence in his work. He's money in the bank for your uncle. Of course, we must worry about your uncle's generosity. I hope he understands this is not a sure thing. Nothing is."

Napier knew all about Nicoleta's uncle. Zacco had a reputation for breaking legs and cutting off ears. Napier didn't mention the problems of replicating Frieze's formula. Not yet. He wanted to prepare Zacco, and would tell the strongman himself when he was ready. He knew Nicoleta would tell her uncle everything he said, that she was in San Francisco to spy on him. He used that to his advantage by saying what he wanted Zacco to hear.

Nicoleta wore the black lace panties Napier had purchased at Frederick's on the way over. She was without a bra. Napier watched her breasts bounce as she combed her hair.

"Fuhgeddaboudit! Uncle Joey's got more money than God. His business with Dos Negros has him rolling in cash. He's gotta put the profits someplace."

Nicoleta finished with her hair and relaxed in the chair. She thought Napier was quite sexy despite their age difference. His body was firm, he still had color in his hair, and he was smart. Uncle Joey said Napier knew how to get things done. She loved his hazel eyes. He was a good lover—considerate, passionate. She thought maybe she could have real feelings for him, and he for her, that it wasn't just her uncle's money or the convenience of being thrown together, but she also knew what she had to do. She couldn't let things go too far too soon.

"Krump's worried about what your uncle might do if we fail."

"Elvin gives me the heebie-jeebies. He'd rape his own daughter if he had one." Nicoleta crossed her slim legs at the thought. Napier observed she didn't get much sun. The delicate, hairless, white skin, the ebony hair, the bright red lips—all these stark contrasts and the risks she represented made her incredibly sexy.

"We're all made of the same clay, you know. None of us is without the vilest of emotions." Napier's eyes switched back and forth between Nicoleta's jiggling breasts and the view of Washington Square outside the window.

"What about you, Russell? Are you capable of rape?"

"It's not something that appeals to me. I can't imagine ever resorting to such a vile thing. If Krump ever laid a hand on you, I would kill him."

Nicoleta walked over, sat on Russell's lap, and played casually with his hair. "Yes, my dear brave Russell, I do believe you would."

16.

Congressman Shipley

One of the Justice Department attorneys speaking off the record told a member of the press that having Congressman Shipley testify before the House Subcommittee on Organized Crime was "a bit like having your cotton crop investigated by a boll weevil." Shipley was a committee member, but he had worked to sabotage the Justice Department's efforts ever since his nemesis, Robert Kennedy, created the Organized Crime Strike Force. Rumors that Kennedy had been assassinated by organized crime elements surfaced when he was shot a few years back, but none of them stuck.

When the time came for Shipley to speak, he laid out his major argument: "Organized crime is a vastly overblown concept, gentlemen. The federal effort against it is too big a weapon. Innocent people just engaging in normal business practices are too likely to get caught up in this complicated web."

Shipley was full of purpose, confident and self-assured. "Sometimes I have the feeling," he went on, "as we go down the path into all sorts of uncharted areas, that if there had been no Mafia, the federal government would have had to invent one. This is especially true with the National Crime Information Center, which has, in the past few years, collected volumes of information on perfectly innocent U.S. citizens."

Already some committee members were nodding their heads in agreement. The Justice officials watched helplessly as Congressman

Shipley diverted the discussion away from organized crime and into the popular areas of invasion of privacy, government overreach, and government abuse of citizens' private rights.

"When you get into the exotic fields that the organized crime unit has got into, it is quite conceivable that anyone who ever was in the same theater or elevator with an organized-crime-identified type is going to find that moment in his life frozen into some government computer, to remain forever a part of the organized crime files."

By the end of the meeting, the Justice officials found themselves playing defense. The committee directed them to put into place procedures to insure that the individual rights and privacy of ordinary citizens would be protected in any future investigations. As he walked out of the meeting, Shipley gloated with satisfaction. Once again, he had thwarted the government bean counters. His next job would be dealing with the pesky reporters. The press was always trying to trip him up. They swarmed around him as he emerged from the meeting.

"Congressman Shipley, is it true that you are connected to mob interests through Joey Zacco, one of your constituents and supporters?"

"That's a despicable lie. You boys are always wallowing in the dirt, hoping to find some mud that'll stick. I have no business interests with Mr. Zacco or with any other alleged criminal. I have been an exemplary public official, always putting the public interest first."

"You deny that you know Mr. Zacco, a man who is connected with the importation of illegal drugs into this country?"

"Look, I get several requests from constituents every day for assistance with problems they are having with the government. I turn them over to my staff. I can't remember every name or issue that my office might have dealt with over the years. As for illegal drugs, you should talk to the Mexicans. They're the ones who profit from that trade. A couple of years ago President Nixon started Operation Intercept to deal with the movement of drugs into this country. I was one of the first congressmen from the other side of the aisle to support him. The program, however, was quickly scrapped at the behest of the Mexican president and a few potheads out in California."

"Are you aware, Congressman, that BioPharm, a company manufacturing Laetrile in Mexico, is being investigated by the Justice Department for possible criminal connections and illegal importation of Laetrile into the United States? Isn't it true that you, along with Mr. Zacco, are a stockholder in BioPharm?"

"Absolutely not. I have no business or personal connection in BioPharm or, as I've already stated, with Mr. Zacco. None at all. Look it up. Do your homework. You're grasping at straws, gentlemen."

"According to our sources, you have been petitioning the Senate to hold a committee hearing on Laetrile on behalf of BioPharm. How do you explain sticking your neck out to go to bat for a cancer drug you know nothing about, promoted by men you claim are virtual strangers?"

"Look," Shipley answered, "if Bonnie and Clyde had a cure for cancer, wouldn't you listen? I'm finished with your questions, gentlemen. I have far more important things to do with my time than to stand here and let you engage in character assassination at my expense."

His statements were aired on the news that night, accompanied by a response from a spokesperson for the Mexican government asked to comment on Congressman Shipley's allegations.

"It's a lost cause until you can control the demand. The problem is in the United States, not Mexico. We Mexicans don't use marijuana or heroin. Some people are just made as addicts. I haven't even seen a marijuana cigarette, and I was raised here and went to school here. I understand that in your schools even little children smoke marijuana and take pills and everything. The thing is, where do most of these young people in the United States get that stuff from? Do they come to Mexico to get it? No, sir. They've got it right there in San Francisco, Los Angeles, Chicago, all over. How does it get there? Having the police force you have, how is it possible to have so many drug addicts in your country? If we were to apprehend, right now, all the people who sell narcotics in Mexico, tomorrow we would have new ones, because there is money in it and there is demand for it. This is what makes free enterprise, as you Americans call it."

17.

Mida

Mida's father, Aurelio, did not return from work as usual. She and her mother, Dolores, were worried. Everything had been a mystery since Aurelio had taken a job for a rich man, managing some clubs downtown. He would not tell them the man's name or anything about his job, but they knew that it must be dangerous because Aurelio was making more money than ever. He told them they would soon be able to move across the border where they could have a better life. Neither Mida nor her mother wanted to move. Their family and everyone they knew lived in Mexico, but Aurelio had big ideas. He was a proud man, and Dolores, as his wife, would do whatever he wanted, though she argued with Aurelio when he took the job.

"This is where the Americans spend their money, Lola. It's the only way we'll ever be able to get ahead."

"I don't like what they do in those clubs. What can I say to my friends? I'm ashamed, Aurelio."

"It isn't for us to be ashamed. It's the rich Americans who created this problem."

"It's not just the Americans that are to blame. The whore is a Mexican, the bartender is a Mexican, and you are a Mexican. It's not *just* the Americans. What they do in those clubs is a sin against God. I don't like it at all."

"I won't talk about it. Only a little longer and I'll have enough to change our lives. Then I'll stop."

Dolores could only shake her head. She could not argue with her husband.

Then came last night, when Aurelio did not come home. Mida knew something was wrong when she realized her mother had stayed up all night.

Mida put on her white uniform for the job at the clinic. She went to their tiny bathroom to do her makeup, and was standing before the mirror when she heard a scream. She rushed to the kitchen as her father came in the door, his hand in a blood-soaked bandage.

"¡*Dios Mio!* What has happened, Elio?" Dolores was frantic.

"It's okay, Lola. I've had a small injury, that's all." Aurelio trembled like a cowering animal. Mida knew something terrible had happened.

"I quit my job at the clubs. I know this will make you happy." Aurelio went straight into the bedroom and closed the door.

"Go on, Mida. You run along to work. I'll take care of Papa and explain everything to you when you come home."

Dolores turned toward the stove and began to assemble the ingredients to make breakfast for Aurelio. Mida kissed her mother on the back of her neck. Dolores cried wet tears and did not turn to kiss her daughter goodbye.

"I'll see you when I come home, Mama. I love you and I love Papa, too. Everything will be all right. I know I can get more time at the clinic until Papa gets another job."

After Mida left, Aurelio came sheepishly out of his room and sat down for breakfast. He had changed the bandage. Dolores knew better than to quiz him about what had happened. He would tell her when he was ready.

"I'm going out to look for a new job. I can't afford to be just sitting around."

"Shouldn't you rest first, Elio?" Dolores didn't look at her husband. She cleared the dishes from the table and took them to the sink.

"I'm fine, Lola. Doctor Robles told me I'll be as good as new in no time."

"Thank God you went to the doctor."

"Don't worry, Lola. The job was no good for me, for us. You were right. I'll soon have another one. We may not be able to move as quickly as I hoped, but our lives will go on."

Dolores turned to look at her husband. She forced a smile. Her large eyes were full of love. Aurelio's face brightened. In that moment, she saw him just as he was on the day of their wedding. She could feel the life coming back into his body. When he was ready, he would tell her what had happened. She would not ask. She had learned that we are not always meant to know everything, but to accept what God brings.

After Aurelio left, Dolores finished with the kitchen. When that was done, she went on a mission of her own. While Aurelio took off toward Plaza Santa Cecilia, where he had friends who might be able to help him, Dolores walked all the way to the Puerta Blanca cemetery. It took her two hours to make the journey. At the shrine of Juan Soldado, she picked up a small rock and prayed to the saint to heal Aurelio and help him through his troubles. She took the rock home and placed it on their family altar. Once the wish had been granted, she would return the rock to the cemetery. It was the custom.

The song *Nights in White Satin* wafted down the hallway. Nelson entered Eric's room, adjusted the bedcovers, and watched Eric's eyes fluttering.

"He still in that half-sleep that the sickness brings," said Nelson to himself. "A few dreams crashing over him like waves in the ocean leaving him jarred and jangled as they ebb and flow."

Nelson retreated back into the hallway, humming along with the music from the speakers.

18.

Ofelia

Clinica Buena Salud

1972

It was the first time he saw her. Something about her face, the way she just stood there. A memory flashed, his arm. When he answered the knock at the door to his room, a beautiful girl with a warm smile surprised him. This was not Mida.

She saw the perplexed look on his face. "You expected Mida? I'm Ofelia. From now on, I'll give you your Laetrile injections if that's okay. I guess she didn't tell you."

Okay? Yes, okay. He tried to control his emotions.

"Of course it's okay. Don't worry about it. I'm happy to meet you. No harm done."

Had he said that before? He remembered the words.

Ofelia had brown eyes with large pupils—deer eyes. Eric wondered if she could see in the dark. She had black hair and skin the color of milk chocolate. He nearly reached out to touch her. Her teeth glowed a brilliant white. She spoke perfect English. *Here's a fine sedative for a broken man's nerves.* He was captured entirely.

He had to ask: "Have I seen you before?"

"I don't think so. I wasn't here when you arrived."

"How long have you been here?"

"A day, or part of a day."

"Do you remember when I last saw you?"

"Excuse me, Mr. Martin. Did you speak to me?"

Eric was dumbfounded. He stepped back to let her inside. He felt disembodied, like a spirit, transparent, as if he were floating in the air. "Excuse me, could I ask you to sit down?"

"Oh, yes, of course. I don't know why I'm dancing around like this. It's not something I usually do. In fact, I don't remember ever doing it before."

He smiled awkwardly. He was embarrassed but didn't know why. "I'm sure I've seen you before, but I can't remember when or where."

"I don't think so. Didn't you just arrive?"

He felt foolish and clumsy. He tried to calm himself but his heart pounded. Everything changed when he'd opened that door. It was like falling through space while he stood perfectly still.

Ofelia noticed the conscientious way Eric had organized his room. He'd been at the clinic hardly any time at all, and despite his illness he'd found a place for everything and put everything in its place. It was unusual to see such order. Most of the patients left their things in such a muddle.

"Your room is so neat and tidy. What's that book you're reading?"

The book of Russian stories Eric read on the plane lay on his bed.

The characters floated above the book.

"Keep your head on, man. She likes it when you talk cool."

"What? Who? Nelson?"

"She gonna follow you right on outta here, man."

Ofelia couldn't fathom what was going on. *Was Eric speaking to ghosts? Is there some flying bug in the air? Why is he waving his hands around? I don't see anything. Oh, well, I do admire men who read. Reading is like having a dozen lives in which to sample a dozen existences.*

"It's a book of short stories called *Fantastic Tales*. The events take place mostly in the character's imaginations."

"That's it. You cookin' now, man."

He'd never had such an immediate reaction to a girl. *Why now, when I'm sick and dying? Is it some cruel demon playing a joke?*

Ofelia was accustomed to odd behavior among the patients but Eric acted very strange indeed. He kept making eye contact and smiling. He couldn't stand still. *I think he's flirting with me.*

"I enjoy authors like Garcia Marquez and Borges," said Ofelia. "I find more truth in the dreams and visions they write about than in realistic fiction."

"I haven't read Marquez, but I like Borges. I like that his intricate stories can make you dizzy sometimes. Borges can be a little heavy, though. I'm not sure he's the best therapy for someone in my position."

She raised her thick dark eyebrows. "You must read Marquez. I'll bring you some of his stories tomorrow. I think you'll like them."

He was entranced. He felt weak in the knees, his mouth was dry, his stomach full of flutters. He stepped forward and handed his copy of *Fantastic Tales* to Ofelia.

"Here, take my book. See what you think. I just finished the last story today."

"What makes you like this book, Eric?"

When Ofelia reached out to take the book, their hands touched. His face warmed. He looked into her eyes and she blushed. She was so surprised at her feelings that she forgot to take the book. Eric stood there holding it, a confused look on his face.

"I can't really explain it. This illness has me in a pensive state of mind, a state of high sensitivity where I see things differently. I don't know if this makes any sense. Peculiar and fantastic stories are easier to relate to now that I'm sick."

"Oh, that makes perfect sense. I've heard many patients say they feel more aware of things previously hidden. I look forward to your book, Eric. It's very kind of you to think of me. I'll be sure to return it quickly."

He was charmed; more than charmed, bewitched. He'd never had such feelings before. *What is this?* He felt light, happy, anxious, and confused all at once.

"It looks like I'll be here for a while. Take all the time you need with the book."

He likes the same things that I like. I wish I could stay and talk with him, but I have my other appointments.

It was time to give the injection. Ofelia did the job expertly. It took just a few minutes to inject him and clean up. Soon she packed to leave.

"Must you go so soon?"

Eric felt awkward. He wanted her to stay but didn't know how to say it without sounding forward.

"Tell me something about yourself. How long have you worked at Buena Salud?"

He held the book in his hand as if it were a pudding that needed to set before he could give it to her. Eric had never been in love. He hadn't been much impressed by women. He'd had sex, sure, but when it ended, he thought it was natural to be on his way, back to the more important things in life. Everything was different with Ofelia. His feelings frightened him. It wasn't just because he was sick. He'd trained himself to live life stoically, to suppress the kinds of feelings that could lead him astray. There was too much danger there.

"I've been with Doctor Milagro for five years," said Ofelia. Suddenly she was carried away by a whirl of pleasure. *What on earth is happening to me?*

Eric thought she was the loveliest creature he'd ever seen.

"Do you live here at the clinic?"

"Live here? Oh, no. Only the patients live here. All the staff lives offsite. I live at home with my parents and my brother."

What a relief, she isn't married!

"I'm happy to meet you, Ofelia, very happy. I look forward to your next visit. It's at one o'clock, right?" He swirled on high. It was like being snatched up from the Earth inside a tornado. He couldn't wait until she returned.

"Yes, I'll see you again at one. Enjoy your day, Eric. Remember to drink your juices. Mida will be in around 10:30 to give you a cleansing treatment."

Ofelia beamed with pleasure as she left, but she was concerned. She tried to put her feelings into perspective. Eric was a handsome young man. He was very well organized, and shared her interest in books. Her heart beat violently. She quickly became upset. *He's charming, but what is there to be done? There is nothing to be done. This is all too crazy.*

It was too much for Eric to bear—too painful. This beautiful girl appeared out of the blue and caught him off guard. He must have looked so ugly and sick. God, what a thing life is. Just when he started to understand passion, his body was too weak and sick to accept it.

Why did he always think what to say after the moment to say it had passed? A series of thoughts came to mind. He should have asked her to walk with him to the cafeteria for a coffee or to show him around Tijuana. He should have asked her something, anything. He might have asked what other books she liked.

Like a total dunce, he'd said nothing. He stood outside the door, confused and silent, while she walked away. He took a few hesitant steps in her direction, stopped, and watched.

Sinyavsky, the author, flew around the bottom of the book trying to put things back into their proper places. He winked at Eric with a wry smile. His eyes apologized while his characters, acting like little children, misbehaved. Sinyavsky pushed them all back into the book and slid onto the cover into his proper place under the title.

Ofelia gave the impression of being oblivious to the emotions brewing inside, but the twitching fingers with which she held the book exposed her true feelings. She turned toward him and laughed uncomfortably, then walked away.

Eric gazed languidly into the dust, shuffling his feet, hands in his pockets, happy and unhappy, pleased and tormented.

The next few days were a jumble of discontinuities. The moments when Eric and Ofelia were apart seemed never-ending, but time flew when they were together. His thoughts rushed about as if on a surreal train ride with occasional brief stops but no clear destination. Ofelia was full of unexpected anxieties. She was guided along by the familiar routine of her work, as always, but interrupted by pestering emotions that interfered unpredictably in a way that baffled and disturbed her.

One day Mida arrived just as Ofelia was heading home.

"Good morning, Mida."

"You're half an orange, Ofelia. What's going on?"

"What do you mean?"

"Your body is here but your mind is not."

"You're tempting God, that's what you will tell me."

"What on earth do you mean, Ofelia?"

"That I'm in love or that I think I'm in love. I don't know."

"With Marcelino, of course."

"No, not Marcelino."

"Not Marcelino! But who then?"

"Oh, to go on this way is impossible!"

Ofelia stomped off shaking her head back and forth like a little dog with a bone. She was heading to La Luz, a bookstore off Revolución, to get something for Eric.

Mida watched her curiously. She thought she saw tears in Ofelia's eyes. Oh, well, there was no time for idle speculation. Mida had her own problems and they were quite bad enough. Something horrible had happened to her father. He would not talk about it, she knew, but she had to find out. She absolutely had to find out.

19.

Depressed

One Week Later

Scattered thoughts tormented him during the night. Strange assemblances. He stared at the window. His reflection stared back, a Jekyll and Hyde fabrication, a bloody mass of muscle and veins, marvelous and absurd. His whole life was absurd, everything he went through. He was a madman possessed with an insanity that ordinary people could never understand.

Eric awoke in a funk. It was as if he walked through mud. He was an amoeba blobbing around in the dark. He'd slept on the floor because of the unrelenting back pain, hoping the extra support would help. When he woke he was stiff and sore. He adjusted his body so that he could raise himself up with minimal pressure on the bones and joints. He drank in the dangerous elixir of doubt and self-pity and became quite drunk. Saturated in sweat, he breathed heavily as if he'd just finished a long race.

Ofelia arrived to give him his early-morning injection. She found him seated in his chair, unshaved, uncombed, draped in a thin gray robe, no socks on his feet.

"Eric, you look awful! Did you have a bad night? Why, your bed, it hasn't even been slept in!"

Gripped by shame and inadequacy, Eric didn't want her to see him like this. He'd begun to look like a desperately sick man, emotionally shattered, drained, traumatized, and worst of all, embarrassed.

"I slept on the floor. The pain in my back made the bed too uncomfortable. I'm better now."

It was a lie. He would never get better. It was a cruel joke fate had played on him. How could anyone so beautiful and perfect understand? He alone knew the truth of his pain. He couldn't speak of it, not to Ofelia.

"Let's get you cleaned up. You're a handsome man, Eric. You're no invalid. You haven't been here long enough. The medicine hasn't taken effect yet. You'll notice the positive changes in a few more days. I'm sure of it."

Ofelia drew some water into a bowl. She took a washcloth, razor, soap, and brush from the bathroom and placed them on the table next to Eric's chair. She shaved him, washed him, and combed his hair. It made her happy to help him in this way. It also gave her a chance to see him up close. Her heart was touched. Behind the fear and sadness, she saw strength and sensitivity in his eyes. She was helplessly attracted in spite of all the warnings she had received not to get too close to the patients. Her feelings couldn't be controlled any more than the weather. She stood with her hands on her hips and smiled.

"That's better!"

Eric was grateful. He felt tingles on his skin when she was close. She pulled him out of his chronic despair simply by being with him.

"Thank you, Ofelia. You accept this joyless burden with such... equanimity. I apologize. I know I look terrible. It isn't that bad, I assure you. Look—I've snapped right out of the foul mood you found me in. I'm ready to face the day now." He smiled and pranced around like a boy who had just received the gift of his dreams.

"You should be a little less hard on yourself, Eric. I enjoy being with you, but I must go. I'll be back at one o'clock for your next injection."

"Ofelia, when do you eat lunch?"

Eric had rehearsed this all night as he tossed and turned. He had practiced every word so that he wouldn't screw it up.

"Lunch? At noon, why?"

"I thought we could meet on the bench in the courtyard and have lunch together. I'll bring something from the cafeteria. We could talk about books or anything else that suits you."

Ofelia considered how sick Eric had looked when she first arrived.

"Are you sure you'll feel up to it?"

"I'll be ready. It will give me something to look forward to."

She knew it was against the rules. Any relationship that might be brewing would be complicated. Still, she couldn't see any harm in making a sick man happy. She enjoyed his company. It would make her happy too, she couldn't deny that. She could deal with any complications later.

"That sounds like fun. At noon then, on the bench."

Ofelia walked away slowly. *This could be the beginning of a great mistake.*

Eric stood at the door and watched Ofelia as she left. When she was out of sight, he closed the door and opened the book of short stories by Marquez. He tried to think about what to say at lunch. The butterflies in his stomach made him lightheaded. His brief moment of joy exploded when the pain struck. He reeled backward and collapsed onto the bed. Then came the worst possible revelation. He was a fool, an idiot. Who did he think he was?

"There are other patients, Mr. Martin. Don't you know that? My world doesn't revolve around you."

Later, when he felt better, Eric climbed the hill to the chapel, eager but apprehensive. It upset him to need help and attention from others. Ofelia had cleaned him as if he were a child. Now he was going to see a priest, something he thought he'd dispensed with long ago. Where was the strong and independent man he thought he was? He trudged along, head hung in shame. He was dying. What difference did all his plans make now? Life's a shadow, an illusion, a dream, just as Macbeth said.

Eric had worked himself into a state of agitation by the time he entered the chapel. His depression had passed. He stood upright and strong as if no illness could attack him. He heard the sound of a Celtic harp. Father Jordan strummed the chords at the altar.

Eric waited in the back of the chapel. As his excitement cooled, he felt ill at ease and ridiculous. He was ashamed that he had no friends to speak with at a time like this. His stepmother, Karen, was smart and always willing to talk, but their relationship was professional. She'd been married to his father longer than his birth mother had. They'd developed a close relationship, but always at a distance. Eric loved his real mother dearly, but they lived in different worlds. His half-sister and half-brother from Karen were too young. They would never understand his situation. He was closest to Devon, his half-brother on his mother's side, but Devon was eight years younger, married with children, and still in college. There were a few people at work, but they were no more than acquaintances. He trusted Manny, but Manny couldn't get close in that way. Manny had little interest in philosophizing. He was a realist who was not afraid to get his hands dirty, a blood-and-guts doctor.

Eric needed someone to stop the nightmares grinding away in the immense mill of his head. He didn't want to bore his friends or impose his problems on those he cared about. They all had their own lives. They had their health. He was jealous. Why not admit it? He hated their good health, the years ahead they had to live, years he didn't have. He knew this despair was born of anger, jealousy, and fear, but it gripped and held him just the same.

When Jordan finished playing, he spotted Eric at the back of the church and waved him forward. Eric was overcome by shame and embarrassment. He didn't know what to say. He stood paralyzed. He stared at Jordan, frozen in thought.

"Aye, lad, I understand your fear of churches. It can be difficult for heathens. I'll come and meet you by the entrance. Give me a minute to take care of this wee harp. How'd ya like the lilting melodies of old Ireland?"

"Lovely, Jordan. I had no idea you played. Stay where you are. My phobia of religion isn't what's keeping me from coming forward. It's just that I'm uncertain about what to say."

"God knows your thoughts, my boy."

"But that's my trouble. I don't think I believe in God. Being here feels hypocritical."

"We each approach God in our own way. What troubles do you have?"

Eric walked to the front of the church. Jordan's jolly round face and snowy white hair came into focus.

"I'm not sure I know my deepest troubles, Jordan. Cancer, of course, but it's not the only one."

Eric sat on a hard wooden pew below the pulpit while Jordan sat on a step leading down from it. They faced each other, but not at the same level.

"Nor do any of us, Eric. But God knows. You needn't have faith. Don't struggle for it. You may be one of those for whom dogma in any form is so repulsive that it would have the wrong effect. You can't be damned for that."

"I used to joke with my brother, Devon, about the growing population of China. I said it was like an unbalanced load of laundry that would cause the world to spin out of orbit. Now I've spun out of my orbit, Jordan. This illness is like a weight distributed unequally that makes me stagger around like someone drunk or sleepwalking."

"Believe me, my son, your situation is not hopeless, though no one could blame you for thinking it is. And even if things don't work out as we hope, death... well, fear of death is not due to the timeless constitution of the human mind. Unfortunately, it's historical and cultural conditioning and the Church, with its misplaced emphasis on hellfire, that's to blame. I don't mean to trivialize what you're going through, lad, not at all, but there may be a blessing in the darkness around you. Any rich life consists of a series of deaths and transformations. When a part of us dies, another part is born. Take each day as it comes. Each moment of consciousness is an amazingly precious thing. Sometimes life's greatest sorrows can lead to life's greatest joys."

"That sounds suspiciously like resurrection, Jordan. Look, knowing that I'm going to die someday and knowing that I'm going to die soon are very different things. I'm thirty-three years old. I've just started to live and now I'm dying. I'm afraid this is the only life I'll have and it doesn't seem fair. I guess I'm here partly to get your opinion."

Jordan had his personal ideas on life. They were not always consistent with the teachings of his church. "The spiritual view is that man is divine in origin with an immortal soul. The materialist view is that man is an evanescent accident with no moral nature except that created in him by his experience and culture. As mortal human beings, we have no way o' knowing which view is correct, Eric. What holds and constitutes Christianity is a body of myths. We each interpret these myths differently. Most Christians believe them, some don't, but all revere them. As a matter of faith, we believe there is an immortal soul that survives the death of the physical body. I'm not blind. I'm as convinced as anyone that a corpse canna come back to life, but I do believe the immortal soul goes on whether or not I can imagine how. But that is not the point. Whether or not we travel through eternity, we do, at the very least, have this moment here on earth. You are alive now, and that's what matters. What you must do is to make the most of that, my son. You must make each day count even if it is to be your last."

"I know, Jordan, but I think constantly about death. It's coming faster than I'd wish."

"None of us knows the future, Eric. In a rich country like America, death is associated with old age. In Mexico, like most o' the world, death occurs all along the life span. No one is immune. Life is fragile, unpredictable, and none of us can know for sure when death is coming. On the other hand, with God's grace, the unexpected can change things quickly."

"I'm angry, angry at being sick, angry at a medical system that's cold and insensitive and ineffective. I'm angry at everyone who isn't sick, angry at their nauseating good fortune, at their inability to comprehend what I'm going through."

Eric's stomach cramped up. To hold himself steady he held onto the pew. He hated unloading on Jordan. He wished he were more courageous. Why couldn't he face death stoically like the great philosophers? To read philosophy is one thing; to live it is another, especially when death is rattling your cage. Eric's heart had been a cold stone through most of his life. Now, it burned. Dying was not dramatic, not heroic. There were moments of intense pain followed by listless boredom and useless worry.

"It's okay to feel the rage, but don't dwell on it, Eric. We must take what God gives. Life's very uncertainty is its greatest asset. Human beings are not windup clocks. Things have a way o' turning around just when you least expect it. I've seen it. We're all mortal. We live in order to die, but death has to be earned. It's the one spiritual experience that cannot be stolen from us, Eric. Your illness could be like a messenger that's come to show you a way to deeper truths."

It was years since Eric had been in a church. The baroquely painted angels and elaborately carved saints no longer worked the same magic on him as when he was a child. Jordan didn't need the magic to make his point. Had he used the same old tricks, they'd have repelled Eric. Jordan spoke as one man to another, unlike the priests Eric had once known. Jordan's wisdom and modesty worked in a special way. He was spiritual in a secular sense. Eric felt a camaraderie. That startled him but also pleased him; not that he was going back to the church or was about to get on his knees to pray. That idea was ridiculous, but Jordan had accomplished what Eric had been unable to do on his own. Eric had scaled the hill to the church while on the brink of complete despair. Jordan gave him a measure of reassurance, even a kind of goal. If he could steady himself through the storm, Jordan was right: everything could change very suddenly.

"Thanks, Jordan. Your words mean a lot. I'm frightened and angry at the prospect of death, but you're right—things could change for me here. In fact, they've already changed."

Eric's thoughts turned to Ofelia and lunch. Taking each day at a time was the way to beat back the despair.

"Don't second-guess your true feelings, the instincts that brought you here. Follow Doctor Milagro's advice. You're just beginning the treatments. Attack the disease with vigor. Fight for optimism. Give it a little more time."

Jordan stood up. "Let's go outside."

He put his arm around Eric and walked him out of the church. Once there, Jordan pulled a cigar from his pocket and lit it.

"Don't give up. It can take weeks before the results of the treatments become apparent."

They shook hands, but that felt insufficient to Eric. He put his arms around Jordan and hugged him triumphantly without giving this uncharacteristic act a thought. Jordan hugged him back. Ashes from Jordan's cigar fell onto Eric's shoulders. He was too full of feeling to notice. It was awkward putting his arms around another man, around anyone actually, yet it felt right. Eric let his head fall onto Jordan's shoulder. If he had let himself cry, his tears would have been tears of joy.

"I'm so glad I came."

"So am I, Eric."

On the way back down the hill, Eric planned what to say at his luncheon date with Ofelia. He had to make up for the poor impression he'd made earlier. He wanted her to like him. If he had nothing to say, it would be a catastrophe. His heart stopped cold, then beat like a kettledrum.

20.

Lunch with Ofelia

After tending to Eric, Ofelia was preoccupied and restless as she worked with the other patients. This sometimes happened when she grew bored with work or was anxious to get home, but there was another reason this time: Try as she might, she could not take her mind off Eric. She knew an intimate relationship with a patient was forbidden, but, like the forbidden fruit in the Bible, such rules just intensified her feelings. She had to sort everything out before lunch.

Mary was first. There is nothing glamorous about dying from cancer. Personal pride, dignity, and strength disappear with the deterioration of both mind and body. Nerve damage caused a burning sensation in Mary's legs and fingers. Ofelia spread warm oil all over Mary's legs and kneaded them to get the knots out. Mary was delirious and couldn't get out of bed. Her once majestic spirit, flying high with hope and faith, had crashed to Earth. Ofelia spoke softly and tried to be reassuring. It was too much of an effort for Mary to answer. The pain had affected her vision, and she wasn't sure who was in the room with her.

"It's Ofelia. I'm here to give you an injection."

Groaning, Mary shook her head. "No good," she managed to mutter. But she put out her arm to let Ofelia do what she had to do.

Mary struggled to speak. "They... don't work anymore. I might as well go home." Those few words exhausted her. By the time Ofelia left, Mary was asleep.

Things were better with Cat. She was the stoic one, somehow finding a way to accept everything as it came.

"How's it going today, Cat?"

"To the mind in the body on the sickbed, Ofelia, the pain that shadows this disease has no meaning or purpose. It's an irreducible sensation that defies words."

"You look pretty today, Cat. You've had your hair done."

"I amuse myself with my hairdressing. I had it done differently, the hair twisted on top of my head and spreading out naturally. It's a charming novelty, don't you think? Of course it's just a wig." Cat laughed.

Outside the window, poisonous snakes oozed in the grass, and queer lizards turned their heads in strobic thrusts, while inside the room Ofelia went about her job methodically. She tried to put Eric out of her mind, but failed. She was unusually clumsy and forgetful. She knocked over a vase when she put her case of instruments on the table.

"Oh, Cat, I'm so sorry. I'll clean this up and get a new vase. I think the flowers are okay."

"Don't worry, honey, they're nothing special. Are you all right, dear? You look a little frazzled. It wouldn't be that young man, Eric, would it? The two of you remind me of my late husband and me when we first met. We couldn't take our eyes off each other."

Ofelia turned bright red. "I hope you're not insinuating anything inappropriate on my part, Cat. I'll be right back."

As Ofelia left to fetch another vase, Cat yelled after her. "Don't bother. I don't want the flowers anyway. They're from a friend I don't much care for. I only kept them to be nice. And don't worry about what I said. Mum's the word, dear, but just between us, it's always best to follow your heart, no matter the rules."

"You're so sweet and gentle, Cat. I admire your dignity."

"Don't kid yourself, honey, it's all fake. You should see me when I first get up. Look at these skinny legs and flabby thighs. Who would guess that I once ran marathons and hiked mountain trails? The only way I could do that now would be to climb on a broomstick like a witch."

"I don't think that would be advisable in your condition," said Ofelia with a smile.

"In my condition, honey, even a broomstick would turn flaccid at the first glance."

After injecting Cat, Ofelia left to see Ira. Cat spoke to her on the way out: "Don't fret, Ofelia. If you have feelings for him, go after him with all you've got. I've never let convention stop me. As I near the end of my life, I'm very grateful to be able to say that. I'd hate to think I missed out on something worthwhile simply because some fool thought it improper."

Ofelia didn't answer. She smiled and walked out. Her heart jolted. It was love. She knew it. She wondered if Eric could sense it too, and what he made of it.

Ira was testy as usual.

"What a mess of hope and doubt I've become. It's no good at all. I'm going to die, and soon! *Oy vey!* All these drugs! *Gornisht helfn.*"

"Don't talk like that, Ira. You're feeling better every day." Ofelia spoke as if what she said were true, but she knew Ira was right.

"Am I? Maybe I do feel a bit stronger." Ira reached out to touch Ofelia's hair. He imagined an angel swooping down to caress him, and thought of himself as a young man again rising to embrace her.

"Please hold your arm still, Ira. I want this to go as smoothly as possible."

"Apricot pits! How do apricot pits cure cancer? I should have never smoked. I should've watched my diet. There are so many things I should've done, been kinder to my family, my son, even my poor dear wife. Look, now there's no one to help me. So? Who needs help? What good would it do? I worked all my life. Every morning I started running. I ran all the day through. Never a rest. Now... now that I'm dying, I don't want to rest! Where does it come from, this comedy we call life? I don't need it. Agh, if only I'd lived differently."

Ira knew the Laetrile didn't stop the cancer. He wanted to make a point with the doctors up north by coming to Mexico to spite them. Their grotesque burning and baking and stewing of his juices, their nauseating toxic cocktails; his decision to come to Mexico put them all in their place. He was a man who could make his own decisions.

But now there was nothing left to do, no place left to go. He'd reached a dead end.

God help me, Ofelia thought. She only wanted to get away from Ira. He made everyone around him so miserable.

"You have nothing to be ashamed of, Ira. You've lived an honorable life."

"Honorable? Who needs it? I've been a fool. I could've died a martyr. I could've let them use me in some science experiment or something. They might have found a real cure. I would've been in all the newspapers, died a famous man. I would have been somebody, but now I'm nobody."

He was covered in sweat. He was feverish. His gray hair had slipped out of the ponytail and lay haphazardly on the pillow in a tangled mess. "This is what cancer does, you see. It turns our bodies by degrees into something less appealing and more alien than we could ever imagine."

He threw off the sheet and showed Ofelia the bruises all over his legs. The shock of it nearly caused her to faint, but she reached for a damp towel and doused his forehead, then covered his legs again with the sheets.

"I'm going to give you a sedative, Ira, to help you sleep. You'll have to take this by mouth."

He didn't move. His enormous eyes looked up at her when he opened his mouth. She placed the pill on his thick tongue and helped him drink from the glass she held for him. After he swallowed, he rolled onto his side to stare at the wall. He wanted to be alone, completely alone.

"Sleep, Ira. It'll be good for you." She left the room feeling guilty that she couldn't do more.

Morning rounds were over. It would soon be time for lunch with Eric. Ofelia went to the washroom to make herself beautiful. She felt like a young girl, crazy with the need to be conspicuous. It was entirely foolish, but she couldn't help herself. She heard music coming from the lobby and found herself silently mouthing the words.

"I'm crazy for trying and crazy for crying and I'm crazy for loving you."

There are times when she could reject all the intellectual pleasures of the world, even art, to live a life in the sun, with music and love. Oh, but he wants to speak of books, and I haven't read his book yet. *Damn!* A chill went through her.

♋

Eric sat on the bench, waiting for her. "You look so happy, Ofelia. Do you have any idea how beautiful you look to me?"

She couldn't help but smile at this compliment. "I know from experience that I'm happy when I wish it. Wishing it is the whole trick, Eric. You look much better yourself. Your talk with Father Jordan must have done you some good."

"Aha! You saw me go up the hill? You must be spying on me."

"Yes. Part of my job is to make sure you don't wander off into the jungle with the lions and tigers."

Eric heard a faint rustle in the bushes at the edge of the courtyard. Ofelia laughed when she saw him look in that direction. She wanted to embrace him, wanted to touch his skin.

"I'm not much for religion. I stopped going to church years ago. I think of Jordan as a friend. He did make me feel better though. I'm happy I went to see him, but it felt awkward."

Eric wondered what it would be like to have Ofelia as his wife. He dismissed the idea as impossible nonsense.

Ofelia said, "I go to church only to please my parents. I believed fervently when I was a child, but I can't make myself believe now. May God forgive me if I'm wrong. To my simple mind, it's just the way things are. I can't change that."

Eric had a roll and some fruit from the cafeteria. Ofelia had a chicken sandwich that she'd packed from home.

"That looks good! I haven't had meat since I've been here. Would you like to share?"

"You're wicked, Eric. You know that's against the rules."

His eyes gleamed brightly. "You're only alive when you're breaking the rules."

She thought of what Cat had said. It pleased her that Eric liked to flirt.

"Men just march straight ahead, without fear, without reproach. You may wear the trousers, but you'll see that in me you have a real foe!" She held her sandwich just out of his reach.

Eric pretended to sulk. He held up his plate of fruit and blessed it. "*In Nomine Patris, et Filii, et Spiritus Sancti...* amen."

Ofelia tried to keep a stern face, but she broke out giggling. In the end, they split lunch and agreed to keep the secret to themselves.

"Do you think disobeying the rules will turn me into a tarantula?"

Ofelia looked confused, and then it dawned on her what he meant.

"You read Marquez! Oh Eric, I'm so sorry. I haven't had time to read your book. I promise to read it very soon."

"It isn't a problem. Not long from now I'll be nothing more than an imaginary dot on your horizon."

Ofelia's expression went dark. "You're cruel to me, Eric. So cruel! That's not what I meant at all. I want to discuss the things that are important to you. Don't be so anxious to fly away like Marquez's old man with his giant wings."

She wondered what he wanted her to say. That she loved him? That he had possessed her mind? They'd only known each other for a week. "Love" is a very ancient and old-fashioned word. Does anyone love anymore as they used to? She needed more time to discover her true feelings—and so did Eric, whatever he thought. Love would come, if it came, because it must.

Eric read her mind. She was right. Instead of standing mute as he usually did, he'd opened his mouth and inserted his foot, the kind of blunder he always made around women.

"Ofelia, I'm sorry I said that. I meant it as a joke, but it was in poor taste. I guess I just feel strange. I haven't much experience sitting on benches with beautiful young women."

It was time for Ofelia to go back to work. They stood up and looked at each other in silence, not knowing what to do next.

"Well, that's a good thing. I might be jealous if I thought you did this with all the girls."

He drew close to her. They stood there uneasily for a minute until she put her arms around him. She didn't know how hard to squeeze or how long. The world shifted with that embrace. They parted calmly, but there was excitement all around.

He kept his thoughts to himself and walked back to his room. His heart pounded....

"Hey, man, you wakin' up? What you been smiling 'bout? Things lookin' up?"

"All the way to the clouds, Nelson, all the way to the clouds."

"I don't see no clouds, man, just that young nurse walkin' away. She been here checkin' you out, man."

Nelson arranged the pillows to make Eric more comfortable.

"Hey, did you watch that Archie Bunker show last night? Everybody talkin' bout it. Sammy Davis, the ole Candyman, kissed that fat honky on the cheek. Wonder what that nigger-hater George Wallace will have to say about that."

Eric had already dozed off. Nelson eased out of the room into the hallway and collided with Nurse Marta.

"Are you blind, Nelson? Watch it. You almost knocked me down."

"Want me to kiss you on the cheek like the Candyman did to Archie last night?" asked Nelson with a laugh.

"Keep your paws off me. Now get back to work and watch your step around here or—"

"Or what, Miss Marta?"

"It's *Nurse* Marta. Get back to work, that's all."

21.

Devon's Visit

Devon heard Buddy Holly's *Party Doll* blasting through the door of Eric's room. He knocked and Eric opened the door immediately. The brothers embraced.

Devon saw twin beds like the ones they'd had in Sugarvale before Eric left for college. There was a round wooden table with matching chairs, an overstuffed couch, and an ancient TV encased in a wooden frame with shiny silver knobs. A small kitchen had been set up in the corner. Air conditioning allowed them to keep the windows and doors closed. Outside in the courtyard the smell was toxic.

The last time they were together, Devon accused his brother of running off to Mexico like a crazy fool. Eric walked away in a fit of anger. They hadn't spoken until a few days ago when Devon called to say he was on his way down for a quick visit. "Are you angry that I'm here?" he asked.

"I'm not angry anymore. I'm over all that. It's good to have company, but don't flatter yourself that you'll convince me to go home."

"I spoke with Mom before I came here. She loves you, Eric. We all just want what's best for you."

"This whole thing has given me plenty of time to think. At first, I'll admit I was terrified, terrified that my life was over. At Stanford I got really pissed off. In my last test they shot air up my ass into my intestine. The pain was so bad I screamed. They treated me like an old car trapped in a garage full of wannabe mechanics. They tinkered, disassembled me, and pulled me apart. When they saw there was no fix, they thought about whether any of my spare parts might be useful. I became a teaching tool for the high-school shop class. The whole thing was an exercise in reduction on behalf of science till I put a stop to their experiments."

Eric didn't expect Devon to understand the horror of living with cancer. Some things can't be shared. Devon and Eric had different fathers, both of whom had left soon after their sons were born. Devon's father often came around with gifts. Eric's father never came, which led to a jealousy Eric simply couldn't shake.

"I realized that conventional medicine has no way of dealing with this disease. I was just a piece of meat on the butcher's slab. I tell you this because it's the last time it will happen to me. I'm done with all that. What I've learned while I've been here would make you cry, Devon. They don't claim to have a cure, but I've heard they've brought some hopeless ones all the way back. Some of the shit these poor people went through before they came down here is terrible— what sad stories."

Devon was unnerved at the questionable atmosphere he saw at the clinic. He didn't know what to say. He understood the appeal of alternative approaches like Laetrile, but everything here seemed so unprofessional and peculiar. He couldn't understand how his brother could fall for such obvious nonsense. He felt an obligation to change Eric's mind, but he didn't know how. The last thing he wanted to do was to alienate Eric, but that's what would happen if he moved too fast.

"I want to help, okay? We all want to help you, Eric. I'm not here to change your mind." *A lie, of course, but just a little white lie.* "I simply want to know how you feel, to hear what you have to say, to see what we can do to help you."

Eric was disappointed in his brother. He had wanted Devon to explore the world before getting married and having kids. Devon got hooked his junior year at college, and that was that. Devon soon realized he'd fallen into a trap. He saw his options slip away as the noose tightened around his neck. The marriage was on the rocks. Eric saw the train crash coming from the very start. One bad move begets another until the whole sequence collapses like a set of dominoes.

Stay away from girls until you've made your way in life.

"I understand how you might find things odd here," said Eric with a smirk. "The doctor doubles as a minister." Eric saw the look on Devon's face. "Yeah, I know. He told me on the first day that Jesus Christ himself is the director of the clinic. I'll admit it made me uncomfortable."

"You're joking."

"No, I'm not. You'll be even more surprised to know that I've become friendly with a Catholic priest."

Devon was stunned. Now he knew for sure Eric was losing it. On Sundays, when they were young, Eric slept in to avoid church. He'd stay home and fix breakfast, making a big mess in the kitchen. He was especially difficult at Christmas when he would rant and storm out of the house. Sometimes he returned with gifts, looking guilty, but he always retired to his room before any of the presents were opened. Devon couldn't imagine Eric would trust his life to a doctor who doubled as a minister or that he would befriend a priest.

"Don't give me that look." Eric winced defensively. "What of it? Maybe it's just the kind of craziness that's needed. I'm comfortable here. I was never comfortable at Stanford. Something clicks that hasn't clicked for me in a long time. I don't think you can understand it unless it happens to you."

"You've found religion?"

"It's not as simple as that. I'm beginning to understand things differently. To see life differently. And why not? What can I lose? The doctors at Stanford told me there was nothing to be done."

"You told me they'd offered a new treatment that might cure you."

"Grasping at straws!"

Devon's father had paid for Eric's college education. Eric was grateful but ashamed. His own father hadn't helped. He did buy Eric a car for his high school graduation, and Eric was happy until he realized that his father had only made a deposit. Eric had to work nights and weekends to keep up with the payments. He would never acknowledge how his father had screwed up his life, but Devon knew how much it hurt him. Eric grew a hard shell around his feelings and kept all his emotions inside. This inability to connect with anyone closely was what Devon thought might have made his brother vulnerable to schemes like Laetrile. Smart people do dumb things when they're desperate for love. The people who ran the clinic could be cons or fools. They certainly weren't medical professionals in any normal sense of the word. That was obvious. Whatever the case, Devon considered them dangerous. They were the enemy because they led sick and dying people like Eric away from the real medicine that provided the only legitimate chance of keeping them alive.

"I can only stay the night, Eric. I know your experience at Stanford was upsetting, but there are other good doctors and hospitals. I think you should give that a thought if things start to go downhill here. This place is very strange."

"Why do you think a treatment that leaves me intact, in good health, and better educated about how to keep my body free of disease is strange? Very few people survive the medical establishment's chemicals, surgical treatments, and radiation, Devon. You said you weren't going to try to change my mind, so don't. The doctors at Stanford tortured me. I'm not going back there no matter what. I'd rather die than go through that again. I'm gonna make it, damn it! I'm gonna beat the *fucking* odds. I have to. Things are starting to happen in my life, good things. The doctors at Stanford have lots of cases, but I only have *my* case, and I'm not going to turn it over to technicians with hearts of stone."

Devon saw he was helpless and useless. He needed a better plan. Eric was losing the ability to make rational decisions.

"If I don't survive, at least I can choose how to die. I know this clinic seems odd, but that doesn't make it a scam. I met Russell Napier, who manufactures the Laetrile. He's sharp. I like him. Doctor Milagro may be an odd duck, but he's a fine man and a competent physician. He's got a real heart, a heart that beats, unlike those cold fish at Stanford. When you're sick and dying, it's good to be surrounded by people with hearts. The doctors at Stanford are revenue generators.

The patients here aren't the deluded bumpkins you think. Sometimes you just have to think outside the box. There's another thing I should tell you: There's one girl here, a nurse, who gives the injections. I like her a lot. I think we might have something going. You'll meet her tomorrow and see for yourself. I'm happy here, Devon. I'm gonna stay. The sooner you accept that, the better things will be for both of us."

"You wouldn't let *me* do what *you're* doing without challenging me, Eric. Think about it. What if the shoe were on the other foot?"

When they were boys, Eric had been Devon's role model. Devon couldn't imagine that Eric had now fallen under the influence of quacks and religious zealots and some girl he hardly knew. Devon blamed Karen; she'd peppered Eric with her foolish ideas about spirituality and interconnectedness and macrobiotic diets—the last things Eric needed to hear. It was exasperating and heartbreaking for Devon to watch these changes take hold of Eric's once-sensible mind.

"I've never interfered in your life, Devon, even when we disagreed. I wanted you to visit Europe, to see some of the world, to take time to get to know yourself before you got married, yet I stood up as your best man when you asked. Remember? If you were in my situation, if you'd been through what I've been through, seen what I've seen, you'd end up doing the same thing. I'm not some madman that's run off on a wild goose chase. I know that's what you think, but it's not true."

"I don't think you're crazy, Eric, just stubborn. Your decision to give up on Stanford and to come here seems cracked. You must admit it's totally out of character. What happened to your belief in scientific truth, the scientific method, and all that?"

"I haven't given up on it, not at all. Science has very practical uses. It works. There can be no doubt about why a plane flies or how televisions function, but there's something at the core of life that science can't touch. I used to think the idea that life has meaning was a crutch, a way of propping up weak people to get them through the day, that religion is popular because it caters to a need to hold onto something, no matter how false, just so we can go on living. I don't know what I think now, Devon. At the deepest level it's possible that nothing makes any sense at all. But what if it does? I could go crazy just thinking about it, but when you're sick and death is pounding on the door, you're forced to think about it."

Devon went mute. There was no way he was going to change Eric's mind, certainly not on this trip. He'd only make things worse by trying. He needed to reaffirm their deep love for each other first. "I want what's best for you, Eric, no more, no less. I'll be there for you whatever my opinion."

"I know you think I'm nuts, but the docs at Stanford can't help me, Devon. They're out of options. I wish they'd had the decency to let me go home and die in peace. Instead, they dangled this new treatment idea in front of me so they could keep me there to carry out their Mengele-like experiments. They have no solutions. Laetrile is my only real chance. I've read about it. I've seen the positive results. I refuse to die in a hospital on a morphine drip with a life that's turned into a miserable parody. I want to live the time I've got left in my own way. If that means chasing after windmills, I'll chase them."

Devon could see where Eric was coming from and why, but he wasn't about to give up hope of getting him back home when there was still a chance of a cure. There had to be a way to figure all this out, gather more information, and develop a better argument to convince his brother.

"I'll take my chances here. Frankly, they're all full of shit, the doctors up north and the healers in Mexico. Go back home. Forget about all this. I don't want you to go through it. My life's become a mean little tragedy."

Eric put on a show of strength, but inside he worried about the decisions he'd made and he was poisoned by anxiety. Devon didn't know it, but he had made an impact. Eric knew that Mexico might be a mistake. Even with the good things that seemed to be happening around him, he couldn't entirely convince himself he'd made the right decision. Everything grew more complicated as the minutes ticked by. Minutes and hours and days. How much time did he have? Damnit! How much time?

Devon turned his attention to the girl. What was going on here? Adding a girl to the toxic mix of Eric's disease and his fragmented mind was a disaster. Devon thought she might be part of a conspiracy to fleece his brother. The scoundrels at these faux clinics were capable of anything. He would wait till he met her before making a decision, but he had a bad feeling about this.

"Don't push me out of your life, Eric. We've gone through too much together. I've got to go home tomorrow. I'll get a leave from the university, then I'm coming back to stay with you. I'll be here as soon as I can. I love you. I want to be here to help you through this. We'll get through it together. All I want is what's best for you."

"What about Mia and the girls? You can't just leave them."

"Mia took the girls to her mother's place. We've decided to take a break from each other for a while."

"I'm sorry, Devon. You should stay in Berkeley and tend to your family. I'm okay on my own. You need to put things back together. I know how important those girls are to you. But remember, if you do come down, no more arguing about the clinic, okay? My mind's made up. I'm staying here. You need to accept that."

"Yes," said Devon reluctantly, "but I'm coming back as soon as possible."

Outside the window a Mexican boy and girl were playing with a chocolate-brown hairless dog and several puppies.

"What kind of dogs are those? I've seen them around down here."

At times when they were growing up together, Eric had been prone to moodiness and anger. Devon adjusted to those moods. He loved Eric unconditionally, and would do whatever he could within the rules his brother outlined, but he wouldn't give up.

Eric walked to the window, and put his arm on Devon's shoulder. "Thanks for coming. I know you only want what's best for me. I'm happy you're here. I need you here. If I'm up to it, maybe we can do a few things when you come back—have some fun like we used to growing up."

Eric glanced over at the boy and girl and the dogs playing in the shade of a large pepper tree. "Those dogs have quite a history. They call them Aztec dogs. The official name is *Xoloitzcuintle*. They're indigenous to Mexico. The Aztecs considered them sacred, and they were sometimes buried with the dead as guides to the underworld.

They're supposed to possess healing qualities. I've been told the ancient Indians ate them as part of a religious ritual."

Devon's eyes widened. On Eric's face was that devious smile he knew so well. "You always study everything before you go into it. Do you still carry around little scraps of paper with words and phrases scribbled all over them?"

"Sure," Eric said. "It keeps me sharp. Right now I'm using that trick to learn a little Spanish."

"I remember writing you letters when you were at college. You always sent them back to me corrected and graded. I seldom earned better than a C."

"Yeah, I was tough on you, but that was for your own good. I didn't want you to go through what I had to go through with bonehead English. I pushed you as hard as I could. Your writing is what got you all the way to where you are today. You can go further too, Devon, if you put your mind to it."

Eric's face relaxed.

"Maybe I'll write a book to thank you someday. Given the path I've chosen, though, I might not ever get around to it."

"Which path is that, Devon? Don't draw a circle around yourself. Remember that Blake comment about God drawing circles? You must invent your own life, Devon, or you'll be living according to someone else's rules."

They stood at the window and watched the dogs. Devon thought about the time he'd collected a bucket of worms for his grade-school science class. Eric took him to the neighbor's house. The man was a carpenter, and a fire of wood scraps always burned in the backyard. Eric threw the bucket of worms onto some red-hot wire that sat atop the wood. The worms sizzled like bacon. Devon never understood why Eric had done that. It was cruel, and there seemed no reason for it. Maybe Eric had a premonition of what was to come and wanted to show him that life is harsh and some things happen for no reason at all.

The boy and girl packed the puppies into a box and headed toward the front gate of the clinic.

"Oh, God, are they taking those dogs to the cafeteria?"

"Don't worry. They don't feed us dog here. It's all vegetarian."

Eric laughed like he used to laugh before the diagnosis. Devon felt like he was home in Sugarvale again, a young boy with his big brother Eric.

Crossing the border, taking his life into his own hands whether or not the Laetrile was useless, couldn't that be a sort of remedy for Eric in some way? Eric needed to be in control. It was his nature. He had been raised by their grandmother—a Missourian whose relatives had taken both sides during the Civil War. Eric shared her stubborn nature and independent frontier attitude toward life. It was sometimes difficult for those who loved him, but it made him strong.

Devon tossed and turned throughout the night. He was visited by a recurring dream he'd had since he was a small boy. He and Eric were around a campfire with some friends in the foothills outside Sugarvale. Eric wandered off and fell into a deep hole. Devon heard his calls for help, and went to find him. He couldn't get Eric out by himself so he called to their friends. Everyone was busy drinking and having fun. Devon awoke, like always, pounding his head on the pillow, soaked in his own sweat.

That night in the dark, lying in his bed in Eric's room, Devon remembered once taking a wager from Eric. Next to their house in Sugarvale there was a garage full of boxes and junk. One summer night, Eric dared Devon to walk through the garage after telling him the bogeyman lived there. "If you go in at the front and walk all the way through and knock on the back door, I'll be waiting with a dollar for you." It was a test to see if Devon really believed in the bogeyman. He entered the garage, which was dark and scary. The summer heat made it hard to breathe. Devon sweated as he felt his way along. His heart throbbed in his chest. He found his way through, bumping into boxes, tripping over things he couldn't see, and getting tangled up in spider webs. The mind loves to play tricks. He was afraid, but he reached the back door and knocked. When he came out, Eric was there as promised and handed him a dollar.

"Devon," he had said, "the bogeyman's not real." You need to learn that early, otherwise you'll be hounded by him all your life."

Devon glanced at his brother. Eric slept soundly. What if the bogeyman *was* real? What would Eric do then? He would carry on, Devon had no doubt. Eric somehow dreamt his own sense of existence into being. He insisted on living his own life. Eric believed in one important thing: a man makes the life that's his until his living's done. He would find a way out.

The next morning Ofelia arrived to give Eric his nine o'clock injection. It was Saturday, and Eric had no other treatments until the afternoon. Devon and Eric decided to explore the beach and have lunch before Devon returned home.

"You look much younger than your brother, Devon, and you don't look like him at all. I would not think you were even related."

Ofelia's smile worked on Devon quickly. He was surprised at her excellent English. Eric was right—she was gorgeous and smart.

"Yeah, I'm eight years younger. Eric and I have different fathers but the same mother."

"Was your father an attorney also?"

"No, he owned a hotel; but he was a philanderer, just like Eric's father."

Ofelia looked sideways with her large brown eyes.

"A philanderer is a guy who runs around on his wife."

"I know what a philanderer is. I'm just surprised. Neither you nor Eric seem like that type."

"We're not, but both of our fathers left our mother after less than a year."

"You grew up together with your mother, then?"

"Yes, we grew up together."

"That explains it. You look different but you act alike, your mother's influence, obviously."

Ofelia gave Eric his injection. Devon noticed that little signals passed between them. The tip of Ofelia's nose moved up and down in a charming manner when she spoke. Eric followed it with evident pleasure. Devon couldn't tell if Eric knew what was going on, but he was sure Ofelia knew.

It was an easy walk to the beach, but Devon drove them in his car. The way back was uphill, and he feared the walk would be too strenuous for Eric in his condition. The vegetarian restaurant Mida suggested was far to the north. They could see the border fence. Eric gazed at the pelicans flying over the ocean.

"Those birds are illegal immigrants," said Devon. "They're heading over the fence."

"They're citizens of the world, Devon, like Tom Paine."

Paine was one of Eric's heroes. Eric especially liked *The Age of Reason*. Like Tom Paine, Eric said his own mind was his church. There were no borders inside his head.

On the beach, below the seabirds, two figures walked slowly toward them. The man looked older but tall and fit for his age. The woman, impossible to miss with her long, shapely legs, reached down periodically to pick up a shell.

"That's Russell Napier," said Eric. "I don't know the woman he's with. I'm going to wave them over. I want you to meet him. Maybe then you won't see me as loony."

"I've already told you, Eric, I don't think you're crazy. I want to make sure you're not making a mistake in judgment, that's all. Illness can impact anyone's ability to reason in unpredictable ways. You know that."

Ignoring Devon's comment, Eric rose to get Napier's attention.

"Eric, I'm happy to see you out. This is my friend Nicoleta Burgiardini. We met in San Francisco and she wants to see the clinic."

White shorts, white top, white skin, black hair, red lips—she was the ice queen of the Arctic arrived to cool the tropics. She was much younger than Napier, but it was obvious they were a couple. Strikingly beautiful but raw and primitive like an untamed tiger, Nicoleta appealed to Eric and disturbed him at the same time.

"Welcome to our little afternoon party, Nicoleta. All I'm allowed these days is juice and vegetables. Please forgive my appearance; I'm slowly turning all the colors of the rainbow. This is my brother

Devon. I'm afraid he thinks you're the devil, Russell. Perhaps you can win him over."

Nicoleta felt a camaraderie with Eric. Her aunt's illness had increased her awareness of cancer. It frightened her that someone as young as Eric could be afflicted with the same disease. She stepped forward to hug him before she realized what she was doing. The hug surprised Eric, but he didn't mind it at all. He noticed a citrusy smell when she drew close. He felt how firm and muscular her body was. He was embarrassed at how his illness had turned him into a slug. Nicoleta didn't hug Devon but shook his hand. Eric wondered if she felt some obligation because of his illness, and wondered whether Ofelia felt the same. Was that all there was between them, a nauseating sympathy without any deeper feelings? He couldn't believe that. There was more, he was sure.

"So, you're a believer in the government telling you which drugs to use, eh?"

"I try to keep an open mind, Mr. Napier, but since you brought it up, why is there so much opposition to Laetrile?"

Eric watched Nicoleta shift her feet back and forth in the sand. He felt he'd seen her before, but wasn't sure where or when.

"Conventional medicine focuses on the tumor. The surgeons think if they cut away the tumor and blast what's left with drugs and radiation they'll cure the patient. We think differently. Cancer is a metabolic disease. The cure for such a disease requires a different approach. The reason conventional medicine fails, even with all its vast resources, is because the process is misguided from the beginning."

"Nicoleta," Eric said, trying to recall where he'd seen her, "I'm sure you don't want to spend your afternoon discussing Laetrile. What brings you to Tijuana? Do you live close by?"

"I'm from Jersey. Russell wants to show me around the clinic."

Napier listened to Nicoleta approvingly. He slid his hand down her back to her white shorts. He stopped there, but didn't pull his hand away. It remained in place, caressing her gently. Nicoleta blushed.

"I'm kinda interested in the Laetrile 'cause my aunt in Jersey is being treated with it for her cancer. She's been, like, so happy with the results that I went to San Francisco myself to meet Doctor Elvin Krump. He's the famous chemist who invented it. He's awfully smart, but I guess you know that."

Napier's smile broadened. Devon saw he was no match for the two of them—Nicoleta's red lips and white skin, Napier's golden tan and hazel eyes. They inhabited a world he knew little about, yet he sensed something amiss in paradise. He made note of it and vowed to come back better prepared to protect Eric from... what? He couldn't put his finger on it, not yet, but he would—he would.

Nicoleta chewed a wad of gum as she spoke. New Jersey and the gum triggered the memory: Eric had seen her photo in an article about Napier. There had been accusations of mob connections. In the article, Napier brushed off the allegations with a single sentence: "If we were connected to the mob, Laetrile would have been approved years ago."

Devon stepped forward and looked Napier right in the face. "Well, Mr. Napier, Eric's at Buena Salud now. He's taking your Laetrile. I hope what you say is correct. I'll hold you accountable if it isn't."

Unfazed, Napier laughed to lighten the mood. "We all look forward to Eric's recovery."

Devon stepped back. "Yes, we do, Mr. Napier. I hope we see some positive results soon."

"Your government's tests on Laetrile have been seriously biased, Devon. Don't let them fool you. The studies use terminal patients who've already failed to respond to conventional treatments. In many cases these patients have been damaged so severely by radiation and chemo that they're beyond any help Laetrile could provide. The authorities refuse to test Laetrile in combination with the metabolic therapies we recommend. It takes the complete spectrum of treatments to get results. If our methods were tested properly against the conventional approach, we'd win hands down."

Napier and Nicoleta excused themselves and walked up the hill toward the clinic. Eric's eyes turned sad as they left. How little we ever understand about our own life, about anyone's life. It's impossible to follow another human being all the way. At the actual moment of death, there's no one to help us down the stairs.

A jacked-up truck full of rough young Mexicans roared down the hill. An unfortunate dog, loitering in the street, couldn't get out of the way fast enough. The owner of the restaurant ran out with a chef's knife, screaming obscenities as the truck sped on. The boys taunted him as he tried in vain to catch them. Head drooping, he returned and looked down at the dead dog. His wife joined him, and together they carried the animal to the side of the street, covered it with a blanket, and returned to the kitchen.

Devon went back inside the restaurant to pay the bill, then drove Eric back to the clinic. He was already packed. It was time for Eric's afternoon injection. They said goodbye when Ofelia arrived. Devon started his long trip back to Berkeley, anxious to put his affairs in order and return to help his brother.

As he drove, Devon reminisced about the times he and Eric played ping-pong baseball in their backyard. Sugarvale was one of those ubiquitous Sacramento Valley farm towns that people drive through but remember little about. Eric came up with the idea of taping a ping-pong ball with the white athletic tape used for wrapping ankle sprains. It was impossible to hit a ball like that very far. Their small yard was just the right size for a one-on-one baseball game. Eric had always been good at coming up with novel ideas. He used wooden crates for hurdles, bought a stopwatch, and timed Devon as he ran the hundred-yard course Eric had laid out. Eric created an imaginary football game using nothing but colored construction paper. He cut out tiny rectangles of different sizes to represent the different players, fatter for the linemen, thinner for the ends and backs. Different colors represented different teams. Little ink marks up the sides of the paper pieces mimicked the uniforms they saw on TV. They couldn't afford one of the fancy electronic football games sold in stores. They played for hours, the game unfolding entirely in their imaginations. They had a swing set, and would swing as high as they could, then jump out as far as possible. Eric named it the swing jump after the broad jump. They set up a high-jump pit with wooden stands and a bamboo pole and fresh sawdust. Devon tried out his skill at the Fosbury Flop, but he was too short and stocky to make a go of it.

Devon pictured Eric alone in his sparse room at the clinic. The change from Sugarvale and Sacramento to Mexico must have been drastic. He understood why the relationship with Ofelia was so important for Eric: She offered respite from the elderly and dying around him. A little happiness was fine as long as things didn't get out of control. Even if Ofelia wasn't acting out of deceit, Devon worried she could hurt Eric emotionally. He'd never had a close relationship like this before, and was obviously head over heels and vulnerable.

When Ofelia gave Eric the injection, she looked carefully into his eyes.

"You're somewhere far, far away, Eric. Where, where are you?"

"I don't know. Sometimes I feel like I'm in two worlds at once. I can't quite understand it. I'm here but not here like a tree limb that branches off in different directions."

"Well, come back to this world, I miss you! You should take a rest, you look tired."

Ofelia left. He was alone. Soon he fell into a deep sleep.

Trumpets blare. An old man sits on the adjoining bed.

"Everyone around here has their schtick," he said, "even the cooks."

Eric turned toward the voice. No one was there.

A creature ran through the grass outside, occasionally using its large wings to rise into the air.

The old man climbed up on the wall surrounding the courtyard. The beast ran past. The man toppled to the ground, his features hidden in a white cloud of fog. Shrieking, the beast ran away. A rainbow rose from the man's head. His face shone like the sun. His feet exploded like pillars of fire, then he disappeared with the beast. A sound like thunder issued in their wake, and then all was quiet.

"He cut out, man, off to meet his maker, gone to his reward."

"Nelson? Nelson!"

Eric snored loudly as he slept.

22.

Rafael Negros

Joey Zacco's first trip to Tijuana was to *Agua Caliente* casino with his father. He was just a kid. His father wanted a look at the gambling operations across the border from San Diego. Zacco senior learned well. He went on to set up some gambling clubs in Cuba. The money came rolling in until Castro ousted dictator Fulgencio Batista. The bearded revolutionary kicked out Zacco and closed down the casinos just like Mexican President Cárdenas had closed Agua Caliente some years earlier.

Napier supported Castro and the revolution. He'd helped Castro's forces by allowing them to intercept guns shipped from the United States that had been bound for Batista. In the 1950s, acting as a mining consultant for a firm with interests in Cuba, Napier had a chance to see firsthand the oppressive world of Batista. He understood the rebels' grievances, though he disagreed with their communist ideology. Today, on the wall in his office at Clinica Buena Salud, hung a framed document signed by Dr. Manuel Urrutia, provisional president of Cuba, commending Napier for his "help in furthering the liberation of Cuba." In these undercover operations, Napier had even had his own codename, *Esquimal,* meaning "man from the north."

Castro might have been defeated had Napier not stepped in to help. Zacco's casinos might still be operating. These past differences didn't stop Zacco and Napier from working together. There was tension between them; they weren't friends—there were no friends in Zacco's world, just associates. His relationship with Napier was all business, and as long as it was profitable, Zacco didn't dwell on the past. The Cuban revolution happened. It was history. History doesn't pay the bills.

The Dos Negros sent a driver to fetch Zacco from the San Diego airport. Soon he stood on the patio of the hillside mansion owned by Rafael Negros and looked down at the beautiful Playas de Tijuana.

Rafael walked out onto the patio wearing a red guayabera shirt, tan slacks, and sandals. He was tall and handsome and very popular with the ladies. As Rafael drew close, Zacco noted the unmistakable signs of drug addiction: The sallow features, puffiness under the eyes, and runny nose confirmed Zacco's suspicions that Rafael's habit was getting worse. Rafael was much younger than Zacco. He spoke with characteristic Latin charm and respect, but the words came out in slow motion, a bit garbled. "*Sa-lu-tos,* Joey. De-ligh-ted. You. Could. Come."

Zacco didn't like anything about the Mexicans. He considered them imposters, a crude parody of the life he'd chosen. He abhorred their personal habits, considered them filthy and lazy. So far Rafael had kept things under control, but Zacco didn't trust him. The profits held the relationship together. Zacco put his biases aside, but he was ill at ease in Rafael's presence. Rafael's brother, Tomás, was even worse; he was a disaster—all action, no brains. They were like two flashy celebrity attorneys. Once, in an interview with the American press, Tomás opened his mouth and nearly ruined everything. When asked if they smuggled drugs into the United States, he'd bragged: "If it's easy, we're not interested. We like the difficult things, the challenges. We're very dangerous men, my brother and I. We are like two rattlesnakes." The camera focused on his evil grin as he rolled a cigar around in his mouth. Zacco had learned early in his career how to keep a low profile, something the Mexicans couldn't understand.

Zacco stood on the patio in his signature gray suit, perfectly pressed white shirt, and silver tie. Bags under his eyes accentuated a prominent aquiline nose. His mouth hung open as if he were about to speak, his actions carefully designed to play the role of the elder gentleman, a man who has seen everything and survived. A little breeze began to blow. Noises from the beach rose up, a cacophony of sounds like an orchestra tuning before a performance.

"I was admiring the spectacular view from this hilltop of yours, Rafael."

The two shook hands and sat down. Rafael found it hard to stay put. He jumped up and walked back and forth along the ocean side of the patio. The balcony was like an old friend that sustained him, bolstering his unsteadiness. He slid his hand along every notch and joint of the railing, inspecting it as if it were a valuable artifact.

"Your family, I hope they are... well?"

Rafael walked deliberately from one side of the deck to the other like a blind man who knew his way in the dark.

"We're all fine, thank you," Zacco replied. "My sister, Rose, has improved with the Laetrile. I'm thankful we can help her."

Rafael lurched from slow motion to hyperactive. He was like a motorcycle with a clutch that jumped between two extreme positions. "Would you like a cold drink? We're at your service, my friend." Rafael's nostrils flared slightly as he spoke.

"I'll have a beer if you'll join me."

"My pleasure, Joey." Rafael waved to a young man in the corner who brought the beers on a silver tray accompanied by some snacks. Zacco thought the gesture too dramatic, but he did love Mexican food despite his disdain for Mexicans. He worked hard to stay in shape, but always allowed himself a little leeway when he traveled below the border. He noticed that Rafael didn't touch the food.

Tomás soon arrived along with Napier. They all patted each other on the back, and small talk ensued till everyone got comfortable. Several minutes passed while they sipped their beers, munched on the snacks, and found their way around each other. Napier was the first to bring up business. "I've just met with Krump. He's in denial. He considers Frieze a harmless old fool, but Frieze is crafty. He's back in production. Milagro says Frieze's Laetrile is superior to what we have. We need to find him. It would be best if we could bring him back into the company, but either way we must get our hands on his formula."

"Would you like the kee-lor bee to sting him?" asked Tomás with a malicious smile. Unlike his brother, Tomás never touched drugs. His vices were women and violence.

"No. We need the formula, Tomás, *sin violencia*. We want to persuade Frieze to work with us on a friendly basis. Reconciliation may be impossible, but we should try that first. It's the best solution. Frieze might cooperate if we approach him properly. Krump is getting old and lazy. He doesn't have Frieze's knack for getting things right. He's popular with the crowds at cancer conventions, but he lacks the Frenchman's knowledge and skills. He's stuck in the glory of his father's past."

Napier knew that any of these men could snuff him out on a whim. They had money and power and were experienced killers, but he'd carefully developed the confidence and charm to deal with such men. He'd been in similar situations dozens of times and survived. It was a marriage of convenience: They needed a way to launder their drug profits; the Laetrile business gave them respectability. Napier had the leeway he needed to work through tricky situations.

"Is Frieze's Laetrile really so much better?" Zacco hated the idea of competition. In his world nothing less than absolute control was acceptable. There were times when it was necessary to depend on others—no one, not even he, could go it alone. In such situations he had a strict rule of accountability: failure by those he depended on had fatal consequences.

"I'm afraid it is, Joey. Krump is working to replicate Frieze's formula, but his research is going nowhere. I wish his father were still alive. He had the drive and talent. We managed to set aside a good supply of Frieze's serum, but unfortunately, it's almost gone. There's barely enough for your sister Rose and a few important patients. We've been using Krump's Laetrile for the others and the results have not been satisfactory."

The look on Zacco's face persuaded Napier to slow down and proceed with care. He methodically laid out the situation. "Krump suffers from delusions of grandeur. We all know that. His best use is as a spokesman; the crowds love him, they hang on his every word at conventions, but to influence the regulators, we need to get hold of Frieze's serum, and for that we need Frieze himself."

Zacco's eyes narrowed into a scowl. "I thought Krump's father invented Laetrile."

"He did, but Frieze improved it. Krump is using his father's original formula. Krump fancies himself a famous chemist, but he doesn't have what it takes to get what we need. Frieze does."

Rafael picked his teeth with a fingernail. He rose and stood at the railing, and wiped his hand on his shirt. His face twitched as he spoke. His pupils were so small that he squinted to see the rest of them at the table. "This Laetrile bees-ness, why so complicated? Why not more easy like heroin and marijuana?"

"Laetrile is a legal business, Rafael—a business without complications where you can launder your drug profits with no problems. There's no room for error operating under a government spotlight. It's not a problem in Mexico, but it is in the United States. To make a real fortune we need to take the company public. Then the drug profits will be easy to hide. For that, we need Frieze."

Rafael touched Zacco's sleeve like an affectionate cat. "What you think, Joey?"

Zacco hated the idea that anyone was indispensable. It was like having to roll the boulder of Sisyphus uphill each time something needed to be done.

"Okay, so we need Frieze. You own this town, Rafael. How do you propose we find him?" Zacco gave a sick smile. Tomás had finished all the appetizers. Rafael waved to the waiter. He brought another tray of beers.

"Are you trying to get us all drunk, Rafael?"

"More appetizers coming, Joey. No worry."

These Mexicans disgusted Zacco. They were sloppy and lazy; worst of all, they were reckless. Tomás was like an impatient sheepdog. He charged in every direction with no clear plan. Zacco planned every move down to the minutest detail. He knew there was no room for error in his business.

"That Catholic priest at the clinic knows more than he says. My men can pinch him and apply a little pressure," said Tomás.

"Slow down, Tomás." Zacco couldn't believe his ears. "We don't want to use a meat cleaver to crack an egg, amigo. The people here respect their priests. We don't need that kind of trouble. Maybe you're on the right track though. I know some officials higher up in the Church. They owe me a few favors, and they might be able get the information we need with no fuss."

The waiter opened a door on the far side of the deck. Hector Hernandez emerged and stood by Tomás. They made a dreadful pair. Vultures would pale at the sight of therm.

"Hector can find Frieze, but what if he don't cooperate?" As Tomás spoke, the words danced off his tongue encased in little balls of spit.

"We need him alive and unharmed, Tomás. He alone has the formula. It's not just the business we need. He *is* the business."

Napier was getting through to Zacco, but Tomás was hopeless. He lived in a world of knives and bullets, and anyone could see that Rafael was undependable. He fidgeted and jumped around like a nervous horse.

A fresh plate of appetizers arrived. The jaundiced look disappeared from Zacco's face. He was brutal and violent like the others, but older and wiser. He'd learned to be patient. His experience with intricate negotiations inside the criminal world helped him grasp Napier's position.

"Let's put out discrete feelers among people we can trust—people that won't make Frieze get suspicious. You and your men can find anyone. When we come up with his location, we should be able to snag him. It shouldn't take deadly force to bring in an old man making a few jugs of Laetrile in his basement."

Tomás lifted his head like an Aztec image and held it to the sun. Rafael, in a rare moment of lucidity, said, "Is wise approach, Joey."

Tomás hated this conciliatory tone taken by his brother. He could find Frieze, and if he wanted to he would kill him. Getting the formula was Napier's problem, not his. Tomás looked as mad as a centipede, but he held his tongue.

While the others offered their opinions, Hector stood by silently. He knew these men better than they knew themselves. Over the years Dos Negros had relied on him to conduct more and more of their business. He'd learned to speak as little as possible and to follow instructions precisely, and had become so familiar to the Dos Negros that they spoke as if he were not present. This made him privy to their innermost secrets, which he put together like the pieces of a jigsaw puzzle.

Zacco stood up. "We are in agreement. I have to leave. I have an appointment and an early flight back. Would you lend me your driver for a few hours, Rafael?"

"Si, Joey. Safe travels. I stay in touch."

At last, thought Zacco. *Rafael's back with the rest of us.*

They all shook hands. The meeting was over. Zacco watched Hector walk away, that gruesome smile chiseled onto his face like some archaic corpse resurrected. "Mexicans," he grumbled under his breath, "an inferior race, but they have their uses. I wouldn't mind having that Hector on my team at home."

Objects flew about as if a great wind had unearthed them from their moorings. Blurry outlines floated through a mist. A white light blinded him. When he could see again he found himself attached to an enormous plastic bag on a metal stand. From inside the bag, dozens of eyes looked down on him, intruding on his privacy—snooping, prying, evil eyes on distorted faces. The silence gave way to frantic voices. He soon saw the horror of his position. The white walls of the room filled with images of wild animals that came at him in packs. He lay strapped to the bed, powerless to do anything in his defense.

23.

La Mesa Penitenciaria

It's Sunday. As usual, Hector Hernandez picks up his brother, Marcos, who will not look out the window as they drive along. He's afraid of the wild animals, their sharp horns and beaks and claws like daggers. He hears them at night when everyone else is sleeping, sees their eyes glowing in the dark. They live all along the roads.

The purpose of the journey is to visit their father at *La Mesa Penitenciaria*. Their mother no longer accompanies them on these trips. La Mesa is on the opposite side of town. Hector drives an old car on Sundays. Marcos likes the fancy red car better, but Hector says it isn't a good car to take to La Mesa.

Hector and Marcos park in the lot next to the Penitenciaria. Marcos does not like the heavy-gauge chain-link fence. Guards with rifles wave them through. Marcos protects his secrets from the invisible eyes that float inside the links, the eyes of the wild animals. Men search him with their cruel, fat hands, frisk him head to toe. They want to steal his magnets, but he leaves the magnets at home. They are one of his magic secrets. The second chain-link fence has no eyes. It isn't scary at all. Marcos walks straight into the main courtyard. A man waits for them inside. His name is Hiladeo.

"*Hola,* my sons. Looking forward to these Sundays keeps me alive. Thank you for not forgetting the miserable wretch that is your father."

Marcos looks and listens but does not speak. Hector says this man is his father. Hector has never lied to him so it must be true. He has no father at home. It is a strange place for a father to live, but his father does have friends here.

There are stores and restaurants inside the fence. It looks like a little town. Marcos sees men with guns. A jukebox is blaring. An ice cream vendor arrives. Hector buys three cups and passes them around. Families share food. Everyone talks with excitement. Some play guitars and sing. Hector and Marcos stand quietly eating ice cream with their father, and Hector slips some money into their father's pocket. Hector gives their father money to spend in the stores and restaurants so that he can have something special to eat. A few men come to speak with Hector. They want him to help them. He listens thoughtfully and says he will try. Marcos is proud of his brother. Hector is important. Everyone respects him, everyone asks him favors.

"There is a gringo here serving three for marijuana. A man in a gray suit came to see him yesterday. I heard them talking about Dos Negros."

Marcos tries not to listen. Words can be misunderstood. Father Jordan told him, "In the beginning was the Word." The story went on and on forever. Listening takes too long. Marcos wants to walk around.

"The colonel is at it again," says Hiladeo. The colonel is the director of La Mesa. He runs the prison with an iron hand.

"What do you mean?" asks Hector.

Hiladeo looks around to make sure no one is listening. "The bribes, the murders. I can't say much right now, it's dangerous."

"Don't worry, Father, I will make sure you are protected." Hector throws his ice cream into the trash unfinished.

Angry men in beige trousers and tan shirts march through the courtyard. Marcos knows they're angry, because their hair lies flat like a bird's crown before the bird becomes hostile. He knows many things from studying the birds in the big tree at home. In the courtyard, an older woman with bags of groceries sets up an umbrella and a large cookpot over an open fire and proceeds to make tamales. A man pushes a *carretone* offering tacos and soft drinks. After the ice cream, Marcos is not hungry. He does not like it when people stare at Hector, but it also makes him proud that his brother is not like everyone else.

"Don't worry about the man in the gray suit," says Hector.

In the Penitenciaria, everything comes in pairs, like in Noah's Ark. Marcos learned about Noah's Ark from Father Jordan. Marcos walks to the small church nearby. Hector lets him go alone. He looks for Father Jordan, but the church is empty. He sits on a bench and watches two men playing cards in the courtyard. Two small children chase each other. Two goats and two cows forage along the outside wall. Marcos walks across the yard to where the workshops are located. In one shop two men make tambourines. Last time, they let him hold one and showed him how to make drum and jingle sounds. He liked the sounds. Today no one notices him. He walks on to the next workshop. Two men make bongo drums. One stretches leather to fit wooden tubes while the other glues it on. The tubes are different sizes and make different sounds. Still farther along, two men build small wooden boats with decks and sails. Marcos dreams of floating in a small boat like a message in a bottle. It would be like exploring the world alone until he was found. Marcos walks back to Hector and Hiladeo. He does not speak. Words get you into trouble. One family has slaughtered a pig and is cooking it inside the prison yard.

"Time to go home, Marcos. Say goodbye to your father."

Marcos looks at Hiladeo. He knows him only from these Sunday visits. Hiladeo lives inside these walls made of cement blocks. There are other men living inside the walls. Marcos does not like the men in brown pants and shirts who carry the guns. They always stare at him. Some women live here, but not many. One has a baby. Marcos thinks she is nice. There are a few gringos here. The other prisoners call them *gabacho* (Frenchy). The gringos are not friendly. They look very unhappy.

Marcos doesn't really know Hiladeo or remember anything about him. Hiladeo looks sad, but he is kind to Marcos. He does not stare at him or treat him like other people do. Only a few in this world understand Marcos and see him as he really is, like Father Jordan and his brother Hector. Hiladeo also sees him in this way. Marcos steps forward and hugs Hiladeo. Hector softens his twisted face, which sometimes scares people, but Hector's face is something special that God gave him, just like he gave Marcos a special character to play and an important job. Father Jordan explained all this to Marcos.

On the way home, Marcos thinks of telling Hector about the Frenchman, El Diablo, who moved into the neighborhood, but decides not to say anything. Words get you into trouble. He will talk to Father Jordan first. He doesn't want to cause trouble for Hector with El Diablo.

24.

The Bus

Penalt returned to El Azteca the night before the bus left for San Kuuchamaa. He'd been propositioned numerous times, but he didn't want a girl off the street. He'd heard stories about the women in Tijuana being dangerous, and wasn't going to take the chance, but the itch for a little fun kept pestering him. El Azteca was a first-class hotel. A good friend had told him the girls there were safe, whatever that meant in a town like this. He hoped his friend was right. An attractive girl sat alone at the bar. She looked at him when he entered and gave him an encouraging smile. He took the stool beside her and ordered a beer.

God, how awkward it is to pick up a girl at a bar. It'd been so long he wasn't sure how to start. He decided on the direct approach.

"Hi. Can I buy you a drink? Your glass looks empty."

"Si," she smiled. "Rrrum and Coca-Cola." He liked the way she twirled her r's.

He ordered two rum-and-cokes. He really wasn't good at small talk, but he couldn't just ask her straight out if she wanted to go back to his room. Having made up his mind not to spend the night alone, he was willing to engage in a little foreplay.

"Are you visiting Tijuana, or do you live here?"

"Live in Tijuana, born in Oaxaca."

The bartender, a young man dressed in a neatly pressed white shirt and stylish black slacks, set the drinks in front of them. He was working intently on an order of fancy drinks for a table in the dining room. Two men at the other end of the bar carried on a conversation in Spanish. The bar itself was beautifully carved from reddish mahogany. A spotless mirror reflected the bottles lined up in front of it on thick glass shelves. The girl's pretty face reflected back from the mirror behind the bottles.

"What's your name?"

She smiled and looked him over as if making up her mind. Penalt felt shivers of excitement rising between his legs.

"Cristina. And you?" Her white teeth gleamed in the light shining from the lamps above. Her black hair picked up the colors of the bar. She fit in like a piece of fine furniture. Penalt could almost taste the strong, sweet perfume she wore.

"I'm Roger. I've never been to Oaxaca. I hear the food and mezcal are quite good there. I'd like to go someday. So, what brought you to Tijuana?"

As Cristina turned to look behind them, Penalt noticed the toned cords in her neck. The movement caused her blouse to poke open and he caught a glimpse of her breasts. She turned back and smiled when she caught him looking.

"*Vamos allá.*" She took her drink and strolled to a table away from the bar. Penalt followed, watching her hips. He felt like a young boy on his first date. He hoped for a better outcome. The bartender glanced at them and went back to polishing the glasses.

"I sleep with you for money. You like sleep with me?"

Penalt almost choked on his beer. Cristina laughed.

"Well, I've never paid to sleep with a woman before."

"Always first time, Roger." Her breasts were visible again through the gap at the top of her blouse. When she sat in the chair and crossed her legs, her skirt climbed halfway up her thighs. Penalt knew he wanted her, but the whole thing seemed ridiculous.

"I'm sure I couldn't afford you."

He was torn between unquenchable desire and knowing that what he was doing was stupid and wrong. Desire won. He couldn't stop himself.

"Fifty U.S. dollar. You won't forget night."

He couldn't swallow. It felt like there was a marble in his throat. What if she had a disease?

"I clean girl. I go doctor all tine. Sleep only clean men. Use condom."

Penalt wasn't going to bargain. He was leaving the next day. He looked around the bar. It was nearly empty.

"All right." As soon as he'd said it, he started to feel strange. What the hell was he doing? He wondered if there was a pimp outside waiting to rob him, or worse.

He went to the bar, paid the bill, and bought a bottle of rum and a few bottles of Coca-Cola. As they walked together to his room, he looked over his shoulder occasionally, but no one followed. Once inside the room, Penalt poured a couple of drinks and they sat out on the deck. He excused himself to use the toilet. He doused his face in cold water. If he wanted to enjoy the night, he had to pace himself.

Cristina stood on the deck enjoying at the view. He walked up behind her.

"You're too beautiful to be a prostitute. What's your real story?"

"Many truths in Mexico, Roger. I come here to be maid, promise to cross border, to start new life. All lies. They force me to sex. I lucky. I escape. My friends no escape. Some girls who try are kill. Many girls bury here."

"That's a horrible thought. Why are you still here?" Penalt realized he was drinking way too fast. His glass was almost empty.

"I too need eat. I try be dancer, but more money for this. I get used to it. Is just business, no? I choose men careful."

"Don't you need a man for protection?"

"I work lone. I protect myself. I have friend if I need. Is better for me."

Penalt felt very tired. He slumped down in the chair. Things quickly became blurry. He tried to speak but couldn't get the words out of his mouth. Realizing he'd been drugged, he tried to get out of the room, but before he could rise from the chair, everything went black.

Penalt awoke in a panic. His head throbbed. Cristina—if that was even her name—was gone. It was dark. Sure he'd been robbed, he turned on the light and saw his wallet on the table by the bed. Hands shaking, he lunged toward it, and found all his cash and cards and ID intact. He poured out everything on the bed and looked more carefully. The girl had taken fifty dollars. Penalt couldn't find the card the little man in the bar had given him, but he could have lost or misplaced it. It didn't matter. Everything important was still there. She'd played him, but took only what they agreed to. At least he wasn't dead. And she was right about one thing: he certainly would not forget the night. He had no time to ponder; he had to be on his way. He dressed quickly, packed his suitcase, and went to the lobby to meet his guide. Instead of the guide, there was a note at the desk. It was an apology with further instructions. The guide couldn't make the bus, but would meet Penalt at the village in a few days. He told Penalt to go on without him.

Despite the setback, there was no choice but to go. He couldn't wait a week for the next bus. He walked the few blocks in the early-morning darkness, oblivious of the dangers that lurked in dark corners, and stood next to the empty bus on the west side of Plaza Central. It was quiet and peaceful at 4:45 AM.

People milled about. The driver was nowhere in sight. A few women and small children stood next to him. Two older men smoked their cigarettes a few yards away. Penalt stayed near the entrance to the bus. He wanted to be sure he could get a seat. More and more people arrived in the next few minutes. At five o'clock sharp the driver appeared. He started the engine to warm up the bus, and motioned for the passengers to load up. Penalt stepped inside and took a seat near the front.

The bus was soon full, but people continued to climb aboard. Soon the aisle was filled with people who sat on boxes and buckets. A young girl appeared and said something to Penalt. He couldn't understand her. He thought she was there to collect the money for a ticket. He reached into his pocket for some pesos. She didn't take the money. She showed him a paper and rattled off something in Spanish. A man behind them who spoke a bit of English explained that the girl had a ticket for his seat. No one informed him that he needed to buy a ticket in advance. The guide should have taken care of it. He got up and stood in the aisle. A young boy soon came, took his money, gave him a white mayonnaise bucket, and motioned for him to sit. He hoped this start to the day was not a sign of worse things to come.

Penalt was the only gringo on the bus. Everyone carried something—bags of groceries, dry goods, clothes. The woman across from Penalt had a sack containing a live chicken that cackled now and again. One boy carried a transparent bucket of fish swimming in murky water. A short, stocky man with greasy black hair had a box of tools and machetes. A young man in the back held a pathetic-looking guitar. It quickly became close and warm in the bus, and smelled like sweaty clothing. Penalt was afraid he might be sick. The top of the bus was crammed with odd-shaped bundles and bags tied up and tied on, while the lower compartment was full of suitcases and boxes. Before boarding the bus, Penalt had helped a woman stuff three huge bags of laundry into the compartment below.

As the bus pulled out, Penalt felt a mixture of excitement and apprehension. His nausea disappeared. This was the day he'd waited for. He had no idea what to expect. There was nothing to do but sit on his bucket and enjoy the trip. From time to time he stood up to get a better view, still light-headed from his fiasco the night before.

Soon they were past the stores and houses of the city, moving between shacks and hovels spaced farther and farther apart until they too disappeared. The overloaded bus wound its way up through the chamise, ceanothus, manzanita, and other flora of the chaparral until they came to a creek. The water reached to the top of the tires. Fearless, the driver forged ahead without pause. Penalt thought they'd surely get stuck, but they got across without a hitch. From then on it was a wild ride over a narrow mountain road with blind curves obscured by thick scrub oaks and sharp granite boulders. Periodically they'd pass a few poor souls, dressed in rags, walking along the road. It seemed at times the bus was about to plunge into one of the canyons that punctuated the mountain. Penalt closed his eyes and bargained with God, strange as it seemed for a man who hadn't prayed in years. He promised that if God got him through the day there'd be no more escapades like the night before. The bus climbed higher and higher through dense brush. They passed through an ancient grove of giant cypress trees. An elderly woman in a seat close to Penalt kept puking on the floor and all over her black garments.

The boy with the guitar strummed a few notes, which lightened the mood somewhat. An hour passed, then two, then four. By now the bus was rolling along at the top of the hill. On the way up they'd met a bus headed down, and they'd had to backtrack to a wide spot in the road where they could pull over to let it through. Penalt developed a great respect for the driver, who safely navigated every difficulty. Around ten o'clock they arrived at a small clearing in the middle of nowhere. The driver pulled over and shut off the engine. Everyone got out. Penalt looked around and spotted a sign with an arrow pointing farther uphill: SAN KUUCHAMAA 10 KILOMETERS →. Around the sign, Matilija poppies swayed in the gentle breeze like white silk baskets holding little nuggets of gold.

Penalt asked when they would be leaving for San Kuuchamaa. The driver told him this was the end of the line; he was on his own to get to the village. Penalt retrieved his suitcase from the bottom compartment, and he helped the lady with her three giant bags of laundry. She thanked him and told him her son would arrive soon with their truck. They would be happy to take him into town. It was his first lucky break of the day.

Roger Penalt had no way to know what lay ahead. He'd been hired to do a job, so he sat with his bundle in the back of the truck and watched whatever unfolded around him. He was soon to discover that God took the bargain made on the bus very seriously. Events were coming that would change his life, but for now he saw only the smiling faces of the others with him as they leaned against one another to steady themselves while the truck bounced cheerfully along on the bumpy road. Everyone was laughing. Everyone was happy.

25.

The Appointment

"Why is he still alive?"

"The world is unpredictable, always in a state of flux."

"What does that mean?"

"I don't control everything. I've created uncertainties to make their lives more interesting."

"You told me it was settled."

"That's not what I said."

"You mean—"

"There's always room for something unexpected. I like it that way."

"How can that be? I thought you controlled everything."

"You're always in such a hurry."

"I've already told him. This makes me look like a fool. How can I do my job when you're always changing everything?"

"Just like Jonah! Three days in the darkness and he still didn't understand."

Seconds turned to minutes, minutes to hours, hours to days. Intravenous Laetrile, special diets, unpronounceable supplements, cleansings, purges, interminable juices—the treatments went on. They told Eric changes had occurred; Doctor Milagro spoke of a new X-ray that showed improvement, a reduction in the number of metastases. He'd told Mary the same earlier, but she'd left, ill and declining, and Eric heard she'd died at home. There'd been many deaths since his arrival. A few lucky ones had their miracles—they were the ones who sang the praises of Laetrile. Survivorship bias was a topic Eric had studied in business law. He wasn't fooled by the testimonials.

He'd become so thin he had to be careful getting around. In this weakened state everything appeared more intense. Beauty was sprinkled about like sparkling salt crystals. He savored each tiny grain. Ofelia invited him to move into a bungalow owned by her family. It was located near the beach in a grove of coconut palms close to her parents' lavish home. Ofelia's brother, Orvaline, also lived at home. He drove Eric to appointments at the clinic. Interspersed with the palm trees outside the bungalow, colorful flowers bloomed, flowers with foreign names and exotic shapes planted by Ofelia's father who collected them on numerous trips all over Baja. Rare species of flowering cacti with names like *Biznaga-barril de Emory* and *Biznaga-barril de Lima* rose out of a rainbow of iridescent succulents covering the ground. The birds and squirrels studied Eric curiously, looking in the windows and doors to his room. He had never paid so much attention to the natural environment.

Doctor Milagro said Eric needed to stay in Mexico to continue the treatments, but the real reason he stayed was to be near Ofelia. They hadn't discussed their feelings for one another. Their only time alone had been when she gave him the injections or when they sat on the bench and talked in the clinic courtyard. Eric wanted to be with her every day. He felt goosebumps whenever she was near. It tortured him not knowing whether she felt them too. Love was more painful than he'd ever imagined, like being stretched on some medieval rack.

The constant anxiety ceased only for those few moments when they were alone together and held hands or hugged briefly.

The Cabrera family lived in a way Eric could not have conceived of when he was growing up. Eric's two-story bungalow was a small guest cottage near the large elegant main house. Over the years, Mr. Cabrera had constructed an elaborate compound on land that had been in his wife's family for generations. The land, which dated to the days of the revolution, had been given to Ofelia's great-grandfather, Silveria Rodriguez, for his service under Pancho Villa. When Rodriguez took possession of the land it was a plantation of coconut palms. Over the years the property had become valuable as the area around Tijuana grew and the tourists arrived. The family owned the land communally as an *ejido*. It was a strange arrangement—one large parcel held by all the family members in common. It served the useful function of keeping the land from being sold off to the Americans in small parcels for vacation homes. Amelia Rodriguez Cabrera, Ofelia's mother, was the undisputed head of the family. Her only sibling, Luis, had been killed some years back in a bar fight with a former gardener who'd gone crazy in a drunken stupor. Amelia alone, along with her children, carried the bloodline back to Silveria.

Eric gazed out to sea. Everything had happened in such a short time. He felt like the boy in the sorcerer's apprentice, controlled by a magician with a weird sense of humor whose purpose was to teach him a lesson. Time sped up and slowed down in fits and starts with no apparent connection to the reality around him. There were moments when he felt as if he were outside of time, lost in an isolated pocket of space where it was impossible to get his bearings. One moment he was lost in a black cloud and the next he floated through a blue sky. He wove his life like a spider building its web, unsuspecting and unaware of the larger forces surrounding it, forces capable of smashing it in an instant.

"What you starin' at, man? Look like you're waitin' for the Second Comin' of the Lord."

"Is that you, Nelson? I'm glad you're here. We need to talk."

"Speak up. I can't hear ya, Jack."

"I don't know what to do about Ofelia. Sometimes I don't know if I'm a ghost or a man. What kind of a life could she have with me? It's so damn confusing and upsetting. I think she loves me, I hope she does, but maybe what I see as love is just compassion and pity. That's the last thing I want from her."

Nelson looked around to make sure no one else was listening.

"Hey, she can't stand your pain and anguish no better'n me. Ain't that what they call love, Jack? Go for it. Give it your best shot."

Confusion. In the shadows, birds sang, scratched, pecked, screeched, went about bird business, and offered a fleeting glimpse of brilliant color. The sound of a car on the road outside, the volume increased as it approached and declined as it sped away like an ocean wave. An ominous insect, big, black, furry, wobbled about in three-dimensional space, a soft wind battled the sun.

Mexico seethed with dark and light. Out on the road, wings flapped. A vulture looked up from a rotten carcass. A raspy hissing sound threatened from its mouth. An iguana sat motionless, sinister, eyes closed on a barren rock, expressed a will outside its own nature, the will of the baking rock itself. Eric closed his eyes. He pursued the dream, searched for peace in a war with death. He walked on the beach and felt the sand. He drank cold juice in makeshift cafes. The sun rose and fell. Death chased him. He stumbled about like Bergman's Antonius Block, played a chess game with Death.

Sometimes I win, but there is no end to this dismal game.

His mind drifted. The details of his life flew by: thirty-three-years—attorney—Sacramento—opportunities—connections—legislative aid—junior partnership in sight. A storm rose out of the calm. The diagnosis blew in like a hurricane, ripped through his unexceptional life. Doctor Rice, immaculate and stylish in a white lab coat, spoke with the sting of a bee: "The cancer in your colon has metastasized. I'm afraid it's inoperable." Three grueling days of excruciating tests; the words blasted, burned, and bludgeoned Eric's brain, the news delivered like Sergeant Joe Friday: "Just the facts, ma'am."

The voices of a chorus ring out, a chorus of defective cells that grows inside him. "Kill him! Kill him!" they shout. The doctor stands back, no longer effective. He washes his hands like Pontius Pilate, retreats into the reticulate chambers of medical science. Peace, peace, there was no peace.

"You are alive now, and that's what matters. What you must do is make the most of that."

In a parallel universe a monkey watches him from across the divide—illusion or reality? He could think, therefore he was alive. Was the monkey alive inside his brain? Is a thought alive, or was Descartes full of shit?

A Mexican street... a crumbling wall... peeling plaster... adobe bricks... wooden doors... rust-colored columns... a jutting shelf... black iron metal grates... a courtyard... darkness... behind the locked door, a life.

Unconsciousness is death's rehearsal, when you're knocked silly or when you fall asleep. Eric fought sleep every step of the way. He didn't want to die. He dreamt he was awake. These dreams of lying awake were so convincing that when he finally did awaken, he was completely exhausted and went right back to sleep, only to repeat the process.

One minute you're awake, the next you're asleep. The crossover is undetectable. *Is that death?* Initially signals demand your attention, an itch, a pain, cold, heat, and you respond by scratching, moving, pulling the covers up or down. The signals weaken. Thoughts run through your mind—something left undone, unsaid. It's common to relive the events of the day. Such thoughts become less distinct, then random. Dreams are the brain's futile attempt to shape these random thoughts into a coherent story. At some point, the random thoughts cease. There is nothing—total emptiness—you're no longer there.

Epicurus said death is a state of nothingness, so there is nothing to fear. Getting there though, that's the scary part.

On the plane flying to Tijuana, Eric had read a story, "The Icicle" by Abram Tertz. He recalled a vivid scene where the candles on a Christmas tree flicker out one by one. Tertz compares the candles to individual lives that fade away.

> Some burned out as gaily as they had lived and even gave a generous spurt of flame, brighter than before, at the end. Others started economizing half-way through, as if they knew what was coming and hoped to put off the end as long as possible. But this didn't always help them and an occasional thrifty wick would suddenly choke in its own wax a good two inches from the bottom.
>
> There were others that only grasped the full horror of the situation at the very end and began to dart from side to side in their tin holders, casting outsize reflections on the walls and ceiling, entirely using up all their vital juices and gases, and which then suffocated in their own prematurely decomposed remains, their death agony being a most unseemly spectacle.

A motorcycle roared by with a sudden blast. A lonely rooster crowed at the encroaching sun. A pack of grouse-like birds chattered among themselves in the underbrush. An uneasy silence replaced the clamor. All that remained was the sound of a far-off dove. Then, a human voice called from the patio. It was Orvaline: "Eric, I'll meet you in the Jeep. It's time to go."

"Right. I'll be there in a second. Let me grab my things."

Having known Eric less than a month, Orvaline knew his impressions were speculative, but he had some strong opinions. Eric was careful, responsible, and organized, but lacked emotion, except for an anger that Orvaline attributed to the illness. He had an appreciation of nature as far as it was visually apprehended, but he understood life only empirically. He lacked passion. In a way this was typical of the Americans Orvaline met. Mexicans had nature and art. They celebrated animals and ancestors alike. Theirs was a culture in which dreams and reality had actual connections. For the Americans life was a puzzle to be solved. There could be no inscrutabilities.

Rocky hills and dark valleys were to be avoided—too much danger in the unknown, too real. On the flat plane everything moved forward with a numbing practicality. There was, however, one place where Eric's emotions peeked through the curtain. He was falling in love with Ofelia, and Orvaline was not happy about it.

Eric climbed into the passenger seat of the open-air Jeep.

"Let's go the long way around. I want to see the sights."

"No time, your appointment's in twenty minutes. We'll have to take the beach route."

They sped along a tiny road. A few locals walked toward the beach, small bundles on their backs. One rode a bicycle that had been modified into a portable cart. It passed too quickly for Eric to see what the man carried.

Mexico changed Eric's perspective on everything. His illness was the truth he couldn't escape, but everywhere he looked he found other channels to explore. It bothered him that Orvaline seldom spoke to him, wondered if Orvaline resented having him around. It disturbed him to be thought of as the ugly American.

"Orvaline, have you been to the States?"

"Sure. I go to San Diego all the time to pick up supplies for Napier and to go to the bank. I take the mail for him, since it goes faster if posted in the United States."

"Have you ever thought you'd like to live there?"

"Why? I'm a Mexican. This is my home."

"I've heard lots of Mexicans want to live there. Many people in Tijuana travel back and forth every day to work at jobs across the border. Some risk their lives to sneak in and stay."

"I'm not one of those Mexicans."

"I think I would like to live in Mexico," said Eric.

"No, you wouldn't. You've only seen the tourist side, the fake areas we've created and promoted. They hide the real thing. You know nothing about the real Mexico. There's the heat, the lack of water, the corruption, poverty and abuse, the filth, and the lack of basic services. No one can speak freely; everyone learns early to stay in place. Nothing is secure. It's a feudal system. You wouldn't like that at all."

"Then why do you stay?"

"Mexico has a soul. America has McDonald's."

"Come on, Orvaline. America has much more than that."

The road wound in and out through the palms. All at once, over the barren hill, the clinic became visible. Eric noticed garbage strewn along the road. The stink of burning trash invaded his nostrils.

"Maybe Mexico appeals to me because I'm trying to regain *my* soul."

"Here we are, Eric. You should think about how you lost your soul in the first place before trying to find it in a country you know nothing about."

The clinic was enclosed on all sides by barbed wire. There was a guard at the front gate. They were building a new wing. Construction in Mexico was ubiquitous, but it progressed at a snail's pace.

Business appeared to be booming at the clinic. Cancer patients from all over the world came for the miracle cure promised by Laetrile.

Eric climbed out of the Jeep. He thought about Orvaline's comments. Was he right, or was he simply angry and jealous at the gringos invading his country—at their opulence, their haughtiness, their lack of respect? It was hard to know what Orvaline really thought. He didn't volunteer his private thoughts to Eric.

"I'll come back to pick you up after I get a few things in town."

"Thanks for the ride. Listen, I don't want you to think I'm just another ugly American. I want to be friends. Sure, I need to learn some things, a lot of things, but I hope you'll give me a chance."

"You're living with my family, Eric. You have a chance. Don't blow it. I'll pick you up right here on my way back." The Jeep sped off toward Centro.

Don't blow it? What did he mean by that?

Eric had tests on a regular schedule, blood profiles, X-rays, urine analyses. There were specialized tests only available in Mexico. Doctor Milagro explained the cancer immunological tests that were patented. It seemed odd to Eric that his American doctors didn't know about them. Were they for real? Was anything here for real? He took two grams of Laetrile daily and adhered to a strict vegetarian diet with organic juices, all approved by the clinic's nutritionist. At home Ofelia prepared his meals exactly the same way. Boxes of supplements lined the shelves of his bungalow. He returned to the clinic weekly for the tests and for cleansing enemas. The regimen was tedious and humiliating. Eric imagined that the Laetrile enveloped his cancer bit by bit, surrounding and conquering the crablike tentacles with the precision of *Wehrmacht* soldiers. When Eric was young he'd had two gruesome picture books of the world wars. There were buildings devastated by bombs, trenches full of the dead, starving prisoners in the concentration camps. Everywhere he looked, he saw total devastation. That was when Eric became aware of death. He couldn't help but think about all those millions killed during the war while he was a child. He was spared, was given a life. Why? What had he done with it?

Eric had been too young to serve in the Korean War, and by the time the Vietnam War rolled around he'd already completed his military service in the Army Reserves. It had only been a couple of years since innocent college kids were killed at Kent State and Jackson State. Devon participated in some of the antiwar protests at Berkeley. Devon could have been one of those kids murdered by the government. And what did Eric do? Nothing. He didn't fight, he didn't protest. He was busy building a law practice.

26.

Penance and Grace

Doctor Milagro was giving his orientation seminar in the Buena Salud cafeteria. "There is a harmony in the metabolism that reflects the eternal mystery of life. When you are able to see the whole in its infinitely fine order, you will understand that effective treatment of the disease, like treatment of the soul, requires a holistic approach. There is one to whom you can go and be sure of your deliverance. God in His mercy will save your body like He saves your soul. You must simply ask Him and believe in His power to do so.

What is there for those who don't believe? Is there is anything to make life easier? Death cleaves the soul from the body as the butcher cleaves the meat from the bones. The only good that death brings is that it puts us all in our place.

A dozen faces listen to Doctor Milagro, a dozen different expressions of hope and fear. In one corner, an American woman, alone, hands folded on her lap, a beautiful yellow dress, stylish amber hair, a string of golden beads, modest but expensive, around her neck. *This can't be happening to me, no, not to me!*

An old man sits at a table, mumbling to himself. From time to time he turns to face the wall and lets out a low, mournful cry. An obese woman lost in the agony of anticipation breathes heavily and dabs continuously at the sweat on her forehead. A man in tan slacks and a crisp white shirt, a businessman, changes facial expressions as a series of thoughts run swiftly through his mind: *I suppose they'll try to move the Helfinger account away from me now. I'll have to convince them that I can find the time to get it done. If I ask my secretary to cancel those advance orders for the camelhair suits, they'll think I've lost hope. Better to let the order stand even if I never wear them.*

They all wanted to know what they would find further on. Eric wanted to know too.

"Don't you ever stop asking?"

"No, I never stop."

"But you're getting no answers."

"There *are* no answers."

"God wants us to be well."

"Then, why does he kill us?"

"The wages of sin is death."

"But why now?"

"Your time is up."

"It's impossible to live like this."

"Life is an ugly thing, but it's what we have and we must make the best of it."

"Yes, but now she's dead."

Milagro continued: "There was a time when you heard 'cancer' and thought *I'm dead, it's over,* or the tests come back and you are kept in the dark. Family and friends hide the facts because they think you can't handle the truth, but you're here now because you know, you know this disease threatens, that it has pulled you out of the life you once had, the life you thought would go on forever. Well, I'm going to tell you something the doctors at home cannot tell you, something they are not allowed to say. Your life is not over. And why won't they tell you that? They are controlled by the medical associations, that's why. They've conspired with the government to suppress the one true treatment for your disease. Your doctors are afraid to speak of Laetrile because they fear the law, a law written by the paid lobbyists of the pharmaceutical industry to protect the profits of a few vested interests. Don't blame your doctors. They're good men and women. They want to help you, but they're hamstrung by the law. Many of you are here with their blessings, I know that. I know these doctors. In fact, many of them work with me behind the scenes, but they can't tell you that. They have looked into the facts. They know the truth about this disease, 'El Grande C,' that afflicts you."

The doctor paused to take a sip of water. The faces in the crowd were fixed on his every word. He told them about the miracle of Laetrile and how God had arranged nature to benefit mankind, how He had placed Laetrile inside the pits of apricots, peaches, and bitter almonds because of His love for us. "God is a great physician who has never lost a case that I know of. The opponents of Laetrile scare you by telling you it is full of cyanide. What they don't tell you is that the unique chemistry of Laetrile insures the cyanide only attacks the cancer, not the rest of you. The cyanide in Laetrile is your friend."

He went on to describe the regimen, the diet, the supplements and vitamins, the injections and the enemas. He made sure to work in a bit of humility, a warning: "Even the miracle of Laetrile cannot save everyone. Some of you will die. We all die sooner or later. People have been known to die of the common cold or after eating a bad mushroom. Sometimes it's just bad luck. Maybe you have some odd strain of cancer that doesn't respond to fruit pits. Anything is possible in this world. People ask me, if God loves us, why do we suffer and die? The truth is, I don't know. God sees more than we see. He knows more than we know. Some things we must accept."

No doctrine had been invented to make life easier, not the sum of Doctor Milagro's views, not the result of any long search, religious or philosophical. There was love, but Eric lacked some vital force, a force he could not summon. Love, religious feeling, the inexplicable passion that arises spontaneously in some people—all eluded him. He could not make that bloody appeal of one human being to another. Personalities manage to retain their basic contradictions no matter what.

God damn it! God... damn... it. He would make this work. If anything Milagro said was real, if any of his feelings for Ofelia were real, he would make it work.

He'd been told the coffee enemas were an essential part of the cure, yet he shuddered every time he was asked to lie upon the enema bench. He felt like Dimmesdale or Hester Prynne standing at the public stocks at midnight, exposing their sin to the world. He wondered why it was that physical redemption, like spiritual redemption, required an arduous humiliating regimen and submission to public suffering, why he had to endure such misery.

He paused outside the door of the treatment room and thought of Stanford. He would try anything to break free from this terrible disease. Mary had called in a faith healer. One patient told him there was a man in the mountains outside Tijuana who could remove the disease by simply touching you with his hands. It sounded crazy, but what if it was true?

Mida was waiting when he entered the room. She knew from the look on his face that something was wrong. "What itches?"

"Everything, Mida. Every damn thing is one big itch!"

Eric was bitter and angry, and couldn't hide it, not even for Mida.

Mida shook her head. "To be angry will not make you well. Lie down. Let's have our party in peace."

Mida gave him the enema. He'd grown accustomed to her seeing him naked in this awful, weakened state. She was always bright and cheerful and knew the right things to say.

"Oh, Mida, how unpleasant this must be for you. It's so embarrassing for me."

"Is no problem. Anyone can be sick. If there's cure, why worry?"

"But is there? Is there a cure?"

"You will have the cure."

Eric was ashamed when he ran to the toilet. He could imagine what she saw, what she heard and thought, despite what she said.

How many times does a man shit in a lifetime? He didn't know, but for him it was two or three times as often. Mida was graciously gone when he returned, pants pulled up, trying to look as normal as possible.

He walked to the cafeteria to get some juice. He had to drink as much as he could get down every day. The patients were still at the large table in the center of the room with Doctor Milagro. "In God's first instructions to newly created man, man was told to eat 'the herb-bearing seed' and 'the fruit of a tree-bearing seed.' Notice the emphasis on seed! When God described His newly created plant kingdom in two short verses, He specifically mentioned seed four times. The divine emphasis on seed leads us straight to Laetrile. All plants are chemical factories that make manmade chemical factories look crude by comparison. But the seed—the chemical wonders in seeds stagger the imagination! There are those who laugh, but you, you surely believe this truth suggested by the Word of God and confirmed by biochemistry. Why else would you be here? You are among the very fortunate few to have God's natural cure."

They all looked so hopeful. Milagro planted optimism in their brains. It was part of the cure. With the nasty business of the enema behind him, even Eric was optimistic.

A few former patients rose to share their stories. The doctor had arranged this to build the confidence of new arrivals. To hear stories that resounded with such conviction and earnest concern for the welfare of a new patient is a powerful source of hope and empowerment. From his courtroom experience, Eric knew that eyewitness testimony was often unreliable; still, the persuasive power of a fellow cancer sufferer who asserts with urgent sincerity, "I was cured" is strong, almost irresistible.

"Because of my colon cancer," said Joe from California, "I required a colostomy. Wearing a bag to poop in was not my idea of living, but I did what I was told. The doctors wanted to cut me again, but I heard about Laetrile from a friend and decided to give it a try. Six months later, instead of lying on my deathbed, I was back to normal. They even reconnected my colon. It was the first time the hospital had performed a reverse colostomy. Laetrile gave me back my life."

Beverly from Idaho spoke next. "When I told the doctor that I was going to get Laetrile, the doctor was greatly upset, and told me my leg would have to be amputated. He assured me that without the surgery, I would live at most twelve weeks. At the first Laetrile treatment, the tumor in my leg grew larger. It went from around the size of a walnut to the size of a lemon, and there was a little bleeding for a few days. Sure, I started to worry. Who wouldn't? But after five weeks of injections, the tumor became smaller. After another five weeks, I couldn't even feel it. I still have my leg and I'm cancer-free."

The man sitting next to Beverly stood up. His name was Milton, and he was older than the other two, with red hair and freckles. "I was told my prostate would have to be removed. I figured an operation would probably just spread the disease, so I opted for Laetrile after my daughter-in-law told me about it. I followed a strict diet that was supposed to replenish my pancreatic enzymes."

A lone goat called from the field across the way. There was something eerily human in the "meh-eh-eh" that recurred at regular intervals—a sound like Sampson might have made when he was tied to grinding machines.

"Three years later," said Milton, "my tumor was gone. Believe it or not my hair turned from white to red again. I think it was the result of my better diet."

The stories were inspiring, but no one at the clinic mentioned the failures. Where were those Eric had met that first day—Mary, Ira, Cat? Who would tell *their* stories? The failures were sent home to die, and no records were kept of them. He walked back out to the gate, thinking about Ofelia.

A small boy ran up to him as he walked away from the clinic.

"Hey, joo! What informations joo want? I got special place for joo. *Muchas señoritas.* Here, joo look, mister."

"No, thanks," said Eric. He tried to walk away. The boy ran after him with a card.

"For joo, mister. Very safe, clean. No *banditos*, no *problemas*. Pretty *chicas*, them like joo, go see. Sexy chicas, very sexy." As Eric pushed him away, the boy shoved a card into his pocket.

A woman was walking into the clinic. She looked like a new patient.

"Hey, joo!" the boy said to her. Gimme me five pesos. I light the candle in church for joo. It work. Clear up joor sickness." The woman smiled and gave him some pesos.

"Gimme five more and I get priest to pray for joo, pray for the cancer go 'way." He put out his hand. She laughed and gave him another peso.

"I happy for joo, señora. Joo be in good shape soon. Joo got all time in the worl'." The boy smiled from ear to ear. Skinny, with a big round head and missing a few teeth, he looked like Jack Pumpkinhead in *The Wonderful Land of Oz* as he danced off down the street.

Eric stood outside and waited for Orvaline. Far off on the twisting road, he saw a motorcycle approaching. It weaved in and out of sight. Soon he could hear the engine, and the unknown became familiar in a flash—it was Jordan.

Eric tried to hide behind a burgeoning pepper tree with leathery green leaves and little balls of bright red fruit. Jordan was a friend. Their talks had helped Eric through some rough spots, but all this religion made him fidgety. Superstitions no longer had any positive effect on him. He had yet to construct some sense of existence on his own, but that was no reason to go back to the inane illusions of his youth. All the psychic tinkering at the clinic weighed on him. Did Doctor Milagro and Father Jordan really think the old unity was going to return and survive in this modern world? No doubt Eric had some religious sensibility, but not of the traditional kind. He didn't care if his life was a mass of contradictions, his feelings for Ofelia, for Jordan, Doctor Milagro, the doctors back home, Mexico, America, and all the rest. Contradictions were the sign of a healthy mind, weren't they?

"Top o' the mornin', Eric. Bless my soul, our paths crossed just as I was looking for you. Tomorrow I'm travelin' to *En Ninguna Parte*, and you, my son, are coming with me! It'll be a glorious day for the both of us."

Eric looked at the twinkle in Jordan's eyes, at his mischievous grin. "I'm not riding on the back of that motorcycle."

"I daresay. It's a very difficult drive. We'll have to take my plane. I'll pick you up at the Cabreras' at nine a.m."

"You have a plane?"

"Officially it belongs to the Archdiocese, but I'm the only one who uses it. There are many isolated villages that need the services of a priest. I'm the only priest in Tijuana who can fly a plane. Thank God for it! I was a chaplain, you see, in the Air National Guard before I was assigned to Baja."

"Why did they send you here, Jordan? This godforsaken place doesn't seem like a prime assignment to me."

"I'm in a wee bit of a hurry. I'll see you tomorrow. Did you know that tree you're standing behind is called a pirul tree? They grow wild in Mexico. They're important in traditional medicine. The branches are used to sweep a person's body. They say this casts away all bad luck and the evil eye. The practice is called *'una barrida con pirul.'* I'll break a branch and sweep it o'er you if you like."

"How can you believe in these crazy Mexican folk customs?"

"Many people here combine the ancient remedies and religion with modern medicine. There's a sort of rivalry between all of us here to heal you, Eric. I say, let there be no want of anything. I may be ignorant of medical science, but I daresay more is better than less. I heard of a physicist once who told a friend that superstitions work even when you don't believe them. The physicist had a horseshoe hung above his door. I thought it was a quaint little nod to custom on his part."

"I thought you priests were hellbent on destroying the traditional beliefs of the heathens."

"I can see why you might think that. The church has made plenty of mistakes. I've always felt religious beliefs should be flexible. I don't hold with hellfire, Eric, or eternal damnation. When I travel to some o' the more remote areas, I make a point to remove any curses that some other priests may have put on the local healers. It makes everyone feel better. I have visited some of the Indian communities across the border in the States. Many of the relatives of our local Indians live there. It's very sad. Congress outlawed the Native American religions in the last century. The poor Indians up there aren't allowed to keep their sacred objects, even the pipes and eagle feathers. They can't gather together to practice their ancient rituals. I help them with their secret meetings in case the fundamentalist cops break in. When that happens I just tell the officers, as a Catholic priest, mind you, that what they're doing is orthodox. After all, we all pray to the same God."

"So all gods are the same, Jordan?"

"Some narrow-minded people who really don't understand God make foolish and hurtful mistakes. They can't conceive how anyone could live without the particular God they have in their own heads, and they look at those who don't share their views as if they had an immense hole inside. They use hateful words like heretic, infidel, and atheist, and consider those who think differently to be sad, incomplete human beings. Then they try to save them with their antiquated notions of faith. It doesn't work, o' course, so as a last resort they persecute them. In the old days they threw them on the rack and burned them at the stake. We've become more civilized, but the persecution continues. It seems to me God wants more from us than that."

Jordan sped his motorcycle off toward town.

Eric looked at the large pirul tree beside him. Its gray bark was twisted and rough. The branches drooped with heavy red fruit. The limbs reached out in all directions like a many-armed Indian god. Two quail roosted high on a limb, nearly hidden by the mass of foliage. The ground below was thick with dead leaves and rotting fallen fruit.

Life is made up of little things, just as the body is formed of molecules. Each life is a string of moments. While we remember the past and ponder the future, life exists only as a single instant in the present. If we fail to seize that moment, we fail to live. When all the molecules that make up the body separate and fly off into space, the body dies, but all those instants of time that made us, they still exist. They're out there somewhere. It was just like Jordan to disappear before Eric could ask the big questions. Jordan was right about one thing: the Church had a bad record with the people it didn't understand.

Orvaline arrived in the Jeep. They took a different route home through the neighborhood. A nostalgia for Sugarvale and a sense of melancholy passed over Eric as he watched the locals in their daily routines. A young boy guided an elderly blind man who walked along slowly with his cane. What the man saw and what Eric saw, how different each view of the world must be. The Mexican people didn't hide their old, their cripples, or their freaks. They didn't celebrate or denigrate them. Those who were different were treated just like everyone else.

Eric admired the photographer Diane Arbus. He was saddened when he heard she'd killed herself a year ago. She photographed oddities but didn't exploit them. She said freaks made her feel a mixture of shame and awe, that there was a quality of legend about them, like a person in a fairytale who stops you and demands that you answer a riddle. *Yes, exactly!*

Tsar Peter the Great was another person fascinated with oddities. Eric had read that the tsar created a collection of dwarfs, giants, and freaks from all over the world. It was meant to show ordinary people that humans came not from God or devilish actions but from the regular development of nature. Peter was ahead of his time—in other parts of the world, deformed children and their mothers were being burned alive as devils or witches by pious Christians.

Everything that lives is holy—holy the supernatural extra brilliant intelligent kindness of the soul! Whatever there might be beyond this life, there is consolation in just having lived and uttered a protest.

On a bench outside a corner grocery, a dwarf sat next to an obese woman in a bright orange dress. Two scrawny dogs fornicated in the street, but no one paid any attention. A young boy, maybe the brother, pushed the distorted body of a child in a broken-down wheelchair. Rickety grandmothers were helped along by anyone who happened to be going their way. The youngest children walked naked alongside their mothers, who wore intricate floral prints in odd mixtures of bright colors, delighting in their eccentricity. How delicious it all was, to be alive, to be thinking, seeing, enjoying, walking, eating, and how different from the current sum in your bank account or the prospects of a career.

Just pay attention.

27.

El Hombre con la Sonrisa Congelada

"You're repulsed by my face."

"What I feel is sadness."

"You're the one who put this mark on me."

"The mark is your own doing."

"What happened was an accident."

"You were careless."

"I didn't understand the magnitude of what I did at the time."

"Now you understand."

"I can't bear it."

"You must live with your mistake."

"I've lived my life for him."

"No, you live your life for them."

♋

Hector managed operations for Dos Negros down to the smallest detail. He would travel anywhere to get the deals done. From the opium dealers in Badiraguato to the heroin and marijuana trade throughout northern Mexico, everyone knew Hector, El Hombre con la Sonrisa Congelada, the man with the frozen smile.

The money was easy. A kilo of marijuana sold for sixty pesos at the source, about $4.80. It wholesaled for $100 in L.A., and a panic like the one in 1969 could raise the price to $350. Heroin was even more attractive. A kilo of 80–90 percent grade sold for $10,000 to $12,000 at the source. The original kilo was turned into thirty-two kilos by cutting it five times with milk sugar, instant coffee, or cocoa. Sold on the street at about 3 percent potency, the original kilo yielded over $600,000.

Two Dos Negros trucks and five men wound their way down to Sinaloa. In both vehicles there were guns and ammunition to trade for heroin. Two men in one truck stayed in Culiacán with the supply of weapons. The other truck ascended into the mountains with Hector and the other two men. In Culiacán they bribed the mayor, who paid off the soldiers at the inspection points. When they arrived at the village, they met with a group of farmers who knew Hector. He and his men had their guns out and so did the farmers. This was détente. No one was going to do a bad deal. The farmers had kilos of marijuana all lined up in bricks.

"How many kilos are you going to take? We have the best stuff at the best price." Hector wanted only the heroin, but he knew he would have to take some of the marijuana first. It was old, and they were anxious to get rid of it.

Hector took a machete and whacked a brick in half to look at it, then did the same to another brick. He wanted to see how much sugar had been mixed in. It looked like pretty good stuff, dry and not too much smell to it. There wasn't a lot of garbage packed in, seeds or stems.

"We'll take five hundred kilos, pay the usual sixty pesos."

"Take more," said one farmer who was taller than the rest. His dark eyes were set deep in his head. A knife scar descended from his ear to his chest. He was the leader.

"I don't have money for more," answered Hector without showing any emotion.

The farmers discussed this among themselves. They were very poor, and Hector knew he could bargain with them. The tall farmer stepped toward Hector, towering over him.

"Take a ton. You can pay us when you come back on the next trip."

"I may not be back." Hector appeared anxious to be on his way.

The tall man leaned toward Hector, stood very still, glared at him. Hector held his ground.

After several minutes the tall man relaxed his stance.

"We need guns and ammunition, amigo. We can trade heroin. If you come back in a week with guns and more money, we can do a deal."

Hector knew about these impoverished farmers. They lived in little *jacales* scattered throughout the mountains and valleys. They needed guns to protect themselves against the *banditos* who roamed in these mountains looking for money and drugs. Even their women were good with guns. Hector couldn't trust anyone with heroin. It was too easy to cut. He had to watch carefully; otherwise there was no way to know what had been done to it.

"I'll send my men back in the truck with the marijuana. They can return in a week with the guns and money for the heroin. We'll take five kilos. I stay here and watch you cook the *goma* into heroin so I know for sure what I'm getting."

"You cannot stay with us!" The man was inflexible. He was afraid Hector would attract attention. The soldiers sent in by the government to burn fields of marijuana and poppies were always trying to shake them down. The farmers bribed them so they would burn only the fields that didn't have enough water or were rotten or had already been harvested. This allowed the soldiers to claim they were doing their job while the farmers could still make a living. Everybody won with this unspoken agreement. Sometimes, however, the soldiers demanded more money after they had already agreed to a deal. There were also rival groups of farmers who raided the farms, especially if they thought a big deal was about to go down.

"I have to stay with you. I'll keep out of sight, but I want to see the whole process so I can be sure the heroin is pure."

Reluctantly, the farmers agreed. They knew Hector was powerful. The Dos Negros operation controlled the narcotics traffic in Baja California and the brown Mexican heroin that supplied the Pacific Coast and Southwest. Through their connections with Zacco, they did most of the business in the Midwest and the East Coast even though they competed with the European and South American suppliers. Neither the soldiers nor the rival groups of farmers wanted to anger Dos Negros by crossing Hector.

Through an intricate series of networks greased with bribes and political connections, Hector was able to move large quantities of marijuana and heroin to isolated airstrips near the border. Seasoned pilots flew the contraband across and quickly landed on one of the countless small airfields that covered the Southwest. The drugs were then sold to distributors. The planes flew back to Mexico, carrying guns and consumer goods and spare factory parts that were illegal to import into Mexico. There was never a worry about the Mexican Customs inspectors on the other side. Even if they caught the Dos Negros pilots bringing in the illegal goods, they were easily bribed.

The key was for the planes to fly low between the mountain ranges and the canyon corridors and to pass beyond the range of the truck-mounted sensors. Using these techniques the Dos Negros-Zacco pilots did a booming business. The U.S. federal agents had no way to stop them. These pilots sometimes made several trips a night, low and slow by the light of the moon, landing on deserted airstrips or right on the sagebrush-covered desert. Each flight could yield as much as $50,000 US before expenses.

Hector had planned for ten long years. He carefully recorded every contact he made, every plan he executed, and every dollar he earned for the bosses. He knew he could dethrone the Dos Negros. They had become soft, wallowing in their wealth, their drugs, and their women. They had forgotten where they came from and what they'd had to do to get to the top. This made them vulnerable.

There was a time when Hector went through the self-questioning anyone would who chose a life of evil, but over the years he had learned to accept violence and life on the edge. He'd seen Dos Negros at their worst. He knew what they could do. At first he couldn't imagine doing such things himself, but he could no longer deny that he'd become just like them, only stronger, smarter, and more disciplined.

He sometimes wanted everything to return to the way it had been, that he and his father and mother and little Marcos could start over again, that every bad memory could be lost, but those years were gone forever. Time could not be turned back. This was his life now.

The Dos Negros made mistakes. Tomás had killed a Mexican official for ordering the burning of fifty acres of marijuana. A few bribes would have restored the peace, but Tomás had to go for all-out war and that's what he got. The politicians in Mexico City were embarrassed. They imposed an unprecedented government crackdown. During those difficult times, the Asians entered the market with their hashish and stronger strain of marijuana. They nearly put Dos Negros out of business. Hector handled the sensitive negotiations and eventually worked out a compromise. Despite all the trouble, Tomás had learned nothing. He was as foolhardy as ever.

The days passed, hot, humid, fly-ridden. Hector watched the farmers unceasingly. They did everything right. The exchange was made when his men returned. The next step was to set up the trucks for the return journey to the border. Trucks to be used as decoys were filled with fruit and vegetables. The trucks with the drugs were packed with ripe tomatoes on top. Occasionally the police, usually bribed by the other dealers, would stop them. The competitors were always trying to sabotage their efforts. The decoy trucks would rush ahead, barreling through the roadblock. The police would chase them, allowing the drug-laden trucks to drive on through without being inspected. If one of them was stopped, the driver would complain that the police were ruining his tomatoes. This usually put a stop to the inspection, but there were cohorts, drivers in other cars, who carried guns just in case. They always arrived at the border safely.

As Hector watched the men load the plane on the Mexican side of the border, he thought about how to stage his coup. Everything depended on the timing. First he had to make sure his family was safe, and he had to get his father out of jail. He had plenty of money to bribe the governor, but the first step would be to persuade the Cabrera-Rodriguez family—a sensitive matter but crucial to the plan. Next he would move his mother and Marcos to his uncle's place in Morelia where they would be protected. It was a better place for them to live anyway.

When everything was ready, he'd make his move. He looked at the new plane, a Lockheed Constellation. It was a giant. Though Less maneuverable and more difficult to get across, the advantage lay in its capacity. After the cabin had been refurbished, this aircraft could carry twenty tons of cargo in a single mission. With this capacity he could smuggle enough heroin on one flight to supply the entire US market for several years. Tonight was a test run with marijuana. If things went as expected, Hector would be the scorpion with wings. He would be unstoppable.

At night, the desert had a remarkable effect: it was a silent place of heat and strangeness that worked its magic on the mind. The stars populated the sky like notes from a ukulele. The air was still and thick, like an exudate emerging from the tissues of an ancient reptile. Time passed slowly. Hector was impatient, but he calmed his nerves. He knew the journey was just beginning. He knew he'd carry it through to whatever end God destined for him.

28.

Itandehui and Carlos

The monster climbed out of the pit using its small reptile-like arms and legs and found its way to the surface. Avoiding the light, it hid in the jungle shadows.

An unexpected sound startled Carlos.

"Who's there?"

Silence. The air smelled of rotted flesh.

Carlos finished moving the jugs of Laetrile up the mountain to the storage shed by the pool. His lungs were heavy with fluid; he coughed painfully, pulling up the phlegm that impeded his breathing.

"Who's there?"

He heard an unfamiliar growl.

"Come out of the dark, *pendejo!*"

A cloud of smoke rose from the jungle floor. A swarm of golden-colored locusts formed all around him. They lifted him and carried him down, down, down in circles slowly into the canyon.

"Ugh! Where are you taking me?"

Dizzy from the rapid descent, Carlos found himself alone in a dark cave-like space at the bottom of the canyon near the base of a large rock. Overhead the bright sun peeked through a small hole and illuminated the rock's flat surface. Polished smooth, shining like a mirror, it revealed a horrific creature, part lion, part bat, part scorpion. Carlos froze when he saw the creature's visage—it had a human face, a woman's, wild and fierce.

"Who are you? What are you?"

The reflection faded. Carlos awoke shivering with fever, a numbness encumbered his head. It was an ominous warning. He went straight to Itandehui and told her of his dream.

She turned white. He'd never seen her so disturbed.

"The evil spirit has returned. It's angry because its world is changing. I feared this would happen. I saw it myself on the day you brought the Laetrile with Ana Louisa. The spirit cannot do its work alone. It needs a human form. It's looking for a living body."

Carlos felt sick and weak. It was hard to breathe.

Itandehui did what she could for him, but his malady had gone too far. She watched as he left to see which direction he would choose. He went south, in the direction of death. She sat, eyes closed, and stroked the soft black fur of the jackrabbit's foot as she awaited the dream. This time the dream did not come.

29.

At the Palapa

Birds disappear to escape the midday heat. The air radiates up and down like bubbles in a jar. Insects crawl into dark spaces for protection from the sun. Eric sits in a chair shaded by the roof of his palapa. He looks out to the ocean, visible through the palm trees. Nothing moves. The world no longer rotates. The sun is focused on him alone. Of course it's an illusion. The sun's rays are impartial. They cover half the world at a time, together with an infinite array of other planetary objects. The sun cares nothing about him or anything else its golden rays might touch.

Orvaline is asleep downstairs. Ofelia is at work at the clinic.

Eric dozes, glides between sleep and wakefulness. In a dream he carries wooden blocks back and forth. They slip out of his hands one at a time, *thump, thump, thump*. He tries to pick them up. Down they fall again, *thump, thump, thump*. Next thing he knows, he's awake. Above his head, the ceiling fan wobbles, *bump, bump, bump*.

Reality and illusion are cousins. Perhaps Eric himself was no more than a grand illusion, a very, very convincing one, but an illusion all the same. His suffering though, that was real. Of that he was sure.

Ghosts speak in the courtyard behind the locked door. The monkey reclines in a dark corner. The monkey grows larger and draws close to Eric's face. He jerks his head away. A cold wind rattles the leaves of a large green tree. Beyond

251

the courtyard, children sleep on the sidewalks, curled up in tiny balls like cats. Beggars troll the streets. A knife slips into a man's chest. The monkey shrieks and scampers back into the darkness.

Eric reaches for the juice. He drinks a quart every hour, and pees continuously. A dark curse echoes throughout the garden.

The sky has grown completely black;

It's time to think of turning back.

Fall down or scream or rush about—

There is no way of getting out.

Ofelia returns from the clinic. Soon she will give Eric his second injection. He's dying. It's logical. We all die, but why must he die now? It's too horrible to think of being buried in the cold earth when he looks into Ofelia's warm brown eyes. He's in love but too indolent and nerveless to do anything about it.

She calls softly, not wanting to wake him if he's asleep. "Hola, Eric?"

"Come on up, Ofelia."

She rushes up the stairs, anxious to see him.

She can't believe God will call him soon. He's all she thinks about—how wretched it would be to not be with him. Her hopes and dreams turn to dust at the thought.

She appears at the top of the stairs still dressed in her white uniform from the clinic, the way he first saw her. "The injection's ready." She's carrying the needle in one hand and the necessary materials in the other. "How were your treatments at the clinic today?"

"I feel smashed like a water balloon run over on the street."

"Oh, Eric, you make it sound awful. I'll ask Mida to treat you more gently next time."

Her smile brings on the butterflies. He feels soft wings tickling inside. The Promethean cycle of dying and rebirth plays out for him each time he's with her. To live to die, to die to live, how senseless it all seems. The happiness she brings is bittersweet when death lurks in the corner.

Away, ah, away!
Go, wild man of bones!
I'm still young, go, dear!
And do not touch me.

Eric goes to the clinic for the enemas and the treatments. He doesn't want to be humiliated in front of Ofelia. But he lets her give him the injections because that's when she's closest to him. Only then can he slow the journey into oblivion. When she isn't with him, there are times he wants to scream or throw a chair through the window. Once, he thought he'd succeed in everything, but he sees now he's failed at everything. He wants more: a ladder balanced against the moon, and the strength to climb it into the sky.

Ofelia's presence stuns him. Is she real? He's had so many visions. He blinks. When he opens his eyes she's beside him, with her chocolate skin, her black hair, shining and glossy, the soft little hairs on her upper lip hardly noticeable, her encouraging smile that penetrates right into his heart. He sighs.

"How did Milagro get that name anyway? It's a good name for a doctor."

"Mexico is the land of miracles. Do you know the story of Juan Diego?"

"Tell me." Everyone knows the story, but he wants Ofelia's version, wants to hear the words as she speaks them.

"The Virgin of Guadalupe appears to an Indian and asks him to have the Mexican bishop build a shrine to her at the very spot where she appears. Three times this happens. Of course, no one believes an *Eeendian*."

Eric can't help but laugh.

"This is a serious story, Eric." She likes to see him happy. She puts her hands on her hips.

Eric feels transparent, like a phantom, and wonders if she actually sees him. Butterflies appear everywhere. They float all about the room like giant flower petals.

"There is a sign, and now you see the shrines everywhere. The Virgin is the most important religious icon in Mexico, bigger even than the Christ."

Ofelia knew Eric was falling in love with her. She could see it in his face. If not that she loved him as well, she might have been content with the life she had before. It would be so much easier that way. But she did love him, and that's what made her suffer. It was all so strange. Take away this anguish and she would be a thousand times more miserable. It was the suffering that made her happy, ridiculous but true.

"Ofelia, do you believe in miracles?"

"That isn't the right question. If it's possible, that's enough."

"But stories must be based on facts."

"There are deeper realities, Eric. A world without miracles is an incomplete world. Life consists of more than facts."

"But... how can a story be true if it's just made up?"

"We all make up stories every day. That's life. All stories are true in some way. If not, they wouldn't be stories."

Eric turns his arm toward Ofelia and waits. He feels a tiny prick as the needle penetrates his flesh, then a subtle flowing as the serum is released. He and Ofelia touch. The room becomes brighter, more intense. It lasts only a few seconds, but the feeling lingers—skin on skin. He's amazed. He feels himself growing hard as Ofelia's breast grazes his arm when she leans over him to drop a piece of cotton into the trash. Outside, the ocean pounds against the rocks. Inside, the ceiling fan answers, rocking to and fro on its mount. Eric feels beads of perspiration forming on his brow. His mouth fills with saliva and he swallows. *My God,* he thinks, *I'm alive!*

Ofelia's heart beats faster when she gives the injection. Penetrating his skin with the fine needle becomes an acute moment of carnal intimacy, two bodies merging into one. She's anxious, restless, a quivering passes through her stomach. Her breathing quickens. Birds are cooing rhythmically out on the balcony. Eric's face twists slightly as he squinches his eyes shut. Ofelia holds onto his arm, caresses it, hesitates to let it go. He opens his eyes. She feels as though he has melted into her. She laughs nervously. Her face is flushed and warm. She swabs his arm with alcohol and applies a dab of white cotton with medical tape.

"Don't resist the idea of miracles, Eric. They happen all the time." Her voice is shaky.

"After my diagnosis, after my time at Stanford, I pretty much lost hope. It was the most horrible time in my life. The American doctors couldn't cut away the cancer. They told me radiation and drugs might help, but they weren't persuasive. You could see it in their eyes. They knew they were up against something they couldn't beat. I came here in desperation, not knowing what to expect. Then I met you. You're the one thing that makes me truly happy, Ofelia."

Ofelia blushes again, afraid this time she's losing her composure. "Anyone could give the injections. Patients always latch on to their nurses. It's a natural thing."

"No, it's more than that. I know you feel it too."

Eric doesn't know about Ofelia's boyfriend. He works at another of Doctor Milagro's clinics. They aren't engaged, and she doesn't really love him. They've been going out for quite a while. Her parents like him. A relationship with Eric would complicate things. Ofelia isn't afraid of complications, but she's been warned about the risks of getting too close to patients. The ill, like newborn chicks, are prone to fall in love with whomever they first see when they open their eyes.

"You're a special patient, Eric."

Ofelia was strongly tempted to skirt the rules, but she knew that the wrong move could destroy everything.

"Is that all I am, Ofelia, a special patient? You have stronger feelings for me than that. Don't deny it. If Doctor Milagro's rules are keeping us apart, have Mida give me the injections. I don't want to be your patient; I want to be as close as we can be, as close as you want us to be."

He'd said it. The next move was up to her.

"You'll recover soon. You're looking better. When that happens you'll go back to your former life and we'll never see each other again."

"So that's what you're afraid of? Don't be so sure I'll leave. I think a lot these days about my former life. My life is much better now with you, even with the illness."

Ofelia gathers up her things to leave. Eric wants her to stay. He stares into her eyes. She stares back. She knows what he feels and what she feels. Where can it possibly go? She wants to cry, she wants to scream. She stiffens and silences her body and walks down the stairs in confusion.

Her smile gives Eric just enough hope. He thinks she'll come around, but the delay is horrible because it gives him time to drag out all his doubts. Each one claws and tears at the love he feels. He knows that reality doesn't coincide with the forecasts about it, that forecasts are often the opposite of what turns out to be the case. With perverse logic he starts to invent obstacles to their love, hoping the mere invention of such obstacles will prevent them from happening. Faithful to this feeble magic, he invents, so that they might not happen, the most outlandish arguments against the love he wants Ofelia to feel for him. Of course, the whole thing backfires. He finishes by believing his imagined obstacles are actually prophetic and is tormented by his thoughts.

"Do you remember that time I bribed you with a dollar to walk through the garage and tried to frighten you with the bogeyman?"

"Yes, I remember."

"What made you do it, how did you get through?"

"I wanted the dollar, so I did it."

"That wasn't really the reason."

"No. I wanted you to love me."

"I wish I could be like you."

"How so?"

"Unafraid to put my feelings out there."

"My life isn't so perfect."

"Nor mine."

30.

Professor Snipe

Devon waited outside Professor Snipe's office. A student emerged, wearing a long flowery dress and a pair of tan Birkenstocks. She glanced at Devon, then quickly walked down the hall and turned the corner. From inside the room, the professor called for Devon to enter.

"Thanks for meeting with me, Professor Snipe. I'm Devon Jennings. I was referred to you by Professor Verne Dahl in the Economics department."

Snipe thumbed through a report on his desk. He had a pointed nose, beady eyes, and ears that were too small for the head that rested atop of his long neck. His drab tweed jacket was strewn over a plush sofa, leaving only a hard chair for visitors.

"Verne? Oh, right, Laetrile." Professor Snipe was absorbed in whatever he was reading and didn't look up. "Hmm. Well, what do you think of spontaneous remission, Jennings? What do you think of diagnostic error? Better yet, as an economist, what do you think of the Hawthorne effect?"

Snipe sat up in his plush upholstered chair and looked at Devon. He rocked his chair from side to side while his bald head bobbled about on his neck.

"How do you mean?"

Devon had come to Professor Snipe in hopes of getting some information that would persuade Eric to return to a hospital in the States.

"Well, young man, patients can recover from cancer on their own for no apparent reason. Do you agree with me there?"

"That's quite rare, isn't it?"

"Patients can be misdiagnosed. When they recover from whatever ails them, they attribute their good fortune to the treatment they received at the time. Even a prominent scientist like Linus Pauling believes that nonsense about vitamin C. Do you follow me, my boy? Why, sometimes just paying extra attention to a patient can have a positive effect, like the change in work habits at General Electric that led to the discovery of the Hawthorne effect."

Snipe's office was a wasteland of discarded books and journals. He himself was the prototype of the absentminded professor. Still, he was *the* expert on Laetrile—a bit of a bumbling expert—an odd combination of the sublime and the ridiculous, like the philosophy professor who shows up to teach a class with jam all over his face.

"I don't understand, Professor. Are you telling me that the benefits attributed to Laetrile can be explained by such things as spontaneous remission and misdiagnosis?"

"We don't know, Jennings. We just don't know. It's a sign of advanced intelligence to be able to say 'I don't know' in the face of uncertainty, my boy. Too many conclusions are drawn on the basis of insufficient evidence. The data can be difficult to disentangle—too many statistical regressions without the brainpower to do a proper analysis, the kind of thing you do over in the Economics Department. Ha, ha! And another thing, the side effects of chemotherapy and radiation are horrible. When patients stop this type of treatment, as many do when they run off to Mexico for Laetrile, there is going to be a period of time when they feel better simply because those side effects retreat. The federal and state governments haven't a clue how to handle this Laetrile nonsense. The demand for Laetrile has mushroomed even though it's worthless and dangerous. Curiously it's an issue that unites the far right and the far left. Eisenhower would never have allowed such a thing happen, but he's gone, and a bunch of goofballs run the government today. Laetrile has become the poster child for desperate cancer patients and for those who enjoy sparring with our baffled elected officials. Enforcement of the current laws is next to impossible."

Professor Snipe stopped swiveling in his chair. He put his elbows on the desk and rested his face in his hands. His beady eyes shot right through Devon.

"Is it really your opinion that Laetrile is worthless and dangerous?"

"I don't know," Snipe replied. "You see, I'm not afraid to admit that, son, not at all, but my opinion, if that's what you ask for, and I should tell you an opinion is not a fact, but for what it's worth my opinion is that the evidence does seem to lead in that direction. If I may ask, what's your interest in Laetrile? Are you planning some type of economic study? I could help you get hold of some interesting data that might help you sort things out."

"My interest is strictly personal. My brother, Eric, is currently at the Clinica Buena Salud in Tijuana getting Laetrile treatment for his colon cancer."

"Good God, my boy! Talk some sense into him. Get him into a legitimate hospital like Stanford or the UC Med Center, some place where they pay attention to the evidence."

"That's just it. He walked out of Stanford after two discouraging weeks. His cancer is inoperable. He felt he was abused in the interests of science. He refused the radiation and chemotherapy and opted for these alternative therapies. I've been down to see him. He's very stubborn."

Professor Snipe closed his eyes and took a minute to gather his thoughts. When he finally spoke he sounded professorial. "Your brother has a point, my boy. Yes, he does have a point. Those research hospitals, they're always setting up obstacles to jump over to justify their grants, you see. They're at the cutting edge—my God we couldn't live without them, could we—but they do treat patients a bit like sheep. It just goes with the territory, I think. I can't recommend Laetrile as a reliable cancer treatment, but I can't entirely dismiss it either, can I? We don't have all the facts, but the ones we do have…

well, I've already given my opinion on that. Now, do you have any other questions? I have a class soon."

"What about Doctor Milagro? What do you know about him?"

"Ah, a charming Latin Casanova. He's very good, especially with the female patients, you know, they all love him, and then he's got God in his pocket just in case. Oh, I hope I didn't offend you, anyway, he claims great success, but he has very little documentation, my boy, very little. He's had some legal problems, quite rightly in my opinion, but, of course, I'm no expert on legal issues, far from it, but he's had a rough go after the Jinks affair."

"What was that?"

"My goodness, you haven't read about it? What's this world coming to with no one reading the news anymore, running off down to Mexico without even getting the facts. Oh, forgive me, it's just a pet peeve of mine, you're not alone, no one reads the news anymore. Mr. Jinks was an unfortunate young man who suffered from leukemia and was undergoing chemotherapy here in the States. He responded well to the chemo, but his girlfriend—they're always the ones to make the trouble, aren't they—his girlfriend wanted him to try the Laetrile she'd heard about from her dentist. Imagine that, a dentist giving advice on cancer, he wasn't even an orthodontist. So, off they went to visit Milagro last year. The facts are murky. The couple claimed Milagro took Jinks off the chemo. Milagro insisted it was the girlfriend who wanted to stop it. There you are, those facts again, so difficult to untangle. No wonder they all ended up at the attorney's office.

The illustrious doctor said he advised using both. Whatever the truth, Jinks died shortly after being treated at Milagro's clinic. Jinks's family got it all over the news, and there was a big stink. It isn't possible to lay blame, of course, it never is, is it? Milagro's reputation suffered, but he still packs in the faithful, a true Mexican phoenix. Oh, the power of faith, my boy, it can move mountains, or so I've been told. Anyway, Jinks's parents brought a lawsuit against Milagro. It was settled out of court. The whole thing died down quickly after that, so I guess I can't fault you for not having read about it, especially since you're an economist. Ha, ha! That's a joke, son; no disrespect to the economists, but they don't read much outside their field, do they? I hope you haven't picked up that occupational hazard. Professor Dahl and I get on quite well, but he's completely focused on the dismal science. He's a math guy, loves the chalkboard. In another life he might have gone in for whimsical machines and moons like Paul Klee, but he uses his squiggly lines and numbers to decipher the economy. I guess you probably know that already."

"My brother's an attorney. He's smart and talented. He had... has... a great career ahead. I don't want to see him die unnecessarily because of an emotional decision to chase down a quack treatment. I don't know how to help him. He seems very determined. What do you think about the claim that Laetrile is a natural cure? Is it true that some natives in remote areas who only eat seeds and fruits full of natural Laetrile never get cancer?"

"Such fantasies are the stepchildren of the idealistic philosophers like Rousseau and Gauguin and other such dreamers. One died of a hemorrhage while walking in the woods, the other of syphilis while dallying on the beach. Nature can be very dangerous, my boy. Cancer is a disease of old age, you see. Your brother is an unfortunate exception. Most people die of other diseases long before cancer gets around to paying them any attention. That's especially true for the primitives who inhabit those lands of nostalgia, areas where most die of completely preventable maladies owing to the lack of basic medical attention. When the statistics are tallied correctly, those who do live longer get cancer at the same rate as the rest of us. Be assured, I've had the number crunchers work that out for me."

Professor Snipe pushed his chair back and stood with his hands on his desk. "You may not remember that tuberculosis was incurable at the turn of this century. It was commonly believed at the time that sanitation, sun, fresh air, rest, proper food, and better personal hygiene could prevent or cure it. Of course, none of these so-called *weapons* were of any significance, as you can well imagine, my boy. It was the antibiotics discovered later that eradicated TB, wasn't it? I'm afraid I don't have much faith in the healing power of ground-up apricot pits."

"But, Professor, we don't have any reliable cure for cancer, do we?"

"We have no cure as yet. The tragedy is that people who have nothing to believe in will believe in anything."

"Under normal circumstances, Eric would never have gone off to Mexico like this, to some crazy clinic for a bogus treatment." Devon threw up his hands in frustration.

"Ah, but you see, my boy, here is where I can put on my other hat, being a man of many hats, of which I am quite proud. I wouldn't try too hard to change your brother's mind or feel too bad about failing to do so. Let me tell you a dirty little secret about the medical profession, son: They don't eat their own cooking. I had a good friend, a highly respected orthopedist, a mentor of mine who discovered a lump in his stomach. It was a complete surprise, as such random tragedies often are. He had a surgeon explore the area, and the diagnosis was pancreatic cancer. The surgeon was the best in the country; he'd even invented a new procedure for that very disease, a procedure that could triple a patient's five-year survival statistics from 5 percent to 15 percent, but with a poor quality of life. Now, let me tell you about my friend. He was brilliant, a medical genius. He read everything about his disease. Then he made a decision that surprised all of us. He was not interested in the treatment offered by the surgeon. He went home and closed his practice the next day. He never set foot in any hospital for the rest of his life. He focused on spending time with family and feeling as good as possible. Several months later he died at home. He never got chemotherapy, radiation, or surgical treatment. Now, what do you make of that, my boy? Sounds crazy, doesn't it? My point is, how can you know what you would do under similar circumstances? How can I know what I would do? Ultimately, it's up to each of us to make our own decisions about life and death."

"I'm sure Eric has good reasons for his decision, but I want to help him get well. I'd feel I was letting him down if I didn't try to change his mind."

"Don't beat yourself up. You said he was a smart young man. Give him a little credit. We each make our own sandwich, and we have to eat it. Can't blame it on anyone else, can we? If we make tuna fish and find out later that we hate tuna fish, well, we just have to eat it anyway or starve. It's the way things work, my boy, just the way they work."

"But what about a change of mind?"

"Your best course of action, in my personal opinion, is to support your brother in his decision. Allow him to enjoy what life he has left as he chooses. He'll figure it out. He might change his mind, but it's up to him. It isn't up to you and it isn't up to me. There isn't any better advice I could give you. I've enjoyed speaking with you, but now I must leave for a class."

Professor Snipe took Devon out into the hall, turned quickly to the left, did an abrupt about-face and walked off in the opposite direction.

Devon was confused. He'd expected Snipe to give him a list of persuasive reasons for Eric to return to the States for conventional treatment, but the meeting turned out quite differently. At a loss for what to do next, Devon walked through the campus and came upon a large fountain he'd never seen before. In luxuriant wastefulness, a bulldog was biting great chunks of water and letting it dribble back out of its mouth. Devon stood and watched till the dog had drunk its fill and wandered off alone.

Devon went home to pack for a second trip to Tijuana. This time he was going to stay and see things to the end. Mia and the girls were gone. He hoped the time apart would give them both an opportunity to think things through. He missed Margot and Shawna, but Eric had to be his priority now. The cancer was quickly eating through his brother, erasing the time they had left together. The past played back in Devon's mind like a defective slideshow with the key scenes missing. At the end of the reel, the pictures stopped. Devon wanted to see the future. Just when you want to see what comes next, everything goes black.

31.

A Dream

Ofelia is gone. Eric slumps in his chair and tries to remember her smell, the warmth of her body when she drew close to give the injection, her eyes, her smile. The sun sinks a quarter degree per minute.

Every action leaves a line in the brain, creates a life of its own. The lines divide the brain into separate histories, which sit like ornaments on a tree, each with a purpose of its own, each with a story to tell. The air is still. Thoughts roll along like rocks at the bottom of a stream, made visible by the rays of the sun and distorted by the water.

A distant raven caws while Eric savors Ofelia's scent on his arm—proof that she was there. Intellectual honesty is impossible between lovers. The heart messes with the brain. Eric was in new and unfamiliar territory.

"I can make you better, Eric. Do you believe that?

"Yes, Doctor Milagro, I believe it."

"Good. Together we will fight, you and I. Together we will beat the cancer. It will know it's finished when it feels our resolve. Do you trust me? Will you fight with me?"

"Yes. I know you can make me well."

From its perch in the future, death laughs at life, at the odd joke, at the puzzle with its pieces strewn all over the floor.

32.

Doctor Rice

"Doctor Rice, thank you for taking my call."

"I have your brother's file on my desk."

"Eric is in Mexico where he's taking Laetrile and undergoing alternative therapies for his cancer. I'm trying to get him to return to the States to undergo radiation and chemotherapy as you suggested. I'm afraid he's stubbornly against the idea. What's your thought on these alternative therapies? Is the prognosis really that much better if he stays at Stanford?"

There was a silence before Doctor Rice answered. "In the medical field it sometimes looks like there's a simple solution to a complex problem. That's what the patient most hopes for. It's usually wrong, but that seldom stops people from giving it a try. Laetrile has no proven medical value. With proper treatment, your brother could live for several months, perhaps a year, possibly longer. There have been some cases of complete remission, but I wouldn't want to create false hopes. Every day, better drugs are developed and the options widen. We offered Eric an experimental treatment that has shown promising results. He walked out of the hospital before giving this any serious consideration. We were very disappointed with his sudden and unexpected departure."

"I agree it would be best for Eric to return to the hospital, but I'm not sure how to persuade him. His mind is made up. Frankly, he couldn't tolerate the pain and the constant testing."

"Eric's condition is not hopeless. While there may be complications from the treatments, we have remedies for them. Those extra months we might be able to give him would be very significant for someone in his situation. Laetrile is nothing but quackery. Your brother will make his own decision. Neither you nor I can force him to return. Unfortunately, his cancer will progress further while he's in Mexico. By the time he decides to come back to Stanford, it could be too late for us to help him."

Devon was devastated by these words. He felt such an obligation to do the right thing but the right thing was anything but clear to him. He kept hoping there was some in-between solution, some compromise where both treatments could work together to cure Eric.

"I'll keep working on him, Doctor Rice. Thank you for your opinion. I have two more questions: Could Eric continue his Laetrile treatments while taking conventional therapies at the same time? Can you refer me to a doctor in San Diego, closer to where Eric's currently living?"

"Laetrile is illegal in the United States. We can't treat him while he's taking an illegal drug. There is one doctor in San Diego who might be able to help you. I'll send you a letter of recommendation. I consider the idea of pursuing both treatments at the same time medically unsound. You must understand that Laetrile is not only worthless but dangerously toxic because of its cyanide content. There are no set standards for the manufacture of Laetrile, and no way to know the actual makeup of the serum from one batch to another. What we do know is that all the various serums tested to date have proven ineffective and dangerous. If Eric were my brother, I would discourage any further use. Sometimes personality conflicts develop between doctors and their patients. If Eric were to return to Stanford, we would have another doctor take over his case. The doctor in San Diego can explain all this to you. For Eric's sake and for yours, I hope you're able to change his mind. He's a very intelligent and sensitive young man. I wish you and him the best."

Devon put down the phone. He was packed and ready for Mexico. He knew it was unlikely he could change Eric's opinions, but he might convince Eric to see this doctor in San Diego to get a second opinion. That'd be a start.

A few weeks earlier, in Sacramento, Eric was reading in the dark back room behind the kitchen in his father's house when Devon entered. They talked about football and Berkeley, the last real conversation they'd had before the diagnosis changed everything. Later, at the hospital, they'd sat for hours and seldom talked at all. Through the window they watched birds land on the grass, what little grass there was around the building. A young boy bounced a blue and white ball against a cement wall. The ball swished back and forth in a series of parabolas. A nurse walked out. The stern look in her eye made it clear she was no one to argue with. She told the boy to stop. He didn't, of course, and she grasped him tightly by the neck using her right arm, lifted him off the ground, and carried him inside. He howled in pain. She looked toward Devon and grinned as she dragged the boy into the hospital, apparently enjoying the moment.

A few days after that, Eric had flown to Mexico. Now Devon was on his way there again, this time to stay. He was going to see this through to the end. Who knew the real facts, the real answers—Professor Snipe, Doctor Rice, Doctor Milagro? Sometimes you do something and you don't know where it will lead, but you keep doing it, doing something, because you must do something.

33.

Dinner with Ofelia

A world goes on at the horizon, a parallel universe. Eric sensed it even though he couldn't see it. Thoughts worked their way to the edge and back again, flowed like waves in a pool, emerged out of a singularity, a steady stream of waves, each with a message working to get through.

A green grasshopper jumped onto the railing. Some mangy flies, wings too large for their bodies, discovered a hole in one of the posts and began to build a nest—their private sanctuary away from danger. Near the roof, a furry black bee danced to imaginary reggae music. A lazy sun took its time to set. A lonely b-a-a-a emanated from the goat tied up across the way—a prisoner protesting in its cell.

Orvaline's younger brother, Osvaldo, was helping one of Mr. Cabrera's men with their five cows. Giant horseflies attacked the animals mercilessly when the weather was hot and there was no wind. To provide some relief, Mr. Cabrera had his men walk the cows along the beach late in the afternoon when a breeze came off the ocean. It gave the cows a chance to fight off the flies with their tails. Eric laughed aloud when he'd first witnessed the majestic promenade along the beach, little children running back and forth between the cows, playing catch me if you can. Watching the cows' tails swish at the flies transported Eric back to an earlier time. He was wistful and sad. A train ran through fields and woods and towns and painted stations. The quickly changing panorama created a sense of moving swiftly through time. Hurled forward, aware only subconsciously of the flight he was on, he forgot for a moment the actual trajectory of his life.

"Eric! Are you ready for dinner?"

Ofelia's call from the bottom of the stairs ended this little reverie. He was anxious to see her.

"I'll come downstairs to eat in the garden."

People seldom wonder why they wake up each morning and go about another routine day. They abandon themselves to habit. Like the ant, they collect. Like the spider, they spin. Death is not very likely before old age, so people fall into the bad habits of assuming they'll live forever and living with no sense of urgency. They use their precious time poorly. Like useful bees, some collect, transform and give back. Others, no more than larvae, crawling, wriggling, eating— live in two dimensions and die unchanged from the day they're born. A few transform and take a single flight before they settle down to live as ants. The lucky ones go through changes like the lowly caterpillar, which turns itself into a butterfly and soars into the sky.

Eric sat at a table built from the trunk of a coconut tree. Orvaline had a talent for building things—tables, beds, even the palapa where Eric lived—all out of local materials abundant on his parents' property.

Eric strove to contain his excitement when Ofelia arrived with his food. He didn't want to look foolish or too eager. The relationship with Ofelia had started to blossom, but he still had much to learn about how to act around women, especially one he was in love with. An orange sun settled over the fronds of the palm trees.

"Will you sit and talk while I eat?"

"Of course, Eric. No one should eat alone. It's bad for the digestion."

Ofelia wanted Eric's company as much as he wanted hers. She'd come to depend on their conversations for the excitement otherwise lacking in her life. When she'd first met Eric, he was distant and withdrawn. She watched him open as they grew closer. It pleased her that he shared his private thoughts.

"Tell me, Ofelia, what do you call someone like Mida in Spanish? She never stops talking. She's as noisy as a parrot when I'm with her."

Ofelia laughed. "A *guacamaya*. I think, in English, it's called a macaw. Don't be put off. Mida has a good heart."

"Oh, I know that. I like her a lot, but sometimes, as we say in English, she drives me nuts."

Eric's eyes twinkled as he spoke. It cheered Ofelia to see him happy.

Eric was drawn to the reflections of the sun in Ofelia's eyes. He sensed he was beginning to win her over.

"She's wise like a crow."

"What do you mean?"

"Have you ever watched a group of crows dance in large circles, one hops in, another hops out as if they're having a powwow? Crows can be sassy and bold. They can also wreak havoc by pillaging and plundering, but they're very intelligent birds. They can be funny and clever and compassionate. Mida may ramble on endlessly like a guacamaya, but in her heart she's a crow. I've seen the way she treats the patients. Old or young, man or woman, she gives them all her love."

"I like how you accept life as it is and adjust. I'm always trying to control and change it."

"Don't make yourself sound like an engineer. Control and change have their place, but stoic acceptance creates the deepest insights. I'm sure you know that. It's the reason the past has such magical power. We can't change it. The beauty of its motionless and silent pictures glows golden against the sky like the leaves of autumn."

"That's a beautiful way to put it. You make me so happy when I'm with you."

Ofelia didn't want to wait any longer. She thought she would die if he didn't kiss her. "You must know how I feel," she said. "I invited you here because I like being with you. I hope I'm not being too bold in saying that. Sometimes I'm afraid I like you a little too much."

Ofelia blushed and turned away.

Eric was astounded. Did she actually say she loved him? He rose out of the chair. He watched her eyes. She didn't back away when he approached. He took her in his arms and kissed her on the lips. She kissed him back. Surprised and shocked, neither knew what to do next. Ofelia stepped back, wobbly. Eric reached out to steady her. He couldn't decide if she was happy or unhappy. He hoped he hadn't botched everything.

Ofelia was usually not unsure of herself, but now, had she let him to go too far too soon?

"You'll get your miracle, Eric. I have to leave now to help my mother."

"Come back tonight so I can see you."

"Not tonight; I'm needed at home. Tomorrow."

"But I won't be here tomorrow. Father Jordan is picking me up first thing in the morning."

"Father Jordan? I didn't think you were religious."

"I'm not. He wants to take me on a trip."

"A trip? Where?"

"He mentioned En Ninguna Parte."

Ofelia burst out laughing. "Eric, in English, that means nowhere."

"Huh?"

"Nowhere, Eric. That's where Father Jordan says you're going."

Eric looked as if he'd sat on a pin.

"Well, the joke's on me, I guess."

Ofelia giggled and walked away. She could only think of him as she left. She wanted to kiss him again. She felt him all over her skin. She wanted to be free, to free her emotions, to expose everything she kept inside. He was handsome and he made her heart leap, but she didn't love him only on account of his face. Love on the surface alone can't last, because the surface won't last. Her love for Eric had burrowed deep inside her.

Eric felt an unfamiliar mix of delight and torment, happiness and pain. She left him just when he wanted her to stay. Had he made a mistake? No, she'd kissed him back. Why did she leave, then? This whole business of love was so impossibly complicated.

How long have you been here?

A day, or part of a day. I remember when I first saw you.

She blushed. I must be on my way, Mr. Martin.

33.

Devon in San Diego

The drive south was long, hot, and boring, up and down through hills and towns, monotonous stretches between. Devon's engine roared the familiar refrain of those he loved: *Eric, Mia, Margot, Shawna; Eric, Mia, Margot, Shawna.*

He used the time to mull over the advice he'd received from Professor Snipe and Doctor Rice. He'd done some research on his own in Berkeley before leaving, but the more he learned the further he seemed from his goal of finding an argument that would persuade Eric to return to conventional care.

Eric, Mia, Margot, Shawna. Eric, Mia, Margot, Shawna.

Devon was headed to the Cancer Treatment and Cure Convention in San Diego. After that, he'd meet with Doctor Doggett. He hoped to find the magic bullet there. He didn't want to arrive in Tijuana without a clear plan.

The convention was held in the giant auditorium at the De Anza hotel. As he entered the hotel, Devon noticed a couple standing at the front entrance. They looked as lost as he was. The woman suddenly got her bearings, broke into a smile, and showered the man with enthusiastic compliments. "Oh, darlin'! Thank yoou! I just knew it. I knew from readin' that article in *Woman's Day* the doctor was wrong. Look at all these nice people here. These are my breasts and it's my life and I'm gonna find out how to fix 'em the way I want without that nasty ol' surgery. Oh, honey, you just wait an' see! You're gonna be sooo happy we didn't listen to Doctor Peavey."

Her husband wore a cowboy hat and boots. His face lit up when his wife threw her arms around him and gave him a bear hug.

"Oh, honey baby! Thank yoou! Thank you for bringin' me down here! I know we did the right thing. My hope and salvation is right here in this auditorium, and we're gonna find it. Yes, we are!" She galloped off ahead of her cowboy, and Devon never saw them again.

Rival healers were set up in booths all around the auditorium. Every imaginable alternative treatment was represented. In the immediate vicinity of the door Devon saw booths promoting cleansing programs, healing waters, bee propolis, massage therapy, laxative therapy, wheatgrass therapy, biomagnetic therapy, and iridology. Some of the booths were small; a single presenter stood or sat in a snug cubbyhole and handed out brochures. The really big companies had booths sprawling with multi-displays. An intense agoraphobia gripped Devon. He sweated and shook as he wove his way through the crowd.

He was about to leave the conference when two presenters waved at him to join them. Both were plump and jolly and wore matching Polynesian shirts in a rainforest design—a mass of green foliage interspersed with little blue, red, and golden frogs. They stacked up their boxes of rainforest supplements, boxes decorated in the same design as their shirts.

"You'll hear all sorts of contradictory advice around here, young man, but you only need to know one thing: Cancer is caused by toxic waste. Our rainforest supplements eat cancer cells. The scientists don't know how they do it. If they read their Bibles, they'd know. It's spelled out in Revelation 22:2."

Devon took the brochure. Over the jitters now, and ready to explore, he walked inside toward the other booths. An entire subsidiary group of products and services had grown up alongside the various cancer cures. One booth advertised life insurance for the terminally ill. In combination with the viatical settlements advertised at the same booth, the life insurance was designed to provide short-term cash to cover the costs of the cures, costs that health insurance would not cover. There were air ionizers, water distillers, and rows of nut grinders, peelers, slicers, blenders, millers, and mixers of all types to aid in the preparation of "God's natural cure for cancer."

Some of the vendors and attendees walked around wearing last year's pink T-shirts with *Just Cure It* stenciled in green letters on the front and *The FDA Should Go Away* in black letters on the back. Others wore the new shirts handed out at the door, brown with yellow and green letters—*Fight Cancer: Eat the Seeds*.

Most attendees looked bewildered, but some faces lit up when they saw a friend they'd met at a past conference. A few political types had come to see and be seen. Most people stood in small groups and spoke about the one subject on everyone's mind.

"The first thing I did when they told me I had cancer was sit down and cry," said a timid-looking middle-aged woman who spoke to her friend. "My mother and two sisters had surgery for breast cancer. They both died later in a horrible way. I ignored mine as long as possible because I thought there was no hope."

"You've got to have a positive attitude and be strong, dear," said her friend. "If a wandering carcinogen happens by and sees an opportunity, he'll sneak inside you and set up house. You can't give him that chance."

The first woman began to cry. "I know, but I can't help it. These bad thoughts just take me over. I'm seeing a shrink. I hope it's not too late to turn things around."

Devon noticed that most people at the conference were white and conservative. Many looked like John Birchers. There was a whiff of religious fervor in the air. Plenty of country folk like those he'd grown up with were there, the kind of people suspicious of city folk, government bureaucrats, and so-called professionals. A few long-haired Birkenstock types were there too, but they looked out of place. Groups bunched together like competitive teams at a tournament next to the vitamin booths (*vitamins aid in disease prevention*), advertisements from local health food stores (*eat the best, leave the rest*), and chiropractors (*align yourself with health*). Placards and signs floated about in the air to remind everyone of the constitutional right to life, liberty, and the pursuit of happiness. Freedom of choice was a big theme here.

Devon quickly became disoriented by the circus unfolding in front of him. He spun around and collided with a man in tan shorts and a Hawaiian shirt.

"Confusing, isn't it, son?"

"Gosh, yes—low protein, high protein, vegetarian, non-vegetarian—how do you choose? I had no idea there were so many cures for cancer."

"Name's Jordan," he said, offering his hand. Devon was surprised by the firm grip.

"Hello. I'm Devon. Sorry I smashed into you. My brother's in Tijuana, taking Laetrile treatments for his cancer. I'm trying to find out more about it. Do you know where I can find the Laetrile booths?"

Jordan's blue eyes opened a little wider. "That I do, lad. I'll be happy to walk you over there. Which clinic did you say is treating your brother?"

"He's at Buena Salud with Doctor Milagro."

"My word! Would his name be Eric?"

The shock of surprise showed on Devon's face.

"How did you know?"

There was a twinkle in Jordan's eyes.

"You might not think it, son, but I'm a Catholic priest. I minister to the patients at Doctor Milagro's clinic. Eric's a grand young man. He told me his brother would be at the conference. He's looking forward to seeing you. He told me to say hello if we ran into each other, and that we have by the grace of God. He's looking better every day, your brother."

"I'm glad to hear that," said Devon. He was distracted by a man speaking with a psychotherapist at the next booth.

The man was thanking the therapist: "You know, my doctor says you're a communist, but you don't look like one."

Devon tried to refocus on Jordan. A few cigars stuck out from his shirt pocket. He certainly didn't look like any priest Devon had seen before. "Well, I'm pleased to meet you, Father. It's good to hear that Eric's improving, but I'm not exactly happy with his decision to go to the clinic. To give up on conventional treatment, well...to speak the truth, I'm very disturbed by it."

"Lots of my friends just call me Jordan, son. I don't know your thoughts, but Eric tells me he's uncomfortable with religion. I don't want that to come between us. Look, I can well imagine your concerns. I know about all the quacks and charlatans that prey on the sick. God knows they're everywhere. They're all over this place for sure—all you have to do is open your eyes and look around. I come here every year to gather information so I can steer people like you and your brother away from the obvious swindlers. Your skepticism about Laetrile is a reasonable response, but you need to gather the facts before you set your mind. Let me say, lad, I've seen positive results at the clinic. Laetrile has helped some, not all, of the patients. Each case is a bit different. Wait till you speak with your brother and Doctor Milagro. Listen to what they have to say, then you be the judge. Don't let the nonsense here at the convention prejudice you against it. There are many sides to the story. I suspect you've only heard the anti-Laetrile arguments. You should give the other side a fair shake as well."

They walked along together. Devon's skepticism grew as he saw one strange sight after another. A poster displayed on a large table read: THE FACTS ABOUT FLUORIDE. Next to a stack of brochures Devon saw a pile of white T-shirts with SAY NO TO FLUORIDE on the front. The "O" in fluoride was red with a large "X" inside.

"To tell you honestly, Father... I mean Jordan... I don't much like these odd remedies for the terminally ill. The victims of cancer should be with their families in real hospitals where they can get the best care offered by professionals using modern scientific methods."

"Remember, my son, Eric decided to go to Buena Salud on his own. Eric's no fool. I believe he thought long and hard before making that decision. He tried Stanford and rejected it. Modern doesn't necessarily mean best. We all know that many desperate and vulnerable people are taken advantage of by quacks with evil motives. Slick salesmen have been around since long before the time of Christ. Modern hospitals have them too."

Jordan stopped to pick up a brochure titled: "Do You Have a Carcinogenic Personality?" A spirited conversation was going on between the man behind the booth and a woman who had stopped by. "To be healthy, ma'am, you must think healthy thoughts all the day through or you'll face dire physiological consequences."

"I know," said the woman. "My heart goes out to those who have already produced cancer in their bodies. I hate to say it, but it's their fault. They created it."

"I'm offering this free handout, ma'am. It's a list of happy phrases to recite whenever you feel low. I call it The Cancer Prevention Cheat-Sheet."

Jordan took Devon by the arm and pulled him away from the table.

"Once these folks reel you in, they'll badger you till your ears burn! Look, son, we both know there are plenty of unscrupulous people, motivated only by greed, who sell useless remedies just to make a buck. Not all of the people here are like that, o' course. Some are taken in by their own propaganda; they sincerely think they're helping. As for your brother, he's smart enough to make good choices."

They passed a booth promoting organic health foods. Devon accepted a brochure that read: "Food low in nutrients will have the same long-term effects on the body that used oil does on the automobile—lower performance and greater wear and tear." A pretty girl handed one to him. Her green eyes were accentuated by large-rimmed glasses, giving her a wholesome, studious look. She was tall, with long, straight brown hair tied back behind a horsey face, and had a great tan. You might think she'd just walked in from the farmer's market wearing her dark blue apron with the ID badge that proclaimed in large block letters that she was Ramona Carson from La Buena Organica Co-op.

As she spoke, her green eyes sparkled. "You are what you eat, you know that, don't you?"

"I guess so," said Devon. "*Der mensch ist was er isst.*" It was the only German he knew. He wondered if it was to be taken literally. His wife, Mia, ate only fish, mostly shrimp. Did that mean multiple antennae would soon be sticking out of her hair? He chuckled at the thought. What if you ate a little of everything—meat, vegetables, fish? Would you become some bizarre chimera, half horse, half pig?

The girl thought he was laughing at her. "What was it that you said?"

"Oh, just a German phrase I picked up."

"Well, dietary deficiencies arrive primarily from eating less-than-whole food." She gazed at him provocatively as she spoke. "This is why the federal and state governments have mandated the artificial enrichment of white flour. How silly is that? We put good food through a process that destroys all its essential nutrients, and then, forced by government dictates, we restore some of the things that have been processed out. That's just totally crazy, don't you agree?"

She was cute. Devon liked the attention. He wasn't impressed with the arguments, but he led her on as if he were in agreement.

Jordan watched from a distance, amused.

"You see, there's absolutely nothing we can do to alter the infinitely complex machinery of life. All we can do is supply the missing components and hope for the best. Imagine you're out on the freeway in a Cadillac."

She marched along behind the table, moving her arms as if steering a car. When she bent down to pick up the pencil she'd dropped, her skimpy yellow shorts rode up in back. Devon had a revealing look at her long, slender legs and the curve of her butt. She had his full attention.

"The hood is locked and you're out of gas. All your knowledge of mechanics isn't going to help. All you need is to pour gas in the tank, step on the starter, and hope the gas gets sucked into the carburetor and the engine works as designed."

She was vertical again, her face a little flushed from bending over. "When the machinery of the cell begins to falter or fail, you do the same thing. You put in those factors normal to the operation of the body. You don't try to tamper with God's machinery."

She seemed satisfied with her recitation. Devon wondered how often she'd told the story and whether she always dropped a pencil when a man was on the other side of the table.

He tucked the brochure into his pocket. "Thanks. I'm sorry, but I've got to move along."

He wondered what she would make of Jerome Rodale of *Prevention* magazine. Rodale had died of a heart attack on *The Dick Cavett Show* last year, right after saying he was going to live to over a hundred. Who really wins the race, the Paleolithic meat eaters or the Neolithic cereal eaters? Throughout history the masters and lords, the warriors and rulers, have all been meat eaters, while those who lived on roots and tubers, potatoes and maize, turnips, carrots, and cabbages and a few nuts and berries had to supplement their insufficient diet by chewing on coca leaves.

As Devon continued along with Jordan, they passed two men discussing prostate cancer. The larger of the two said, "Remember that shrink who claimed regular orgasmic spasms of sufficient potency are essential to preventing cancer?"

"Oh, yeah," said the other with a grin. "Something about a connection to the healing rhythmic energy of creation!"

"I'm all for that!" said the first man enthusiastically.

"Me too!" said the other, and they slapped each other on the back.

"I think Eric's made a terrible mistake, Jordan. The doctors at Stanford offered him a new treatment that might save his life. He didn't even consider it. Instead he came down here hoping for some miracle. I can't believe the nonsense I'm hearing at this conference. Most of the people I see here are completely nuts."

Devon had to duck when two men walked through a side entrance carrying a podium, followed by two more with a microphone and speakers.

"You might expect a priest to tell you to put your trust in God and wait for the miracles, Devon. For sure, God does provide them, but he doesn't pass them around like rusks with the morning tea. Many Christians fall into the trap o' just waiting for God to do everything for them. God will provide according to His own will and in His own time. In this world, we must take responsibility for ourselves. You're right to be cautious. I see all the desperate people here. I agree with you that anyone with an illness like your brother's must be attentive and careful, but I also know that many o' the surgeries for cancer are a waste of time and energy and money. The treatment they offered Eric at Stanford was experimental. Medicine has no proven cure for cancer. At this stage it's all a guessing game. Desperate people will seek desperate solutions, sometimes without thinking them through, but that doesn't mean every alternative is worthless. I'm sorry your brother is ill. He's a fine young man—more than that, he's become my friend. You should recognize that even the best hospitals in America have no cure, nor do the clinics in Mexico. Each of us is called on to sort out the options for himself. Your brother made a choice. Let's give that some time. Things for him are beginning to change for the best in many ways. You'll see that for yourself soon enough, and draw your own conclusion."

Jordan walked Devon across the room to a row of tables. Approaching the podium was Mr. Laetrile himself, Doctor Elvin Krump. A crowd formed around him as he walked into the room, eager to hear him speak. Jordan whispered to Devon: "The man's an icon among these people. His father was the first to discover Laetrile's anti-cancer benefits. He's carrying on his father's work. Krump works with Russell Napier, who owns the company that manufactures the Laetrile for Buena Salud. I'm sure you'll want to hear him."

A tall man, a well-groomed reporter with a black beard, shoved a microphone in Krump's face: "Doctor, do you think Laetrile will be legalized in the United States?"

"I won't give up the fight until we win," answered Krump as he sauntered along. An attractive blond in a long purple dress walked with him. The two of them entered like royalty. Krump himself was pudgy, with a pasty complexion and straw-colored hair that hung on his head in a mass of waves and curls. He had the look of a powerful but befuddled Roman emperor. His loose white shirt puffed out around his ample waist, and his pale purple pants, a bit too long, poured down over his brown shoes. Sweat marks had formed on the back of his shirt.

Another reporter accosted Krump. "Is it true you're forming a committee to lobby Congress for legalization of Laetrile?"

"Senate hearings are scheduled. I'm not in a position to discuss the details at this time."

The woman with Krump tried to sweep a path toward the podium, but the group around him persisted. He had to push his way through.

"I've heard this speech before, Devon. By the way, there are three different types of Laetrile displayed on the tables over there." Jordan grinned. "You see, we have right-handed Laetrile for the John Birchers, and left-handed Laetrile for the hippies. Clinica Buena Salud uses the formula developed by Elvin Krump, which splits the difference right down the middle."

"I take it that's a joke, Jordan. The problem is, Eric's cancer is dead serious."

"In no way would I diminish the horror of Eric's disease, but there *are* different serums. I sense your unease, so I'm just tryin' to lighten the mood. Listen to Krump speak. I look forward to seeing you again at the clinic. I have to go now, son. I've got other business here."

Father Jordan left. Devon didn't see him again during the conference. Krump's speech could have become long and tedious had he not been unceremoniously interrupted. "It's certainly a pleasure to be here at the Cancer Treatment and Cure Convention," he intoned. "As I look back through time, I can recall the number of miraculous victories we've had in those intervening years. It's as true today as it was all those years ago that Laetrile is—"

"Meester Krump! Meester Krump! Doctar!" A small man in the crowd, with a voice that crackled as if it came through a bad radio connection, turned his head from side to side as he tried to lock his squinty eyes onto Doctor Krump, who avoided the man and went on speaking.

"Every chronic metabolic disease that will ever be controlled by man must be controlled by means that are a part of the biological experience of the organism. When we are eating less than adequate food, we know better, and when we continue, we are engaged in sin. This is the basis for practically all of our physical, mental and spiritual difficulties. And, when we develop cancer we will receive the results of this transgression in the old fashioned Biblical sense— the wages of sin are death."

"Meester Krump! I beg of you, pleeze hear me. I have evidence, evidence I say, that your Laetrile is not the recipe your father perfected. It lacks certain—"

One of the conference organizers approached the little man and took his arm to lead him away. The crowd was getting impatient. Some yelled, "Let him speak!" Others wanted him removed. "Get that troublemaker out of here!" "He's a government plant!"

The man shouted in desperation as they led him off: "I have evidence, I say! A few vials... a lost formula... pleeze, let me speak. I obtained them from a healer in the remote mountains outside—" Before he could say more they dragged him away.

Devon thought the man had been treated unfairly, and wanted to hear him out. Maybe there was something to his story, something that could help Eric.

Krump picked up smoothly as if nothing had occurred. "Let me give you a categorical or axiomatic truth to take with you, one that is totally uncontradictable, scientifically, historically, and in every other way: No chronic or metabolic disease in the history of medicine has ever been prevented or cured except by factors normal to the diet or normal to the animal economy. Many erstwhile fatal diseases have now become virtually unknown. They have been prevented and cured by ingesting the proper dietary factors, thereby preventing the deficiencies that accounted for these diseases...."

The crowd around Doctor Krump eventually dwindled. They seemed an impatient bunch, and went off to other exhibits.

Devon walked outside the auditorium into the hot sun. He was happy to have met Jordan. He still questioned Eric's decision, but he'd heard the same advice from both Professor Snipe and now Jordan. This opened his mind to the idea that Laetrile might not be so crazy after all. There were no cures for Eric's cancer, even the conventional doctors had told him this. Stanford offered some unproven cure, but at what physical cost? Laetrile had been tested. The results had come up wanting except for one mysterious trial that Karen told him about. That left the door open—the door through his doubt. Who knew what lay on the other side, an enchanted garden or a deadly pit?

Devon's eyes had adjusted to the darkness inside the hall. He balked at the bright sunlight outside. He had to compose himself. Time to meet Doctor Doggett.

35.

Journey to the Mountain Village

Darkness, hopelessness, death. Before Eric awoke, he imagined an abandoned pile of daguerreotypes, a silent movie of his life.

Thump, thump, thump. Thump, thump, thump.

The crickets stopped, and the first birds of morning tested their voices. He heard a few cars with their sleepy drivers on the road outside. With quiet precision, one degree at a time, the sun rose and shot out the tiny photons of light that squeezed into his room.

A strange noise came from the corner, a rough, rolling, bouncing, followed by the sound of little feet running, a miniature Mesoamerican *juego de pelota* going on around him. He'd heard it before. He got out of bed and turned on the dim light, investigated the closet, and found nothing. He surveyed the room, opened the sliding door to the deck and looked out, but whatever was making the sound had vanished. Eric closed the door and walked into the bathroom. Periodically, the mysterious noise returned while he shaved, washed his face, combed his hair. He took another look around the room. Nothing. He brushed his teeth with the purified water in the pitcher on the sink, then dressed and went downstairs thinking about spirits and elves, and tried not to look foolish.

Orvaline was on the patio.

"There was a strange knocking around in my room this morning. Do you think it was a ghost?" Eric laughed uncomfortably.

"It's the squirrel. He has a small nest above your closet. Sometimes he comes to crack the nuts he stores there."

Culture, age, circumstance, naïveté—they all conspired against any strong bond between Eric and Orvaline. A tension persisted between them like the lingering odor of smoke in a room long after a fire. Irrevocably connected to everything that kept them at odds was the obvious unmovable wedge between them, Ofelia. Orvaline refused to accept the relationship; Eric would not back off.

"Well, that's a relief," Eric said, but he saw by the way Orvaline looked at him that something was up.

"Eric, I think you should know that my sister has a boyfriend. She's been going out with him for over a year. My parents expect them to be married."

Down snapped the iron trap of doubt, Orvaline's deliberate creation of anger and jealousy. Eric was stunned. Orvaline saw the opportunity, and twisted the knife. "I know you like her, Eric. She thinks she likes you too, but it's all wrong for her. She'll see that soon enough. I saw it when you first came here. I'm telling you the truth when I say I wasn't happy about it. It bothers me you're sick. I'll just say it: I don't want you to hurt her. You're an American living in the United States. She has her life, you have yours. She'll never move to California. Her family's here, her life's here, she belongs here with her people. Could you really live in Mexico? You haven't even thought about how the future could work. Don't ruin her life. My parents have traditional values. They will not let you take her away. Neither will Marcelino, who loves her. His name sounds Italian, but he's just another Mexican. He works in the lab at one of Milagro's other clinics. He's a good guy, but he'll be very jealous if he finds out the game you're playing, so watch your step. I thought you should know."

Orvaline stood silent and smug. It was obvious the revelation about Marcelino had planted a seed, a potentially poisonous seed that unsettled Eric.

Eric considered carefully how to respond. Orvaline was clear: He wanted the relationship to end. Ofelia had a suitor whom the family approved of; they did not approve of Eric. Eric chewed at the hair on the back of his hand while he worked to regain his composure and formulate a plan.

A gray squirrel jumped off the roof of Eric's *palapa* onto the broad, flat leaves of a large papaya tree, bounded along a limb, jumped into another tree, and scampered about changing direction half a dozen times before it disappeared into the jungle.

How Eric handled Orvaline's revelation would be crucial. Eric wanted to be open about his intentions without destroying the possibility of a friendship with Orvaline. He was angry with Ofelia. Why hadn't she told him about Marcelino?

"You're right, Orvaline. I haven't given enough thought to the future. Ofelia and I have feelings for each other. We're not playing a game. An honest relationship has developed between us. I'm not surprised you've seen it. You have your opinion, which I respect, but you must also understand that Ofelia has her opinion, and she will make her own decision. I appreciate your telling me about Marcelino. I would never hurt your sister or embarrass your parents. I have no intention of taking her away from you or her family. I've been acting instinctively without considering how complicated this could all get. I'll certainly think about that more carefully, Orvaline, but you can't expect our love for each other to just disappear because you're unhappy about it."

Orvaline knew he'd shocked Eric. It was what he'd wanted to do. He knew Ofelia was blinded by the novelty of an American swooning over her, like so many of his friends had been blinded by the promise of money and a better life up north. His own parents were impressed with Eric's career; held him up as an example for Orvaline to emulate. He hated that. Anyone could get an attorney's license, it wasn't such a big deal, but love, that was a big deal, that was family, children, life. He couldn't watch his sister ruin everything, ruin even him, for if she got married and went away, that's what would happen. Everything would change. He was proud he'd stuck up for his sister and parents. He was sure they would thank him one day.

Jordan arrived in a turquoise VW van. He was dressed in his usual khaki shorts and Hawaiian shirt. In the rear of the van there was a black-and-white Dominican habit along with a few things he'd packed for the trip.

Orvaline got in one final jab before Eric left. "So, you understand, Eric. Be careful. Don't make a mistake."

Orvaline walked back to his parents' house, pleased with himself. He hadn't convinced Eric to break off the affair, but he'd slowed things down. Orvaline was convinced that nothing had happened yet. Ofelia might be naïve around boys, but she was no fool. He was worried, though, when he saw how lightheaded and silly she was around Eric. Ofelia could be very stubborn when she got her mind set. Orvaline couldn't let her lose track of reality.

Eric walked to Jordan's van. His life had just been upended. How easy it is to twist and squeeze life into something different with a few words. *Screw it,* he thought. *I'm just going to enjoy the day.*

He would ignore all the worries, focus on the adventure ahead, and make the most of the day with Jordan no matter what. He could twist and squeeze on his own. *Thump, thump, thump. Thump, thump, thump.*

"Is something wrong, Eric? You look like you've been hit by a truck."

"You might say that. Look at you, with all your gear. What do you call yourself, Jordan, the Flying Padre?"

"Well now, I've always been a great fan of Sally Field. There was that famous line of hers on the TV show—how did it go? Ah! 'When lift plus thrust is greater than load plus drag, anything can fly.' I call my plane The Flying Anchor."

Eric climbed into the front passenger seat. He had a bag with juice, supplements, and some things Ofelia had packed for the trip. "That's an odd name. How did you arrive at it?"

"Well, when the engine stops, you see, the plane drops just like an anchor." Jordan spoke out of the side of his mouth as he chomped on a cigar. The startled look on Eric's face produced Jordan's familiar grin.

"You are a devil disguised as a priest, Jordan. You should be ashamed of yourself, taking advantage of a terminally ill man."

"Oh, I think you'll get over it."

Jordan navigated the Borges-like labyrinth of streets in and around Tijuana. He seemed to know just which alleyways to use to avoid the snarled traffic, and deftly avoided potholes big enough to bury a burro. Eric had seen little of Tijuana since his arrival; he'd spent most of his time at the clinic and the Cabreras', and looked forward to seeing more of the city and its surroundings.

"I understand you're taking me to nowhere today."

"What? Ah, En Ninguna Parte. I didn't know you spoke Spanish."

"I don't. Good joke, Jordan. Ofelia had quite a laugh at my expense when I told her. What do you really have in store for me? There isn't any plane, is there? You're going to drive up the mount and give me a sermon, right?"

"I have no intention o' preaching to you, Eric. I know your feelings about that. There *is* a plane and you'll soon be on it. We're going to San Kuuchamaa, a wee town in the mountains. Very interesting. The town was built with the wealth from the surrounding silver mines, but those were played out years ago. The Spaniards left. Not much remains now but a few poor Indians and *mestizos* who scrape together a life from the corn and chilis and vegetables they grow. It's a poor but proud community. I've ministered to them for years. I thought you might like to see it. Getting out o' the city and taking in some mountain air will do us both good."

Eric suspected this was more than a casual outing. Jordan wouldn't take him off like this without a reason. Eric was ready for an adventure. He was happy to get away from the routine of the clinic, and he had lots to think about before he confronted Ofelia with what Orvaline had told him.

There was more activity than Eric expected at this hour. There were rickety delivery trucks, bicycles with baskets bulging, several older-model cars, and lots of people walking. Most headed to the shops and stores and restaurants in and around Centro to make deliveries or begin their workday.

"I'm curious, Jordan. Is that your real name, or is it a religious name you chose? Priests do that sometimes, don't they?"

"My given name is Michael O'Connell."

"What caused you to choose Jordan?"

"I knew I wanted to be a priest from as early as I can remember. You may think it's quaint, but I'm a sucker for the Jesus story. Not the hellfire and brimstone, mind you. I've never been able to believe that God would command the impossible and then torture us for eternity because of the human failures he built into us. I became fascinated with Giordano Bruno, the sixteenth-century Dominican friar who so angered the ecclesiastical authorities with his ideas on the universe and religion."

Jordan was in his sixties, portly, but in good shape for a man his age. Eric figured Jordan had seen parts of Baja that few others see as he traveled around in his Flying Anchor. The sun came through the window and cheered him. He thought about the day ahead. Illness and love take their toll. He hoped he was up to whatever Jordan had in store for him.

"I began to consider Bruno a role model. I admired the man's independent spirit and intellect."

"Napier told me an old friend calls you Tartuffe. Are you really a priest, Jordan?"

"My word! Napier told you that, did he? My goodness! Oh, I'm a real priest, Eric, different from some I suppose, but that doesn't make me an imposter. It's none o' my intention to lead you or anyone else astray. That old friend of mine is the Mangy Parrot. I call him that because he reminds me of the main character in Lizardi's book of the same name. He's had a very interesting life. I want you to meet him sometime. Now, where was I?"

Jordan nearly ran the van off the road when Eric mentioned Tartuffe. How much did Eric know about Frieze, and how had he heard about him?

"You were telling me about Bruno." Eric noticed Jordan's discomfort at the mention of Tartuffe. Eric hadn't seen the play, but he knew Tartuffe was a trickster and not exactly trustworthy.

"Indeed I was. The upshot of it is this: Jordan is the English version of Giordano, and Jordan is also the sacred river of Judeo-Christianity. Such a charming coincidence, don't you think? There is a statue of Bruno in Mexico City. Have you been there?"

"No, I haven't."

290

"A shame. Anyway, when I first saw that statue with Bruno's penetrating eyes, they burned right into my soul. I heard: 'Listen, listen, if you have an ear. Think, think, if you are drawn. Wake, awake!' Right then I found my purpose in life."

"But Bruno was burned at the stake."

"Sure enough, he was. When he was alive, Bruno was full of marvelous ideas and very much loved by the people for his brilliant speeches. His popularity and new ideas frightened the Church authorities. I was drawn by his indomitable spirit and inquisitiveness. The Church's inability to understand Bruno, and its subsequent persecution of him, that was one of their great sins. Imperfect are we all, Eric, and prone to mistakes, from the lowest to the highest."

Tartuffe, Bruno... Eric began to see Jordan in a different light.

"So, they assigned you to Tijuana because you chose Bruno as your role model?"

"Since you're bent on it, I'll tell you the all of it. Sometimes the light plays above the stream while we keep our secrets under the surface. As you've heard, the Mangy Parrot calls me Tartuffe. It's true, I do have a double life. I have a secret, you see: a wife. Her name is Ana Luisa. We've kept it quiet, but the Church knows. They were embarrassed, so they sent me here to push me out of the way, hoping this old sinner would disappear. I suppose they regarded it as a punishment. They didn't know what God had in store for me. Being here became a great blessing, Eric—what a great, grand blessing this banishment has become."

The news made perfect sense to Eric. Now he understood why he was comfortable with this priest: Jordan was a normal human man with the same needs and desires as Eric's. He spoke the first words that came to mind. "I suppose a priest having a wife is better than a pope having a mistress. You're married, right?" Immediately Eric wished he hadn't said it.

Jordan smiled. Unburdened of one secret, he was ready to unload. "Yes, we are married, lad. Ana Luisa and I have a son. He's an attorney just like you. One reason I took such an interest in your situation here is that you remind me so much of him. He lives in San Diego. We get together as often as we can. Sometimes he brings his car down for the Tijuana Road Races. I want you to meet him, Eric. I think you'd get on well with each other."

"You really are full of surprises, Jordan. No wonder your Mangy Parrot calls you Tartuffe."

"Aye. We all have our secrets. I've made my peace with God. What about you, lad?"

Eric ignored the question. "I look forward to meeting your son, Jordan. If he's anything like you, I'm sure to like him."

"Two attorneys—young, smart, energetic—both single. He's a bit of a loner like you. Most think his real father was killed, and I'm ashamed to say I let the lie stand. Officially, I'm his godfather. A few close friends know the truth, but we don't speak of it openly. Lord help me, I love my family with all my heart, but it doesn't stop me from loving God or even the Church, and it hasn't stopped me from administering the sacraments, not yet."

Downtown, all the buildings were two stories, a shop on the ground floor, living quarters upstairs. There was a drugstore on every corner. They did a good business with Americans who came for items illegal up north. The ghostly groans of drunks, mingled with the smell of urine and beer, wafted over the cobblestone streets along with the rotting food and trash in the gutters.

Jordan navigated through it all until, with a quick final turn, they arrived at a tiny airstrip. There was a rugged dirt runway and a hut that Eric assumed was for storage. The large metal hangar where Jordan stored the plane was locked with several bolts and chains.

Jordan parked the van and unpacked some fuel cans. "Do you feel fit enough to help me carry these to the plane?"

"I think so." Eric hadn't slept well, and felt weak and tired. Orvaline's revelation rattled his brain. He sensed trouble ahead. Why hadn't Ofelia prepared him? He drank from one of the juice bottles he'd brought along, and washed down his morning dose of supplements.

After Jordan filled the gas tanks, he took off his shirt. Naked from the waist up, he was a sight to behold. He walked out onto the runway, his head bobbing on his long neck while his belly protruded. Eric held back a laugh. Jordan looked like a plucked turkey.

"What on earth are you doing, Jordan?"

"The Good Lord doesn't tend to the runway, Eric. I need to throw some of these larger rocks off to the side. They raise hell with my efforts to avoid a catastrophe taking off and landing. You could help if you want."

"You're kidding."

"Jolly well not. Thank the Good Lord for the exercise, my lad."

Jordan chuckled as he walked off and Eric followed. It took about half an hour to remove the rocks. Eric wasn't ready to bring up his discussion with Orvaline, so he returned to the Mangy Parrot. "You were going to tell me more about the Mangy Parrot, Jordan."

"The Mangy Parrot? My, my, indeed I was. Well, let's see, where to start? His real name is Frieze, Louis Frieze, a Frenchman."

"I supposed he was French, since he calls you Tartuffe."

"I first met Louie Frieze at the clinic. He supplied the Laetrile to the clinic then."

"Did he work with Napier?"

"Yes, but they had a falling out."

"What happened?"

Jordan headed for the plane and soon they were both strapped in. "Time to be on our way, Eric. I'll tell you more when we we're up in the air, but for now enjoy the takeoff. You might be in for a few surprises if you're not used to small planes."

"Surprises?" asked Eric. "Like what?"

"Oh, you never know when some silly animal is going to run out in front of the plane. It's usually not dangerous, but it can be a sight."

Eric looked down the runway. He didn't see anything, and wondered if Jordan was pulling his leg, but just as they were accelerating, the wheels bouncing up and down on the rough runway, Eric spotted a rabbit on the left. It stood there watching them. They passed it in a blink. Eric got the point.

As they lifted off, the engine vibrated so fiercely that Eric wondered if it was going to drop out of the plane. He looked at Jordan who calmly chewed on his cigar.

"No worries, Eric. Some vibration's normal."

"Some?" said Eric. "That's a lot more than the Beach Boys' *Good Vibrations.*"

"If my memory serves, that song was about a girl. Do you have something to tell me, Eric?"

Eric retreated back into his shell, mesmerized by the scene unfolding in front of him.

They banked to the left and rose up. Eric felt like a bird. He thought of Blake: *How do you know but ev'ry Bird that cuts the airy way, Is an immense world of delight, clos'd by your senses five?* His brother was always quoting Blake, a poet Devon came to love after being exposed to his poetry by an exceptional high-school teacher. Eric was exhausted but also exhilarated. He looked down at the tops of the palm trees, tiled roofs, tin shacks, and the crooked roads of Tijuana. "From up here you can sure see the expanse of the city," he said.

"Tijuana became a Mexican state in 1952 when you were a teenager."

"Right," said Eric. "I was just fourteen."

"The city has grown by leaps and bounds since then. First, it was the drugs and the sex clubs and the booze. Now it's the *maquiladoras,* those factories where big international firms hire cheap Mexican labor. The vice remains, but Tijuana has transformed itself into an industrial city. Lots o' people come here from southern Mexico hoping for a better life. Unfortunately, the Mexican malaise follows."

"How did the Mangy Parrot get here?"

"Frieze is the renegade son of a distinguished family in France, a country he calls the old land. A distant uncle, Joseph Louis Frieze, was one o' the first graduates of the *École Polytechnique.* Later he became a protege o' the famous chemist Berthollet. Louie inherited his uncle's love for science, but had to cut his studies short because of an argument with his father over a love affair. That's when he traveled to Mexico."

"What happened, did he marry the girl?"

"Oh, the heavens took no pity on that poor girl. I'm afraid she died. It destroyed Frieze. For a long time, he struggled to survive, then finally pulled himself together and resumed work as a chemist.

He developed his own formula for Laetrile. On your first night at the clinic, do you remember telling me how you heard about a more effective serum?"

"Louis Frieze?"

"That's the story, my lad—and that's why you must meet him. He's in hiding at the present time. The argument with Napier makes things risky for him. Napier's a fine chap, but his two partners, those Dos Negros brothers, they are a couple of bad eggs." At the mention of Dos Negros, Eric's ears perked up. Jordan continued: "Frieze doesn't know what might happen if they find him. My poor friend must stay out of sight."

There was some turbulence. Eric's stomach grew queasy. He feared he might vomit, but that soon passed and he started thinking about Ofelia. "Tell me about the Cabrera family."

"Very prominent Mexicans they are. Ofelia's great-grandfather, Silverio, was the brother of Abelardo Rodriguez. Now, there's a good story. Abelardo rose to the presidency in the mid-thirties. The dam and the new airport here are named after him. Silverio and Abelardo had a row. Ofelia's family didn't rise as high as Abelardo, but they are powerful in Tijuana. Ofelia's mother, Amelia, Silverio's granddaughter, had only one sibling, a brother, Luis. He was killed in an ugly bar fight. The incident was a double tragedy because the man who killed Luis had been the family's gardener for years."

Eric's stomach seized up when they hit more turbulence. Jordan steered right through it.

"Jordan, I need to ask something."

"Well, go right ahead, lad."

Eric kept his feelings hidden in darkness like an oyster's pearl. He added layer after layer inside the closed shell. Love now forced it open. This was the sort of conversation that did not come easily for him. "I suspect you know about my feelings for Ofelia?"

"Aye. The two of you seem very happy when you're together, Eric. It's a grand sight for an old man's eyes."

"Orvaline told me this morning that Ofelia has been dating a young man for a year. Her parents expect them to marry. Given my condition and knowing what I now know, I feel selfish pursuing her further, but I'm in love, Jordan, for the first time in my life. I don't know what to do about it. I'm sure Ofelia feels more than just friendship for me. She let me kiss her last night."

"Let me tell you, Eric, I don't think your illness has anything to do with it. Ofelia will make up her own mind. She's a smart girl. Love is one o' the best things that can happen to anyone, no matter the circumstances. You're not selfish to pursue her, son. Ofelia's a different person since she met you. I see her laugh all the time, and she looks so happy. Yes, I think Ofelia does love you. I see it in her eyes. Whatever relationship she had before doesn't matter. She can handle her parents, sure enough, but she needs to know your feelings before she can know her own. Tell her. Let her decide."

Eric sat back. The steady drone of the engine put him to sleep.

What you sayin'?

I love Ofelia, Nelson, but what if I die soon? Where would that leave her? I don't know what to do.

Nelson hadn't seen the Hispanic nurse around lately. He'd heard she was fired. He'd been told he was going to be fired too, but he wasn't going to let that stop him from taking care of the patients who needed him.

"Look at you, Jack. I thought you was an attorney, fixed up other people's lives. Now you jumpin' up and down and cryin', "I gonna die! I gonna die!" For Chrissake, remember who you are, man. Don't matter when you go, we all go sooner or later. What you needs is to make your life whole. If death take you, then you ready.

36.

The Mountain Village

Jordan steered the plane inland. The ocean gave way to trees and thick brush as the plane rose higher into the mountains that jutted up from the coast. Gray cliffs rose from the jagged canyons interspersed with desolate mountainous terrain. There was an occasional break in the pattern, where a stubborn farm held out against the persistent jungle. On a few of the highest mountains, communication towers had been erected. Narrow roads careened about the mountaintops and disappeared down into the forest below.

The landing was rocky, but better than Eric had expected. He was at ease even though he'd never before flown in a small plane. Jordan was a skilled pilot with years of experience flying around Baja. The runway was nearly hidden, a thin straight slice through the foliage. There was no sign of human life until Jordan and Eric exited the plane. A white Jeep emerged out of the lush green, a dark-skinned Indian at the wheel. Jordan tied down the plane, put on his black-and-white habit, and walked toward the car. A short Indian with an angular face stepped up to embrace him. They spoke in Spanish for a few minutes.

"This is Carlos, Eric. He speaks only Spanish and the local Indian dialect. He's a friend of my Ana Luisa, and he knows these mountains inside and out."

Eric extended his hand. Carlos grasped it with two small brown palms, his head bowed, oval eyes looking down at his feet.

"*Mucho gusto,*" said Carlos, in words barely audible followed by a series of deep coughs.

"Mucho gusto," replied Eric.

"Don't mind Carlos, Eric. He exhibits a bit o' timidity around strangers, but once he knows you, he'll fight like a little bull to extricate you from any trouble you might encounter in these wild parts."

Eric and Jordan took their seats. Carlos jumped in without opening his door. It was tied shut because of a broken handle. The Jeep zigzagged in and out for about twenty minutes along a narrow road leading uphill. The jungle brush parted and Eric saw the entrance to the small town. Cobblestones overgrown with moss encircled a grove of giant parota trees. Jordan asked Carlos to stop so they could get out and proceed on foot. He told Eric that two centuries earlier the Spaniards had promenaded into this town on horseback. The road had been much wider then, and people stood on both sides greeting the magnificent horsemen.

Today's entry was less majestic but still impressive. Purple-striped pipevine flowers grew out of thick long stems that encircled a mass of trees and ferns. All this vegetation encroached on the road, attracting big blue swallowtail butterflies. White stucco buildings with red tile roofs began to appear on either side of the road.

"Now, Eric, the people here are generous in their welcoming o' guests and visitors alike. Don't be surprised by what you see. I've come to love these people with all my heart. They're so isolated that many still speak their native dialect. Spanish is a second language. Some speak a wee bit o' the king's English. I'll endeavor to translate as we go along."

The silence was lucid, the air serene. Then that changed. Children appeared out of nowhere. Their parents ran out behind them to greet Jordan and Eric. Dogs barked. Jordan was surrounded by well-wishers. People knelt at his feet to confess their sins. Two older men roared in laughter, something about pulling his car out of a riverbed last year.

A young man approached. "Do you remember me? You gave me my first communion. Come to our home, have a beer."

A stout woman emerged from the crowd and offered Jordan some *chicharrones,* fried pork skin.

"You're not going to eat that, are you, Jordan?"

"You're always thinking o' disastrous results, Eric. You can't look a gift horse in the face and refuse the gift." Jordan pounced on the fried pork with a gusto that would have put Friar Tuck to shame. Eric politely refused. Feeling awkward, he asked Father Jordan to explain he was ill and on a strict diet.

The group quieted as a tiny old woman walked out of the crowd. Her eyes projected wisdom. She seemed to know that Eric was coming. Everyone parted to let her through. Eric looked quizzically at Jordan.

"There now, Eric, you are to go with her. Her name is Itandehui. She's the most famous curandera in all of northern Baja. I have arranged for a healing. No harm done, son. People come from all around, walking for days and weeks, to have her heal them. She'll take you to her home and give you a curing massage. Afterward, she'll give you some bitter tea. Drink it. I'll explain later. Don't worry. Go. God be with you. I'll meet you after."

"You set this up, Jordan?'

"Don't ask questions. Just go, lad. I'll explain later. I'm off to lunch with some friends."

Unsettled by this turn of events, Eric followed the old woman along a dirt road to a small shack on the edge of town. He smelled something like incense wafting through the air. The shack was little more than a hut made of branches and adobe bricks with a roof of thatched bark. A rickety wooden fence engulfed in vines separated the shack from the jungle. Unlike the other buildings in town, the hut was covered with leaves and twigs that had accumulated over the ages. Itandehui led Eric past the gate and through an opening covered by a large animal skin. He found himself inside a single dark room. He could see what must have been a kitchen in one corner where a trickle of light came through a pane-less window. There was a wood-burning stove with bundles of tied sticks alongside.

The dirt floor had been raked clean. A pile of corn husks sat in one corner. Dried goatskins had been placed on the floor. On the opposite side there was an altar against the wall, with a shrine of nested crosses and candles of various colors that gave off an eerie light, the only light in the room. Smoke from the incense on the altar permeated the atmosphere.

Itandehui motioned for him to lie down on the goatskins. Next to them, she placed a clay *olla* of burning sage leaves that filled the room with a different kind of smoke. She knelt beside him, pulled up his shirt, put her hands to his stomach, and held them there for a few minutes with her eyes closed. She started a somber chanting. The strangeness of it all put Eric into a sort of trance. He couldn't describe exactly how he felt, but he knew he was going to experience something entirely different from anything in his past.

Itandehui unbuckled Eric's pants and began to massage his upper abdomen with her thumbs, pushing his skin down slowly, then letting it snap back into place. He looked at her dark, wrinkled face and thought about the eyes of the woman he'd seen begging downtown. He'd given her only a small coin, and now wished he'd given more. He felt as if he had crossed the gulf between two separate worlds. Itandehui's eyes, like the eyes of that woman, pierced the outer layers of his body and touched the monster inside. Her hands worked its claws loose. He felt the monster shrink back. Eric was the beggar now, and she was giving him the gift of life.

Itandehui repeated the motion with her fingers again and again. Eric grew comfortable, relaxed under the effect of a very vigorous massage. Itandehui motioned for him to roll over onto his stomach. She rubbed along both sides of his abdomen, then his calves, with a similar top-to-bottom motion. She removed his shoes and massaged his feet. He heard the bones pop. *Where,* he wondered, *does she find the strength in that small body?* He felt awake inside a dream. Everything was magical and mysterious but completely normal.

Eric's thoughts wandered while smoke floated in the air. He lost track of time, and found himself in a curious place, familiar yet unfamiliar. Around the perimeter everything was black. A dim light encircled him.

There were banana trees. The monkey was there. A dead
butterfly rekindled into life and flew into a strange fig-like
tree that grew out of the crevice of a rock on the side of
a hill.

A voice came out of the darkness. "Whoever comes is sent
to me by God."

He saw his grandfather rise into the air like heatwaves
above hot pavement. His grandfather transformed into
a disembodied eye. The eye looked down at him. It grew
bright and moved about the dark room like a Chinese
lantern. The eye closed. Everything disappeared. A somber
silence was the last he remembered behind the locked door.

Eric's nostrils filled with smoke. Inside Itandehui's hut events
progressed silently and slowly like vegetables growing. Itandehui
finished the massage by pressing firmly along Eric's spine from top
to bottom. She ended each rotation by pulling at his skin and letting
it snap back. Eric fell back into a trance.

He floated along the corridors. He watched Nurse Marta
enter a secret room in an abandoned part of the hospital, a
small area tucked behind a stairwell. She had the only key.
With a Mona Lisa smile on her lips, she carefully unlocked
the door and entered, unseen and unheard except by him as
he hovered over her. He could read her thoughts.

She used this room to store her coveted stock of filched
medical supplies—things that were hard to find, always
scarce and on back order. She had a stash of special wound-
dressing kits, an extra EKG machine, a new blood pressure
machine, a variety of drugs and medications that were
usually locked away from the nurses, extra patient charts,
which she used when she wanted to reconstruct a patient's
history, incident reports that she could fill out to get her
enemies into trouble, a box of Sharpies never available
when you needed them to mark up the patients for their
tests and surgeries, extra boxes of pens and notebooks.

She looked moody as she surveyed the room, and swung
wildly back and forth between anger and joy. She thought

about how the patients, the doctors, and the other nurses talked behind her back. All she wanted was friendship and appreciation, but she got neither. The most upsetting thing this week was that young patient, Eric what's-his-name. He disappeared before she could work her designs on him. She vowed to find him. It was all she could think about.

She sulked while she admired the special things she kept in her room—a bizarre private collection of patient trophies and mementos.

When a patient slept, was confused by sickness, or died, she thought nothing of stealing locks of hair or vials of blood. Clothing with the strong scent of a hated patient, or the private articles of someone she fancied, were particularly valuable when she went to prowl for those who'd escaped her ward.

She was wild, different from any creature Eric had ever seen. She was wicked, but he also felt her vulnerability, and was surprised to see the sensitivity with which she fondled her stolen objects. She showed a tinge of grief when she crushed the watch she'd stolen from his room. She spoke in a garble of words he couldn't at first understand, the words of someone possessed.

"The poor man. It's for his own good. He doesn't know what he's done or what he needs."

Through her nostrils she exhaled loneliness, the demon that consumed her. She spit out pestilence from her mouth, twisted her nails into talons sharper than drills, and when, in her anger and despair, she made tight fists with her hands, drops of dark blood splattered onto the floor. She looked up and bared three sharp rows of jagged yellow teeth. She looked right at him but didn't see him.

Eric opened his eyes. He sweated and shook. He realized he'd been in a deep sleep. He couldn't move. He'd been covered with a blanket and was tangled up in it. He worked himself free and rolled onto his back. Itandehui emerged from a corner. She knelt beside him. She had some large green leaves which she placed on his lower stomach. She motioned for him to lie completely still. She pressed the leaves against his skin and held them there.

> She began to chant in words and tones that sounded like some ancient prayer. A great wind rose up, and the corn husks in the corner flew about the room. The candles on the altar went out. Eric became enveloped in a thick fog as the walls of the room dissolved. He felt hot stones pressing against his body, felt something enter his abdomen. It raced through his veins, through his heart and his head. It centered itself in his chest and then it left him.

> He looked toward his stomach. The soft green leaves had shriveled and dried into a fine white powder. Itandehui carefully brushed off the powder and collected it into a jar, which she sealed and set aside.

Eric was stunned. Nothing in life had prepared him for what had just happened. There was no rational explanation. Something cracked in the world he knew, letting in light where it hadn't been before. His body shook. He was suspended in space with no firm ground to stand on.

Itandehui gave him a cup and motioned for him to drink. He thought about Giordano Bruno: "Listen, listen, if you have an ear. Think, think, if you are drawn. Wake, awake!" Itandehui watched him drink the thick dark liquid in large sips. It was very bitter tea. When Eric finished the tea, Itandehui motioned for him to lie down, She put the blanket over him, moved to the corner, and sat on the reed mat, her legs crossed and her hands on her lap. She closed her eyes while Eric dozed off again.

When he awoke, his eyes had adjusted to the darkness of the room. He was able to see things he'd missed when he first came in. On one was a shelf with piles of dried leaves and powders. There were feathers and small bones and buttons, a few clay ollas, and gourds, reed baskets, and abalone shells filled with dried herbs.

Father Jordan arrived. "If you're able to get up, you may need the toilet. It's out back through that open door over by the stove. I'll meet you out front when you're done." Eric walked out through the back of the cottage. Itandehui was nowhere to be seen.

Before they left, she appeared out of the shadows and gave them a plastic jug full of liquid. Eric wanted to pay her. Jordan said it wasn't necessary.

"What's going on, Jordan? That has to be the strangest thing that's ever happened to me."

"Now, mind my words. The jug contains some of the Mangy Parrot's Laetrile. It will help you, Eric. I'm no doctor or scientist, but I've seen the results. I pray every day that Louie Frieze will change his stubborn mind and make his serum available to more people. Right now he only provides his serum to Itandehui and a few other healers. He's angry and afraid after the events with Napier and Krump."

"How can you work with the clinic if their Laetrile is worthless?"

"It isn't at all worthless, Eric. It's all we have unless Louie changes his mind. Napier and Doctor Milagro do their best. Elvin Krump's serum is better than no Laetrile at all."

"Maybe I could set up some legal arrangement to protect Mr. Frieze and his discovery. Things are moving very fast for me, Jordan. I'm not sure what I think about all this. It's peculiar and strange. It was an enormous leap for me to move from Stanford to Clinica Buena Salud, but what happened today is a quantum jump. I don't understand it, not at all."

"No, you don't, and you can't, not in the world you've come from. Itandehui is one o' the last authentic curanderas. Many so-called healers are unable to summon the spirits like she can. It requires years of work and study. Those who don't have the patience for this often turn to drugs for their visions. Many in the mountains of this area have tried to gain their healing power by using *toloache*. It's a powerful medicine derived from a beautiful purple flower called *datura*. It looks harmless, but its beauty is deceptive. Used improperly, without adequate preparation and fasting, it's very dangerous, even deadly. The locals call it the crazy weed and forbid its use. Authentic healers depend on dreams for their powers. You may think I've been hoodwinked, but I've seen these methods work. I trust Itandehui. If I didn't believe in her skills, I would never have arranged this trip."

Eric didn't look convinced.

"Of course you're skeptical. It's natural to be doubtful of what we don't understand. The great point is, Eric, I've seen the results. I brought you to the mountain today because I believed it was the right thing to do. Give it some time, lad. If you feel better, maybe you'll think differently."

Carlos arrived to take them to the plane. As they left, they ran into a young American walking past Itandehui's cottage. In a bizarre twist it turned out that he was from Sacramento and lived in the same apartment complex as Eric. He even knew Doctor Marx. Eric remembered Manny telling him about a neighbor who was on his way to Mexico. What a surprise that he was here in San Kuuchamaa.

The man, Roger Penalt, said he wanted to learn about folk medicines. Jordan agreed to introduce him to Itandehui. While Jordan spoke with her, Eric and Roger chatted about Sacramento, Tijuana, and the differences between cultures. Their discussion was just getting started when Jordan motioned for Penalt to walk over and meet Itandehui.

Eric was flabbergasted. Lots of strange things had happened since the diagnosis. He'd come to accept that coincidences were a part of his life now. He quickly forgot about it as Carlos drove him and Jordan away. His thoughts turned to Ofelia.

Eric and Jordan were soon belted into their seats and heading back to Tijuana. The little plane rose up from the grass runway through the thick jungle, past the tops of spindly trees and ragged mountaintops, then veered toward the ocean. Down on the ground, everything looked small—rectangular fields crisscrossed by winding roads, clumps of trees and foliage, little bodies of water too inconsequential to call lakes, and the occasional gorge with a stream meandering through it. Above, the sky was immense. The ocean was demarcated by a chaotic coastline of rocks and bluffs and beaches spread out like a huge electric quilt buzzing and flashing in a pattern explicable only to the quiltmaker. *Was there a quiltmaker,* or was life some self-organizing phenomenon, inexplicable and without plan or purpose?

Life was a great puzzle. Eric knew he could never unravel it. This day had met his expectations and more, but something unreal about the experience left him unsettled. He remembered Martin Luther King's "mountaintop" speech, and for the first time understood what it meant. He knew something literally incredible had happened. He knew Jordan had taken him for a healing, but it was more than that. Jordan plunked him down into another world where he experienced something he instinctively knew from his past. There he reconnected with some nameless truth he'd long ago learned but had allowed himself to forget.

"I think with the trip to the mountain you were trying to sneak God in the backdoor, Jordan."

"I have no objections to bringing Him in through the front door, but that's not my intent. Come, Eric, don't try to guess my purposes, guess your own. Why did you agree to come? What, if anything, did you learn?"

"I suppose I came for an adventure. It was certainly the strangest adventure I've ever had, and the most confusing. I'm not sure what I learned. I'm still trying to figure that out. I don't know if I believe any of it, I mean the supernatural parts. Faith is not easy for me, Jordan. It goes against all my instincts."

"A belief in the supernatural—even based on experience—is not faith, Eric. How shall I say it? In the name o' God, it is faith, but it's not the kind of faith you mean, though it might lead to true faith."

"Then what is faith?"

"You might try thinking of it as a messenger. Yes, a kind o' messenger."

Eric was changed. How he had changed he could not put into words. Maybe it was the bizarre nature of the whole experience. For the first time since his diagnosis, he felt at peace with himself and with the world around him. As sappy as that sounded, there was no getting around it. He didn't mention it to Jordan, but yes, he had been visited by a messenger.

The rest of the trip home was a blur. They didn't speak again. When he arrived back at the bungalow, Ofelia was waiting for him. It was obvious she'd been crying.

"Ofelia, what is it?"

"Oh, Eric!" There were tears in her eyes. "I didn't want to tell you about this." The corners of her mouth turned down. Her lips quivered, the usual bright smile absent. She struggled to hold the sadness inside, but it poured through.

"About what?"

An odd mixture of lust and love, passion and compassion, pulsed through Eric's veins. Sad, vulnerable, innocent—all she wanted was a strong shoulder to lean on. Why was she so beautiful? Her skin mesmerized him. The bright colors she wore made him feel warm and strong. He wanted to embrace her, pull her body close, protect her from whatever troubled her.

"About Orvaline."

He was captivated by her pouty mouth, by her childlike fragility. She seemed to be saying: "Go ahead, caress me, I won't resist." He still reeled from the experience he'd been through. He tried to pull himself together.

"What do you mean, Ofelia? What happened? Tell me."

"He left this morning, as he often does, to go on a trip into San Diego for Napier. At the border they chose his car for further inspection. He's been arrested."

"Arrested? Why?"

"They said he was trying to smuggle Laetrile into the States."

"Was he?"

"I don't know. He makes these trips for Napier all the time. There's never been any trouble before. He says he delivers the mail and does the banking."

The word "arrested" straightened out Eric's conflicted emotions. He immediately assumed his attorney mode. "Let me take care of this. Where's he being held?"

"Right now he's in jail at the border crossing."

"Can I use the phone?"

"Of course."

They went inside Ofelia's parents' home. Mr. and Mrs. Cabrera were waiting for them.

"I'm sure this is just some kind of mix-up," Eric said. "I'll contact my office and have someone look into it. I know we can get Orvaline back home." The Cabreras looked doubtful but grateful. Ofelia's father took Eric into the kitchen where there was a phone on the wall. On the table there were cornhusks and masa flour, chopped vegetables and chicken. It looked like the maid had been in the midst of preparing dinner before she was told to stop. Eric guessed they got the call about Orvaline and put everything on hold.

Eric called his stepmother, Karen. Given her feelings about Laetrile, he knew she'd be receptive.

"Karen, it's Eric."

"Eric, what's happened? Are you okay?"

"I'm a little tired, but no worse than when I left. Maybe better—yeah, I think I'm better. I'm calling about something else, though. This family I'm staying with has a son. His name is Orvaline Cabrera." He spelled the name so Karen could write it down. "He's been arrested at the border. The authorities have accused him of smuggling Laetrile into the States. I don't think Orvaline knew anything about it. A Canadian man named Russell Napier runs the manufacturing plant here. He supplies the local clinics. He's working to legalize Laetrile in the States, but I suspect he's been sending it to his patients up north even though it's illegal there. He probably gets a good price for it under the circumstances. He sends Orvaline on routine trips to San Diego—banking, mail, supply purchases, that sort of thing. It's my guess that Napier's been using Orvaline as a carrier without his knowledge. Do you think you could find a way to get him released into the custody of his parents? He has no record and is an upstanding young man. I'll see that his trips north are brought to a halt, and I'll certainly have a talk with Napier about it."

"I'm sorry, Eric. You know how I feel. Laetrile should be legalized, but that isn't how the establishment sees it. The federal government outlawed it a few years ago. Governor Reagan's attorney general is adamantly against it. They're making a point by vigorously prosecuting anyone involved in importing or using Laetrile. Russell Napier is high-profile. They're going after him; that's probably how this Orvaline got caught. This might not be easy."

"There must be something we can do!"

"Do you really trust this young man? Do you really want to pursue this?"

"He's been helping me get around in Tijuana. His sister is a nurse at the clinic, and she's been helping me with the Laetrile. I've become quite close to her and her family. Yes, Karen, I definitely want you to help."

Señor Cabrera was watching and listening. He smiled nervously.

"Eric continued, he comes from a very prominent and respectable family. I'm sure the Laetrile, if it was there, was hidden in the packages without his knowledge."

"I'll make some inquiries and get the details," Karen said. "I doubt they'll just let him walk away. I'll send Steve, our Mexico guy, down to see if he can find some holes in their case. If they've made any mistakes, Steve will find them. He can also negotiate the conditions of release if that's possible."

"Thanks Karen, I knew you would help."

"Tell me about yourself, now, Eric. Are you really feeling better?"

"My brain and my body communicate in the strangest ways, Karen. There's no pain, at least for now. Breathing is still difficult, but I'm getting along. I've lost a lot of weight on this diet. That's lowered my energy level. This morning I flew in a small plane with a priest from the clinic to a remote mountain village where a remarkable thing happened. An Indian woman, a healer, gave me a massage like I've never had before. Apparently she has access to a special type of Laetrile made by the priest's friend. She gave it to me in a cup of tea. Father Jordan assures me it will cure me faster. I know this all sounds strange—it's strange to me too. I'm tired and weak, but I think this may actually be a turning point of sorts."

"A priest?" Eric noticed Karen's surprise.

"It's a long story. Anyway, I'm determined to beat the cancer. I've heard lots of good things about the Laetrile treatments from the other patients. I know the approach down here is the right one for me. They give us enemas every week. It's humiliating, but it's better than chemo or radiation and has none of the side effects. Thanks for helping, Karen. Take any expenses out of my savings. There should be plenty in the account. You have my power of attorney."

"Okay, Eric. Take care now, and stay in touch. Let me know how things evolve. It's been too long since I've heard from you. Call or write more often, promise? We're all pulling for you here. I know you made the right decision."

"Will do. Thanks, Karen."

After the call, Mr. and Mrs. Cabrera asked Eric to dinner. Normally he would have jumped at the chance to spend time with Ofelia, but he was too tired after the long day with Jordan. He apologized and left for his palapa. Ofelia followed him outside, where she held his hands and looked into his eyes.

"Thank you, Eric. My parents are very grateful for your help. You do look tired, get some rest."

He couldn't resist taking her into his arms. She was so gentle and lovable. Though deprived of his normal strength, he was surprised at how easy it was to lift her. She floated in the air like a feather. He let her go, but not until he'd stolen a kiss.

"Goodnight, Eric. Sweet dreams!"

There was a coquettish twinkle in her eyes. Before he could decipher what it might mean, she was gone.

Eric felt like a man on the moon. The day had been a triumph. He walked around in his room carefree and confident, whistling an old Cat Stevens tune, trying to remember the words. Everything was turning around. He washed his hands and face, took off his clothes, and went to bed. Relaxed and happy, he was soon fast asleep.

Eric woke to total darkness. There was a sound at the door. It opened. He sat up, immediately alert and on guard.

"Shh! Leave the light off, Eric." It was Ofelia. As she slipped out of her clothes, her body became visible in the tiny streams of moonlight that found their way into the room. His excitement grew. He felt a strange combination of desire and fear. He wanted her, but wasn't sure he was able to perform. When she climbed into bed beside him, his worries vanished.

"Ofelia, you don't have to do this. What I did for Orvaline, I did because I like him and your family. I wanted to help."

"Eric, I know you like me. I like you too. Relax."

Ofelia's warm body made Eric hard immediately. All the fantasies he'd dreamed of rushed through his mind. The erection surprised him, given his condition. He'd been limp as a drowned snake since his diagnosis.

He didn't want to hurt Ofelia. He struggled against his instinctive urge to mount her, but parts of his body long neglected awoke and began a persistent clamoring for attention. Eric and Ofelia explored each other like two schools of fish swimming around in a warm lagoon, intersecting at a thousand points, locking and unlocking at will, traveling in circles, in straight lines, randomly caressing and finally colliding in those final seconds of bliss when everything went blank.

"Eric, relax."

He was relaxed. He'd completely forgotten about Marcelino, about Orvaline, about his disease, about everything except Ofelia. He could see her white teeth as she smiled. Bits of light beamed in through small cracks around the windows and doors, illuminating the two of them as if they were characters in a play—lingering, laughing, feeling, molding, while at the same time watching from front-row seats.

After they made love, Eric collapsed to sleep. When he awoke the sun was up and Ofelia was gone.

37.

Surprises and Delays

Penalt helped the woman's son throw the bags of laundry over the wooden rack into the back of a road-worn flatbed truck. The boy was young, with almond-shaped eyes, black straight hair and white teeth that shone. He wore scuffed work boots and blue jeans, a white T-shirt and a denim sweatshirt with a hood hanging in back. The boy jumped into the rusted brown cab. His mother sat opposite him. Penalt rode in the back with the laundry and a few other passengers. The truck hauled them up the hill to San Kuuchamaa. It bumped along over a dusty, heavily rutted road stopping every few minutes to pick up another neighbor walking up the hill. By the time they reached San Kuuchamaa, the back of the truck was filled with people and animals and boxes. The locals talked excitedly as they rode into town.

They drove through town on a cobblestone street until they came to a large square, which was built on a slight grade. A beautiful church stood at the top of the hill, its belfry rising into the sky. The belfry looked down on Penalt and the others like the face of some deity peeking out of the clouds. Around the square a few small stores were open. People milled about outside, smoked and talked in groups. It was cooler in the mountains, but the sun peeked through the clouds and warmed Penalt's back. Across from the church, the only hotel in town looked empty.

Penalt lifted the laundry bags back over the sides of the truck and handed them down to the woman's son. When he jumped off the truck, the woman offered to put him up at her house. He would've accepted but his instructions were to stay at the hotel, so he politely refused, thanked her, and offered a few pesos to help with the gas. She shook her head. He thanked her again, then walked with his bag to the front entrance of the hotel.

He rang the bell. Behind the front desk a small dining area was visible through an open curtain. At one of the tables he could see three people lingering over lunch. He assumed one of them was the owner or manager. A man came running when he heard the bell. His effusive greeting was a sign there were probably few other guests. Penalt's intuition was correct. He found out later he was the only one.

"Hola, Señor. Room ready. We got message for you."

The man's stomach hung over a thick leather belt. He wore a brown shirt tucked sloppily inside. The shirt was wrinkled and lumpy as if the man were a freshly stuffed scarecrow. His black hair, tangled in untidy curls, covered his large head. Back at the table, Penalt saw a beautifully dressed woman. She looked exotic, like an actress or a dancer. The third member of the group, a priest, was dressed in Dominican garb, a bit portly, very jolly looking.

"Thank you. I have only this one small bag."

They walked along a stone walkway through an open courtyard to the room. When the man swung open the door, a mural on the wall behind the bed was the first thing to greet Penalt's eyes. It was faded but still brilliant. In a familiar scene, Indian women picked colorful flowers and collected them in handwoven reed baskets. It reminded him of an exhibit of Diego Rivera's paintings he'd seen back in the States. Real flowers had been placed on the nightstand. They blended with the mural and made the room seem like part of a stage set. An elegantly polished armoire stood proudly in the corner. A glass pitcher with fresh water on an inlaid wooden tray sat on the table by the armoire, with water glasses and towels alongside. The room was quite sufficient for Penalt's needs.

The owner handed Penalt an envelope, and stumbled over a few practiced words in English: "You come far way, all this far from *los Estados Unidos?*"

"Yes, from the United States."

"*Muy bonita* day, si?"

"Very beautiful. I think I'm going to like this place very much."

"First time in ol' Mayheeco, si?"

"Yes, my first time."

"You here all week? Tell me wha' you want an' I get you."

"Thank you."

Penalt sat on the bed. He was tired from the bus ride up the mountain, but in a marvelous way. If there were any doubts about taking on this job, they were quickly dispelled by the sights and sounds he saw along the way and by the atmosphere around the town square. Penalt was anxious to get to work. He opened the envelope and found another unexpected message.

> Sorry. Unable to come. My good friend Alberto, he come in Jeep soon. Contact you.
> Miguel

Penalt learned quickly that Mexico was the land of unexpected outcomes. One had to adjust. It was late afternoon, and he could explore the village with this unexpected free time. He washed up, then changed into a pair of Levi's and a Bob Marley T-shirt. In the lobby there was no sign of the three people he'd seen earlier. He walked out the door and into the square, where he stuck out from the short dark-skinned locals like a robin amidst a flock of sparrows.

When he walked around the square, Penalt had his first encounter with a healer. He was inquiring about the medical herbs and plants he saw, when an old woman approached him and said that she had a patient, a young girl, who was "*en problemas.*" She could show him how the herbs worked if he wanted to see. She wanted money to show him.

He knew it would be foolish to take part in what this woman proposed. She might know something, but her eagerness made him uncomfortable. He refused, which turned out to be a good decision. The healer was a fake. He would hear later that the girl died. Had Penalt participated, he'd have been persona non grata in the village.

At the edge of the square a bridge led out of town. The road ended and a narrow trail climbed up an imposing mountain into the jungle. The mountain blocked the village from the direct rays of the sun. Penalt started to walk up the trail. High above, the clouds burned off and the sun blazed fiercely. Penalt cupped a hand over his eyes so he could gaze to the top. Unexpectedly a black cloud rolled over the mountain, obscuring the view. A rush of cold air swept past Penalt's face. He might have considered these as sinister signs, but he just figured rain was on the way. He turned and started back to town, hoping to find a dry place where he could have a drink and a bite to eat while he waited for the weather to change. As he turned away from the mountain, the sun reappeared from behind the cloud. He didn't see it—something else caught his eye.

On his way down he passed a small hut. At its gate, he saw the priest he'd seen at the hotel, accompanied by a young man about his own age. He quickened his pace to catch up with them. He assumed they spoke English, and thought they might give him some information about the town. The young man was thin. His ashen complexion made him look ill, but he looked friendly.

"Hello, there! I saw you at the hotel, Father. Name's Roger Penalt."

"By Jove, so you did. I remember seeing you arrive. Father Jordan here. This is my young friend Eric Martin."

The three shook hands. Penalt noted Eric's handshake was weak. He looked as if he'd just been put through a wringer.

"Where are you from, Eric?"

"I live in Sacramento." Eric thought the name Penalt was familiar, but he couldn't place it right away.

How unusual, thought Penalt, *that someone from the same town has come to the same remote village.* He wondered if it had anything to do with Yawnix, but kept his thoughts to himself. "What a coincidence," he said. "I live there too. It's a small world, that's for sure."

Eric thought it strange indeed.

"I live at the Rivergate Apartments on the east side of town," Penalt said. "How about you?"

"Gee, I live there too, in the apartment next to Doctor Marx. I remember now: Manny said a neighbor was leaving for Mexico to learn about alternative healing methods. That would be you, I guess?"

"Sure enough. I'm interested in these healers and their unconventional techniques. I decided I'd better take a look before my life got too complicated."

Jordan hoped Eric wouldn't spill the beans about the Laetrile. Louie Frieze would not be at all happy to find out the Americans were onto his secret. Jordan stepped in to change the conversation. "Well, you've found the most beautiful spot on the mountain, Mr. Penalt. May I ask what brings you here specifically?"

Penalt saw the gallon jug Eric held, and wondered if the liquid in it was medicine. Penalt's heartbeat quickened at the thought.

"I have an interest in the healing methods of the curanderas. I understand one of the most experienced healers lives right in this town. I'm hoping to persuade her to take me on as an apprentice. I've gathered quite a bit of information from the vendors at Mercado Principal in Tijuana. I think I'm ready for the next step."

Jordan couldn't be sure of Penalt's true motives. He knew there was a search on for Louie Frieze and the Laetrile formula.

"I'm told many o' the large pharmaceutical companies from the States have been searching for new cures in the wilds of Mexico and Latin America. I suppose you're representing one of them?"

"I'm here for my own reasons. I've taken time off from my job to follow this dream I've had for years."

Penalt was uncomfortable with the lie, but his instructions were clear. His mission was a secret. What he'd said wasn't so far from the truth. The more he thought about it, the more he realized he really did have an interest in following up on the cures and plants he'd seen in Tijuana.

"I've been working as a research chemist in a different field. It was terribly boring to sit alone in the lab all day. I want to explore the world while I'm still young and unattached. Some of my friends told me of positive experiences they've had with the healers here in Mexico. That piqued my curiosity. I was skeptical at first; I'm the scientific type, you know, but the more I looked into it, the more irresistible it became to search this out. The people at the mercado told me about a healer who lives here. I want to see firsthand how these folk-healing methods work."

Jordan had to size up Penalt before he could consider any action to help him.

Penalt knew he'd had a stroke of luck, but he had to be careful. He tried to look relaxed and a bit naïve. He didn't want to seem too anxious. "If you have the time, maybe we could have a drink together and you could give me some pointers about how to get along here?"

Jordan's eyes veered up to the left as he tried to recall if he'd seen Penalt before. He hadn't. "Well, to be sure, we'd like to oblige you, but we're just leavin'. Do you speak Spanish?" Jordan was going to help him. He had a sense for people. He saw no harm in introducing Mr. Penalt to Itandehui. She could take care of herself.

"Just a little. I tried to brush up on it before I came here, but frankly I'm not very proficient yet." Penalt squirmed. He wished he'd studied harder.

Jordan lit a cigar. That wry little smile formed on his face. Penalt didn't seem to have any hidden motives. It was impossible to fool Itandehui. She could smell a rat if that's what Penalt turned out to be. He'd introduce Penalt and let Itandehui decide whether she could trust him.

"In the name of goodness, it's your lucky day, my boy. The healer you're seeking lives right here in this wee cottage. I can introduce you if you like."

"Why, yes, that would be wonderful!" Penalt could hardly contain his excitement at this good luck.

"Right. Give me a moment. She's a bit shy with outsiders."

Jordan walked back to the cottage to speak with Itandehui who was standing by the front door observing them all. She had a way of sizing up strangers with uncanny accuracy. Jordan explained that the young man had an interest in learning about healing methods. Itandehui didn't seem surprised.

Penalt, who'd been engaging in some small talk with Eric, looked toward Jordan and Itandehui. She looked him over carefully and said, "I'll teach him what he wants to know."

Jordan made the introduction. Carlos came to take Jordan and Eric to the plane. Jordan looked back as they drove off, and saw Penalt trying hard to communicate with Itandehui in his broken Spanish. He laughed at the scene—a large American man struggling to speak with a tiny Indian woman who herself hardly spoke Spanish. Surely these are the connections that make life worth living, that bring the world closer together. The whole afternoon shaped up as a success.

Penalt had no idea how much his life was about to change.

38.

Saturday Lunch

Saturday lunch at Ana Luisa's had become a tradition. Louie Frieze claimed he had no real interest in leaving his house, dismal as it was, but Jordan and Ana Luisa knew these lazy afternoons were important for all three of them. It was risky and difficult for Frieze to venture out, and Jordan and Ana Luisa had their own reasons to be discrete, but all three could enjoy the trust and friendship and food on these Saturday afternoons without having to worry about the rest of the world looking in.

"With all my heart I thank you, Louie, for that last shipment to Itandehui. It was a kind and admirable gesture. A young lad, I count him a friend, is on his way to recovery because of your serum. You've made this old man very happy."

Ana Luisa brought out a plate of the cheeses she'd received in exchange for the medicines and services she provided to the local farmers. She put the plate on a wooden table under the well-tended oak tree. One of her favorite textiles covered the table. It was embroidered in primitive hues from the dyes made of cochineal, marigold, indigo, and *campeche* wood, a gift from friends in Oaxaca. The wineglasses were handcrafted from simple colored glass. Jordan had a sturdy claret he'd found in a shop in San Diego. It had been imported from Bordeaux. He knew better than to offer the wines of Mexico or America to the Mangy Parrot.

"I don't know, Jordan. Sometimes I think everything I do is for nothing. I am hounded by Napier and Krump. They are the scoundrels, but I do the suffering. I'm too weak and too old to start over. It is time to stop. I do not have much faith in anything anymore."

"There, there. You must make the best o' the situation. What good is your work if you don't share it with those who are in need? I wish to heavens you'd listen. My son, Danny, is willing to help. This young American lad could work with Danny. Together they could protect you and your work. Blood alive, man, just ask! They could get your serum out there to those who need it most."

Ana Louisa graced these two sparring partners with her soft smile as she floated around the table. "Jordan is right, Louie. This serum you've worked on your entire life is your legacy to mankind. I've seen how it cures all around Baja. A true miracle! It's time to share it with the rest of the world now."

"Death is blind, my friends. The good, the bad, the young, the old—the Grim Reaper eventually takes us all. In zees world, I have seen more evil than good. It is true, some innocents die, but most of us become despicable long before death takes us. The world would be better off if our deaths came sooner. Cancer exists for a reason. Who am I to interfere? My work only delays the inevitable. It gives ze devil a little more time to work his designs on us."

"Enough, Louie. You don't believe in the devil. Don't be denyin' your genius. To be sure, we're all sinners, but we also have it within us to become angels like Ana Luisa. Show a little optimism, man."

"I'm no angel, Jordan, except perhaps to you. As I've said before, Louie is an old dry shoe." Ana Louisa broke out in laughter as she spoke. "An old dry shoe without ears, Louie, with tangled laces and cracks in the worn leather. Is that how you want to be remembered?"

"Anatole France taught us all we need to know about angels in his book, my dear Ana and my sanctimonious Tartuffe."

"You're incorrigible," said Ana. "Let's not argue further. The day is too beautiful for that. Let's enjoy lunch."

Frieze took a brown bag out of the wicker basket at his side. He had befriended a local fisherman, a man who'd helped him get the supplies to make his Laetrile. The man took the local fish, stuffed it with juniper leaves, then smoked it over a coal fire. Eucalyptus leaves soaked in seawater were placed on the coals to give the fish a rich smoky flavor. It reminded Frieze of the fish he ate as a young boy in the south of France.

"Oh, I guess you're both right. I am a sad, melancholy old man, a cynic. I 'ave seen too much of ze world not to be."

"Right enough, but there is nothing better than to be happy and to do good while you live, Louie. You've shared your discovery with so many who would've died without it. Indeed, you carry your marks and scars. I know they are a witness to the battles you've fought, but don't let that stop the good you do for so many. Take pity on their poor souls, my friend; they need your help."

"Yes, Louie. Jordan sees what I see: that God has a plan for you. You must follow it whether you believe in God or not."

The summer heat approached its maximum strength, but the shade from Ana's ancient oak blocked out the fiercest rays of the sun. The atmosphere around the table was serious but festive. Ana went to the kitchen and returned with a plate of fresh local fruit and a real French baguette she'd taught a local woman how to make in the style that Frieze loved. She poured the wine and they all filled their plates.

"People worry too much about death. Sleep is good, but death is better, my friends. You know I'm right. What would be ze best is to not be born at all. To be born is a curse. What are we but a lump of mud that comes awake for a moment, then returns to the muck?"

"I know no such thing, Louie." Ana Luisa gave him a grim look.

"Nonsense, Louie!" said Jordan. "It's a wonder that any mud can sit up at all, my friend. To come into existence is not a sin. It's a great thing to enjoy life and search for beauty in the natural world, and it's marvelous to struggle for excellence, even if we die in our struggle."

"Listen to Jordan, Louie. You are so much more than a lump of mud. You can't really believe that is all you are, can you?" Ana Luisa had always had a soft spot in her heart for the gruff chemist. She could understand his lack of faith but not his unrelenting pessimism and bitterness with life itself.

"Such eloquent arguments, I zink your roles are rehearsed. You conspire against my will to be free. What does your Church say on the matter? Our existence is seen as evil, as a fall, as original sin. The Church has no more regard for life 'ere on Earth than I do. It teaches us to seek paradise after death. Why not just die now and speed up that journey?"

Ana Louisa grew sad. This was no longer fun, no longer a game. She knew Frieze was serious. She walked away into the garden to find some beauty there to console her.

"Come now, Frieze, take a drink of this Bordeaux. You know nothing about the Church. You've not seen the inside of a church since you were a boy. God knows how much longer we'll be able to enjoy our life together. Take advantage while you can."

Jordan uncorked the bottle. He started to reach for a cigar, but a stern look from Ana Louisa, who had returned to the table, made him reconsider.

Frieze took a sip of the wine and rolled it around in his mouth. He stood up with the glass held high and a little smile on his face. "I relent. No more gloomy mood, my friends. Here is a little something from Pierre Motin."

Bacchus we thank thee who gave us wine
Which warms the blood within our veins;
That nectar is itself divine.
The man who drinks not, yet attains
By Godly grace to human rank
Would be an angel if 'e drank.

"Well done!" laughed Ana Luisa. The mood was lightening and she was once again happy they were all together.

"Thank you, Ana. You are ze most beautiful woman! Why you choose to live with zees preachy Tartuffe, I never understand."

"It's your duty, Frieze, as one of God's creatures, to live as well as you can and to use your great talents for all mankind." Jordan spoke what he thought was an obvious truth.

"Not to be born at all, Tartuffe. That would be the miracle. Anyone who opens 'is eyes to the miseries of the poor can't help but see there are fates far worse than death. Had I never been here, no one would miss me, and I would have missed all the misery and sorrow in this sad world."

"Sometimes, my Mangy Parrot, I think you are a contemptible creature."

"Ha! Should I punch Monsieur Tartuffe in ze nose for this insolence?"

"Wait until after dessert, Louie. The afternoon is young," said Ana, whose face was flushed after a sip of wine.

As Frieze sat down with a scowl, Jordan said, "This fleeting world somehow strangely concerns us, Frieze. It seems to need us, if only just once. That is enough to make this life irrevocable, indeed, at least for me."

"Tell me about your young friend, Jordan. How can you find anything compelling about an American? Most of zem don't even know ze difference between Bordeaux and Pinot Noir."

"Jolly funny, Frieze. Jolly funny! He reminds me of my own son, very serious and very sensitive. He doesn't deserve to die so young. He won't die now, because this time you let down that mulish obstinacy of yours."

"Are you calling me an ass, Tartuffe?" Frieze stood up with clenched fists.

"What if I am?"

"Then I will punch you in ze nose, dessert or no."

Ana Luisa stood up. "Come, come, gentlemen. Let's not spoil lunch."

"He's a living storehouse of intelligence, Frieze. I tell you, he can help you. He can protect you from the evil forces that are searching for you as we speak. He can help you set up a company to produce and market your Laetrile in a way that will make you proud. Think of it. Thank God for it. Please, for me, won't you consider it?"

Ana Louisa turned pale. Jordan had been too direct this time.

"Zere is no God to thank. That's all in ze imagination. What evil forces do you speak of? Is zere something I don't know?"

Father Jordan looked at Ana Luisa and saw the fear on her face. They both knew that a recent change in events had put Frieze at greater risk.

"I'm told Napier is getting desperate, Louie. He's run out o' the supply of Laetrile he stole from you. More patients at Buena Salud are dying. The Senate hearings are about to commence. The Dos Negros brothers are on the hunt, and I'm afraid you're the game, my Mangy Parrot. Come, don't close your eyes, don't shrink from it. Mind my words. Take me up on my offer."

Frieze put down his glass of Bordeaux. The light went out in his eyes. His face turned pale. He returned the piece of bread to his plate and sat quietly, deep in thought.

"If zey are looking, zey will find me. It is impossible to 'ide 'ere."

"We have to get you out of town. I've already got Danny working on it."

No one had much appetite after that. They went on eating mechanically until the food and wine were gone, but without enjoyment. The party was over. They all knew that the clock was ticking. Jordan drove Frieze back to his decrepit quarters. The Mangy Parrot agreed to accept help if it was offered.

"Let Danny figure it out, or this American friend of yours. I'll stay at home in 'iding until I 'ear. I don't want to die at ze point of a knife."

39.

Doctor Doggett

Devon parked in a nondescript lot alongside a dreary cement medical building. Sad green shrubs with little white flowers were planted throughout, the spaces between them optimistically allowing for future growth. The soil below the leaves was covered with tiny rust-colored pebbles. To avoid walking around the entire lot, he charged through one of these spaces directly to the entrance. Once inside, he sat in a chair covered with nauga skin surrounded by large framed abstract paintings. *The nauga is ugly, but his vinyl hide is beautiful.*

The conference did little to raise his spirits. He'd learned some things from Elvin Krump's presentation, but his concerns remained, especially after the interruption by the odd little man whose claims stuck in Devon's mind. He'd have liked to hear more. The world of Laetrile was utterly bizarre. Devon hoped Doctor Doggett had some useful information. He needed more before he could once again confront Eric. While he waited in the lobby, he read his copy of the letter from Doctor Rice.

Dear Doctor Doggett:

This letter is to introduce Mr. Eric Martin. He is a thirty-three-year old lawyer from Sacramento who presented a few months ago with bilateral supraclavicular lymph enlargement. A lymph node biopsy performed at Sutter General Hospital revealed metastatic adenocarcinoma. Chest X-ray showed hilar and mediastinal adenopathy and a diffuse increase in interstitial markings. The patient was then referred to Stanford for further evaluation. His history was rather benign, with some vague abdominal symptoms of "feelings of waves" across his abdomen on several occasions since about Nov. 1971. He has a long history of functional bowel complaints. He has also had a dry, nonproductive cough for the past several weeks. He denies anorexia or weight loss or change in bowel habits until the last week before learning of his diagnosis. His physical exam on admission was negative except for the bilateral supraclavicular adenopathy. Initial lab findings were not remarkable except for a mild anemia. His workup included a negative sigmoidoscopy and UGI. His barium enema revealed a lesion in the ascending colon, presumed to be the primary lesion. His only problem in the hospital was a temperature, about 38–38.5 degrees C. Sputum, blood, urine, and wound aspirate cultures have all been negative. Chest X-ray showed the development of a small pleural effusion. A lateral decubitus X-ray before he left shows free-flowing fluid. The plan was to do a diagnostic tap today. The patient, however, left our hospital abruptly before the thoracentesis could be done.

I believe Doctor Frank Stockdale has talked to you about Mr. Martin. Until his last day in the hospital, Mr. Martin took his diagnosis quite passively. However, he became very anxious and angry and left Stanford without the usual exit procedures. His brother, Devon Jennings, on whose behalf I am writing this letter, informs me that Eric is now in Mexico undergoing alternative therapies. I will let Devon provide the details. Mr. Martin is a very sensitive, cooperative, and intelligent person, and I am sure his brother will do what he can to encourage him to return to conventional treatments.

Good luck with this unfortunate patient. If there are any further questions, please let me know.

Sincerely yours,
G. J. Rice
Department of Internal Medicine

Devon read the letter twice. He wanted to be sure he understood every detail. Afterward, he collapsed back on his chair, his heart split into shards. How could he blame Eric for running away to Mexico? The medical system was cold and dirty like the slush that forms in roadside snow in winter. A gloom settled over him. He failed to hear the receptionist when his name was called.

"Doctor Doggett is ready for you, Mr. Jennings. Mr. Jennings? Hello?"

Inside the doctor's office, Devon was dazzled by a collection of stone masks. They were replicas of the life-sized masks commissioned by Akhenaton and Nefertiti during their rule in Egypt. A form was taken directly from the sitter's face, and a gypsum copy was made from the mold. The copy was then finished by the sculptor in various details, especially the eyes, since they had to be closed when the impression of the face was taken. Devon was strangely moved when confronted by these real people, people who'd lived 3,000 years ago. He didn't know their names or anything about them, but he saw his own humanity in their faces. Akhenaton had an unbridled hunger to know how he and other people really looked. This hunger for the truth became stone.

"Let me cut to the chase, Mr. Jennings."

Devon warmed to Doctor Doggett at first sight. He was professional, but he also cared in a way that was completely absent in Dr. Rice. He spoke directly to Devon rather than down to him.

"I know from our phone discussions that you would like me to treat your brother concurrently with his treatment at the Mexican clinic. What he's doing in Mexico is illegal in the States. I'm sure you understand I can have nothing to do with that. I'll be direct: Your brother's cancer is advanced and terminal. You know this already.

I'm sorry to remind you, but he likely has only a few months to live regardless of the type of medical treatment he receives."

Devon flinched. He knew it was true, but hearing it like this directly from Dr. Doggett deflated all his hopes.

"Doctor Rice mentioned an alternative course of treatment, something new that might help."

"Yes, that's right. We are currently in trials with a combination of immunotherapy and newly developed chemotherapy that shows promise in cases like Eric's. However, we would first have to get him into the trial program. He would be required to stay here in the United States. The side effects can be quite nasty, even intolerable for some, and we cannot be sure this treatment would increase his life expectancy. It doesn't sound like he wants that."

"In other words, his situation is hopeless."

"I didn't say that, Devon. Eric's decision to seek treatment in Mexico is not as unreasonable as it might sound. I try to keep an open mind—not so open that my brains fall out, but open enough to at least consider what others sometimes instinctively dismiss out of hand. I don't condone Laetrile or any of the alternative methods they pursue across the border. Many of these treatments are completely useless, some dangerous. However, there are other factors that also come into play. If your brother passionately believes in the power of Laetrile to cure him, he may experience physical as well as psychological benefits. Avoiding the pain and suffering associated with the more aggressive treatment options available here in US is in itself a factor that must be weighed against the benefits, particularly given your brother's circumstances. Eric's choice should be judged by taking into account his mental framework and all the quality-of-life factors."

"I understand, but he's my brother. I don't want to lose him. If I were able to persuade him to visit you, would you see him?"

"I'd be willing to assess his current condition and to monitor him periodically. I will not treat him or advise him on the treatments he's receiving in Mexico. An impartial opinion might help him more accurately understand what is happening to him as he moves forward."

"Okay. This seems like a good plan. It gives me something to shoot for. I'll be back in touch after I speak with him. Thank you, Doctor."

"I'm afraid there is no magic bullet, Devon. I don't want to give you or your brother false hope. As I said, I'm happy to meet with him. If the only result is some peace of mind for Eric, that in itself is important."

"I'm clear on that, Doctor. I hope we see each other again under different circumstances."

"I hope so too, Devon. Good luck with your brother."

40.

Marcos

Marcos climbed the big tree in the vacant lot next to the Frenchman's house. The tree was a refuge where he could hide and feel safe. It was also where he could gaze at the world around him through his own eyes, not the eyes of others who couldn't see his world. No one else ever went there. The lot, long since abandoned, was filled with weeds and underbrush, smaller trees, garbage, old cars, and discarded household paraphernalia. Like the detritus of those parts of dreams that mean nothing, images flashed in front of Marcos as he surveyed the field below.

It was from here on Friday evenings that Marcos watched the wild men queue up outside the Alameda house. They were men on fire, with hot coals in their stomachs and devils in their eyes. A witch stood at the door with a coin box. She was cold and black, a menacing obelisk with a small head and dead eyes. One of the wild men approached, paid, and entered. Later, another did the same when the first came out smiling, looking shy and weak, tame, small, and cowering, like a dog that had just lost a fight. Marcos had no idea what strange things went on inside the Alameda house. The wild men smoked and fidgeted and laughed outside as they waited their turn.

In the mornings came ducks and penguins. They walked along the road to school in their black-and-white uniforms. They quacked. They bleeped. As they passed by Mrs. Martinez's house, wild pigs with giant tusks barked, wagging their tails while the ducks flapped their wings and ran away scared and screaming. During the day, steel boats paraded along the street. They were just trucks, but Marcos saw them as giant piñatas decorated like shiny fat fish with black rubber fins. He knew things other people didn't know. The piñatas twisted and turned to avoid the giant *hoyos*. Sometimes one would tumble into a deep hole and get stuck. The wild men would come and push it out. All the neighbors would cheer. Among the leaves where Marcos hid, tiny angels with rainbow-colored wings sang joyful songs in a strange language. He understood all they said, but dared not speak to them.

It was from this hideout that Marcos first learned about the Frenchman's underground pit. When he waited long enough, the Frenchman would emerge from his workshop, grope his way around the weeds and rocks behind his house, find the hidden door, open it, and descend into the cavern below. Marcos had never been in that room. He did not know what the Frenchman did there. He knew where the door was, and knew where the key was hidden. He wanted someday, maybe today, to find out what the Frenchman did in the underground room.

At first Marcos thought the Frenchman was an evil wizard. He did the things that magic men do. He carried around beakers and vials and boxes filled with an odd assortment of powders and liquids that he burned and boiled and mixed. Bright colors flared up through the windows when Frieze was working at the stove. Evil shadows reflected on the walls. The Frenchman wrote things down and kept records. Each day, usually early in the afternoon when the sun's heat was at its peak, the Frenchman would carry boxes out to his underground pit. Marcos was curious about the boxes. He wondered why they had to be stored out of the light.

The Frenchman worked day and night. He didn't go to church on Sundays. Marcos decided he was doing the devil's business. After the fire burned the Frenchman's face and legs, Marcos suspected he was the devil himself. The book that Father Jordan read to him said the devil will be cast into a lake of fire and tormented day and night forever. It happened to the Frenchman. No one believed Marcos, so he kept his thoughts to himself. It frightened him to think the devil could be right there among them. He thought he should do something. If he could get into the hidden room, he might find a clue, something to take to Father Jordan. If the devil had come to destroy them, there might not be time. Marcos was special. Father Jordan told him so. It was his role in life to destroy the devil and save the world. The angels on the tree limbs confirmed this to him with their songs.

When Marcos awoke from his dreams, he was sitting in his tree. His eyes, blurry from sleep, focused on Louie Frieze as he came out of the house and looked carefully in all directions. Frieze toggled a box to a corner of the yard, stopping to rest every few minutes. He pulled a key out of a hollow in a scraggly old pine that towered over the yard. On one side of the tree, he cleared away the needles and dirt until a wooden door was visible. The key opened the lock, and with great difficulty Frieze swung the door up and threw it back against the fence. The *thump* of the door heightened Marcos' senses.

He was startled at first, but when fully awake, he realized the Frenchman was down in the pit. The sun was at its zenith. The rainbow-winged angels sang, "The path of the just is the shining light, that shineth more and more unto the perfect day." Marcos knew what he had to do. He climbed down from the tree and sneaked quietly over to the fence surrounding the Frenchman's property. He peeked through a crack and saw the Frenchman was still down in the cavern. He carefully climbed the fence and made his way to the pit. He couldn't see below, and was afraid to stick his head into the darkness. He took a deep breath, slammed the wooden door shut, and secured the lock. Something was moving down in the pit. He expected there to be wailing and gnashing of teeth. He covered the door with pine needles and dirt, then climbed back over the fence. Safely on the other side, he ran down the road. When he looked back the rainbow-winged angels were gone. Black crows were flying furiously over the Frenchman's house. The wild pigs barked. Marcos was frightened. The ducks were coming back down the road. He tripped. Hiding in the grass he saw a fierce monster, part man, part animal, crawl up from the depths of the earth. It had a wide mouth with rows of sharp teeth cut like those of a saw. It had the tail of a dragon with quills that spread out in every direction. It looked at him angrily with eyes of sapphire. Marcos froze. Then the monster smiled at Marcos and bounded off in giant leaps without looking back. Marcos stood up quickly. He ran in the opposite direction all the way home.

Part III

Remember

Remember me when I am gone away,
Gone far away into the silent land;
When you can no more hold me by the hand,
Nor I half turn to go yet turning stay.
Remember me when no more day by day
You tell me of our future that you plann'd:
Only remember me; you understand
It will be late to counsel then or pray.
Yet if you should forget me for a while
And afterwards remember, do not grieve:
For if the darkness and corruption leave
A vestige of the thoughts that once I had,
Better by far you should forget and smile
Than that you should remember and be sad.
—Christina Rossetti

41.

On the Way to Meet with Napier

Eric lay in bed half-awake; Ofelia's scent lingered on the sheets, the lyrics of Simon and Garfunkel's *For Emily* passed through his brain. He climbed out of bed and went downstairs to boil water for tea. A dead moth lay on the counter. Tiny ants dismantled its body. The darkness and corruption of death are food for the living. Eric measured one tablespoon from the plastic jug and put it into his teacup. He wondered if Itandehui had a magic elixir for someone falling in love. Falling was the right way to put it. For Einstein, gravity was a twist in space, a vertigo not unlike what lovers experience.

He swallowed the bitter tea in small sips.

The faster it goes, the easier it goes. To a bad step, rush it.

Outside, a gardener raked dead leaves away from the base of a giant fern. Osvaldo teased his little dog with a bone. He threw it up and the dog jumped, then he snatched it away just as the dog was about to catch it. Osvaldo shrieked in pleasure and repeated the taunt again and again.

Ofelia arrived in the Jeep to drive Eric to his meeting with Napier. They met each other with embarrassed smiles. Ofelia bit her lip, hoping Eric would speak first. She thought of his firm yet gentle touch when they made love, how his forehead wrinkled and his nose twitched as he thrust into her. Just the memory was enough to arouse her. She pushed her tongue against her teeth to keep from screaming or laughing.

Eric got into the Jeep without a word. Ofelia drove off toward the clinic, stealing glances at him along the way. Eric pictured the strands of hair heedlessly falling about her face when she sat on him, and how their tongues caressed when they kissed. He felt quivers of excitement again, but he couldn't let loose of the jealousies and doubts triggered by Orvaline's revelation.

Ofelia imagined living without Eric's brown eyes to stare into. She asked herself if she really loved him or if it was just her imagination. She thought what it would be like to marry someone else and then, one day, to meet Eric by chance on the street, to see those same eyes but at a distance. Oh, no, it would be too horrible! She must never let that happen.

Eric was the first to speak. "What about Marcelino?"

Ofelia jerked to the side of the road and slammed on the brakes. "Who told you?"

"What does it matter? You have a boyfriend. He wants to marry you. Your parents want you to marry him."

"Marcelino and I have been going out, it's true, but that was before I met you. Now, everything is different."

Eric didn't know what to say. He had no intuition or conviction like the people he'd read about in books. Love was new and it confused him. It was as if he'd entered Dante's dark wood where there was no clear path.

"Whatever Orvaline said to you, Eric, he did it to hurt you."

"Why doesn't Orvaline like me?"

"Orvaline lives in a Mexico of brown people, where fish jump out of the sea, where fruit hangs on the trees for the taking, where the hot sun warms you and the rain cools you. He can't imagine anything else. My parents want him to get ahead, to succeed in life, to become something, but he lives his fantasy like a child. When you arrived, my father told Orvaline you were an example of the successful young professional he wanted Orvaline to become. That infuriated Orvaline. It made him jealous and angry."

"Your father will change his mind when he finds out about us. Orvaline said our relationship would be complicated."

"All relationships are complicated, Eric. Marcelino is only a friend. He could never be more than that to me."

Ofelia drove back onto the road. A bus went by in the opposite direction. Sunlight reflected off the front window and momentarily blinded Eric. By the time they reached the clinic, Ofelia had grown quiet and withdrawn.

"Are you upset with me?" Eric asked

"I know how sick you are, and I know we have very different lives, but I also know there is something real between us. You can't deny it. However much time we have, I want to spend all of it together. Don't you want that too?"

A squirrel ran along the limb of the tree opposite the clinic gate. Eric watched it jump from limb to limb.

"I knew I loved you the day you gave me that first injection. My love grows deeper every day. Of course I want to spend my life with you, but how long will that be? I love you too much to tear your heart apart. You deserve more than I'm able to give."

"You won't tear my heart, Eric. I'm whole because of you. I'm so upset that Orvaline tries to destroy us with his deceptions. He's such a jerk. Last night meant everything to me. Let's begin with that. A week is better than nothing. A month, a year—I want whatever we can have. I hope for more, but anything is better than nothing at all."

Eric leaned over and kissed her on the lips. He embraced her and held her close, keeping his lips pressed against hers. The whole experience of love was a mystery he simply could not figure out. Life, so tentative, so fragile, sustains itself through this comical set of chemical responses that can't be controlled as easily as summoned. Love shows up uninvited, flattering the object of its affection, then turns to torment with cravings impossible to fulfill. The whole experience is so maddeningly irrational. Eric despaired of ever pinning it down. The poets believe a firm persuasion that a thing is so makes it so. He wished he had more of the poet's nature and less of the cold rationality that had guided his life in the past. He wanted a different future.

"Am I so unworthy of your love, Eric, that you can't commit?"

"God, no, Ofelia! It's just that... I don't know. Of course I can commit. I love you more than life itself, but I just don't want my selfish desires to hurt you."

They parted, and Ofelia drove off. Eric knew she was unhappy. He stood alone and squirmed in his misery, then walked into the clinic. Through the window, he watched the Jeep disappear around the corner. Love was thwarted by arbitrary doubts that, in his constant ruminations, he himself created. These doubts were unreasonable, but powerful because he had been at the mercy of them from the moment he'd become aware of his feelings for Ofelia. He didn't want to be a burden, didn't want to upend her life, didn't want anyone he cared for to go through the pain of his death. He was stuck in his tracks right at the beginning of a journey that he wanted more than anything else to take. He needed a good push to get going.

42.

The Search

When they realized Frieze had disappeared, Rafael and Tomás sent Hector to investigate. The two guards ran away, fearing for their lives. While Hector was going through Frieze's things, Ana Luisa arrived to pick up another shipment of Laetrile. She knew Hector's family before Hiladeo had killed Amelia's brother. Many people feared Hector, but she was not one of them. She wasn't worried for herself, but for Frieze. She suspected Dos Negros had taken him away.

"What are you doing here, Hector? Where's Frieze?"

She saw past the hardened smile and remembered the little boy she'd once seen help his father trim the hedges around the Rodriguez property. She saw the way he carefully raked the cuttings into little piles, each exactly the same size and spaced the same distance apart. Hector and his father made art even out of refuse. *Art,* she thought, *is transformation, not representation. Art transforms reality into the exotic and gives it back to us in the only way that's meaningful.*

Hector didn't seem surprised to see her, which made her wonder if he'd been spying on her all along. She shuddered at the thought that she might have led him to Frieze's hiding place. A shiver ran down her spine when she thought of what they might do to Frieze to get at his formula.

"We found Frieze a few days ago. He agreed to meet with Rafael and Tomás. They persuaded him to help with the new manufacturing plant. He and Napier patched up their differences, and Napier promised to keep Krump out of it. Frieze said he would make Laetrile for the clinic. We knew he might try to leave, so we posted two guards outside. I don't know how he got past them."

Ana Luisa didn't believe a word of it. Frieze hated Napier, and would never have agreed to work with him. If he'd made an agreement, it had to be under pressure. Frieze was old and weak, but he was resourceful. He might have said he would work with them to buy time. She hadn't talked to Jordan. Maybe he knew something about it. She looked around and saw the supplies and tools scattered throughout the workshop. Frieze had obviously left in a hurry. There was no sign he'd taken anything, but where would he go? What would he do? And how could he have gotten past the guards?

"There's nothing here for me now," said Ana. "If you find Frieze, tell him I was here to see him. You'd better tell me the truth, Hector. If anything bad has happened to Frieze, I'll see that you and Dos Negros pay—somehow I'll see that you pay."

Ana Luisa looked at him in a way that even Hector feared. She and her driver went back to her house in town. Worried, she thought about calling her son in San Diego, but there was nothing he could do. In any case, he would be in Tijuana soon for the car races. Jordan could speak with him if Frieze didn't show up by then. Frieze was not an American citizen, so she thought it very unlikely he would have gone to the States alone. It was all quite strange.

Hector found no clues in Frieze's workshop, just a mess of papers and equipment. He secured the door and drove back to tell Dos Negros. Hector knew they would be furious and launch an all-out search. They'd had him and he escaped. It made them all look foolish.

Frieze was a loner. He couldn't go far without help. Either he'd hidden in the neighborhood in one of the old abandoned buildings, or someone had come to take him away. The logical person was Father Jordan. Ana Louisa seemed surprised that Frieze had disappeared, but maybe she was trying to throw them off course. Hector ordered his men to follow both Jordan and Ana Luisa. No one knew more about Frieze than they did.

Hector found the Dos Negros outside on Rafael's deck when he arrived. "There's no sign of him. It looks like he left in a rush without taking anything. I found nothing to help us. He left a lot of stuff behind. I'm having a couple of men clean out his house and take everything to Napier to see if there's anything useful. I also put a tail on Ana Luisa and Jordan. They might be involved, but Ana Luisa says she knows nothing."

"Frieze is crazy like a fox," said Rafael. "A wily fox."

Tomás banged his hands on the table. His fears had been justified. From the very beginning he wanted to capture Frieze and put him away, even if that meant killing him, but he'd been overruled. Now Frieze had slipped right through their fingers. Napier was soft; he didn't have the stomach for these things.

"*¡Hijo de puta!* We got to find him. Zacco already thinks we're idiots! We have hundreds of thousands tied up in this deal. If Zacco pulls out, *estamos atornillado. ¡Ese jodido francés!* I won't let that Frenchy ruin things for us. Find him, Hector. Do what you need to do. Focus everything on Frieze until we have him back. Get him! You hear me?"

Tomás was red with anger. Rafael paced back and forth along the deck, beads of perspiration dotting his forehead.

"Okay, boss, I'll put everybody on it. With that face of his, people should remember if they've seen him." Hector left. There was going to be hell to pay. He would have to put his plans to stage a coup on hold.

"Who is Hector to talk about faces?" Rafael laughed.

Tomás did not smile. He was angry. He no longer trusted anyone, not even his own brother.

"Listen, hermano. We need to be more careful around Hector. Some of the men say he has too much power inside the organization. If you think about it, he probably knows more about the deals than we do. Zacco always says that no one should be indispensable. It's a good rule to follow."

"Hector has never let us down. I'm not worried about it, Tomás."

"Well, I worry about it. You should listen more to me and less to those worthless politicians you hang out with. They are leeches sucking our blood."

"I do listen, Tomás, okay? But right now I need some rest. I'm not feeling so well. My back aches."

Tomás saw Rafael sweating. He knew why.

"Not okay! Rafael, I've told you a thousand times to stop the smack. It's sapped the ambition right out of you. You're a junkie, just like those *locos* we sell the *drogas* to. All you care about is the dope. You're losing it, hermano, losing it! I'm not going to watch this anymore. Pull yourself together, or else."

Tomás charged down the stairs and left. Rafael felt the nausea grip his stomach. His entire body began to ache. It started with his ears, then his teeth, then his jaw. The pain traveled right on down to the bones in his toes.

One more, that's all I need, so I can sleep. Then I'll quit....

Rafael stumbled into his office and locked the door. No one was ever allowed in his office. He pulled up a piece of wooden flooring to get at the safe below where he kept the heroin and the paraphernalia. He took out a syringe, a cooker, a bottle of water, a latex tourniquet, and a small ball of white cotton. He lit a candle on his desk, put the powder into the cooker, sucked up just enough water to do the job, and released it carefully into the cooker. Perspiration dripped from his forehead as he heated the solution over the candle until the heroin was dissolved. Next, he set the cooker onto the cork cup holder on the desk. He shook so badly he nearly spilled it.

He was almost ready now. He dropped the cotton ball into the cooker and it instantly sucked up all of the heroin solution. He stuck the needle against the cotton and pulled up the plunger. The cotton filtered out the impurities as the heroin flowed into the needle. He tapped the barrel of the syringe to make sure all the air bubbles rose to the top. He put the cap on the syringe and laid it on the table.

He rolled up the left sleeve of his tan guayabera shirt. A garish *Santa Muerte* tattoo in pink, black, and green stared up at him. He wrapped the tourniquet around his arm twice and stuck the other end under his armpit to secure it. He made a fist and held the barrel firmly against the injection site. Slowly he inserted the needle into his arm where he could see the vein bulging near the middle folds of Santa Muerte's pink inner robe. He pulled out the plunger a little until his blood flowed into the barrel. He loosened the tourniquet by moving his arm slightly and then shot about half the solution.

There was a quick rush. When he shot the rest, his world transformed. He relaxed into the large leather chair and let the mojo take over. His heart quickened. His handsome face froze into a demonic stare. His mind reeled with energy. The murky space around him became crystal clear. All his worries fell away, and his mind grew settled and quiet. He felt an internal fire. It warmed him from a hidden source deep inside his stomach. His body was still. He felt the earth quake around him. As the drug consumed him a euphoric peace spread itself all over his skin like a spider's web.

43.

Jail at the Border

Napier was surprised when Eric walked in without knocking. Brochures were scattered about the desk and on the floor.

"You know why I'm here, Napier. Orvaline's in jail, and it's your fault, you selfish bastard! Did you give any thought to the risks you asked him to take? This is inexcusable. You've turned his family upside down. His young life could be ruined."

"Whoa, slow down, Eric. I'm not what you make me out to be. I know the risks; I think about them every day. When the patients leave the clinic, I can't let them go home empty-handed. Going off the Laetrile would be a death sentence for them. I have a list of doctors who can help these patients, but they need the Laetrile. Sometimes one has to gamble with the law."

"Did Orvaline know? He drove into a trap. He could go to jail for a very long time. This is your mess, Napier. What are you going to do about it?"

Napier raised his eyebrows. He looked out the window. A minute went by. Two minutes. Eric held his tongue.

"Sooner or later I knew this day would come. I'll take full responsibility. I'm an honorable man, Eric. I know you're angry, but just wait. Tomorrow I'll turn myself in. I'll testify to Orvaline's innocence and they'll let him go. I'll get him home. Count on it."

Eric hadn't expected such a quick and direct response. His anger receded.

"What about you?"

"Oh, they'll make a lot of noise, put me in jail, but it won't hold up.

"I'm sorry I blew my top. I guess you're a stand-up guy after all, Napier. I should've given you the benefit of the doubt. I might be able to help. Steve Gillian, an attorney from my firm, is on his way to work on Orvaline's case. He's a terrific lawyer and has a lot of experience in these kinds of situations. Meet with him before you speak to the judge. Here's his card. He'll be there when you arrive."

Napier took the card. He affected a look of concern, but it was all a fake, an act meant to impress Eric, and it worked. Napier had no real worries. He was adept at dealing with these border problems. He had friends he could rely on. The situation would ultimately work to his benefit. He knew he would be quickly released if he went to jail at all, and the notoriety would bolster his reputation inside the Laetrile community. The whole thing would also increase Eric's trust—a bonus.

Eric thought about his own health. He wanted Napier's opinion on some questions that had been piling up. "Have you ever considered whether there's a spiritual aspect to the healing process, Napier?"

Something had happened in San Kuuchamaa. Eric knew there had to be some rational explanation. Maybe Frieze was really onto something, but Eric couldn't speak of that. He had this lingering feeling that Itandehui had actually changed things in some fundamental way. It was crazy, but he couldn't shake it.

"Spiritual? No. I'm absolutely scientific in my approach. Theory, evidence, tests… that's what it's all about for me. If it's not quantifiable, you don't know the importance of anything you find. I let Doctor Milagro worry about God and people's souls."

This was Eric's view too, but it was also the view of the doctors at Stanford, the Nobel laureates, molecular geneticists, and biologists who prided themselves on producing specialists and medical research scientists. The great thrill for them was in diagnosis and the development of their scientific cures. They didn't seem to care much about the patients, whom they considered the boring part of the job. Eric had felt this from the moment he'd arrived there. And now it was

Napier. His game was Laetrile. He wasn't really at all different from the doctors at Stanford, except for his unconventional approach.

"I wasn't talking about God or the soul, Napier. What I mean by a spiritual aspect... well, I'm not sure exactly. I mean, we all tell ourselves stories to get along, right? What if one of these stories doesn't fit the rationalist point of view? Couldn't there be... I don't know, some great piece to the puzzle the intellect can't comprehend? What if there really is something that guides us through the dark, spirits or what have you? Do you think I'm crazy?"

Napier wasn't sure what Eric was getting at, but it sure sounded like he'd been talking with some of the loonies that hung around outside the clinic. It sounded like nonsense, but he had to be careful what he said. He'd seen patients go off the deep end before, but it wasn't something he expected of Eric.

"What you say is interesting. We know the state of health depends on the patient's psychological make-up. Spiritual healers can trigger powerful visual hallucinations using heat, hunger, and exhaustion. Extremes can produce psychological and even physiological responses much like the work of a good psychotherapist. There are rational explanations for such experiences. I don't believe in any ghosts or spirits floating around that we can marshal to make us well, but if the idea appeals to some people, who am I to destroy their beliefs?"

"It's all turtles then, all the way down?"

Napier smiled when he recognized the old anecdote about infinite regress.

"Blood tests, X-rays, long-term results—these are the markers I look for, Eric. People have the right to choose their own healthcare, whether spiritual or science-based. I stick to the science. It's what I know. Doctor Milagro puts a greater emphasis on the spiritual. You should ask him or that Catholic priest you've been hanging out with. I've got no objection."

"Okay. Thanks. Look, I commend you for standing up for Orvaline. Speak with Steve Gillian. He can get help. I'm sure of it."

Eric left not knowing what to think, but he felt better. Napier was going to help Orvaline. That much was clear, and it was all that mattered for now. It was more than he expected when he started.

♋

Two days later, Russell Napier found himself in jail at the border after Orvaline's hearing where he'd explained everything to the judge. Orvaline was his employee. Orvaline had been told he was transporting mail, bank deposits, and ordinary medical supplies, nothing more. Napier told the judge Orvaline played no role in the packaging or loading of items into the car.

"Well, then, who's responsible if not this young man?" asked the judge.

"I am, Your Honor," answered Napier.

"You? Only you?"

"Yes, Your Honor."

The judge spoke to Orvaline. "Orvaline Cabrera, you're free to go. You should be more careful in the future. Be on your guard when you're asked to carry things across the border. Do you understand?"

"Yes, Your Honor, I understand."

"Russell Napier, you are remanded until trial. Bail is set at $50,000."

Steve Gillian whispered into Napier's ear: "I think we can get you out of here pretty quickly. Don't say any more."

"Sorry, Mr. Gillian, I have something to say on behalf of my cellmate."

Napier had a special talent for getting into and out of odd situations. His cellmate was a tall dark-skinned man who'd been accused of smuggling two kilos of heroin. He had a scar on one side where one lung had been removed. He was sick and in bad shape. The man's hearing followed Napier's, and Napier asked permission to speak on the man's behalf.

"Your Honor, my cellmate has only one lung and he has the flu. I know he is accused of a serious crime, but he's going to die if you don't get him to the hospital, the sooner the better."

The judge hated men like Russell Napier, men who tried to control the world with their charm and their money, men who broke the law with impunity. He took his time to respond, and scowled at Napier when he did. "Bailiff, release that man to the guards and see that they drive him directly to the hospital. He's to remain under guard and to be returned to jail as soon as he's medically fit."

As the man left the courtroom to be transported to the hospital, he winked at Napier.

"As for you, Mr. Napier, you will stay locked up in our jail as I said, and will remain there until I have had time to examine all the evidence. Perhaps you will now be persuaded of the seriousness of the crime you stand accused of."

The judge sat straight up in his chair and spoke with the authority of a man who knew the power of his position. The look on his face gave Napier no comfort, but it didn't faze him in the least. Steve Gillian, however, was distressed. He again whispered to his client. "Russell, let me arrange for bail. You don't want to spend one night in this jail."

"Sorry again, Mr. Gillian. The judge thinks he's got me, but I'm not going to pay a dime to get out of here. You watch, they'll release me without bail soon enough."

Napier told Gillian to request the defense be allowed to test the alleged Laetrile that led to the charges. The judge ordered a sample to be produced by the authorities. In the meantime, Napier was led away to his cell. There he remained while everyone waited for the samples.

After three days, the judge reduced Napier's bail to $10,000 at Steve Gillian's request. He again ordered the authorities to deliver their evidence to the court immediately.

"Don't be foolish, Napier. Ten thousand is nothing compared to what could happen to you inside that jail."

"Be patient, Mr. Gillian. I can take care of myself. I know you're looking out for my best interests. I appreciate that, but I refuse to pay a penny. I'm innocent. That judge hates me, but you watch, they'll release me very soon."

The bail was reduced to $6,000, but Napier still refused to pay. Steve Gillian complained to the judge. The samples had yet to be provided. It turned out the evidence was lost. This was no surprise to Napier. He knew the Dos Negros would come through for him eventually. The judge had no choice but to release him.

Napier gloated as he walked out of jail. The press was there to meet him.

"Mr. Napier, will you continue to smuggle drugs into the United States?"

"I do not smuggle drugs. It is not my intention to break the law. The American government is allowing helpless and terminally ill people to die without the medicine that could cure them. These laws are on the books because of the corrupt lobbyists hired by a greedy pharmaceutical industry. It's a real shame. For many, Laetrile is the only hope. I don't know how the US government can stand idly by while their own citizens die for lack of a simple, effective solution that is readily available."

"Do you deny that you smuggled Laetrile across the border?"

"No further comment."

"What these people need is education and a good scrubbing, followed by a few lessons on how we do things in the United States! Why on Earth would he leave us and come to a foul place like this?"

Nurse Marta's yellow hair was matted from the sweat and dust. She bounded along the sidewalk in giant strides. Nelson ran along behind, trying to keep up.

"We're gonna find him, and we're gonna haul him back. Do you understand that, Nelson?"

"Yes, ma'am."

"I seen better faces on an iodine bottle," muttered Nelson.

"Is that a damn scorpion on the ground? Smash it!"

"Just leave him be, ma'am. He'll just sting himself to death anyway."

"For God's sake, Nelson, don't try to tell me what to do. Smash the damn thing before he poisons us! My skin's crawling with all the bugs around here. Where do you think our patient might be?"

"What makes ya think I'd know, bitch?" Nelson whispered.

"What's that? What'd you say? Speak up, Nelson."

"Said I seein' things I ain't never seed before, heard about but never seed. Gonna take some gettin' used to down here, ma'am. I don't know if we gonna find him today. It's gettin' pretty late."

"Don't give up on me, Nelson. There's plenty of daylight left. I'm not going to stay in this hellhole any longer than I have to."

Nurse Marta charged up a hill with her clipboard, and then stopped to get her bearings.

"Hold up a pretty minute, ma'am. I'm coming along as fast as I can." To himself, he grumbled: "Don't ever take off to Mexico with a mean bitch nurse. Shee-it, what'm I into now?"

44.

Hector and Amelia

A rooster crowed in the middle of the night. Eric walked out on the deck of his palapa. From the Cabrera property high on the hill, the lights of the city seemed far away and small. Toward the beaches everything was black. There was no moon in sight. It was impossible to tell where the sea ended and the sky began.

Distant and soulless, the stars danced to a silent symphony in space. Eric leaned his head back and the entire sky came into view. The scene made him dizzy. The very idea that he was one with those flickering stars so impossibly far away, was part of something bigger, made everything else shrink; but he didn't live among the stars. His life was here on Earth. His life was now. The decision to travel to Mexico, to break with the doctors at Stanford, to defy science and throw himself into all the desperate optimisms of last resort had paid off. Rational or irrational, it was true.

Eric stepped back from the railing. The rooster crowed again. Dawn was hours away. The feelings he had for Ofelia were the result of instincts evolved through the ages, but such knowledge didn't change them. Life is more than hard cold facts. If he had learned anything from this damn disease it was that. The swirling stars disoriented him, but there was grandeur in what he saw and what he felt. His life shrunk and expanded due to some quirk in the laws of physics.

He walked inside to pee. He turned on the light. A line of giant amber ants was invading through a tiny hole in the wall. He peed and stayed away from them, then climbed into bed and fell quickly back to sleep.

Ofelia danced around him. She was naked. Her undulating movements were precise, like ritual exercises. She moved in slow, continuous motion. Movement, energy, vibration. The notes of an ancient music put everything in flux. Eric joined in the dance. They spun like dervishes and drew infinitely close to each other. It was a dance of two flowers, shaken free from the bud, alive in their moment upon the earth.

Hours went by, restless sleep. At last, the sun peeked in through the cracks in the door and the window shutters. Eric stepped outside onto the deck of the palapa and was shocked to see Hector Hernandez walking through the garden. Ofelia's mother was walking in front of him. What possible connection could the Cabreras have with Hector or Dos Negros?

Eric went to brush his teeth. He looked at himself nude in the mirror and was revolted. An emaciated human is the most unlovely thing in creation. He'd seen the ceremonial skeletons at the stores in town used to celebrate *Dia de los Muertos*. Here the bones were his bones, the teeth that clacked in the mirror were his teeth, and the cavern behind the hollow eyes where his brain burned was just like those in the paintings by Posada. He stepped back in horror.

The ants were gone. A scorpion wandered around on the floor. Its segmented tail and claw-like stinger rose up in attack mode. Eric was about to smash it and flush it down the toilet, but he changed his mind. He captured it carefully and threw it out the window, then went downstairs to make his tea. Ofelia was outside on the patio.

"Good morning, Eric. You slept in."

She looked neat and professional in her white uniform, the same one she'd worn when they first met. The memory sent a shiver of excitement up Eric's spine. He felt like a caricature of his former self. He tried to keep fit but he'd become so unappealing, so thin and pale. Hard as he tried, it was impossible to gain weight.

"I'm glad I caught you before you left. I saw your mother with Hector Hernandez in the garden. What's going on?"

Ofelia was not amused that he thought her parents were associated with gangsters. "My parents are not mixed up with Dos Negros, Eric. They are good Christians. I hope you think better of them than that."

"Why was he here then?"

"I suppose you have a right to be curious. It's nothing to do with Dos Negros. They were speaking about Hiladeo, Hector's father. He worked for my grandparents as a gardener many years ago. He took a wrong turn, became an alcoholic. The sadness after his youngest son was injured destroyed him. My grandparents had to fire him from the job. One dreadful night when Hiladeo was very drunk, he got into an argument with my uncle Luis and killed him with a broken beer bottle. Hiladeo has been incarcerated at La Mesa Penitenciaria ever since."

"Jordan mentioned something about that. I didn't know it was Hector's father who was involved."

"Hector wants his father out of jail. He feels responsible, because an accident he had with his little brother is what started Hiladeo's drinking. Hector made an arrangement with the governor, but the governor won't act without my mother's consent. Our family still has some pull with those in power. Hector is asking my mother to forgive his father. He wants her to give the governor the green light to free Hiladeo."

"What do you think your mother will do?"

"She's going to speak with *mi abuela* today. I think they will grant Hector his wish. Over the years, the whole incident has been a terrible weight on all of us. They're ready to forgive Hector's father. Before that awful night they had such good times together, my mother, grandmother, and Hiladeo. Hector was different then too. So many lives have been destroyed."

"What a sad story. Your mother and grandmother would be wise to let it go. I've seen many clients destroy themselves with a desire for revenge. Dwelling on the past can poison the soul."

"Yes, I hope they do the right thing."

Ofelia took his hand. Little wrinkles of excitement formed around her eyes. "Eric, I have good news. My parents leave this week for their summer home in Rumorosa. My little brother, Osvaldo, will go with them. Orvaline and I will stay. Devon and Orvaline can entertain each other, which means you and I should have a lot more time alone."

"Orvaline watches us like a hawk. I think he still hates me."

"Don't worry about that. I spoke to Orvaline last night in front of my parents. I told them I've ended it with Marcelino. I told them that you and I are in love! I did! Orvaline and my parents have no choice but to accept it now."

"You told them straight out, just like that?"

"Some people pull the bandage off slowly to lessen the pain, but going slowly only prolongs it. I rip it right off. Life returns to normal faster that way."

Ofelia's childlike ways were deceptive. She was no child. Eric envied her relationship with her parents. He'd hardly gotten to know his father. He loved his mother, but they seldom discussed personal things.

"Do you always give your parents trouble?"

"Yes, always," said Ofelia, with a giggle.

"Then you're a wretched person, Ofelia, truly wretched!"

"Oh, no! I rate myself above everyone. Wretched is not possible for me. I don't want to be at the same level as anyone else. I want to be different."

Eric chased her around a palm tree. She let him catch her. He took her into his arms and they kissed, no longer concerned about hiding their feelings.

"You're different from anyone else I've ever known. I want you all to myself," he exclaimed.

"Heavens, do you suppose I could be in love? Well, of course I am, but you can't have me all to yourself, Eric. You ask too much. I love everything—art, music, books, the sun, the beach. I want to be all I can be. Don't look so silly, *querida*. There's plenty to go around. Come here, I'll give you another kiss."

Eric doubled up in pain. He staggered to the bench.

"Eric! Eric! What's wrong? Tell me!"

"It's the pain in my belly. It'll go away, just give me a minute."

"Can I get you some water, a cold cloth?"

"No, it's going away. Really, I'm okay."

Ofelia's eyes looked at him fiercely.

"Devon told me he spoke with you about Doctor Doggett in San Diego. I think you should go soon. We should look into everything, Eric. Everything. I don't want to leave any stone unturned."

"Yes. Devon already made the appointment, but I'll tell you something: Since that trip to San Kuuchamaa, I know I'm getting better. I'm not sure what happened, but I feel it inside. I don't need Doctor Doggett to tell me what I know is true, but I'll see him for you. Go on along to work now. I'll be fine."

"Well, I'm glad you're going. I want to explore every option. Are you sure I can't get you something before I go off to work?"

"I'm sure. I'm fine now."

He gathered the strength to stand with her and hug her. After she left, he went back up to his room and collapsed on the bed.

"Oh, God! Don't you get your priorities straight when this sort of thing happens?"

"I'm here. No need to worry. I've got a little something to help the pain."

"Nelson? Where... where are you?"

"I'm right here next to you, man. Swallow this and take a little rest. Everything's gonna be okay."

45.

Appointment with Doctor Doggett

Devon drove Eric across the border from Tijuana to San Diego. It was a sunny day along the busy road, and traffic was steady.

"Orvaline says there was a famous robbery on this road in 1929," Devon said. "A group of mobsters held up the money car for the famous Agua Caliente Casino. They used machineguns. It was the first time machineguns were used in San Diego and it caused quite a stir. There was some funny business about the heist. The locals thought the casino owners planned it themselves. The idea was to set the stage for a much larger robbery. The final plan was to blow up the casino for the insurance money, because the Mexican government extorted too large a share of the profits. There were rumors the government was going to shut down gambling. By stealing their own money, the owners could avoid the taxes and get out before the changes came."

Eric didn't respond. He was preoccupied and clearly unhappy about being back across the border. He felt as if he had been ripped out of a lucid dream before he'd experienced a proper ending.

"As it turns out," said Devon, they were right about the government. President Lazaro Cardenas outlawed gambling, and the resort was closed in 1935."

Devon was concerned about his brother's lack of response. Eric loved history, and would normally have been fascinated by a story like this. Instead, he sat mute all the way to San Diego. Devon understood that Eric was unhappy about the appointment, but he hoped Eric would give Doctor Doggett a chance. Instead, when they pulled into the parking lot, Eric grew visibly upset.

"This place is depressing as hell. I don't want to be here, Devon. I'm not coming back. Let's get it over with quickly."

Devon didn't comment. If Doctor Doggett could make a good impression, maybe it would persuade Eric to stay in touch. Devon crossed his fingers.

When they walked into the office together, Devon saw Eric look curiously at the Egyptian stone masks. This was a good sign. Eric's mood changed, buoyed by his interest in archaeology and ancient artifacts.

"Hello, Eric. I'm Doctor Doggett. Devon met with me earlier and filled me in on some of the details of your illness. Also, I received a letter from Doctor Rice that brought me up-to-date on your time at Stanford. I take it things didn't go well for you there."

"Not well at all, Doctor. I want you to understand, I'm only here because of Devon. I'm not looking for a new treatment. I don't want to undergo radiation or chemotherapy or any more painful tests. Let me be clear, something happened in Mexico, and I'm feeling better, especially in the last few weeks."

"I'm happy to hear that. I assume you're speaking about the Laetrile? Tell me about it."

"It works. That's all there is to say. I know it's working because I feel the changes. I'm sorry for taking up your time, but I don't think there's much more to be said or anything you can do for me." Eric rose from his chair ready to leave.

"Please sit down, Eric. I'm happy to hear you're feeling better, and I don't want to put you through any unwelcome treatment. Devon suggested I might take a look at you and offer a second opinion. Nothing invasive. What I could do, if you agree, is test your blood and take a few X-rays, then give you my opinion about whether there've been changes since Stanford. You could find out if these feelings of improvement have any physical basis that can be confirmed by the tests. A negative result would not indicate that the Laetrile isn't working. Your disease is complicated. The tests can't pick up everything, but they might give you some extra confidence. Is that something you'd like? We could do the tests today, and I can discuss the results with you over the phone when they're available, so you won't have to return here unless you want to. What do you think?"

Eric didn't care what the doctors or their tests said. He felt better. That was enough for him. Devon looked at him as if to say: "Well, go on. That's what we came for isn't it?" Eric knew Ofelia was worried. He wanted to reassure her things were really better. A little test wouldn't be much of a bother, but it could also backfire.

"I guess that would be okay. Look, I'll do this, but only if we all agree to some conditions. If the results are bad we'll keep them quiet. I don't want to upset my friends and family. Right now everyone thinks I'm getting better, and I want to keep it that way. No matter what the results, I'm not changing treatments or doctors. Understood?"

"That's fine with me, Eric," said Doctor Doggett. "As I said, I'll just check your current status, that's all. You can do what you want with the results. I have no intention of sharing them with anyone. That's your business."

This encouraged Devon. It was a start. He could figure out the next step later.

"Sure, Eric. Mum's the word, but what if the tests show improvement or even remission?"

"Then we'll tell everyone," said Eric with emotion. A devious smile crossed his face. "That'll piss off Doctor Rice and make the naysayers think twice about what I'm doing."

Doctor Doggett went along with the plan. He had no confidence in Laetrile, but he kept his feelings to himself.

46.

The Road

An unfinished road wound through a patch of hillside jungle behind the Cabreras' property. Eric figured that walking the road every day would help him regain some of the muscle he'd lost to the illness. Moisture trapped from the ocean breezes formed a humid atmosphere in which jungle plants thrived. The road had been started to serve a planned residential community, but the plan had been abandoned, like so many projects in Mexico that start out with optimism and end up in shambles. Eric and Ofelia hiked along the road, surrounded by the creatures and colors of the forest.

The vegetation had been cleared, but was growing back quickly. The site of the abandoned project was now covered with vines made heavy by absorbing water from ancient underground streams thick with minerals that gave the leaves their manifold colors. The leaves made the doomed development look like old Indian ruins peeking out from the underbrush. Eric scratched his calves where he had some itchy gnat bites.

"I think these walks help me," he said, speaking more to convince himself than to state a fact, but it was true—Eric's condition had steadily improved after his trip to the mountain village. Itandehui's world was completely foreign to him, but that didn't mean there wasn't something to it. Most likely it was Frieze's serum. He was definitely better. He'd regained some weight and felt more energetic. He thought back to that afternoon at San Kuuchamaa when his grandfather's spirit floated above him. Itandehui had placed those leaves on his abdomen. Did they really suck out the poison and turn it into a white powder? The imagination plays with the rational mind.

"I'm so happy Devon persuaded you to meet with Doctor Doggett," Ofelia said. "The results are very encouraging! I want to jump with joy."

"Yes, it does put me more at ease, but I felt better and looked better long before those tests. They just confirmed what I knew already."

Eric couldn't let down his guard completely. The cancer was still there. The tumors had shrunk, or so the tests said, and these walks didn't wear him out like they used to. The changes both amazed and scared him.

Ofelia knew his thoughts. "Let's not think about anything else, only about us."

"You're right, Ofelia. It's what I should do. This illness has a special way of creating fear that no trick removes."

"There are no tricks, Eric. My love and your recovery are real. I told you that you would have your miracle. Don't intellectualize it. Believe, and accept the gifts that come. It's not just this or that, but everything that works together to make you well. We have to make a new world on our own, Eric, a world we can enjoy together."

Optimism is like a seed that pushes up through dead leaves, through mold and muck. After months of darkness a new life discovers the light.

"Let's go, Ofelia, before I get weak in the knees."

They continued the walk. The road wound up a steep hill. At the ridge was a beautiful view of Tijuana on one side and the ocean on the other. Birds sat like little jewels on the limbs of trees. Eric didn't know the names of most of them. Two doves flitted in and out of the foliage while sparrows flew back and forth among the trees alongside the road. One bird with brown spotted wings and a white tummy looked like a thrush. Another, with luminescent wings, pestered a larger one with deep red wings and a brown body. Periodically, an entire flock of swallows emerged from nowhere and charged into the jungle in search of insects.

Squirrels ran along the tree limbs in front of them. Flowers were everywhere—bougainvillea, young palm trees, tiny orchid-like flowers popping up through the green ground cover, large white flowers with purple centers and pink stamens. Two redheaded woodpeckers worked over a snag, while giant bees pollinated the blooms on the jungle floor. The plants and birds and insects didn't worry about the meaning of life, what it meant to be alive, what it meant to die. Humans categorize and organize and set up all these boundaries, while nature ignores boundaries and tests the limits.

At the top of the ridge, they climbed out above the fog. Everything below them was obscured, the border between valley and ocean no longer visible. Eric and Ofelia found themselves in a fairytale among the clouds. They sat and talked while the sun caressed their backs. It was the moment Ofelia had hoped for, where everything other than the two of them subsided.

On the way down, they held hands. It was the best time Eric had had since becoming sick. The walk down was steep, so they proceeded carefully. Eric had another bout of cramps, and struggled to conceal it. He didn't want to ruin the moment for Ofelia. Remission and relapse—the cancer toyed with him like a cat with a mouse. He thought of Leon, and couldn't imagine Leon doing this to him, but what did he know about nature? There was that story about the scorpion and the frog. The scorpion promises not to sting the frog if the frog takes him across the river, but once in the water the scorpion stings the frog, dooming them both. When the frog asks why, the scorpion says, *"I couldn't help it, it's my nature."* The heart has its reasons, of which reason knows nothing.

At the bottom, a field of windblown grass was covered with small bugs burrowing holes to make homes. They made a feast for a flock of blackbirds that swooped down on them. Nature gives and nature takes away—a lesson you learned quickly when you walked in the woods.

Ofelia thought Eric was unusually quiet, and wondered if she'd done something to annoy him. Neither could know what the other thought. Under the fraught circumstances of a fragile love and Eric's disease, each assumed the worst.

"I think I'll go upstairs and take a rest."

Why doesn't he want to stay and be with me?

"I'll miss you." She didn't want to burden Eric with her insecurities, but she had to know why his mood had changed so abruptly.

"I'll miss you too. I just need a little rest. I'll be back down later." Beads of sweat popped out on Eric's forehead while he fought the pain in his bowels. He was embarrassed about what he knew was coming.

Ofelia assumed there was something about her that disturbed him and drove him away. Was it her hair, her face? Not knowing was less dreadful, but she must know.

"Eric?"

"Yes?"

"Is everything all right?"

"I feel fine, don't worry."

"No, I mean is everything all right between us?"

"Of course, why would you ask that?"

He sounded angry. She couldn't understand why he was so short with her after such a beautiful time together. She'd done nothing to deserve being kicked away like a stone.

"I just had a moment."

She feared that his feelings about her had changed. Everything about him suddenly seemed cold and distant.

Eric found her inscrutable at times. He sensed she was upset about something he'd done, but he didn't have time to dwell on it. He had an urgent need to get back to his room.

Ofelia and Eric kept their thoughts to themselves. The idyllic mood of the walk gave way to a series of false conclusions that propagated like an edifice of unsightly vegetation. They parted in this unsatisfactory state, their feelings and emotions swarming helter-skelter all around them.

Ofelia noticed a card on the walkway that had fallen out of Eric's pocket. She picked it up. It was an advertisement for a bordello downtown on Avenida Revolución . She trembled when she realized what it was.

So this is how he spends his time! I don't know him at all. He's a liar and a cheat. He's using me just like he uses these girls downtown.

She ran to her room and fell onto her bed in tears. Her pain turned to anger and thoughts of revenge. She could be cold and mean just like him, and she didn't have to say why. Let him stew in his own pain and see how that felt.

47.

Tijuana Road Races

Eric and Ofelia struggled with doubt, anger, jealousy, love and pain. Eric grew further aloof and withdrew into himself. Ofelia blamed this on his little getaway downtown.

"*¡Lo odio!*" she screamed one night alone in her room. "I hate him!"

The red light turned blue, then red, then blue again.
"Light gone, light gone, light gone, light gone. I get no lift!"
Wisps of white rushed about. Ghosts.
"There is no redemptive value in suffering, sir."
A tiny prick as the needle penetrated his arm.
Blue to red, red to blue.
Darkness.

Ofelia returned early from the clinic. Eric was gone. By the time he arrived in a cab, she was fuming. She didn't speak; the look on her face said all.

"What's wrong, Ofelia? What have I done to make you treat me this way? You don't hug me anymore. You don't kiss me. I thought you loved me."

"You're the one who hides in his room. You keep your thoughts to yourself. How am I to know what you're thinking? You leave in taxis. You're gone most of the time. You're the one who threw our love away, visiting your other women. I know about them. Don't deny it."

Eric was stunned. "What other women? What are you talking about?"

Ofelia reached into her pocket, pulled out the card, and threw it in his face.

"*These* other women! *¡Jódete!* (Fuck you!)."

"What?"

"You're just like your father with his *putas feas*. Ugly whores!"

It hit him smack in the face. That day when he walked out of the clinic, that little boy at the gate. That's where the card came from.

"Oh, Christ! I can't believe this. How could you think such a thing of me?"

"Why did you have this card then if you didn't go there?"

From the look on his face, a bit of doubt entered Ofelia's mind. *Could I be wrong?*

"Of course I didn't go there. One day leaving the clinic that young boy that hangs around outside the gate, you know who I mean, accosted me and shoved the card into my pocket. I forgot all about it. You have to believe me, Ofelia. Oh, God, this is so stupid. I can't believe it."

Ofelia had seen that little boy pester the patients going in and out of the clinic. It all made sense. Now, feeling completely foolish, she tried to compose herself. "What a fool I've been! It all started after that last walk. It was such a wonderful day, but you left me so abruptly without even saying why. I thought I'd done something to annoy you. Then, when I found that card, well, I assumed the worst."

She began to cry. Eric took her in his arms. "No, it's my fault," he said. "I've been so blind. I didn't feel well that afternoon, Ofelia. I needed to go to my room. I had diarrhea. I was ashamed to tell you. I've never been good at sharing my feelings, but that's going to change now. I'll tell you everything, I promise. Whatever embarrassment it may cause will surely be better than what we've gone through this past week."

"I'm so sorry, Eric. Sometimes I can act like such a spoiled little girl."

Eric tore up the card and threw it on the ground. "It's over. Nothing will get in the way of our love again, Ofelia, as long as we're honest with each other. No more secrets. From now on if either of us is worried about anything, let's get it out in the open."

Eric found it difficult to keep his promise. He could never be completely honest with Ofelia about his illness. There were times he wasn't even honest with himself.

"You better now, Jack? Things okay now in the room down the hall. Dude unplugged his monitor. I fixed it good this time. Everything gonna be quiet again. You awake?"

Eric spoke from a drugged stupor. Nelson thought it was all nonsense until he realized there was something to it, some kind of story. That's when he started taking notes.

The heat in Tijuana became unbearable. Ofelia's parents and Osvaldo were at the summer home in Rumorosa. Devon stayed in the big house with Orvaline. Their friendship blossomed, which surprised and pleased Eric. The two went on little explorations and were gone most days. Orvaline introduced Devon to areas of Tijuana the tourists never saw. They wandered around the broken-down remains of the Agua Caliente Casino, went to dog and rooster fights, hung out with Orvaline's friends and listened to the music played on the San Diego radio stations—songs by The Beatles, The Beach Boys, and The Rolling Stones. It seemed to Devon as if they had the world at their fingertips. They explored desolate beaches, swam in the nude, and enjoyed the sun. At night they partied hard in the clubs downtown.

The war in Vietnam, savage and apocalyptic, had led to numerous rebellions on college campuses around the country like the People's Park riot that Devon had seen firsthand, and Kent State where four students were shot dead and others seriously wounded. He was conflicted by his revulsion toward the war and his compassion for the soldiers, some of whom were his friends and fellow students. This trip to Tijuana gave him a chance to escape the toxic political and economic atmosphere in the States. He was here for Eric, but the break from the chaos up north was a bonus.

Orvaline and Ofelia took time off from their jobs. Orvaline suggested they all go out to the Tijuana Road Races at the playas in the shadow of the Bullring by the Sea. Eric was keen on the idea because Jordan's son would be there.

The race ran along an upper street, then proceeded north, close to the border, so spectators on both sides could watch and cheer together. The cars sped back along a lower street parallel to the beach where bales of hay were set up as safety barriers. Almost all the spots were good for viewing. They decided to stand along the lower street where they thought the cars would reach top speed. Some enthusiastic local boys sat on the hay bales, and tried to kick the cars as they went by, oblivious of the danger. Some ran across the track in front of the cars to show their bravery. The whole thing was so chaotically Mexican that an accident seemed inevitable. Still, everyone had a good time. Eric spotted Jordan along the track and walked over to speak with him.

"Which one is he?"

"Number 23 in the red MGB. He'll be in the third race." Jordan explained that the cars were divided into classes based on their specifications. Eric saw the pride in Jordan's eyes.

"What's his name, Jordan?"

"Daniel. We call him Danny."

"I'll be rooting for him."

"Thanks, Eric. How are you feeling? You look better."

"You know, Jordan, everything changed after we took that trip to the mountain. My brother persuaded me to see a doctor in San Diego. He did a complete workup and was amazed at my condition. I think it's Frieze's serum. You did right by me. I'll never forget that. Everything has worked out, and I have you to thank for it."

Jordan put a cigar in his mouth. That wry smile appeared on his face. His round stomach moved in and out with each puff. Between puffs he said, "Don't discount Itandehui, lad. She worked her special magic on you."

"You do know, don't you, those things aren't good for you?"

"I'll take my chances. I've got a little pull upstairs."

Jordan puffed away as Eric walked back to the group.

Over the years, Orvaline had gone to several of these races with his buddies. They were the boys from the top of the hill, not a gang, but an exclusive club based on heredity, the sons of the rich families who ran the city. They had the money and the time for car racing, bullfighting, and boxing—all the things the poor kids only dreamed of. In recent years, many of Orvaline's friends had moved to Mexico City for college or to one of the other state capitals for a professional job. Some had even moved up north.

The first race lasted about fifteen minutes. During the break, Eric and Ofelia walked to one of the carts that sold cold drinks. They held hands. As they strolled along, Eric watched the waves break on the beach. Orvaline had at last accepted their relationship, albeit grudgingly. Devon had been a big help. He and Orvaline were getting on so well that Orvaline had little time to worry about Eric and Ofelia.

A girl with blonde hair and fair skin, stood next to Devon. Orvaline glanced at her, obviously distracted by the girl's tight shorts. She had a wild cat on a chain. Occasionally she walked it along the track. Devon asked where she was from.

"My boyfriend's racing today. We came down from Colorado after some friends told us about these races. He loves this kind of thing. I don't care much for it, but I put up with it for him." Up close, Devon could see her pretty green eyes. Orvaline shifted back and forth like he wanted to break into the conversation, but he seemed shy about doing so.

"That's quite a cat you've got."

"It's an ocelot. We got it in Texas." She smiled suggestively.

It was time for the second race to start. Eric and Ofelia returned, still holding hands. Half an hour later the third and final race began. The girl with the ocelot was still there, and Orvaline got up the nerve to speak with her. She had lots of questions about Tijuana, and he was happy to supply the answers.

"My boyfriend heard you can get the full tuck 'n' roll here for about a hundred bucks. Do you know any places that do that?"

"Sure, there are a lot of places off Revolución. If you decide to do it, though, keep a close watch on your car. Sometimes they bury drugs under the upholstery to send up to the States where their friends steal the cars to get at the drugs."

Her eyes opened wide.

The ocelot jumped, and she had to yank the chain hard to keep it still. A dog on the other side of the track was giving it the eye.

"Ooh! They really do that?" she asked innocently in a way that amped up her appeal to Orvaline.

Devon wondered what her boyfriend looked like and if he'd be angry that they were talking.

"Yeah, but don't worry. Usually things go okay. I can give you the names of some reliable places if you want."

"Gee, that would be great," she said, giving him a suggestive smile.

Orvaline wrote down a few names for her and handed over the note.

The race started. Everyone stood up, anxiously waiting for the cars to make the turn and come roaring along the ocean side of the street. As the cars drew near, Eric noticed the red MGB with #23 out in front. He could feel the excitement build.

The dog broke loose and ran across the track toward the ocelot. Eric saw the MGB swerve and brake to avoid an accident, but there wasn't time. It slammed into the dog. The car was so close that Eric could see Danny's terrified eyes as he lost control and flipped over the hay bales. People scrambled out of the way. The MGB hit something, sparks flew, and the car exploded into flames.

Eric grew sick. His heart pounded. Everyone screamed. The *federales* ran down from the corner. A fire truck was on the scene in minutes, but it was too late for Danny.

Jordan saw the whole thing unfold right in front of him. His eyes wild, he rushed the flaming car, oblivious of the searing heat. Eric lunged and dragged him back. Eric felt the blood rush through Jordan's body, and watched the tears stream down Jordan's face. The cigar still glowed on the ground next to his feet.

Eric held Jordan as if he were a child. Ofelia, Orvaline, and Devon ran to help, but there was nothing to be done. The fire truck put out the flames. All that was left was a blackened smoldering mass, a sight too awful for any of them to look. Eric guided Jordan away from the scene. It was too horrible to even think about what had happened. They took Jordan to Ana Luisa's. By the time they arrived, she'd already heard the news. Several neighbors and friends milled around in shock, not knowing what to do. Ana ran out and hugged

Jordan. They cried together, then went inside. Eric and the others went home. The summer that had started in bliss had turned to misery in an instant. It was a shocking reminder that the world has its own inexplicable designs, sometimes brutal, cold, and heartless.

48.

Underground

When the trapdoor slammed down, Frieze hurried up the ladder. He dropped his flashlight and it broke. He heaved, yelled, and banged against the door, but there was nothing, no one, only silence.

It was dark and damp in his underground storage room. He hoped his eyes would adjust, but the blackness was so total he couldn't see a thing. He thought about pushing a pole or stick up through the trap door, but as he groped about in the dark, he could find nothing suitable. He considered burning a hole through it, but he had no way to light a fire—and the smoke might have choked him. The air was dense. It would soon be hard to breathe.

Frieze yelled and banged until he was exhausted and was forced to rest. He heard nothing on the outside. He knew Dos Negros had two men spying on him, and hoped they might come looking.

He slipped off to sleep, but it was very cramped and he kept waking as he changed position. He was thirsty and getting hungry. He hadn't eaten breakfast or lunch before being trapped here. He knew there was no way out. Frieze had built this little room well. It had reinforced wooden beams, a cement floor, and wooden walls. He used this secret space to store his Laetrile so that no one could steal from him again. To throw off potential thieves, he kept a few bottles of the clinic's Laetrile at the house. It would take the dimwits at Napier's lab weeks of testing to determine that what they'd stolen was no different from what they already had at the clinic. Louie had committed his formula to memory. Everything important about his life was here in the underground room. Now, he was here too. He was struck by the irony. He remembered Ana Luisa trying to convince him to hire a housecleaner. Had he followed her advice, his maid would be out looking for him now. He lived and worked alone, and had told no one about the storage room, not even Jordan and Ana Luisa. Without some kind of miracle, he would die here, and so would his discovery. He and his life's work would disappear forever unless by some miracle he was found. He yelled again and banged on the door, but he knew it was futile. He slumped into a corner and thought about his life. He tried to picture what things were like when he'd been a little boy, when he was in college, then later when he was a professional chemist.

In the dusty tomes of the école Polytechnique, Frieze had discovered that in 1830 two French chemists had isolated amygdalin, a substance found naturally in the pits of apricots. They speculated amygdalin was useful as an anti-cancer agent, but nothing came of the idea. Frieze set about perfecting the anti-cancer benefits of amygdalin, but family circumstances forced him to relocate to Mexico. He abandoned his research. Years went by. He settled in Tijuana where he met two men working on alternative cancer cures. They persuaded him to resume his research.

After all the years of disappointment, he became excited. Sadly, jealousy, envy, and greed conspired against him. The men who claimed to be his friends concocted a plan to steal his formula. Frieze found out, broke off the relationship, and went into hiding. He knew he could never trust them again. Jordan told him to get away to where it was safe, but he didn't act fast enough. Ironically, it was not Napier or Dos Negros who threatened him. His own stubbornness was the instrument of his bitter ending. Here he was in the darkness, alone and tired, so tired. The clock ticked. Time passed away—and before long so would he.

49.

The Funeral

The archbishop didn't attend Danny's funeral. The Church preached compassion but banked on propriety. The prelate wanted to avoid the appearance of hypocrisy, even at the cost of friendship and duty. Several priests from the surrounding area did come, probably at some risk, to pay their respects to Father Jordan. His lifelong friend, Father Gomez, performed the service. Father Gomez was known throughout the community for his good work among the Indians in the mountain communities. He often traveled with Father Jordan to remote areas in the hills where together they preached the Mass and provided the sacraments of baptism, marriage, and communion to the natives who had long ago worked Catholicism into their ancient form of religion.

Everyone in the local community knew Ana Luisa and mourned for her. Few knew the real story, but everyone understood Jordan had had a special relationship with Danny. Eric felt a personal kinship with the boy whose ashes lay in the hand-painted urn at the altar. Neither Ana Luisa nor Jordan wanted cremation, but it was necessary because Danny's body had been too badly burned to allow an open casket.

Ofelia, Orvaline, Eric, and Devon sat near the front of the church. Seeing the crash and the fire brought on woeful dreams night after night. It was all they could speak of. There was no escape from the nightmares, and the funeral reignited the awful memories.

Eric sat with Ofelia during the ceremony. Devon's attention oscillated between the back of Doctor Milagro's head and the breasts of his beautiful daughter. She frequently dropped her rosary, and each time she bent to pick it up, Devon got the full view. He was a slave to his libido. The lack of intimacy with Mia, and the bawdy clubs he frequented with Orvaline, keyed him up. He knew it was blasphemous, especially at a funeral, but he couldn't help imagining every beautiful girl in the church naked. It made for an interesting afternoon despite the sad events of the day.

Orvaline sat stoically throughout. Behind closed eyes he saw nothing. His somber thoughts were painful enough. He and Ofelia had met Danny only once, when he and Ana Luisa and Jordan had come to the Cabreras' home for a short visit. It was long ago, yet somehow the funeral affected Orvaline in a very personal way that he could not understand.

Hector Hernandez stood at the back of the church, out of sight of all but a few. Eric noticed him before the service began. Hector's face poked out around the screen that separated the foyer from the nave. Eric thought there was sadness and confusion in Hector's eyes. His distorted face, like the mark of Cain, spoke to the tragic life he'd chosen, but underneath the knotted skin, Eric saw a vulnerable man, one who suffered from an unjust burden fate had thrown at him.

The church, built of wood and bricks and mortar, was extravagant, like many of the older churches in Mexico. It provided an unimaginable opulence in the lives of the faithful who attended the Mass and weddings and funerals. Delicate stained-glass windows depicted the fourteen Stations of the Cross. Ofelia's great-uncle had donated them in memory of his departed wife. A generous patron had contributed three painted wooden statues adorned with gold leaf: Joseph, the Virgin Mary, and the Savior. There were oil paintings of prominent saints. Eric had never paid attention to the saints. He'd once told Devon they were manufactured to order whenever the Church was having trouble keeping the laity in line. On one side of the altar, under the statue of the Virgin Mary, were votive candles and a metal coin box for donations. The golden tabernacle held the sacramental wine and wafers. It wasn't real gold, but it was quite impressive just the same. On the altar's other side, Joseph, the cuckold carpenter, was in mid-stride in his brown robe, his familiar staff in his hand. A life-sized Jesus, nailed to a large wooden cross, looked down on Danny from above the tabernacle.

Hector hadn't known Danny. He'd come because he thought Frieze might show up, perhaps in disguise. Rafael and Tomás attended because of their position in the local community. They sat in the back row. Tomás hated churches, but he and Rafael thought this was an opportunity to demonstrate their compassion to the congregation. No one was fooled—the people here knew what the Dos Negros represented, and despised them.

At the entrance to the church was a stone pathway lined on both sides with ancient olive trees. Ofelia told Eric no one could remember who'd planted them, but they were meant to be a reminder of Gethsemane. Several parishioners claimed they'd had visions while sitting alone on the benches lining the walkway—visions of Jesus, of the Apostles, even of Roman soldiers. An old man baptized in the church as a child harvested the olives each year and cured them in salt brine. When they were ready, he shared them with the entire congregation. The pathway diverged into two semicircles near the front and surrounded a small pond with a trickling fountain. Beyond the fountain, the two paths rejoined and continued on to the wooden stairway.

When they arrived, Eric and Ofelia met Napier. Nicoletta was with him. She wore a black silk dress. It was one of the few times she wore no lipstick at all. Devon tried not to stare as they went inside, but found it impossible. If Nicoletta had wanted to be inconspicuous, she'd failed.

Ofelia's family sent a giant spray of flowers. It was impossible for them to come in person because they were to stay in Rumorosa for several more weeks. Ofelia was ashamed. She felt her parents owed Ana Luisa and Jordan more respect. When she mentioned this to Eric, he told her this was one more way that Mexicans and Americans were different. No one would have worried much about missing a funeral in California. He had missed his own father's funeral. He'd been in Europe at the time and hadn't returned home.

Several healers from the area came to share Ana Luisa's sorrow, as had farmers and Indians. Many had walked the entire way to town. Eric recognized Itandehui. She seemed even smaller and more frail than he remembered. Odd how memory can distort the truth. The healing treatment was vivid in his mind; Itandehui had seemed eternal and indestructible that day. Eric's life had changed in so many ways since then. He had many reasons to be grateful, and despite the sad occasion, he was happy. He wasn't out of the woods yet, but was on the way.

The results of Doctor Doggett's tests were more than Eric could have expected. Nearly at a loss for words, the doctor confirmed that Eric's pathology had changed dramatically. Something astonishing had happened, something anomalous that modern medicine could not explain. Doctor Doggett assumed cancer began and ended in glands and tissues and organs. The way to fight such an illness is with drugs and surgeries. This story didn't jibe with what he saw in Eric.

Several young men from the race attended the funeral, as did the ocelot girl and her boyfriend. They felt terribly guilty. The owner of the dog was not there; he'd left the dead animal on the track and driven quickly away, too ashamed or afraid to be seen.

The funeral was not as morbid as Eric expected. The immediate family, including Ana Luisa and Jordan, were sequestered behind a black curtain. Eric had no idea how things were there, but he could guess. He knew a part of Father Jordan had died with Danny. Everything about Jordan had changed. He gave up the cigars and his wry smile had disappeared. Eric didn't hear the harp anymore when he walked past the chapel. It was as if Jordan's ashes were there in the urn with his son's. Jordan still here, but he was like a puppet with broken strings. Eric wondered if he'd slept at all since the accident. Sleep is a rehearsal for death. Eric met the dead in his dreams, the distorted floating eye of his grandfather, the stern cold stare of his own father, even Azore, the faithful German shepherd that was his constant companion as a young boy. He wondered if Jordan saw Danny in his dreams, if they spoke, or if Jordan dreamed at all.

The wake preceding the funeral went on for two days at Ana Luisa's house. People came to leave flowers and offerings and mementos next to an *altarcito* in the front room. Neither Eric nor Ofelia had seen Jordan. He hid himself away. Eric wanted to hug Jordan, to tell him how sorry he felt, but that would have to wait.

Because of the cremation there would be no interment. After the service, Jordan had stayed behind the black curtain with Ana Luisa. Everyone else left—life goes on. All funerals make the participants think in some way about their own deaths. In the line with the other mourners, Eric walked past the urn. Some knelt to pray. Eric wasn't afraid of death. He now had so many reasons to live. He didn't want to die, but he also knew that immortality was not for him. What counts in life is quality, not quantity. The most beautiful things in life would not gain if they lasted forever.

50.

Confrontation

Eric climbed the hill to the clinic chapel. This was his first chance to speak with Jordan since the accident. After Danny's death, Jordan was hounded like Orpheus in his futile journey to bring back Eurydice. Who among those remaining has not wished to bring back the dead? *It's just selfish vanity,* Eric thought. *The peace of death surpasses the utter lack of peace in life. Raising the dead might be like waking a sick person in great pain—waking him because we feel lonely and want company. Maybe it makes more sense to join the dead than to wish for their return.* Eric couldn't fault Jordan for having the feelings we all have. He'd be just like Jordan if something happened to Ofelia.

The old priest met Eric with a blank stare. The air in the church felt oppressive and stale. Jordan's hands hung heavy at his sides, no longer aware of the delicate lyre that lay at his feet. The brooding expression on Jordan's face was formed by thoughts that raced ahead, stopped, came back, and rushed off again. He stood impatiently listening for something from death's dream kingdom where Daniel rested.

Until Eric's words came out of his mouth, he wasn't sure what he would say. He let his heart be his guide. "Jordan, I know you're a priest. You're so much more than that to me. You are my friend, my mentor, and my guardian. I worry about those demons I see in your eyes."

If there's meaning to be found in the land of mourning, it must be a hollow meaning at best. The abyss opens and hands beckon from death's other kingdom. Belief that the heart escapes this valley of dying stars might sustain hope of a final meeting with those we love, but who would stake a life on it?

Jordan's eyes were pained. He was a man possessed by sorrow and bitterness, but most of all, he felt more alone than ever. He'd lost his faith, and for the first time he experienced solitude, loneliness, and despair.

"What can I say, Jordan? This breaks my heart. You're such a good friend. You've done so much for me. I wish I could do something, anything, that might help."

Jordan's eyes focused far away. "I'm no different from anyone else at a time like this, Eric. Sadness, confusion, anger—there are times, yes, I can say it to you, times I feel that God does not want me, that God is not God, that God does not even exist."

Eric didn't think. He hugged Jordan, clasped his arms around Jordan's great bulk and pressed Jordan's head to his chest as he had on the day of the accident. Jordan didn't struggle or pull back. He sobbed freely. It was an awkward moment, but there was something noble in it that made Eric feel useful in a way he'd never felt before.

"Cry, Jordan. Let it out. You don't have to explain. Faith without doubt is dead faith. You know that better than anyone. I'm sure all believers have times when they wonder if God is there or if he cares. Life is a long dream. There are nightmares along the way. We do our best."

Jordan untangled himself from Eric's grasp. He stepped back.

"They say time heals all. I'm not so sure, lad, but we must go on. Yes, we must go on."

"Remember Mary? I met her when I first arrived. That first day she said, 'Life can be ugly but we must make the best of it.' Healing is slow, Jordan. Our lives and our hearts are impatient."

The ocean pounded in the distance. A gardener planted small palms in tin buckets alongside the chapel. A breeze came off the ocean. The color returned to Jordan's eyes. "I'm happy to see you're looking well, Eric. Thank you for coming. I do feel better just seeing you."

"I'm well thanks to you, Jordan. Doctor Doggett in San Diego has confirmed the progress I feel."

A tear rolled down Jordan's cheek as he spoke. "You're so much like my Danny: You're about the same age, you have the same kind temperament. What I feel most is that your heart, like Danny's, is pure and good."

"No one can replace Danny, Jordan. I know that. I do think of you as a father sometimes, the father I wish I'd had. We're two spirits floating in a fog. I don't believe in purpose or fate, but something brought us together just when we both needed each other. It's the unselfish love I learned from you."

"There's something I must tell you, Eric. The Mangy Parrot has gone missing. Ana Luisa and I are very concerned. It's not at all like him to just disappear. And, there's this: The bishop approached me with a peculiar request. It may be innocent, but it adds to my worries. Just after Frieze disappeared, the bishop asked if I knew where to find him. It seemed odd. I've never discussed Frieze with the bishop so it made me wonder if someone put him up to it. Frieze may never be found. The last time I saw him he was very depressed."

A cool shadow fell over Eric. He knew what this meant. No more Frieze, no more Laetrile. Ofelia had set aside some of Frieze's serum, very little. It would have to get him through. He didn't want to burden Jordan with these new fears, but they were impossible to hide completely.

"It does sound strange. Let's hope he shows up."

Fear is a sinister monster that eats away at the brain like death carves up the body.

Oh, go away, please go! I'm too young. Leave me alone!

Shh! Be cool. I'm right here with you, man.

Nelson pressed the button to increase the flow of medication.

"Eric, are you all right?" Jordan was concerned with the look of confusion on Eric's face.

"I'm fine." Eric had to buck up, to be strong for Jordan. "Look, you told me to find you whenever I wanted to talk, remember? Well, I'm here for you too, Jordan. It works both ways. You know that, don't you?"

"Indeed. I'll manage it and so will you. Come now, Eric, how are things going with Ofelia?"

It was as if a great darkness passed.

"You were right about telling her. We confessed our love to each other. She's already told her parents. I've decided to ask her father for his permission to marry when he returns from Rumorosa."

"I daresay he's a tough old bird, Eric. He has a soft side underneath that stern countenance of his and a wife that can help you. I'll appeal to him on your behalf and to be sure I'll speak with Ofelia's mother. She's a good Christian, has a heart o' gold. She understands the ways of love. I'll get her to work on Ofelia's father."

"Thanks, Jordan. You're a true friend. I'm so lucky. I'll admit I'm nervous. I wish we could just run off and get married without all the fuss, but I know that would be wrong."

After their goodbyes, Eric walked down the hill and out the gate of the clinic compound. That's when he saw them—three young Mexican men. They were waiting for him like three lizards on a rock. He didn't pay much attention until he realized they were following him. The hair stood up on his arms. There was no place to go. In his condition he knew he couldn't outrun them. He'd had an experience with a pack of dogs when he was in college. Alone, they weren't aggressive, but in a pack, the hunting instinct took over. He knew running would encourage the worst in the dogs, would trigger a predatory attack. He walked along slowly, watching the dogs out of the corner of his eye. The pack leader jumped forward and bit him on the leg hard enough to draw blood. Eric didn't flinch. He held his ground, kicked and yelled and shooed them away. Eventually they left. He hoped the same plan would work now.

The three men drew close. The one in the middle seemed to be the leader. He spoke to Eric in English. "Do you enjoy fucking your little Mexican whore?"

Eric was blindsided. "What?"

"Ofelia can't keep her legs crossed around men, gringo. Every time you fuck her, just remember that my prick was there first. You're parking in my garage."

So, this was Marcelino. He had his buddies with him. He was going through the motions to impress them, to demonstrate that he was macho. Eric didn't want to play into their hands, but he couldn't let the insult pass.

"I'm in love with her, Marcelino. Go screw yourself."

It was the wrong thing to say. Eric should have allowed himself to be humiliated, but he couldn't allow Ofelia to be humiliated. Marcelino stepped forward and punched him in the stomach. Eric doubled over. It hurt more than he'd expected. He dropped to his knees.

"That's right, gringo, pray to me. Take your Mexican whore back to the States. I give her to you. I have no use for that puta anymore."

Eric looked up and saw Marcelino's face. There was a glimmer of compassion.

One of the others yelled "*El hombre no esta terminado,* Marcelino."

Marcelino kicked him in the face. "*¡Ahora, esta acabado!*"

They all walked off, their cruel laughter ringing in his ears.

Eric lay squirming in the dirt. He knew his face had been cut. He didn't want Ofelia to know this happened. He stood up slowly, brushed off the dust, and returned to the clinic to clean up. On the way inside he ran into Mida.

"¡Señor Eric! ¿*Que pasa?*"

"Nothing Mida. I tripped walking outside and cut my face."

When Mida snorted, her whole body shook.

"God who gives the wound gives the salve. You want me fix you up?"

"No, thanks. I can wash up in the bathroom."

He looked in the mirror. It wasn't as bad as he'd thought. Marcelino had gone easy on him. Eric was convinced Marcelino didn't want to hurt him. He was putting on a show for his buddies to prove he was a tough guy. He could easily have broken Eric's nose if he'd wanted to. On the way out, Mida was there to greet him.

"I see Marcelino, Señor Eric. He is little rooster. There is no worse struggle than one not done. No worries. Marcelino finished with you, terminado."

Eric felt foolish. "Don't tell Ofelia, Mida. She doesn't have to know about this."

"*El perro ladra y la caravana pasa.*

"What's that?"

"Dog bark and parade it pass. I say nothing."

"Thanks Mida. You're a good friend."

"*¡Si, buenos amigos, verdad!*" She laughed heartily and started to walk away.

"Don't put too much cream on your tacos, Mida!"

Now they were both laughing.

Doctor Milagro came walking by, looking distracted.

"Hello, Doctor. You seem lost in your thoughts. I hope they're good ones."

"Ah, Eric. Yes, good thoughts, very important they are. I am writing a piece for one of the medical journals on preventive medicine. We all need to pay more attention to that. We ignore God's plan at our peril. Western medicine addresses the symptoms, but here at Buena Salud we try to support the immune system so the body can heal, something we should all focus on every day. It is natural to want a quick fix, but we need to incorporate prevention into our lives. That requires more diligence on our part. We could eliminate most of the drugs and surgery. All we have to do is to value the preventive approach and cultivate a positive mental attitude. It's absolutely vital to get to know and understand the body's signals. If everyone took Laetrile on a regular basis even before any symptoms showed up, I am convinced the occurrence of cancer would be greatly diminished."

"You mean, take Laetrile as if it were a vitamin?"

"Si! It *is* a vitamin! Señor Napier has some new products that will introduce Laetrile into the daily diet. They will soon be on the market. I must be on my way. I am off to meet with him. Good to see you. What happened to your face?"

"Just a little scratch. I must be more careful with the steps."

"Oh, yes. Those steps, we must put the better railing."

Doctor Milagro left as quickly as he had arrived. He was a man with a purpose. Mida had already left to meet with a patient. Eric walked back to the gate. Two patients, a man and a woman, were conversing in the courtyard.

"We've all experienced events that don't have any rational explanation. There are some truths that can never be proven true. Godel showed that."

"I thought it was Pascal. Who's Godel?"

"Some mathematician, I think."

"I don't trust mathematicians. They reduce everything to numbers, even love."

"Well, one plus one is two isn't it?"

"That means nothing to me. We'd be a lot safer if the government would take its money out of science and put it into astrology or the reading of palms and auras, if you ask me."

"That's going a little far, don't you think?"

"Look, I didn't come here looking for reason or science. There's no reason in this confounded illness. There's no science that can justify why cancer chooses one of us over another. There's no good sense why my uncle's heart failed him or why my grandchild was born blind. Illness and death, they aren't rational."

Eric walked out the gate. He didn't know what to think. It was the first time he'd sided so passionately with the trees. They stand silently, their roots solidly in the ground. He'd come for Laetrile treatment because he thought it would prolong his life. He didn't believe in magical thinking or flimsy evidence. He'd always trusted in science to find the answers that could be found. Was he a fool for leaving Stanford? Was he on a wild-goose chase, as Devon said? Had he become as looney as these two in the courtyard?

Confrontation

"Speak to him in Spanish, Nelson."

"Huh? I don't speak Spanish, ma'am."

Well, shee-it! I ain't no goddamn interpreter; what's the bitch thinkin' anyway?

"Ask that man what time it is. Go ahead, ask him."

"Uh, 'scuse me, sir, what time you think it be?"

"*No comprendo.*"

Nelson started to dance around with his dictionary in hand.

"Uh, que whora est-ee?"

"Half past tree by the cock."

"I think he says three-thirty, ma'am."

Nurse Marta took off her hat and wiped her sunburned forehead with a handkerchief. Her blonde mane hung down all around her. The hills of Tijuana were jumbled up in a maze of crooked streets and alleyways, and she and Nelson were caught in the middle of it.

"How the hell do they find their way around down here? There aren't even any street signs."

"I s'pose they just knows the way from habit."

"You suppose, do you Nelson? That doesn't help us at all, you dunce. I thought you said the man down at the bottom of the road said it was up this way, but I don't see any clinic around here at all."

You should've brought a goddamn map, bitch!

"What's that, Nelson?"

"I'm not sure he be knowin' what I be askin', ma'am. I don't speak the Spanish too good."

"What exactly did he say, Nelson? I want to know exactly what he said. I'm getting very exasperated right now, and I think you are the cause of it."

"Well, truth be known, ma'am, he didn't say too much, but I'll tell you everything I recollect. I think what he said was, if there is a clinic, it be right up this road."

You've gotta be a junkie to put up with all this shit. No wonder they're trying to get rid of me at the hospital. Those folks are all nuts.

"What do you mean, if there is a clinic? Of course there's a clinic. That's where Mr. Martin said he was going to go."

Nelson chuckled. A wild-goose chase'll slow 'er down.

"What did you say, Nelson?"

"I said, maybe we should go back down and start over, ma'am."

The manticore has the body of a lion, a human head with three rows of sharp teeth, sometimes bat wings, and a trumpet-like voice. Its tail is like a scorpion's, and shoots poisonous spines to either paralyze or kill its victims. It devours its prey whole and leaves no clothes, bones, or possessions behind.

Nelson decided it was best not to get Nurse Marta's dander up.

"I'm not starting over! It must be up here somewhere. Ask that man with the burro. Those look like medical supplies he has strapped onto its back."

"Don day es tah clinico?" Nelson read the words out of the dictionary.

The man's dark eyes peered at him. Nelson wondered if he hadn't seen a black man before.

"What for you ah want clinico? You sick?"

"Amigo, yo tango amigo in clinico." Nelson was getting the hang of the lingo now. He thought that was pretty cool shit. He couldn't wait to tell his friends back home and impress his old lady.

The man spat into the dirt. He spat into his hands and rubbed them together.

"You make ah the map this place? Stir up trouble?"

"No, no. Shit, we got no map, amigo. We just lookin' for a friend."

"You want to founded out the clinic? Well, you walk the wrong place. Clinic on other road."

The man pointed across the canyon to one of the roads on the other side.

"Well, there's your answer, ma'am. I guess we took the wrong turn at the fork. We gonna have to go back."

51.

Rogelio

Rogelio knew the reason for Eric's visit. He'd thought a great deal about his daughter's future. He was not sympathetic to a marriage but he would listen to what Eric had to say.

This meeting was Eric's one chance to win over Ofelia's father. He knew he would have to get everything just right. "Mr. Cabrera, first let me apologize. We can never know when love will come to carry us away. It's not always possible to prepare in advance. I know that's no excuse for not coming to you sooner, but I'm here now. I've come to ask you for Ofelia's hand in marriage. I hope you'll listen to what I have to say with an open mind."

Rogelio gazed out the window. His wife told him Father Jordan thought very highly of Eric. She advised him to be generous. He did not feel generous. He did not trust the Americans. They had caused him only grief.

"You hardly know Ofelia. I have watched her grow from a baby into the young woman you see now. You know nothing of her past, of our family, our culture. You are a foreigner. I suspect you are unfamiliar with many things that are important to us. A marriage between two such different people is not a good idea. There is not enough in common to make such a marriage work."

Ofelia's father wore gray slacks and a blue shirt. Eric glanced down at the shoes. They were of the finest golden leather. The shoes walked around the room with a will of their own. Rogelio was wealthy and powerful, stern and stiff. He wanted to protect his daughter from a future he saw much differently than Eric did. Having grown up without a father, Eric was at a disadvantage. He knew this was going to be a difficult argument to make.

"I love your daughter, sir. It's true I've only known her for a few weeks, but I feel as if I've known her all my life. I love her, and she loves me. I know I'm a foreigner in your country. Your family has been very kind to me. It's not my intention to repay your kindness with ignorance or arrogance. If you'll allow me, I want to become part of your family. I have much to learn, but nothing is impossible if we put our minds to it. I want to marry Ofelia. I want to add to her life and to your family, not subtract from them."

"Suppose what you say is true. Do you even know what love is? We men often confuse lust or friendship or even mere novelty for love. There was a time when women loved men for money, and men loved women because they were the fashion or because of their surroundings. Today, too much is put on the physical and on the immediate emotions. Not enough thought is given to the great work a lasting love requires, to the future. When the novelty wears off, it is the everyday that remains. Love makes one do foolish things, as you say, but there is much more to a relationship than those first days when you are caught up in a romantic idyll. Love brings responsibilities. True love sometimes means walking away. You are ill. What will happen to my daughter if you die? I do not mean to be callous to a man in your condition, but we must talk about such things."

The golden shoes snapped together. Rogelio stood like a statue and stared out the window. Eric took this pause as a signal to make his case. "I had little idea when I was first diagnosed how my life would change. None of us can tell the future, Señor Cabrera. I do not want to die. According to the doctors, my chances have improved. Ofelia knows how sick I am. She knows from the clinic what can happen. We all die sooner or later. Should I die, Ofelia will continue her life. She will have her own resources. I will make arrangements to see that she is comfortable financially."

Rogelio turned to Eric, his eyes deadly serious, burning like some volatile new chemical element, his face flushed red, his blue shirt billowing in the warm breeze that came through the open window.

"I cannot agree." Rogelio's whole body trembled as he spoke. "There has not been enough time. This is an important decision, a life decision. I'm appreciative of what you did for Orvaline, but I don't know you, Mr. Martin. I don't know your family or anything about you. I cannot consent to a marriage. Ofelia is my only daughter. I've raised and protected her since birth. How could I agree to a marriage under these circumstances? It's simply not possible. None of us are ready to decide that, not even you."

"Mr. Cabrera, this is not a matter of lust or friendship or mere novelty. This is not some fatuous romantic idyll. My love for Ofelia is the same as the love she has for me. I assure you I will take care of your daughter. That is a promise you can hold me to. I will respect her. I will not disappoint her or you or your family. Look into your heart. You know we love each other. The power of love is unyielding. There must be a way through this impasse."

Rogelio thought back to the time when he'd asked Amelia's father for her hand in marriage. It was the most difficult thing he'd ever done. He too had run into a wall of stone. Amelia's father considered Rogelio's pedigree too many levels below the pedestal the proud Rodriguez family rested upon. In the end, love won. It usually does.

"What do you intend to do if I do not give my permission?"

"Mr. Cabrera, I won't embarrass you. I won't disrespect you. I would prefer to marry Ofelia with your approval, but marry her I will, if she will have me."

"You haven't asked her yet?"

"Not yet."

"I suppose you know that you have Father Jordan's support. He spoke highly of you. He's a good priest. We need more like him. You also know, I understand, that Ofelia has another suitor, Marcelino, a fine young local boy with a promising career in medicine."

"Yes, I've met Marcelino."

"How did that go?"

"Let's just say we came to an understanding."

Rogelio noticed the fresh scar on Eric's face. He smiled, but didn't waver.

"I could make this difficult. I could send Ofelia away. She has a desire to study in Europe. I could ask you to leave. Perhaps I should."

"I could have asked Ofelia to run away with me, to elope, but I wanted to make my case honestly to you. You are her father. She loves her family. I would never ask her to give up that relationship. We can all come together without taking extreme measures. Give me a chance."

Rogelio saw Amelia looking through the window. Her eyes told him what she felt. "I have some sympathy for your situation. I went through this myself once. Amelia's father gave me a difficult time." He paused, and his eyes glanced left while he pondered what to say next. "I want what's best for my daughter, that's all."

"It's what I also want. I want to ask Ofelia to marry me. If she agrees, Father Jordan will perform the service. My time frame may be a little shorter than you might prefer, but it's what I have to work with."

Both men relaxed. The sounds of birds and insects in the garden mingled with the pounding of the ocean below. Rogelio's head moved slightly. It was barely perceptible at first. He made a slight nod forward. Eric couldn't be sure but it seemed to be Rogelio's way of acknowledging that he might be receptive to the proposal.

"I can't stop you from speaking with Ofelia, but you should know I will have a talk with her. Let's see what she says after that."

"Fair enough."

Eric would move forward. He had faith in Ofelia's love and in her ability to handle her father.

As Eric left, Amelia looked into his eyes. She looked happy but kept her emotions hidden. She walked into the room with Rogelio. Eric watched them embrace. It was something he'd never seen his own parents do. They'd divorced when he was still a baby. After that, they'd treated each other like business associates. He'd never seen the kindness and respect that he saw with Ofelia's parents, each one's honest recognition that the other was unique and valuable. It was what he wanted with Ofelia.

He walked leisurely back to his palapa, winding his way around the trees and flowers. He thought about what would happen next. What if Ofelia was not as strong as he thought? What if she refused him? He knew she loved him, but marriage was quite a different thing. What would Rogelio say to her? She loved her father dearly. Could he change her mind?

Doubt was there, hiding in the darkness. Was he too confident? Had he assumed too much? Was Ofelia ready for marriage and all that it meant? She was so young. Was Rogelio right? Was marriage too great a leap? Alone in his room, he groped his way through the confusion. He computed the countless alternatives until he fell asleep.

"How will I get well without Frieze's Laetrile?"

"Who you talkin' bout, man? You been talkin' up a storm. I been tryin' to help you but that Nurse Marta, that bitch wants to fire me. Things are gettin' dangerous around here. I think there's gonna be a strike or worse."

"...the road ahead... It's so dark. I can't see you."

"I'm right beside you. But, I gotta go before she catches me here."

True love... walking away.

"Nelson?"

Silence.

52.

The Demise of Louie Frieze

How long he'd been underground, Louie didn't know. It was getting difficult to breathe. In the darkness, he found his way among the shelves and the walls with his hands and feet. His skin became sensitive to impending collisions. He foraged around in the pit of death, closed away from the rest of the world, with nothing to do but think. He'd stopped worrying he would go insane from starvation or thirst. That period ended unexpectedly and peacefully—an anticlimax to the angst preceding it.

He resigned himself to the fact he would die here, without any good-byes and without leaving anything of his life's work behind for those who might find some value in it. It was too late, but he now understood what his bitterness and lack of trust and inability to love had wrought.

Outside, the great experience of the world went on, magnificent but completely heartless. Underground, in the dark, everything changed shape. What had been so important in ordinary life became remote and trivial. Echoes of his Saturday afternoon lunches with Ana Luisa and Jordan rang in his ears then faded. The difficulties with Napier and Krump that had consumed so many hours of his life deformed into the squatness of toads.

For Louie Frieze this scene of death became the great confessional. He had sinned against himself, that which he most fully believed in, and now, in these last moments, he asked himself for absolution and a chance to perform a sort of penance. It would take a long time to die. The right atmosphere had to be created. He was kept waiting while his mind was prepared for whatever it might be, the surprise or the lack of surprise. Frieze looked back at his life. Everything was remote and distant, like the shore seen from a ship far out at sea.

Her name is Simone. He sees her green eyes and blonde hair. He experiences the salty taste of her skin, the wet warmth of her mouth, the quiet sound of her breath fragrant with the smell of fresh raspberries.

The darkness and solitude had swept aside his wakeful intelligence and left only emotions, emotions he'd ignored for so long that the pain nearly overwhelmed him.

A man, tall, dark, stern, sits at a desk. His father. The man hovers over a checkbook, and with a few scribbles tries to flick his son away like a cockroach. The boy takes the money and leaves. His father is spared the scandal.

Frieze's eyes and mouth were dry and cracked. He had not even the moisture for tears.

Simone becomes violently ill. She loses the baby. He tries to console her with his love. He runs for help. Rashness is one of the qualities of illness. When he returns with the doctor, the room is empty.

His sorrow rises like steam above a pot. It floats in the air, visceral, until it grasps his entire body and shakes him.

He cannot find her. When she fails to return after several months, he leaves France for Mexico.

The Indians of Mexico viewed death as a continuation of life. They embraced it. To them, life was a dream; only in death did they become truly awake. It's an illusion that the world is so shaped that it echoes every groan of every human being who ever lived. We bear our trials alone and cannot share them. What we can share are the dreams. The dreams were what Frieze had left in France. His life became absolute and fixed, stale and dead, a flat plane surrounded by mountains he was afraid to climb.

This dark cavern returned to him the power of his dreams. Now he understood: If the truth is to be known, the eye must catch fire like the ear, tongue, heart, and mind. How long he had limped about on one leg! So late to come, it was a cruel awakening, but he welcomed it, opened to it and accepted the consequences.

Frieze felt himself slipping away from the constant roar of life. There were times he dozed off, then awoke not knowing if he had died or not. He felt around with his hands for something familiar. *Yes, I'm still here.*

How odd he'd lived his entire adult life in Mexico, a country he never understood or accepted. The food made him sick, the wine was inferior, and the people lived entirely in thrall to crude and ancient superstitions.

Until this moment, he had been immune to those silly fallacies. In this tomb, he remembered having seen the black witch moth on the eaves of his porch just a day before the trapdoor had slammed down. The locals called it *mariposa de la muerte,* the butterfly of death. At the time, he'd dismissed the thought as foolishness. Now the ominous name seemed entirely suitable, and its appearance on his porch a portent.

His mind was restless. Thoughts skipped across the surface like flat rocks on a lake, then sank to the bottom into the darkness and the mud.

An old man traipses along in the town square of a Mexican city. He wears a straw hat with a wide brim to keep out the sun. Khaki pants and a plaid shirt colored in faded squares of black and gray indicate he's not a local. His shoes look a bit worn and he hasn't shaved for a few days. Hair has started to grow on his ears. Near him, a young girl seated on a bench speaks in French to the boy who accompanies her. The man walks toward them and raises his head as if to speak. They look up. She's beautiful, with green eyes and blonde hair. Shocked, the old man hurries away.

Frieze awoke from a deep sleep, surprised to be awake, and slightly annoyed. Like Samuel to Saul in the Bible, he whispered: "Why have you disturbed me to bring me here?" Sounds carry in the dark. It's easy to be deceived. He thought he heard something above, but no longer had the strength to move or even to speak. He was not afraid to die. Christianity spreads the horror of death through its threats of hell and its perennial attempts to frighten people into repentance on the threshold of eternity. Frieze didn't believe such rot. He would soon be nothing, feel nothing, and do nothing for all eternity.

He did regret parting from his friends. He had few, but that made each one more important. He knew they would worry about his mysterious disappearance. He wished he could have prevented that, but he could do nothing now. There are places we must go alone.

They sit, arms outstretched, hands cupped, backs straight against the ancient stones—families, old women. He sees the same woman every year. She wears a red rebozo and a colorful dress, a strange outfit for begging. She looks the same as she did twenty years ago when he first saw her. He's approached by every kind of person: whores, drug addicts, the disabled. These are the empty people, hollowed by hunger and desperation and the trials life has thrown; the seekers searching the diaspora for the remnants of those who are still moved by the vulnerability and despair of people like them who've become beggars.

His arms and legs were stiff. The floor was hard. Frieze pulled his body into the fetal position. He was ready take the hand of death willingly if he could just doze off again into his dreams. The wounds of his life had healed, but lightly. There was not yet peace. He could not be done with it.

If he could say one more thing to his friends it would be to laugh. Only the insane take life seriously. Despite his many disappointments, after all his churlish complaints, the pessimism, the gloom he allowed and even encouraged to surround him, it had come to this one simple revelation: the whole thing is nothing more than a comedy. He laughed a hearty laugh, and heard everyone laugh with him.

It is taught: If one dies laughing, it's a good sign. When Louie Frieze died, he had a short discussion with the God he'd denied.

"What, I'm not dead yet?"

"Is this death?"

"How would I know?"

53.

The Secret

Like ancient flying reptiles, black-and-white frigate birds plowed the updrafts over a calm ocean in the afternoon sun. They soared in ever-widening circles, oblivious of the small but bold sunbirds that followed them around. A slight breeze made the heat bearable, even now at the hottest time of the day. Ofelia sat with Eric in a beach café, drinking cold juice from frozen glass mugs.

The frost on the mugs quickly turned to slush, and dribbled into little pools that looked like coins on the white plastic table. Eric knew Ofelia had something to tell him. He also knew better than to ask. They were celebrating Jordan's good news: Ana Luisa had discovered another jug of Frieze's Laetrile. They hoped this might be enough to completely cure him.

On one of the palm trees jutting out of the sand, a few coconuts sat in a ball of furry brown leaves. Through the warm and heavy air a familiar melody drifted to their table. They finished their juice and sat without talking. The clear, sharp notes of the music floated up to entertain the frigate birds. Mexico had become familiar. It was home.

"Do you want to go back to the bungalow, Eric?"

Ofelia's eyes were happy and bright and reflected little pictures back as Eric watched her. If he focused carefully, he could see the reflections were of his own face.

"Let's stay awhile longer. It's peaceful here. I love the music, though I can barely hear it. I've heard it somewhere before."

"What music?"

Eric blurred the boundaries between reality and illusion. The visual and auditory areas in his head threw surrealist parties of their own volition, bizarre imageries and odd melodies from the past. Fear gripped him when such episodes occurred.

"Oh, nothing. I was dreaming."

Ofelia shrugged it off. She had other things on her mind. "Would you like another juice?"

"Would you?"

Neither seemed anxious to answer. A few quiet minutes passed.

"No."

"Me either."

The waiter came to take the empty glasses. The rings of water soon became drops, then spots evaporated by the sun's heat. Devon and Orvaline were downtown exploring. Eric was surprised at how quickly Devon was turning into a local. A coconut dropped out of the tree. Eric expected it to split open, but it landed softly on the sand with a little thud. The music stopped.

"Marcelino attacked me the other day, when I came out of the clinic after speaking with Jordan."

"What?" Ofelia stood up, her hands on the table.

"He was with two of his buddies. He just wanted to save face in front of them."

"He's such a fool... just a child unable to control himself. So that's how you hurt your face. You didn't trip on the stairs. No more secrets, eh?"

"I didn't want to say anything about it. I had it coming. I stole his girl. It's a guy thing." Eric tried to smile.

"I was not *his* girl to steal. If he told you we made love, it's a lie. He tried, but I wouldn't let him."

"It doesn't matter. We worked it out. Now he can go on with his life, and we can go on with ours."

"It matters to me, Eric."

"I believe you."

Ofelia squinted at Eric.

The beach was long and narrow. The tide was in. Huge waves crashed onto the shore one after another, each new one sucked back by the last. The beach was empty. The waiter had disappeared. There was just the two of them and the black grackles with their shrill whistles.

They both wanted to walk on the beach, but neither voiced the thought.

Time, space, and matter became unstuck. Eric was disoriented. The music returned in a strange series of bleeps and blips. Everything around him changed. The fierce sunlight blinded him. He heard voices, people arguing. His eyes adjusted and he saw unfamiliar faces around him. A hand moved toward him and placed something over his nose and mouth. There was a horrible pain and tingling. He fell into a tunnel of black-and-white concentric circles, descending deeper and deeper until he passed out.

"Let's go walk on the beach," Ofelia said.

"Sure," said Eric.

"If I could just paint," said Ofelia, "I'd paint you in a thousand different ways."

Ofelia sensed he was lost. There are stages of this disease when the body weakens like a dying flower. She put on her hat, and Eric seemed to snap out of it. He paid the bill, and followed Ofelia onto the beach. Before Mexico, he'd never worn a baseball cap in his life. Now, with the fierce sun overhead, he wore one every day. It was embossed with the round face of a Mexican with a thick black mustache. The Mexican's eyes were always staring at Ofelia. Sometimes Eric grew jealous thinking about it.

They could see up and down the beach. It was much longer than it appeared from where they'd been sitting. They walked carefully to avoid sinking in the sand.

"We should have taken off our shoes," said Eric.

A small boat traveled north, bobbing up and down with the waves. A man in a bright-orange shirt tried to steer it against the wind. Distant and small, it looked like a toy boat in a bathtub. Above the flower-dripped bluff, a lonely gull dove toward them. People walked at the other end of the beach. After a few steps, Eric looked back. The café had shrunk in the distance.

"I'm pregnant, Eric." Ofelia had finally worked up the nerve to tell him.

"Yes, I know."

Ofelia nearly fainted in astonishment. How could he possibly know?

"Well, I didn't know for sure," Eric said, "but I felt something different about you. I sensed it, I guess."

"Oh, my God! My parents!"

"Don't worry, I'm sure they don't know. I'm happy about it. We'll get married as soon as possible."

"My father will be furious! He'll send you away. Oh, God, what are we going to do?" Ofelia was walking backward, her hands on her hips.

"Turn around, you're going to trip."

"We should get married. Right now. But you'll never convince Papa. Never. He's too old-fashioned."

"I already have."

Eric told Ofelia about the meeting with her father. She was astonished, but it was news she'd hoped for.

"He told me true love means knowing when to walk away. I couldn't walk away, Ofelia."

Eric dropped to one knee and reached out to hold her hands. "Will you marry me?"

Laughing, Ofelia tried to pull him back up. The tide rushed away from them, the waves cast shadows in the soft sand. Above their heads, under the white clouds, two seabirds sailed, their wings beaded with ocean water.

"Oh, Eric, yes, I'll marry you. I want us to spend our lives together. I love you."

Eric felt every pore on his skin rise up into a separate goose bump. He stayed on his knee, unable to move.

Ofelia managed to pull him up.

"Stand up, silly, before the tide takes you out."

54.

The Hearing

Frieze could not be found. The meeting before the Senate subcommittee could not be postponed. They would have to carry on without Frieze. This meant they'd have to rely on tactics based on emotion, not science. Napier was worried. There were vocal supporters all over the country. The political atmosphere was in some ways favorable; however, going through the hearing without Frieze was a gamble. Napier grew tense when he arrived to drive Elvin Krump to the airport.

"Good morning, Doctor. I'm happy to be back in San Francisco, though I could do without this fog."

"Welcome back, Russell. I'm packed and ready. Have you got things lined up for us?"

Napier had been contacting speakers and supporters to be sure they'd attend. He needed a positive outcome. Good timing or bad, there was no turning back now. Napier had carefully investigated Krump's checkered past before suggesting their joint venture. What he'd found would have discouraged those who lacked Napier's keen business sense. He knew from years of experience that it wasn't the steak but the sizzle that led to success. Krump had plenty of sizzle to reel in those desperate for a magic cure, and that included everyone with cancer. Appearing before a Senate committee, however, was a different matter. That required steak. Elvin Krump would not be an impressive advocate under the skeptical scrutiny of the senators.

Krump had inherited the family business. His father, the so-called grandfather of Laetrile, had worked as a pharmacist before becoming involved in a succession of bizarre but imaginative ventures to market unusual medical cures. The elder Krump was convinced that an old Indian remedy made from parsley was effective against the flu. He'd set up a company and marketed the product as Syrup Leptinol, claiming it was not only effective against the flu but also asthma, whooping cough, tuberculosis, and pneumonia. He was hugely successful until the FDA stepped in and seized the product. They argued the old man's claims were false and fraudulent. Next he and his son promoted pangamic acid, later called vitamin B-15, which they said was effective against heart disease, cancer, and a variety of other ailments. This business was also successful, but the government, ever watchful, closed down operations yet again. Napier admired the elder Krump for his tenacity. The old man had died in 1970 at the remarkable age of ninety-four. Elvin Krump Jr. inherited his father's gift of self-promotion, which included promoting his worthless credentials. After giving an hourlong lecture on Laetrile, Krump Jr. had obtained a Doctor of Science degree from Universal Christian College, a small, now defunct, Bible college in Tulsa, Oklahoma. The school, founded by evangelist Bo Diddley White, had no science department and lacked authority from Oklahoma to grant doctoral degrees. That didn't dissuade Krump from using the title of "Doctor."

"Everything's a mess, Elvin. Frieze is still missing. We have nothing new to offer the FDA. They denied our initial request. My whole strategy was to focus on a new, improved version, but that's impossible now. After the recent thalidomide scandal, the federal government is paranoid about any new drugs. They've made the process for approval much more difficult. The Kefauver-Harris law requires us to demonstrate both efficacy and safety consistent with stringent government guidelines. We have good arguments on our side, but we need definitive proof for the senators."

"I don't think it's a problem at all, Russell. The public is demanding Laetrile. Just read the press. Public opinion is firmly on our side. The senators will be receptive to their constituents. That's where the votes are and they know it."

Ever the optimist, Krump smiled with confidence like a satisfied toad on a mushroom. Napier grew increasingly worried as he watched Krump pull out a stack of documents from his briefcase.

"I have a bad feeling about this, Elvin."

"Shush! Listen to these newspaper clippings, Russell. I've assembled a large collection for the subcommittee." Krump shuffled the papers around. "Take this Oregon state senator quoted in the *Portland Herald:* 'We want to maintain our freedom of choice.' In the *Sun Times* a Florida state representative says: 'Stay the hell out of our business,' and a California state senator quoted in the *Long Beach Chronicle:* 'Our society will be a little bit freer when those who suffer from cancer are finally allowed to use Laetrile legally. They are already using it, but they must go outside the country for treatment at great personal expense and risk.' These public statements will clinch it for us!"

"Yes, Doctor, I'm aware of all that, but you forget that the other side will have their own news clippings. This isn't the kind of proof the senators are looking for. They want scientific facts. The large pharmaceutical companies and the FDA are against us. They have a slew of professionals to testify, with negative lab tests to back them up."

"What's the word from Congressman Shipley? I thought we paid him to line up supporters in Congress."

"Shipley has done the best he can. His influence isn't as strong in the Senate. He did manage to get a press release from Curtis LeMay, George Wallace's running mate in the last election. LeMay said:

"Eliminating cancer through a nondrug therapy has not been accepted because of the hidden economic and power agendas of those who dominate the medical establishment. At the very top of the world's economic and political pyramid of power there is a grouping of financial, political, and industrial interests that, by the very nature of their goals, are the natural enemies of the nutritional approaches to health."

"Well, you see, I told you as much," said Krump. He brought out still more material—testimonials, anecdotal evidence, demonstrations, and notes from various local meetings where people clamored for Laetrile. Laetrile advocacy was taking the nation by storm. Former patients held Laetrile taste-ins at their homes. Bumper stickers were distributed that read: LAETRILE WORKS! YOU BET YOUR LIFE. In some states, shopping bags stuffed with thousands of signed pleas for Laetrile were delivered to state legislators. Krump was certain the Senate committee would be impressed.

Napier was less sanguine about their prospects. "The problem with these comments in the press and so forth," he told Krump, "is that the other side has them too. It'll be up to us to convince the Senators to open the door for us. The best we can hope for is to get another crack at the FDA and hope they give us a fair shake. There's no getting around it—without Frieze's formula, our case is weak."

"You worry too much, Russell. Let's go to the airport. We can work on our strategy during the flight."

Elvin Krump slept the entire way from San Francisco to Washington. Napier used the quiet time to fine-tune their presentation before the committee.

When they arrived at the capital, Krump was starving. They went out for a pricy dinner close to the Amsterdam hotel, where they were staying. After dinner they waited in the hotel lobby for Doctor Milagro and Jonathan Blackstone, the physician who headed the powerful group Americans for Cancer Freedom. Milagro looked pale and exhausted.

"Three more patients died at the clinic this week," he said. "I was unable to get them home, and we had to go through all the red tape to have the bodies transported. You can imagine the problems this caused for their families. I'm a wreck, Russell. I don't know how I can speak with any enthusiasm at the subcommittee meeting tomorrow."

"Don't speak about your failures, Alejandro, speak of the successes. You brought all the good case files with you, correct?"

"Yes, of course."

"We'll rely on Blackstone to give us a boost with his data. Are you up for that, John?"

"I don't know what the problem is at your clinic, Milagro," Blackstone declared. "My patients continue to improve. I haven't seen many failures at all. We can't cure every patient, of course, but the track record is excellent. I know my results will be convincing to the senators. If not, we have other ways of turning up the heat."

They all went off to bed. Napier slept poorly. He missed Nicoletta. She was flying down with her uncle from Newark the next day. They were scheduled to arrive just in time for the hearing.

Seven senators sat in a raised semicircle and faced the audience. Napier and his group sat facing the politicians. Congressman Shipley asked his good friend, Senator Millard, to introduce them. As soon as the introductions were out of the way, Senator Battle threw them a curveball:

"Thank you for coming here today. This Senate subcommittee is here to listen to arguments for Laetrile. You have a big job in front of you, gentlemen. According to the American Medical Association, there is no evidence that amygdalin, otherwise known as Laetrile, is effective against any type of cancer. There is evidence the long-term ingestion of Laetrile, which contains cyanide, is poisonous. Despite this, the public continues to clamor for the right to use Laetrile because you continue to promote it. I'm concerned about your continued efforts to influence a vulnerable public with a worthless and dangerous substance. This committee is not inclined to relax the law without substantial new evidence. I would like to ask each of you here today, will you desist from raising false hopes when an objective test finds Laetrile worthless?"

Each member of the group stood and answered: "Yes."

Russell Napier explained their position. "We'll agree to stop, but only if objective tests are carried out. The tests to date have not been objective; they have been carried out only on terminal cancer patients and without the individual dietary regimen that we recommend."

Doctor Blackstone rose to speak for the group. He used the press release from Curtis Lemay as his guide. "Eliminating cancer through a non-drug therapy has not been accepted because of the hidden economic agendas of those who dominate the medical establishment. At the very top of the world's economic and political power pyramid there is a grouping of financial, political, and industrial interests that, by the very nature of their goals, are the natural enemies of nutritional approaches to health."

There was an immediate negative response. A doctor from Sloan Kettering who had previously testified before the FDA spoke in opposition: "We have conducted test after test according to the most rigorous scientific standards. When all the tests are taken together, there is no substantial evidence that amygdalin, or Laetrile, is in any way effective against cancer. Victims of cancer should not be twice victimized by the promoters of a worthless and dangerous quack remedy.

"Leaving orthodox treatment is the same as suicide. It is choosing to give up on the only credible hope to cure the disease. It is opting for charlatanism and agreeing to be fleeced by a well-organized group of swindlers who take advantage of the terminally ill for their own financial gain. There are many patients in the United States receiving effective therapies who are abandoning these therapies for unproven methods smuggled in from below the border."

Boos and hisses rang out from a group of Laetrile supporters who sat in the balcony. Cancer and the right to seek one's own remedy had become a nationwide cause célèbre, second only to the Vietnam War in the size of the rallies it generated. Chairman Battle banged the gavel to silence the crowd.

Napier, bristling at the use of the word "swindlers," turned red in the face.

An Illinois state senator was next to be recognized by the chairman. "The proponents of Laetrile have organized helpless cancer victims and their families and friends into a political apparatus to abolish the laws protecting Americans from the pseudoscience of modern-day snake-oil salesmen. We cannot allow these extremist groups to run roughshod over desperately ill patients who depend on the government to protect them from opportunists."

Napier requested to be heard, and was recognized by Chairman Battle.

"Senators, I understand your job is to protect the public and to insure that only safe and effective drugs are approved. We agree fully on the importance of that responsibility. There is, however, an equally important charge you've been given. Cancer impacts the lives of thousands, perhaps millions, of Americans. It's so devastating that President Nixon declared a war on the disease, a war that we in the Laetrile community take seriously. I strenuously object to our being called snake-oil salesmen and swindlers. We are hardworking, sincere allies in the war on cancer. We dispute the test results referred to by the last speaker. I ask you to consider the book in front of you, *The End of Cancer* by Glenn Beckman. I ask you to enter the book into the record. It lays out in several chapters the scientific and humanitarian case for Laetrile. Mr. Beckman's research finds undeniable evidence in favor of Laetrile that goes back in time hundreds of years."

Senator Battle responded with a smirk, and gave a wink to the doctors seated across from Napier.

"Let me ask you, Mr. Napier, who is this Glenn Beckman? Is he a physician?"

"No, Senator."

"Is he a professor of science, then?"

"No, sir."

"Well, what is his background?"

"He's a self-educated expert in speech and communications, a successful radio host, film producer, author, and lecturer. It does not take a medical professional to gather the evidence. Anyone with the necessary skills and a willingness to do the research can uncover the truth. Beckman's research is substantial and his conclusions are sound."

"Is it true that Mr. Beckman is a member of the John Birch Society?"

"Yes, that is true, but his political views are not relevant to whether Laetrile is effective or not. He's highly regarded by a wide spectrum of Americans—voting Americans. He is an educator, and has established his own institute of learning in the medical sciences. He spent years gathering information for his book. He traveled the world to investigate people in remote areas who have lived without cancer for centuries because of their diet. He bases his writing on facts gathered in the field and on tests with real people, not rats. Conventional science does not have a monopoly on the truth, nor does it have a cure for cancer. Every new scientific discovery starts with a handicap. The entrenched views of scientists who have their own economic interests work against new ideas. In our case, this is more than an intellectual handicap. Some of the previous speakers referred to the financial gain of those promoting Laetrile. The median cost of conventional cancer treatment, including surgery, chemotherapy, and radiation amounts to many thousands of dollars, not to mention the pain and suffering. Laetrile goes for a dollar a capsule and about ten dollars a shot, and there are no nasty side effects. I'm sure you're aware that the large pharmaceutical companies make billions of dollars, far more than the promoters of Laetrile. They're working against us to preserve their obscene profits from drugs that do not work."

The audience seemed to be warming to Napier, but others were waiting to speak against him.

A prominent Stanford University doctor and professor was the next to be recognized.

"While there is an emotional plea for the unrestricted use of Laetrile as an anti-tumor agent, the scientific evidence to justify such a policy does not appear within it. Senators, let me ask you, would you get into an airplane if the CEO of the manufacturing company said he'd read an ancient Tibetan text and then had a dream about how to build an aircraft? This is more or less the level of the evidence offered by the pro-Laetrile forces. The apricot-pit gang sitting in front of you, including Mr. Napier, who was arrested for smuggling Laetrile into the United States, won't be appeased by any government-sponsored trial, no matter how thorough and unbiased it may be."

Napier quickly objected: "For the record, I was arrested but not convicted. The United States has been relentless in its persecution of those who support Laetrile. The smuggling charge that landed me in jail unfairly for several days was dropped for lack of any evidence. The US government has done everything in its power to harass me, but I refuse to be silenced on a matter of life and death."

A Doctor Klein was recognized to speak in favor of Laetrile. "Distinguished senators, there is no doubt in my mind that we can prevent cancer. Moreover, if cancer has already occurred, we can, in the majority of cases, stop it and destroy it. I have witnessed such results at Doctor Milagro's clinic, where I was on sabbatical doing cancer research. I'm convinced Laetrile is nature's defense against cancer."

"Are you a cancer researcher, Doctor Klein, or a cancer specialist?"

"I'm a licensed dentist, but I have extensive knowledge in this area."

"I presume you are not treating cancer patients as a dentist?"

There were some chuckles among the doctors.

"Of course not. I was observing Doctor Milagro. My personal interest began when I myself was diagnosed with cancer. I was cured at Doctor Milagro's clinic. Despite my initial skepticism, I'm living proof of Laetrile's effectiveness."

Next, Senator Battle addressed Doctor Milagro: "Doctor Milagro, our committee has received reports that your clinic has been smuggling Laetrile into the United States. I would like your response to that allegation."

Doctor Milagro shook visibly as he stood to speak. Gentle and soft-spoken, he was barely audible when he spoke. Perspiration beaded on his forehead.

"I do everything I can to stop the smuggling, Senator, of that you can be assured. It is true I sell Laetrile to my patients when they visit my clinic in Mexico, where it is legal. What they do with it after they take it from my clinic is out of my control. It is possible some have purchased more than they needed for themselves. Some may have resold it in the United States. I do not promote that illegal activity. We are trying to control resale by prescribing no more than a three-month supply per individual. It is sad, of course, because many patients cannot afford to travel back to Mexico every three months."

Senator Battle spoke to the Laetrile group and their supporters: "Gentlemen, I will become your biggest advocate if an objective test proves Laetrile effective. Are you telling me all the independent labs, medical researchers, and government regulators in America are biased, that none of them is credible?"

Napier's group maintained that the entire medical community could not be trusted to give Laetrile a fair test. The majority of tests to date had been done only on mice. The few tests performed on humans were on severely ill patients who were already terminal. The supporting metabolic treatments essential for effective treatment with Laetrile were not followed. There was also a question about the scientific integrity of the tests. Napier pointed to positive test results that were obtained with Laetrile, and then introduced Doctor Kanematsu Sugiura, a researcher at Sloan Kettering who was responsible for these results. Senator Battle questioned the doctor.

"Doctor Sugiura, do you agree with the summary conclusions of the Sloan Kettering report?"

"Which conclusions, Senator?"

"To the effect that Laetrile does not either cure or prevent cancer?"

Doctor Sugiura smiled nervously. "My results don't agree. I did sign on to the report but my results were not in agreement with the others."

Senator Battle asked him how he had obtained his differing results.

"I write what I see," said Sugiura.

"I don't understand," said Senator Battle. "Do you stick by your results, which do not agree with the conclusions of the report?"

"Yes, I do! I hope someone is able to confirm my results later on."

Senator Battle seemed frustrated. "Has any other of your results ever been disputed?"

"I'm here almost sixty years. Nobody disputes my work."

"Why this one, then?" asked Battle, growing increasingly confused.

"My results were accepted for publication, but the Institute does not accept them because no one else there has been able to confirm them."

"Thank you, Doctor Sugiura."

Senator Battle looked to the group of doctors from Sloan Kettering. "Do you think further studies are warranted?" he asked the director.

"We see no further experiments that would change our opinion, Senator. We've looked at all available methods for any evidence of anticancer activity, and we have not found it. Doctor Sugiura's results are anomalous."

"I see. Well, let's move on, then."

Some of the senators made note of Doctor Sugiura's comments. They appeared to be wavering, but none spoke out.

Napier raised his hand to object, but Senator Battle changed the focus of the questioning to financial matters.

"Is it a fact, Doctor Blackstone, that you have received $675,000 in profits from $1.4 million in Laetrile sales over the past two and a half years?"

Blackstone's face remained calm. "I couldn't tell you the exact numbers, Senator, but yes, I am in business to make a profit in addition to helping my patients. What you should be focusing on is not whether my business is profitable but how many of my patients have survived this horrible disease because of the Laetrile they received. I am confident that most of my patients would have gladly paid more if that's what it took to regain their good health."

"I am sure the senators on this committee will consider those results, Doctor Blackstone. Please provide your financial records to our committee."

Senator Battle expected Doctor Blackstone to sit down, but Blackstone continued to speak: "Senators, let me tell you something. We in the Laetrile community are working at the outer limits of scientific knowledge. It can be lonely and dangerous on the frontier. It's easy to become the target of well-meant but inappropriate rules and regulations. When we started to dispense Laetrile, our office became filled with faces we had never seen before—faces of hopeful men and women who had been abandoned by orthodox medicine as hopeless or terminal cases. Some of these patients had no identifiable tumor or lesion but complained of feelings of impending doom, malaise, unexplained or vague pains, headaches, bowel changes, lack of appetite, loss of energy, depression. We found to our surprise that Laetrile could help these patients as well. When those who did have cancer were treated with Laetrile, in many cases we witnessed the cancer cells dying off like flies. We take these results as seriously as you take the results of the animal models at Sloan Kettering. We are not quacks, as depicted by these wealthy doctors. You owe your constituents more than demonizing those who are working day and night to give people suffering from cancer a chance to save their lives."

"Thank you, Doctor Blackstone, for your impassioned plea. It has been entered into the record."

Blackstone continued to stand. "Rest assured, ladies and gentlemen, the people demand Laetrile. They are going to get it whether Big Brother wants it or not. We cannot expect thousands of American cancer sufferers to wait more long years for further tests and red tape. Do we really want another American Civil War?"

"Doctor Blackstone, your time is up. Please sit down. This committee will not be intimidated by threats, and neither will we tolerate illegal activity. Your strong opposition to the current laws is noted. It is our job to protect the ill and vulnerable from unproven and dangerous drugs. We take that responsibility seriously."

An older man, a cancer victim who had traveled from Arizona at his own expense to address the committee, was allowed to speak: "I'm sorry to have to say it, Senator, but you people in authority consider all the rest of us a bunch of dummies. You set yourselves up as God and Jesus Christ all rolled into one. We're losing all our rights. As a free man, I should be able to choose the way I want to die. It isn't your prerogative to tell me how. Only God can do that. This is all about freedom. We lose it by chunks, by bits, by grains. We hand over more and more authoritarian control to the experts every day."

The FDA chief, Doctor Kenyon, jumped in. "I do not believe anyone has the right to debase the concept of freedom by swindling those who are desperate for their lives."

Elvin Krump stood. Given his bulk, he was an impressive sight. "I am Doctor Elvin Krump. Senators, the previous speaker, Mr. Kenyon, has it all wrong."

Senator Battle interrupted. "He's Doctor Kenyon, sir, and you are *Mister* Krump. You're not a doctor. Your honorary Ph.D. does not give you the right to use that title."

Krump was embarrassed. Thrown off his game, he fumbled the rest of his presentation, and much of what he said simply baffled the senators: "Laetrile is at the forefront of a scientific revolution as profound as the germ theory of disease... and the Copernican theory. What vitamin C is to scurvy, niacin is to pellagra, and vitamin D is to rickets, Laetrile is to cancer. It is a vitamin, vitamin B-17. If every American took Laetrile regularly, in twenty years cancer would be relegated to the dustbin of history."

Krump managed to get copies of his former speeches at the various cancer conventions entered into the record, but most of the senators could hardly keep straight faces during his incoherent ramblings.

The crowded hearing went on like this for another hour. It exasperated Napier to sit and watch as the senators and medical doctors skewered each point the Laetrile group tried to make. The M.D.s sat together in a row, some in expensive suits and ties, others in their white medical coats. Napier's small and disparate group of supporters was no match for the professionals, who had made their science-based case the week before on a specially arranged episode of the prestigious *60 Minutes* show. They'd hired seasoned performers who exuded the reassuring charm of the family doctor with lines drawn from the popular TV show *Marcus Welby, M.D.* At the end of the hearing, most agreed the supporters of Laetrile had had a bad day. The most damning testimony was that of Robert Simpson, whose wife, Mary, had recently died of cancer after being treated at Clinica Buena Salud.

"Mr. Chairman and members of the committee, I am Robert Simpson, the survivor of a cancer patient who, in her desperation to live, turned to Laetrile in the last few weeks of her life."

Mr. Simpson went on to describe the progression of his wife's disease and the series of treatments she went through before turning to Laetrile: "It was at this low point when her hopes of recovery had been destroyed and the doctors told her she had only months to live that she came across the book previously mentioned in these hearings, *The End of Cancer* by Glenn Beckman, who is not a medical doctor but a writer and publicist. Mary pleaded with me to take her to Mexico. With money raised from relatives and friends, we flew to San Diego. Then we drove to Tijuana with friends, and stayed at Clinica Buena Salud for six weeks."

Looking pale and worn, Mr. Simpson continued with a ferocious indictment of Doctor Milagro and his clinic: "Over those weeks, we paid thousands of dollars for transportation, consultations, lab tests, X-rays, pharmacy, dietary supplements, and special meals and, of course, supplies of Laetrile. Nothing done for Mary in Mexico made any difference at all in her condition. She died exactly as her doctor informed us she would, just a few months after the treatments available here in the States had been exhausted."

In summarizing his testimony, he spoke with a combination of sadness and rage to make his plea: "Laetrile is a snare and a delusion. It does nothing but raise false hopes. It causes desperate cancer patients to divert their savings to a worthless will-o-the-wisp, and worst of all, it might cause unnecessary loss of life by encouraging cancer patients to forgo conventional proven treatments such as chemotherapy, radiation, and other therapies in favor of an unproven so-called miracle treatment. I ask you to reject the legislation to legalize. Thank you."

Congressman Shipley left the hearing worried and angry, looking for a way out of the mess he'd created. Napier, Krump, Milagro, and Blackstone went their separate ways. Napier spoke only briefly with Nicoleta before she ran off to find her uncle. Joey Zacco left before the end of the hearing. He blamed Shipley for not doing a better job of preparing the committee, and was enraged at Napier and Dos

Negros for not finding Frieze and obtaining his precious recipe. Russell Napier knew the relationship with Zacco had been seriously strained. It would have to be repaired. There was work to be done. He was disappointed, but not defeated, not yet.

After the committee meeting, Laetrile became the butt of jokes on the late-night TV shows and of cartoonists in the major newspapers. Johnny Carson got some major laughs with what would become an iconic bit:

> Following an exhaustive two-year study, Doctor Richard Osgood announced some unsettling news: Leisure suits cause cancer. It seems that perspiration causes the synthetic fiber of leisure suits to release a carcinogenic gas. Children who cling to Daddy's trousers may also be in trouble—but only if Daddy has sweaty legs. How did Doctor Osgood know? Why, he experimented with rats, of course, and to prove it he brought the rats out in their rat-size leisure suits. Unfortunately, Doctor Osgood had no immediate solution, but he is testing leisure suits mixed with Laetrile.

Doonesbury cartoonist Gary Trudeau showed his character Duke planning to make a fortune by purchasing an apricot farm and marketing the pits in Tijuana.

Despite all the jokes and negative comments, pro-Laetrile forces continued to make slow but steady headway among the general population. In Massachusetts, supporters delivered forty shopping bags containing more than 12,000 pleas for legalization to the state legislature. In Wichita, Kansas, Laetrile taste-ins were held in homes, featuring fresh fruits, lima beans, beets, and carrots, which proponents claimed were rich in the substance. In Texas a state legislator was quoted as saying: "Oh, hell, if it doesn't do them any harm and it gives them hope, why not let them have it?" An Arizona state representative told the press, "We're making criminals of those who want to use Laetrile."

Napier regained a bit of optimism after reading these reports. Several individual states, Alaska the first one, bucked the national law by passing pro-Laetrile legislation. According to a Harris Poll, two thirds of Americans favored such legislation, but the federal government remained firm in its position against it. Aside from the setbacks, there had been positive developments. All was not lost. Napier was already working on a plan to set things right. He also knew what might happen if he failed. He began work on a safe exit plan in case events turned against him.

55.

The End of the Smile

The Indian blood that ran in Tomás's veins was darker than European blood. Mixed blood, like any mixture, has its peculiarities. It can produce angels or monsters. When Tomás Negros was conceived, the dark forces joined to produce only evil.

The sun, shining through enormous cumulus clouds, unlocked the elemental pigments from their prisms in space while the heavy air that hung over the ocean dispersed in reflections of blue, pink, yellow, gray, and green. Hector stood on Rafael's deck anticipating what was to come.

Except for the disappointment at the Senate hearings on Laetrile, the Dos Negros enjoyed the best of all possible worlds. Their new aircraft was a welcome addition, but getting it across the border and back without detection was another matter. Hector, always resourceful, found an accomplished pilot who had the needed skill. The geometric growth of the naval base in San Diego increased the income from prostitution and gambling. Competition was nonexistent. Seeing to every detail, Hector made the Dos Negros rich and their lives easy. He had arrived at this breakfast meeting with high hopes. They might even offer him a chunk of the business. He would forget his plans to stage a coup if they offered a fair deal. *Más vale malo conocido que bueno por conocer* (Better the devil you know than the devil you don't).

Mud and heat and a little color and glaze makes pottery, adobe, tiles—the stuff of Mexico. None of it lasts. Everything, even life itself, crumbles and turns to dust. That's nature's way. Tomás sometimes quickened the destruction. He had no regrets. Crushing a human skull was no different for him than smashing a ceramic vase. It was this insensate quality, this utter disregard for anything sacred, that separated Tomás from his brother and from Hector. Hector still had the compassion he was born with, an emotion Tomás had lacked from the very beginning. It was Hector's relationship with Marcos that stirred his feelings in a way that still made the sunrise magical.

In the days before Dos Negros, Hector used to dive in the ocean and explore the secret caves and grottos. It took a leap of faith to take a deep breath and dive downward until his lungs nearly burst, and then, with a parallel movement followed by an upward surge, explode into the trapped air of the cave few dared to enter. It was dark for several minutes until his eyes adjusted. Thin rays of light entered through the splits in the rocks that separated the cave from the rest of the world. He swam around in the huge space for hours, and found rock shelves where he could stop and rest. Outside, the ocean pounded onto the rocks and poured hollow sounds into the depths of the cave. Generations of bats lived there along with fish born with no eyes. It was when he was alone in the caves that he decided to work for Dos Negros.

When Rafael and Tomás arrived together, Hector noticed how similar they looked. Tomás was short, stocky, and menacing, while Rafael was lean and tall and handsome, but those surface differences faded when one looked closer. A single root produced similar fruit. An outer variance might cause a shopper in the *bodega* to choose one over the other, but once cooked into a sauce, the results were the same.

"Sit down, Hector. Breakfast will be served here on the patio."

Hector no longer swam in the caves. He had given his life to Tomás and Rafael, and held nothing back for himself. His only true love was his brother, Marcos, but there was little they could share. Even when Hector had the time, Marcos lived in his strange visions and dreams, a world incomprehensible to Hector. On the few occasions when he managed to decipher Marcos's mysterious world, it was like returning to the silent darkness of the undersea cave.

"How's your father, Hector?"

Tomás was always full of hidden meanings. Hector answered carefully.

"I'm happy he is out of prison. Beyond that, I have no interest. We parted as father and son. I do not expect ever to see him again."

After Amelia and her mother had agreed to drop their objections to Hiladeo's release, Hector paid a bribe to the governor, and his father was a free man. There was no reconciliation with his wife or his family—too much time had passed. Hector gave Hiladeo a little money to get started, and his father left to make a new life on his own.

"How about Marcos and your mother, are they well?"

Hector was concerned. Something was up.

"Yes, they are well. What's all this talk about my family, Tomás? Do you plan to invite us for a party?" The frozen smile on Hector's face relaxed. He looked briefly as he had before everything in his life changed. Tomás knew this as a sign that Hector was vulnerable. A wicked laugh exposed his shining gold teeth in a way that raised the hair on Hector's neck. He knew that look: It was usually followed by trouble. Rafael moved uncomfortably in his chair. There was a strange vibration in the air, like the filament inside a light bulb before it bursts.

A servant brought out plantain *empanadas,* eggs scrambled with *machaca, queso panela,* avocados, and beans—a real feast. Hector's expectations were deflated. He lost his appetite. Tomás ate greedily while Rafael took only a few bites. Hector played with an empanada and sipped a cup of coffee.

"Eat, Hector. A young man needs his strength."

Rafael spoke while Tomás ate enough for all of them.

"What about Louis Frieze, Hector? Have you found out anything?" Hector hadn't mentioned the rumors about the mountain village. He'd found and questioned the mysterious man from El Azteca, and planned to visit the village to check for Frieze. This was the ace he kept up his sleeve.

"No. Nothing. We emptied out his house. We've gone through everything. He just disappeared."

Hector looked at Rafael's fingernails. They were dirty and needed trimming. Hector didn't like men with long fingernails. It made them effeminate in a way he found disgusting.

As the morning progressed, Hector grew more disappointed with the way things went. It was obvious Tomás had a nefarious plan and that it involved Hector. His heartbeat quickened at the thought that somehow they'd discovered he was planning a takeover. He'd been extra careful, but he knew the Dos Negros' tentacles reached everywhere in Tijuana.

Finished with breakfast, Tomás burped loudly and squinted up at the sun. Hector focused on the napkin Tomás had affixed to the top of his shirt. It made him look like a frill-necked lizard. His tongue flicked around grasping crumbs from his upper lip. Most worrisome was that lizard brain. Hector knew it well. The lizard brain is designed solely for survival. It's an ancient brain that operates in only four modes—eat, attack, mate, or escape.

Tomás looked down at the deck. When he looked back to Hector he had eyes of fire, but he spoke calmly. "We are grateful, Hector, for all you've done."

Rafael shifted in his chair like a man with a backache. Hector noticed the sweat on his forehead.

"We want to express our appreciation by giving you a little vacation. We've decided to cut back on your responsibilities for now so you can enjoy more of life. You know, as the Americans say, all work and no play make Hector a dull boy. Ha, ha."

Tomás stopped to pick his teeth.

"Take some time off. Spend time with your family. We'll run the business. When you return, we will work as a team. You've been doing too much and we haven't kept up our end of the deal. That's gonna change."

What was this? Was he being fired? Hector was furious. "I'm not overworked. It'll be a bore for me to take time off. My work is my life. Don't do this. You need me."

Tomás now showed his hand. He was firm and did not allow Hector a way out. "Yes, we do need you, Hector, but there are things we want to do on our own. It will be better for everyone if you accept our offer and take a *vacación*. We will contact you when we're ready to have you resume your duties."

The meeting was over. Hector didn't know what to make of it, but he knew this was not good. Everything would be doubly complicated now. He had to get back in their good graces. It was time to pull the ace out of his sleeve.

56.

Planning A Wedding

Mottled clouds drifted through a pink and blue sky when Eric and Ofelia went to speak with Father Jordan about the wedding. So much had happened so quickly. Sometimes Eric pinched himself just to see if he could feel the pain, to prove he was really there. In Mexico, he'd rediscovered the sky, nature's theater, a work of art going on above him, something he'd forgotten since his carefree days as a child in Sugarvale. When he looked at the sky now it kindled memories of flying kites, climbing in treetops, hiking, fishing, all the beauty of nature, everything in a fresh new context heightened by the exquisite wonder he felt at being alive.

When Ofelia and Eric arrived, Father Jordan offered a proposal: "Danny had some cases he was working on before he died that need to be completed. I want you to step in and take these over... for Danny... for me. After you're married, it will be convenient for you to have an office close to Tijuana. Danny's office in San Diego is paid through the end of the year. It's all set up. His secretary is familiar with the cases. You can still work with your Sacramento group, but you'd have a place close to Ofelia's family. I've discussed it with Ana, and she agrees it would be wonderful if you'd consider this."

"I couldn't, Jordan. I don't know the clients. I didn't even know Danny. I'll help if I can to finish any open cases, but I can't take over his business."

Jordan looked disappointed. "Don't be hasty, Eric. Think about it. A local office might smooth things over with Ofelia's father."

Ofelia glanced with confusion at Eric. "I thought you already had things worked out with my father?"

"I do, more or less. He wants to speak with you alone first. It's his way to feel he's done his best to warn you about the Great White Devil."

"This is no joke, Eric. My father will use every trick in the book to talk me out of it. He'll make me miserable!"

Ofelia stormed about with her hands on her hips shaking her head.

Jordan had returned to the cigars. He rolled a fresh one, not yet lit, around in his mouth.

"Speak with your mother first, Ofelia. She and I have talked. She's on your side. She knows how much you love Eric, but she needs to hear you say it. Then she can work on your father. He listens to her. I'll talk to him too. Your father won't have a chance with the two of us—a committed wife and a Catholic priest—in your corner."

Doctor Milagro walked up the hill toward the chapel. The determined way he strode along made it clear he wanted to speak with them. "Hello, Jordan... Eric... Ofelia." He made a little bow with his head. Two black birds captured Eric's attention as they flew around each other in the tree behind Milagro. They were grackles, smaller than crows but larger than the blackbirds at home. As they circled, their long tails opened like little fans.

"The meeting in Washington did not go well. The Dos Negros brothers blame Napier for the failure. They want to take over management of the Laetrile business. I would prefer Napier to stay, and he wants to. I'm afraid of an ugly fight."

Eric had heard about the Senate hearings from Karen. He knew Laetrile was Napier's passion, and couldn't imagine that Napier would just walk away.

A worried look crossed Ofelia's face. Doctor Milagro was her friend.

"What will happen with the clinic, Doctor?"

"Oh, my clinics are all fine. They will survive, thanks to God. Napier is still here for now. He is very conscientious. Even if he leaves, he will be sure to put things right first. Have you had any contact with Mr. Frieze, Jordan?"

"Unfortunately, I have not. I am so worried about my friend. Do you know anything?"

"Only that Napier and Dos Negros are desperate to find him. They hoped he would surface in time for the hearings, but that was not to be."

At first, Jordan suspected Dos Negros had kidnapped Frieze. But that clearly was not the case. The only explanation seemed to be that Frieze had slipped away to a safe place on his own. It seemed unlikely, but Frieze was a tough old bird who'd survived many dangers over the years. Jordan prayed that he would show up unharmed when the danger had passed, but his hope grew dim as more time elapsed.

Milagro excused himself and walked into the chapel. Jordan told Ofelia and Eric he'd be ready for the wedding. There was work to do and little time to get it done—invitations to be sent, flowers and decorations to be arranged, dinners, clothes. Eric looked up at the sky. His life had changed in a fundamental way. It wasn't just the improvement in his condition, or even his love for Ofelia. His entire way of thinking had been transformed. He felt, saw, and experienced a new connection with every living thing. Somehow he'd missed what had always been right before his eyes, the complicated process of life that went on around him. Such euphoric feelings were unexpected. He had to hold fast to this new world lest it evaporate.

He didn't speak of his illness. He felt unwell at times, but kept this to himself. The vacillations between hope and doubt, the fear of death always near—these took their toll on him. He tried to focus on the wedding. Why shouldn't he be granted time for his own banquet, why should the cancer have all the victories? Ofelia told him he would have his miracle. Well, here it was, he just had to accept it. Life is wonderful and tragic. We march into battle with the heroism of the ant or the bee knowing that we will die. The indifference of nature to our cares is cold but comforting. We get no answers but that may be the very impetus that forces us along.

"For Christ's sake, Nelson, pay attention! How did we get so mixed up that we took the wrong road?"

"Sometimes when a person be thinking about one thing they forget another."

"Well, stop thinking and start walking! I didn't come down here for my health, you know, and I didn't bring you along to philosophize. We have a job to do."

"Sorry, ma'am. I was just thinking that Mexico is so close to the States and so far from God, you know."

"Didn't some poor Mexican say that already? Let's just get on with it! I've never gone in for philosophy. People who sit around and think up that sort of crap never get a thing done."

"It was the Mexican president, Porfirio Diaz, who said it, ma'am."

"The president? Jesus, no wonder this country's in such a mess. Get moving!"

"Okay, ma'am, but by the look of them clouds we gonna get a little rain. Maybe we should find a dry place where we can wait it out?"

"Just keep walking, Nelson. Let me worry about the weather. Your job's on the line. I've had about all I can take."

Ofelia met with her father. Father Jordan had prepared the way.

"To be married and have children! Any Indian woman from the mountains could do that. What about your career, Ofelia?"

"I can have both, Father."

"What about your job at the clinic? What about medical school? What about traveling to see Europe and Asia?"

"I dream and wish for all these things, but with a husband I love and who loves me."

"He's a fine young man, of course. I hope, like you, he will live, but our hopes and dreams are not like the beliefs and certainties of the Church, Ofelia. Eric should not marry in his condition. It is selfish of him to ask you."

"Papa, he's gentle and sweet. He makes me laugh. We like the same books. We have the same thoughts. If he's selfish, then so am I. You don't see him as you were at his age, at my age. You see him as you are now. Close your eyes and think back to the time when you decided to marry Mama. Could anyone have stopped you? Eric is just like you were then."

Her words struck at her father's heart. Yes, he could see it. Amelia, and even Father Jordan, had told him the same. What Ofelia said was true. He couldn't refuse her, despite his reservations.

"All I want, my darling daughter, is your happiness. If it's Eric who gives you happiness, so be it. Let's all be a family together."

"Oh, Papa, I love you so much! I knew you would agree. You are the first man in my life. It will always be so. Now I have one more thing to ask."

Rogelio wondered if he'd given in too easily. Why were all these demands being made on him? Still, he couldn't help but smile at his daughter. She was so much like him in her forward approach to life. It pleased him that he saw a part of himself in her.

"Please, Papa, speak to Orvaline. When Eric first arrived, you made an example of him. Orvaline hated that, and he started to think of Eric as the enemy. Eric arranged for Orvaline's release, but that didn't change the way my brother feels. Please help Orvaline to see Eric differently. Help him to accept Eric into our family."

"Orvaline is his own man. He must make his own decisions. I will not tell him what to decide, but I will tell him how I feel about him and about Eric. Maybe that will make a difference."

In the end, Ofelia won him over. Now the plan unfolded in earnest. She and her mother started the complicated process of making a list of those to be invited. Her parents would reserve the church and make arrangements for the reception. Now she was off to find the most wonderful dress ever to grace a bride!

She adored dressing beautifully, and wanted to do it more often. She liked to see and be seen. Oh, how she wanted Eric to be pleased! She wanted him to feel what she felt, that a life of paradise awaited them.

57.

One-Way Communication

A few days after the hearings, Zacco called Shipley's unlisted telephone at the congressman's office in Bayonne. There was no answer. He called Shipley at home. No answer. A week passed. Zacco called Shipley at his office, again no answer. He called the congressman's home two more times. When a woman finally picked up on the last call to say the congressman was out, Zacco asked that she relay the message to "Mr. Gray at the usual number."

The next day a mutual friend called Zacco.

"Shipley's off on a ten-day trip, Joey."

"Yeah? Where's he going?"

"Europe and Africa. He's no longer a kid, Joey. He's representing the United States all by himself now."

"Yeah? Well, what about me!"

"He spoke at the armory before he left, and they gave him an ovation as big as Kennedy's. He's gonna be the next governor, Joey. Cool off. It ain't over."

"Well, if he doesn't come up with something big, and soon, it's gonna be over for him. The bastard let me down big-time. He didn't line things up the way he said he would. We got trouble, Carmine. You hear? Lotsa trouble."

"Settle down. He's gonna get to you soon, I promise."

"He didn't keep me waiting when he wanted me to get rid of that stiff drawing flies in his garage. I got the goods on him, Carmine. You know it and he knows it. If he don't attend to business, my business, things are gonna get rough in his neck of the woods."

"Don't do anything foolish, Joey. He's on our side. What's up with that Laetrile anyway? My sources tell me it's not very effective."

"Bullshit! It saved my sister's life. They haven't been testing the right stuff, dammit. Okay, okay. Have him get back to me soon, Carmine. I'll pull off the dogs for now, but they're hungry little bitches,, and I can't keep 'em chained forever."

Zacco didn't feel any better after the conversation, but he had learned not to burn bridges. He would give Shipley a little more time... but not much.

The skeletons danced to the light of the fire inside the cave.

I'm bein' followed by a moonshadow, moonshadow,
moonshadow.
Leapin' and hoppin' on a moonshadow, moonshadow,
moonshadow...

They welcomed Eric with their fleshless hands.

And if I ever lose my hands, lose my plough, lose my land,
Oh if I ever lose my hands, I won't have to work no more.

They joined their skeleton hands and moved around in a circle. Their heads all turned at the same time to look at Eric, and he saw into their empty skulls through the hollow eye sockets.

And if I ever lose my eyes, if my colors all run dry,
Yes if I ever lose my eyes, I won't have to cry no more.
Oh I'm bein' followed by a moonshadow...

It all seemed normal. There was nothing unusual about being there. They sang and danced while the firelight followed them along with the moonlight.

And if I ever lose my legs, I won't moan, and I won't beg,
Yes if I ever lose my legs, I won't have to walk no more.
And if I ever lose my mouth, all my teeth, north and south,
Yes if I ever lose my mouth, I won't have to talk...

The laughing and singing and dancing abruptly ended. The skeletons exploded into tiny pieces of bone. Eric awoke outside the cave in the moonlight. An owl looked down on him. The owl was keenly alert as it watched Eric from its perch.

Did it take long to find me? I asked the faithful light.
Did it take long to find me? And are you gonna stay the night?
Oh I'm bein' followed by a moonshadow, moonshadow, moonshadow.

58.

Beginnings and Endings

Day after day passed. The guide didn't arrive, but no matter, Penalt found the life he wanted in San Kuuchamaa. He hoped Yawnix didn't cut him off. He hadn't found the Laetrile, but he didn't want to leave yet. The mountain village worked a peculiar form of magic on him. The changes started with the plant and herb vendors in Tijuana. A full conversion occurred when he went to work with Itandehui. He found what he'd been seeking as if he'd cracked open a shell, yet while his newfound optimism grew, he still doubted. The supernatural parts put him off. He couldn't go all the way. He wondered if he'd ever be able to pull it off, be a healer like Itandehui. He was a lab rat, always searching for the science behind the miracle. This worked against him. In these mountains, the people wore their lives on their sleeves. He kept his feelings close to the vest until his knowledge was complete. In the sterile atmosphere of his lab back home there was no room for emotions, but things were different here. A world he'd thought unnecessary was in fact essential. He had to accept that before he could make headway.

Penalt became a familiar sight to the local peasants and farmers. They laughed when he strolled along, towering over them like Goliath. He rented a small house, and had a box of supplies shipped from California. He knew what Yawnix wanted, but now he had a personal agenda. He hoped there'd be enough time for both.

"You're a fool, Penalt!" said his friend back home at Yawnix. Penalt heard the suspenders snapping over the phone. "You've gone native. It's madness! Either get the Laetrile or get out of there. We can't go on funding you with no results."

"I'm trying." *Too weak,* thought Penalt. "I'm close. Hang in there. I won't disappoint."

Penalt hung up. His friend would never understand. No use trying to explain. *Gone native?* Jesus! Had he really? He couldn't go back, he couldn't go forward. What was to become of him?

His Spanish improved, and he even learned some of the local dialect. He was pleased when Itandehui agreed to be his mentor. Pleased but terrified. The commitment was to be total.

"You must do exactly as I say or you will not see the spirits."

He tried to shake off his doubts. "I want to learn. I will do what you tell me."

"This will be hard for you. You cannot eat meat. You cannot drink. There can be no sex."

"No sex?"

"You need all of your energy to succeed. The spirit world is very demanding."

She smiled and revealed her missing teeth. He knew the world of ghosts and spirits was strange. Must he believe all of it? It was a foreign land where plants and animals could speak, where invisible forces collided with the world he knew. The gulf was wide; what if it was impenetrable? It would not be easy to forge a bridge.

Itandehui spoke an ancient Indian dialect. She spoke Spanish sometimes, and that helped. Penalt made careful notes of everything she said. Slowly, over time, he learned to understand her. He transcribed her words and reformed them until they made sense to him.

Listen to the wind. Look at the eyes that shine in the night. The spirits behind the eyes are watching. They are guides through the darkness. The bat that flies in the black of night sees the unseen. He will show you what is shallow and superficial and what is deep and real. The owl that sings wu hu hoo, wu hu hoo speaks for the spirits. Think back to when you were a child. You heard the voices of the trees and the murmurs of the stream and the warbles of the rocks. When you grew older you forced them out of your mind. They're still there. Listen to them now.

It was much harder than he expected. He'd pushed such things out of his mind long ago, and wasn't sure if there was still a place for them.

"I try, Itandehui. I can't. The journey is too far."

"It's not a journey," she told him. "The source is inside. You're already there. You must only open your mind to see."

Silence has profound messages, stories without words. Between the rustle of the branches, the creak of the tree limbs, between silence and sound, there is the tension of the flesh and the spirit. Portals to other worlds lie within that tension. Your core is there. Not even death can destroy it. Inside, there is a self, continuous and permanent, untouched by what you grasp and what you give away. The past and the future that we dwell on are illusions. The core is the eternal now.

He wrote down everything she said. When he read it back in his own words, he felt he must have missed something. The words by themselves sounded trivial. He couldn't wrap his mind around the essence of what she said—and where was the evidence to verify all these odd things? He had no place to store such wild ideas.

"I don't understand, Itandehui. These spirits, the spirits of the animals and trees, do they exist like we exist? Do they speak like we speak, or are they just visions?"

"Are you are willing to die to find the answers?"

"To die? What do you mean?"

"Wanting to know the answers to everything poisons the soul. Some things cannot be said with words. When you don't understand something, laugh. It's what all the great healers have learned to do."

Everything is in motion. No movement, no energy, no vibration stays unchanged. Nothing continues, nothing ends. Life is a universal movement that flows according to lines of force, ascending and descending. The spirit world is at the heart of the play of the forces.

Penalt did everything she asked. He listened. He followed her lead. He laughed. Nothing helped. He couldn't see what she saw. He watched her work with the sick and injured, but when it was his turn, he failed. A man came to her who could not sleep. He was having "dark visions" and "pains" all over his body. She helped the man lie down on a mat and stepped away.

"This is Antonio. Put your hands on Antonio's chest."

Penalt did as instructed. The man was moaning and turning on the mat. It was difficult, but Penalt managed to keep his hands on the man's chest. Meanwhile Itandehui burned some herbs in a ceramic bowl. She poured a pungent liquid into a cup, and set a large bowl next to the mat.

"Do you feel them, the spirits inside Antonio that are making him sick? Close your eyes. Do you see them?"

Penal neither felt nor saw anything. He became very frustrated. "I don't see them. I don't see anything."

"Step away." Penalt stood back. She put her hands on Antonio's chest and closed her eyes. Antonio began to settle down.

"Hand me the smoking herbs."

Penalt handed her the ceramic bowl. Itandehui removed her hands from the man's chest to receive it. She blew the smoke rising from the bowl all over the man, and continued until the herbs had burned away.

"Sit up, Antonio."

She motioned for Penalt to hand Antonio the cup. "Drink quickly, Antonio, until it's all gone."

Antonio struggled and choked as he tried to get the bitter liquid down. Itandehui used the bowl to catch any that spilled, and poured it back into the cup.

"Drink! Drink!"

At last the poor man finished.

Itandehui had the empty bowl ready. Antonio's eyes grew big. His stomach convulsed and he vomited into the bowl.

"Good," she said. "The evil spirits have left. Go home. Sleep. You will be well now."

Antonio looked at Itandehui as a child looks at his mother, in awe and wonder at her invisible power. He thanked her and left.

Ha, nice trick! thought Penalt. Here was a world he would never understand. Itandehui's reality was too far from the objective reality he knew, too far from his comfort zone. Science couldn't touch it. No one he knew had discovered the levels of reality where she worked.

This was a waste of his time.

Itandehui read his thoughts.

"The spirit world is not done with you, Roger. It wants more. You must go to a higher level, a spiritual level. To go there, you must be willing to risk everything."

Penalt vacillated day to day. He'd given up his job and his time; he was not about to give up his sanity. All Itandehui's strange utterances seemed like foolishness. He'd witnessed a healing and had been hoodwinked. Itandehui would go into a trancelike state, and in some inexplicable way exorcise the demons troubling her patient. Sometimes it was the simple application of herbs and plants. He could understand that, but most of it was preposterous. That an impoverished old woman, living in the middle of nowhere, knew more about healing than the doctors at home with their scientific medicine? The strange visions were a trick to fool people into being cured, some psychosomatic mumbo-jumbo, a placebo effect. That's all she had, smoke and mirrors. Penalt was not about to go nuts. He'd been kidding himself. It was time to leave. He was reluctant, but leave he must.

He made arrangements to return home, but while he packed his suitcases he remembered something from long ago: The first time he'd smoked a joint with friends in college he hadn't felt anything. Everyone around him laughed and carried on, while he sat aloof, stone-cold sober. Then, like an epiphany, the revelation came. Everything changed in an instant. He had an "Aha!" moment like what he would later experience in the lab when some particularly difficult puzzle piece fell into place. Could this be what Itandehui's world was about?

He would stay a few more days, try harder, give her one more chance. If Itandehui was right, he had to give everything. Maybe, as she said, a part of him had to die.

Itandehui knew what to do. This was the man she had seen in her vision. Maayhaay had sent him to be the new healer. A healer must see on his own. She could only make him ready.

"A great healer is never poor, never alone." Her dark eyes shone in brilliant flashes. "We who are healers have a treasure, something most people will never know." A smile passed over her cracked lips. "Everyone chooses one path over another. There are different paths all around us. They move with us through time. We choose one to follow, only one, but the others are still there. It's very difficult to change paths. Very few have the will to do it. What you are trying to do is not impossible. It can be done. I did it. You can do it too."

"Are you really a healer?"

"People think I am."

"What I mean is do you actually heal the sick?"

"Only Maayhaay and the spirits or the patient himself can take the credit for healing. I am no more than a dead chicken."

Itandehui laughed. The dark gaps that marked her missing teeth were like portals into another world. Her gray hair, her wrinkled skin, the odd routines of her life—they set her apart in ways Penalt didn't understand at all yet, but he felt her power. All of his friends would sneer at him if they knew where he was, what he was doing. He had to put that worry out of his mind.

He had a responsibility to Yawnix. He knew Itandehui had jugs of Laetrile hidden away somewhere. A part of him wanted to get on with it, to find the Laetrile and leave. He doubted he had the talent to be a healer like Itandehui, but maybe he did, and if he did, shouldn't he try? Guilt and doubt worked on him, but so did something else, something he couldn't yet articulate, but he felt it. He knew, despite his very legitimate doubts, that he wouldn't leave. Whatever held him, maybe it was nothing more than stubbornness, worked on him until he came up with a new plan. He'd make it to the next level or die trying. He would go up the mountain alone to think things through, clear his head, work things out for himself. That was what he needed.

On the trail there was a fork that led down into a valley. During the time of the silver mines this road had been built to accommodate some of the large wagons that carried ore down the mountain. Over time, it had eroded in places, but it was still passable, though dangerous. Hiking down to the valley would make a good day trip. It would get him away from the monotony of the village and give him a chance to think, to refresh his brain with physical exercise. Then he could make up his mind once and for all to stay or leave. He told Itandehui of his plan. Her response was odd, as if she'd already known.

Penalt left early on the day of the hike. He knew it would be dangerously hot in the valley by the afternoon. The trip would be difficult, but that was good—he wanted a real workout, knew from experience that heavy exercise improved his thinking. Taking as much water as he could carry, he set out, wearing a large hat to shield him from the sun. He chuckled at the thought of himself heading into the desert like the ancient prophets.

At first, things went well. The crisp mountain air stimulated his senses and cleansed his mind. After a time, he came to a sharp curve where the trail narrowed. On one side, a steep precipice fell off into a deep canyon. He stopped to rest, set the heavy water pack down, and gazed out over the valley. A lizard ran over his foot. It startled him, and he jumped, knocking his canteens over the bluff. When he looked down his hat flew off and spiraled into the canyon. How stupid! There was no going back now. He reached for the only remaining canteen but found most of the water had leaked out. Across the plain, he saw a small village. It didn't seem so far away. He figured he could get a new supply of water and another hat there.

It was a long, hot descent, harder than he'd anticipated. At last he came to the flat ground at the bottom. It had the characteristics of a desert. He'd underestimated the distance and the heat, and was exhausted. Going back was out of the question. He walked toward the village, but it didn't get any closer.

Soon Penalt was sick and lightheaded. The heat and insects buzzed around him. Things went out of focus. He looked in the direction of the village, but it jumped around; it wouldn't stay still. He grew dizzy. The desert was stronger and smarter than he was. It played with his mind. There were echoes behind him, but he saw nothing when he looked back. He tried to put one foot in front of the other and couldn't believe what happened: His legs gave out. The intense heat and the rugged, rocky trail caused him to lunge and lurch till he fell flat on his face and passed out.

It was dusk. The sky was turning dark. There were voices.

"Yea, though I walk through the valley of the shadow of death..."

Two figures approached like ghosts floating in the air. Behind them followed two shadowlike apparitions. They were neither material nor spiritual. The atmosphere around him was heavy. It was difficult to breathe.

The ghosts looked like two men, a priest and a young man. Neither saw him. It was as if they were in a different space. The shadowlike creatures floating behind were vague and formless. Strange sounds, secret sounds, confused Penalt, who tried to interpret them as if they were words.

"Who are you?" he asked the shadows.

The phantom behind the priest took the shape of a young man.

"I'm a soul, an imagination, a meditation. They call me Daniel."

When the phantom spoke, the priest clutched his heart with his hands and stumbled.

The young man reached out to steady him.

The other phantom simply leered and did not speak. Lurid stars flickered in the gloomy sky above. This silent phantom drew close to the young man. It spoke so softly Penalt could hardly hear.

"Give me your hand, sweet young man. You've nothing to fear. I'm neither evil nor wild. You'll sleep gently in my arms."

How long he was out, Penalt didn't know. It must have been several minutes. His arms and face and clothes were wet with sweat and covered with mud. There were cuts and bruises on his arms and face.

He woke in a sitting position, but couldn't recall getting into that position. After a few minutes, he rose to his feet. He was very wobbly, his mind in a daze. Everything appeared out of focus. Two men walked toward him. They helped him into a truck. They said they were driving across the plain when they'd spotted him, lost and disoriented. He asked about the village. They said it was a mirage.

"Sunstroke," he heard. They took him to Itandehui.

She had them lay him down on goatskins. She spread out some wild tobacco leaves, then mashed up some dried sunflower seeds and combined them with cottonseed oil. Next she spread the mixture on the leaves and covered Penalt's head with them for about half an hour. She treated his cuts and bruises with a salve he'd seen her use before, and cautioned him not to wash. The two men took him back to his place to rest, where he slept soundly through the night.

Itandehui boiled the flowers and stems of some small sunflowers into a brew and set it aside to cool. When Penalt arrived the next morning, she had him sit erect with his head down while she poured some of the liquid all over his head from his neck to his brow. After half an hour she repeated this dousing. Next, she poured small amounts onto his head and massaged it into his scalp. He started to feel normal again.

She brought out some dried leaves, ground them up, and rolled a cigar that she lit and smoked. She motioned for Penalt to lie still. She blew the smoke into his face and over his body. She fanned it around him with an eagle feather. Again, he slept.

When he awoke, he noticed the changes. He could see things—hear things—none of which had been there before. Itandehui's body looked transparent. He could see the connections inside between the muscles and tissues and joints. His own hands looked strange, like claws. His arms were a mass of tiny points of light held together by an invisible magnetic force. Penalt tried to speak, but no words came out of his mouth. He stood up. As he walked around, everything was out of balance. It was like walking on a tilted plane. The space around him changed. He could no longer distinguish his body from the surroundings. Everything had merged into a misty blur.

Itandehui watched and laughed and clapped her hands. She'd seen it happen only once before—it had happened to her when she was a little girl.

Penalt knew that he'd made the jump. He remembered when he'd first smoked marijuana. Everyone around him was asking: "Do you feel it? Do you feel it?" He wasn't. He didn't know what they were talking about. Then, in a flash, he was. It was a subtle but fundamental change—and you can never go back.

59.

Jai Alai

"I had a vision while I was in the desert," Penalt said.

"You'll meet them again, those you saw."

Itandehui went on about her usual routine as if nothing had changed, silent, resolute.

"I really screwed up yesterday. I'm sorry I caused everyone so much trouble."

She swept the broom across the floor without looking up. When she was finished, she spoke.

"I need some supplies. You will need to go to Tijuana."

"Yes, of course. Whatever I can do to help."

He didn't want to go to town. Still trying to grasp what happened to him, he didn't want to leave just as he'd begun to unravel the mystery. He needed time to think. In town there would be women and bars, all the temptations he needed to avoid. He wasn't excited about the prospect, but he couldn't say no after what Itandehui had done for him.

She knew all about his worries. She had a list prepared.

"Everything will be at the Mercado Principal. Don't stay more than one night. There is work to do."

He wondered if this was a test to see if he was ready. Ready for what, he didn't know.

The locals joked as he climbed onto the bus. Penalt sat beside an older man, skinny, two-day beard, dressed in his Sunday finest. "The way to town is the road to hell, señor," he said soberly. Behind them another man piped in: "Or just a hell of a road." The two slapped their knees and guffawed.

Everyone was happy, excited about the trip, anxious to see relatives, to shop, or just to go somewhere different. The air was close, the odors pungent, the ride bumpy and long. Penalt was relieved when they finally pulled into town. He was also nervous. He wanted to get on with his task and return. Most of all he could not let himself spin out of control.

Tijuana was filled with danger. After living on the mountain, especially after what happened in the desert, he was unprepared. The city hurt like a thorn in his side. He saw two young Indian women with babies tied in sling-like rebozos suspended from their shoulders. The infants took in everything silently with probing black eyes. He wondered if Indian babies ever cried. He looked at them gaze out from under mats of black hair. He was amazed how mute and stationary they hung there, like little dolls. Lucky for him it wasn't the weekend, when the city sucked American crowds over the border for two days of madness. Most of the gringos downtown were hangers-on, men who'd let their hair grow wild, the skinny ones on pills and marijuana, killing time till they could fleece the next group of wide-eyed tourists. On his way to the market, Penalt saw a couple of *Tejanos* coming out of a bar with a *bailadora*. During his week in Tijuana he'd learned the risks of walking down that road. The Texans were heading straight for trouble.

Tijuana was the sex capital of the world, or the abortion capital of the world, or the divorce capital, the souvenir capital, or the ultimate drugstore, depending on your tastes. Penalt walked along in the dust. He passed mounds of turquoise and silver jewelry, sombreros, serapes, guitars, bongo drums, leather goods in every shape and form, pornographic towels, and sexy ashtrays. Half the junk he saw was the same as in the stores up north. There were stalls that sold red-hot jalapeño peppers, fried bananas, charcoal-roasted corn on the cob, and fiery tacos. At last he reached the area of the mercado where he hoped to find the items on his list.

It was dark inside the large-roofed market. It took some time for his eyes to focus, but the smells were immediate, musty, bitter and sweet all at once. He found the jars and baskets and boxes of herbs and potions scattered all around one area. It was crowded, and Penalt bumped into people. There are no straight lines in Mexico. Sometimes a collision would send him off in the wrong direction. When he asked for help finding some obscure item, the local vendors were honest and helpful. They seemed surprised that a gringo would shop there—most of the Americans went straight to the bars and trinket shops.

A lady followed him around buying similar items. He hadn't noticed her at first. After his last purchase, just as he started to leave, she approached him.

"You are Roger Penalt, *si?*"

"Yes. How did you know that?"

"I am Ana Luisa. Itandehui is my friend. She told me you'd be coming. She said you might like to join me tonight for the Jai Alai games. They are very popular here. Everyone comes out for them."

Penalt didn't understand what she was talking about, but if Itandehui had arranged something, he thought he should go.

"I'm not familiar with 'high a lie'."

"It's a game similar to racquetball with professional teams. Jai Alai is very popular here. I'm sure you would have fun."

"I'd be happy to join you. Where shall we meet?"

"I'll be back in front of the market in an hour."

"See you then."

Penalt rushed off and checked into his hotel. He showered and put on clean clothes. Soon he was back at the market, waiting for Ana Luisa. Two Mexican boys ran up to him begging for money. He gave them a couple of coins. A larger pack of urchins was headed his way when Ana Luisa pulled up in her Jeep to save him. They drove directly to the Jai Alai Palace.

"You mustn't give those boys money. I know you mean well, but they should be in school."

"At this hour?"

"School here is in the morning and evening. Too hot during the day."

"Oh, I see."

The car bounced unexpectedly; Penalt hit his knee on the door handle, and nearly fell out when the door opened. He managed to pull it back.

"I don't usually drive," Ana Luisa said, "but my driver has been ill." She gave him a nervous smile as she tried to avoid running into the cars and pedestrians that surrounded them. The car jumped and stuttered and swerved back and forth. Penalt was amused but held back his laughter.

The architecture of the *Fronton Palacio* was impressive. It was a large stadium, Moorish in design, with two giant white arched stone doors. A crowd had formed by the ticket booth. Ana Luisa guided Penalt past the throng. She already had the tickets. They entered through the front entrance, and followed an usher who led them to their seats. The first game had already started.

Penalt was quickly drawn in by the action. The court was about the size of a basketball court. One player spun like a top and hurled a goat-hide sphere to the green granite wall where it rocketed off with a satisfying *thunk*. The opponent climbed up the sidewall to catch the ball in his basket, and then in one smooth motion slung it back to the wall. The crowd was electric. Thunk-thunk-thunk went the volley, until a well-placed ball finally eluded its defender.

It wasn't till things slowed that Penalt noticed Father Jordan and Eric seated beside Ana Luisa. It seemed like a bizarre coincidence until he realized this must have been Itandehui's plan all along.

"Hello, Mr. Penalt." Father Jordan spoke as if they were old friends. "I'm sure you remember Eric? This is his fiancé, Ofelia, her brother, Orvaline, and Eric's brother Devon."

"Please, just call me Roger. I'm happy to see you again, Father. It's a pleasure to meet you, Ofelia, and you too, Devon, Orvaline. I want to thank you, Father, for your help at the village. Itandehui and I are getting on well. I'm learning a lot, some of it very strange and quite extraordinary. There is so much to learn and it's so foreign to my scientific senses that I'm overwhelmed."

Jordan smiled. "I well imagine you are out of your element, lad."

After each point, the losing side crept off the court in shame, replaced by another team from the queue. Then the action resumed immediately, thunk-thunk-thunk.

"These games can get pretty wild, Roger. Relax and enjoy."

Penalt heard yells from the crowd: "You stink, greenie!"

"Drop it, you Cuban monkey!"

"Just one more point, Felipe, or whatever your name is!"

Occasionally a more knowledgeable voice, usually with a Spanish accent, would salute a subtle play: "¡*Chula!* ¡*Chula!*"

Penalt was fascinated. The court was a vast open space, its tall ceiling surrounded by tiers of stadium seating. The oohs and aahs of the crowd echoed between the walls each time a player caught and released the ball. The noise deafened.

Penalt had to yell for Jordan to hear him. "It looks easy enough. All you have to do is catch the ball in that little basket suspended from your arm and fling it back against the wall."

"Not nearly as easy as it looks, my boy," said Jordan. "That basket, it's called a *cesta,* is only about this wide." Jordan spread his thumb and forefinger to show how small. "The walls are made o' granite to withstand the impact of the ball. The ball, they call it a *pelota,* is harder than a golf ball, and the space where it enters the basket is even narrower. It's like trying to catch a flying egg with a large spoon."

It was obvious that Jordan was a great enthusiast of the games. He stood up and moved toward Ana Luisa.

Jordan said, "Move over and sit by Eric and his friends, Roger. You're closer in age and will have more to say to them than to an old couple like us." Penalt watched him grasp Ana Luisa's hand when he sat beside her.

Jai Alai happened in discrete steps instead of in a continuous flow, more like tennis than basketball or horseracing. After a few games, Penalt got the hang of the scoring system. With each point, he noticed how the loyalties of the crowd changed rapidly. The dynamics of the game could be altered instantaneously. In baseball, you can be twelve runs ahead, so giving up one run costs you very little, but in Jai Alai, no matter how far ahead one team was, the loss of a single point could doom them to defeat by forcing them to sit and watch miserably while the opponent won the match. Suddenly a team given up for dead trotted back onto the court, and it became a whole new ballgame.

The fans were inveterate gamblers, large and small. In the corner was a betting clock that counted down and terminated when a loud buzzer sounded, announcing that the betting was closed. There were cheers and boos from the fans as they jumped up and down, spilling their beers. All three walls of the court were in play. Father Jordan leaned over to speak to Penalt.

"You may not know this, but according to the *Guinness World Records* book, Jai Alai is the world's fastest ballgame." Jordan's excitement was addictive. Penalt felt the blood speed through his veins.

"I had no idea," he said. The place was full and the crowd was rocking. "It looks like Jai Alai is the most popular thing going in Tijuana."

"Oh, it is, lad, it is. Some of the most famous American icons have been to the games here—Mickey Rooney, "The Duke" John Wayne, Clark Gable, Victor Mature, and Jack Palance. I've seen them all over the years."

When Jordan turned back to Ana Luisa, Penalt looked at Eric. He blinked. Did he really see what he thought he saw? It was like his desert vision of apparitions and ghosts. Inside Eric's body, shadowy figures circled each other like phantom wrestlers. All the noise in the stadium disappeared, and Penalt felt as if he were alone inside a bubble, so fully engaged by what he saw that he became oblivious of everything else. Not long before his trip to Mexico, he'd heard an interview about chakras and auras with some guru who was riding the biofeedback wave. Penalt thought such things were crazy, but something similar was happening before his very eyes.

Eric turned to him, and the strange visions stopped. Penalt tried to hide his staring by asking a casual question. "So, Eric, what brings you to Tijuana?" Penalt shouted the words so as to be heard over the thunderous crowd. Ofelia looked in their direction.

"I was diagnosed with colon cancer a few months ago," Eric shouted back. "Conventional medicine was a failure, so I came here for alternative treatment with Laetrile. Things didn't go too well at first, but recently I've seen improvement. I'm hopeful. My doctor at the local clinic. and an American doctor I've been seeing in San Diego. agree that there's been improvement in my condition. Only a few months ago I was considered hopeless, so I'm very happy about the changes."

"Was that why you were at San Kuuchamaa the day I met you?"

"Yes. Father Jordan and Ana Luisa set up a healing treatment with Itandehui. She gave me a special type of Laetrile. I can't say any more, but I can assure you it works, at least it's worked for me. Jordan says it's a bit of a secret, the Laetrile, I mean, but since you're working with Itandehui, you must know about it already.

Things were falling into place. Father Jordan knew about the renegade strain of Laetrile, and had taken Eric to San Kuuchamaa so Itandehui could administer it to him. The man with the crossed eyes at El Azteca was right, the one who asked: "Meester, you want to know about the Laetrile?" Penalt now found himself conflicted. He felt an allegiance to Itandehui, but also had an obligation to tell his friend at Yawnix about what he'd discovered. Not yet knowing all the facts, he'd leave things on hold till he learned more.

"I'm happy to hear you're better, Eric. I must say, you're a lucky man! Ofelia is a beautiful woman, and together you make the perfect couple."

Ofelia's cheeks flushed. She lowered her eyelids.

"Thank you. The wedding's set for next Saturday."

"So soon? Wow, congratulations!" A shy smile crossed Ofelia's lips. Penalt had seen more pretty girls this evening than he'd seen in weeks at the mountain village. He tried to control his hormones. Itandehui had told him, "No sex." Now that he'd seen the visions, he didn't want to mess things up. He didn't want to end up like Thomas Merton, the famous monk destroyed by sex. He had to stay on the path Itandehui had set, for now at least. Poor Merton had died alone—perhaps of a broken heart— just a few years back, the same year Martin Luther King and Robert Kennedy were killed. Those were terrible times.

"Thank you. We're very happy," Ofelia said, and Penalt's brief daydream about sex ended. "It would be our pleasure to have you come to our wedding and to the festivities after. It will be at one o'clock at the Cathedral de Nuestra Señora de Guadalupe. You might find some interesting people there, maybe even a date." She laughed.

Just what I don't need right now, Penalt thought.

"That's very kind of you, but I'm afraid I must get back to San Kuuchamaa. I'm only here on a supply run for Itandehui."

Penalt turned back to the game just as two singles players switched back and forth between offense and defense, catching and throwing at the same time.

"What's the history behind these games? I've never heard of Jai Alai before today."

Orvaline joined the conversation. "Some say the games are related to the ancient handball courts of the indigenous Indians of Mexico, but Jai Alai actually originated centuries ago in the Basque provinces of Spain and France. It traveled here with the early explorers."

One game followed another, each more exciting than the last. The crowd stomped and cheered till the noise built to an overwhelming pitch. Penalt joined in at the top of his lungs, his lustful thoughts gone for now.

The pitch grew louder and louder till the final game ended. Afterward, Father Jordan and Ana Luisa drove Penalt back to the hotel while Eric and his friends went home.

Devon was off to California the next day. He'd return to Mexico soon with his mother and grandmother. Eric and Ofelia and Orvaline were busy with their individual roles in preparation for the wedding.

As Penalt lay awake at the hotel, he mulled over the facts repeatedly. Could it really be true that a cure for cancer had been discovered and kept under wraps by the large drug companies because it threatened their profits? Of course it could! The same professionals who denied the connection between cigarettes and cancer were the ones who denied the effects of Laetrile. Money is the devil's lubricant.

The world seemed so dirty and sad. Penalt thought about severing his ties with Yawnix, but if Laetrile really worked, he'd be depriving cancer sufferers of a potential cure. He decided to keep up his double life a bit longer. Tomorrow he'd return to where he belonged, to the mountain, with Itandehui. He was the eagle who visits the earth, shakes the dust from its wings, and returns to the sun. He would find a way to meet his obligation to Yawnix, but he had his own business to pursue first.

"What is it with this giant crow that keeps pestering us?"

"Don't worry none, ma'am. I'll keep him away."

"Well, you'd better, Nelson, if you know what's good for you. You blacks are all alike. I don't trust any of you."

I'd like to truss you like a turkey, bitch! "Now ma'am, this ain't no time for that kinda talk. You mind your words. I have feelings too."

"Oh, shush! I think that's the clinic up ahead. Thank God. We're here at last."

Nelson guided Nurse Marta through the gate. As they walked past the mural, she gave it a harsh look. Nelson blessed himself.

"What on Earth do you think you're doing, Nelson? This is no church—and it's no hospital. Look at this place! It's crawling with insects. Who in their right mind would travel down here for any kind of treatment? Move ahead. I think that's the front door to this... this... whatever it is."

Nurse Marta walked in and immediately confronted Mida. "Who's in charge here?"

"Excuse? You have appointment?"

"Speak English, for Christ's sake. Where's the doctor in charge?"

Nurse Marta headed down the hallway looking at the office doors. Nelson followed sheepishly.

Mida ran after them, wiggling in her tight uniform. "Estop! Nobody go there except those who have appointment! Estop!"

Nurse Marta look a fright. She been too long in that hot sun, the wicked witch. Why don't she melt? "Walk slower, Nurse Marta, let's not anger them up around here."

"Shut up, Nelson! I didn't come here to sweet-talk any of these imbeciles. I came to get my patient. Now where is he? Where's Mr. Eric Martin?"

Nurse Marta's words reverberated around the empty hallway. No one was at the clinic at this time of day except Mida, and Mida wasn't going to tell these crazy gringos anything. She'd let them flail about and find their own way. The fierce go to the bull ring, the tame to the cattle pen.

"Is that you, Nelson?"

"Be cool, man. Be cool. Just go on 'bout your business."

"Is that nurse here with you?"

"Don't worry. No honky nurse's gonna beat this nigger at his own game, not even that ole bitch."

"I'm frightened, Nelson. Where am I?"

"Shh. Go back to sleep. I'll try to keep her busy a little longer."

"What? Who are you talking to, Nelson?"
"I ain't talkin' to nobody, Nurse Marta. You must be hearin' ghosts."
Mida shook her head. These were two crazy gringos!

60.

The Wedding

Mida gazed into the magic mirror. She was transfixed. Her bathroom mirror at home was so small she could hardly see her face, but in Ofelia's house everything was larger than life. The strapless silk dress, papaya pink, fit Mida like a glove. She still had the shape God had given her, even if she'd added a bit more here and there. It was all right—most men liked a little meat on the bones.

Ofelia walked up behind her and stopped to look into the mirror to see if the bright pink lipstick she wore had smudged her teeth. She squinted her eyes and puckered her lips to get a better look. Mida laughed.

"*Querida,* an old friend is the best mirror. You look perfect, but what about me?"

Ofelia reached up to twirl the ends of her long black hair. Mida pushed her hand away.

"A tree that's born twisted never grows straight. Leave that alone. You'll ruin the hairdresser's hard work."

Ofelia giggled. "Poor Papa, I hope his heart is strong when he sees the bills."

"He who wants Heaven must pay." Mida turned in a circle. "So, how do I look?"

"They will think you're the one getting married. Be careful you don't steal the groom!"

They exchanged stories about the way they'd been as little girls. They grew up under very different circumstances: Ofelia had all the advantages, while Mida's family struggled to get by. They'd met when Mida's mother worked for the Cabreras as a cleaning lady. The girls soon became inseparable. At first Rogelio and Amelia discouraged the friendship, wanting their daughter to mingle only in the highest social circles. Ofelia would have none of it. She insisted that Mida would always be her best friend.

Eric was across the garden in his palapa where Rogelio had installed a phone. Manny called to say he'd arrived. Eric told him about the positive results from Doctor Doggett.

"I'm happy for you, Eric, but I must tell you I'm skeptical. At first, when you told me you were leaving Stanford for Mexico, my heart sank. The new treatment Doctor Rice offered was a gamble, but at least it was real medicine. This Laetrile business seems farfetched to me, a crazy idea. Maybe I'm too old and closeminded. Einstein said something to the effect that if an idea doesn't seem insane it doesn't have a chance. For your sake, I hope he's right. I can't understand it, so I'll chalk it up to your good luck. In any case, I'm happy you're feeling better, whatever the reason. I look forward to meeting Ofelia and the rest."

"It's more than luck, Manny. Dig into it deeper. Go and speak with Doctor Doggett if you want. They're onto something down here. Crazy as you may think it is, what happened isn't just a fluke. Whether you understand it or not, I'm convinced. Something more than luck has brought on this cure. You wait, a scientific explanation will come if the right people look into it."

At the other end of the line, Manny raised his eyebrows. The idea of healing without drugs, surgery, or other invasive care went counter to everything he'd learned in medical school. Eric's unexpected recovery was clearly an anomaly. Manny didn't want to spoil Eric's party, but things didn't add up. This could be the lull before a storm. He worried about a relapse.

"You sound great, Eric. Let's talk at the reception."

Eric too was worried, but didn't want to admit it. Things had been going so well he'd forgotten how sick he'd been at Stanford.

Though he tried to hide it, he knew that things could turn on a dime. He was undeniably feeling better, but the cancer could return. That was why he was so anxious to get on with his life. His sleep had been restless for the past several nights. Thank goodness the wedding day had finally come.

There was a knock at the door. It was Devon. "Time to put on your monkey suit, Eric."

"God, I just wish it was over. All the planning and waiting takes its toll. Kafka called impatience the one cardinal sin. If that's true, I must be the world's greatest sinner."

"I'll get you through the day, don't worry."

As an attorney, Eric knew all about intricate planning, but the petty details and constant nitpicking for a wedding was over the top. He could see Mathilda shake her head and hear her: "das Spatzenhirn!"

Precious hours were spent honing the guest list to avoid any errors that might destroy a lifetime of careful family positioning. Painstaking care with flower selection was taken so as not to conflict with the meticulously chosen bridesmaid's dresses. Mountains of food and oceans of drink had to be prepared. Next came the divining of the seating arrangements, as complex as reading the entrails of a goat. The prickly old maids had to be coddled and made to feel as important as the narcissistic single young women. They all wanted to sit next to important and rich young men. Extravagant and worthless party favors would be passed out to the guests to add to their overstuffed cabinets. Musicians and photographers were hired. It was endless and exhausting, but Eric endured it to make Ofelia and her parents happy.

"Do you think Mom and Gram will get along with the Cabreras and all their wealthy friends? I worry about it, Eric said."

"They'll fit in," Devon replied. Orvaline and I get along great. I think Rogelio enjoys the novelty of having all these Americans around. Even though he may dislike us in some ways, we're an eclectic collection he can use to impress his friends. Now, get your pants on. Hide those skinny legs. Did you have any breakfast? You need something in your stomach."

Outside, servants, uncomfortable in their stiff new uniforms, ran around the courtyard attending to last-minute details while two young men stood in the driveway awaiting the prominent guests. Rogelio and Amelia had invited a few dignitaries to their house before the wedding. A member of the president's cabinet and two senators newly arrived from Mexico City were escorted into a salon in the main house. The governor and the chief of police were next to arrive. Devon watched them from the palapa.

"Wow! There's a political summit unfolding down there. Ofelia's parents are some important folks."

"Don't make me any more nervous than I already am. There's no way I can keep up with that. Karen is bringing Bill Berman, dean of the law school, and I've invited an assemblyman and a couple of state senators from Sacramento. There'll be lots of attorneys, but attorneys are a dime a dozen. God, this whole thing makes me nuts. I put up with the fuss for Ofelia and her parents, but I can't wait for this day to be over."

Ofelia wanted the decorations to be simple but elegant. Her mother wanted something far more elaborate. They ended up compromising. Pink and white roses were strung on thin wires to hang over the pews. Runners were draped over the walls of the church. At the top they swung out to meet magnificent light fixtures that hung from the peak of the roof. Big bouquets of cream-colored flowers in massive standing vases surrounded by greenery adorned the entire area around the altar where Eric and Ofelia would exchange their vows.

"I managed to tone down Mama's plans to rebuild the church in her Rococo style." Ofelia watched Mida's face in the mirror. She wanted to see the reaction. "I think Eric and his family will be comfortable. I know he's worried about how two such different families will get along. I must admit I'm a little nervous myself, but I know my parents can be gracious to anyone. I am so excited and looking forward to a wonderful day. I wish Eric would just relax. I don't want this whole thing to be a burden on him. He just wants it to be over so we can be alone together—respectably, that is."

"As soon as he hears thunder, he wants zucchini," laughed Mida. "Men are all alike!"

The limousines arrived, first for the politicians, later for Eric, Devon, Orvaline, and the ushers. Ofelia and Mida and the girls were the last to leave, in a car with Ofelia's parents.

Eric was stunned when Mida arrived all dressed up as the maid of honor. "You look beautiful, Mida! Like an exotic flower. I almost didn't recognize you. Everything suits you perfectly."

"You, mister fancy tuxedo, are the donkey talking about ears!"

Rogelio laughed loudly when he heard her.

"Someday, Eric, someday I want one just like you!" Mida declared. "Ofelia has all best luck! I meet your mother and abuela. They set me up *con su primo, verdad?* We be relatives soon!"

"I was worried that Ofelia's parents might not get on so well with my family, but it looks like they've hit it off."

"I no gold coin, Eric. They learn to like me fine. Faces we see, hearts we do not know. Inside the heart, *el corazón,* there you find the truth. Ofelia's parents, your mother and grandmother, they all got good hearts. They all good people. El corazón, that is where the gold is."

Before the ceremony, Eric spoke with Father Jordan, who was getting dressed in the sacristy.

"Come, Eric, are you ready?"

"I think so. I love Ofelia, but I know so little about love, Jordan. I'm afraid I've lived a fairly sheltered life, always working."

"Well, I can't say much on the matter, but I do have a little experience with love."

That wry little smile appeared on Jordan's face again. It made Eric feel good to see Jordan had recovered some of his old self.

"Thank God for love, Eric. I daresay without it we'd all be poor, base reptiles. There are several kinds of love: The selfish love you grasp with desire; the love you feel for all God's creations, a love he put in your heart; but the best of all is the unselfish love you have with one special person, the love you have for Ofelia. It's an honor for me to marry the two of you. Indeed, it will be one o' the greatest joys o' my life."

"I owe you everything, Jordan. You've helped me through some very tough times. I won't forget it. You're the father I wish I'd had."

"Well, I can't say but that you've changed, Eric, in the short while I've known you. I suppose *matured* would be a better word. You had the strength and goodness and courage when you first arrived. You even had some o' the wisdom—you just didn't know it then."

"Thank you, Jordan. I'll admit, I'm a nervous wreck today."

"Put your worries aside. I'll manage it. It's time to go in. Are Devon and the others ready?"

Ave Maria finished playing. It was silent inside the church. Eric called Devon and the others into the sacristy. They walked out and stood by the altar with Father Jordan, looked back toward the church entrance, and waited. Rogelio appeared with Ofelia. He walked her magnificently toward them. A lone guitar played *Pachelbel's Canon in D*. All eyes were on Ofelia. Napier sat with Nicoleta next to Doctor Milagro and his family. They were in the row behind Eric's mother and Karen. Eric's mother's eyes beamed at him and gave him the confidence he needed to get on with it.

Rogelio guided Ofelia to the altar. He raised the veil and kissed his daughter. He looked at Eric with both sadness and joy, then stood quietly for a moment, staring in wonderment at his daughter. Eric recognized the look on Rogelio's face. He'd seen the same look on people in his office who knew their lives were about to change forever. Rogelio turned and took his seat next to Amelia. At last, Eric and Ofelia stood alone at the altar.

Ofelia wanted to remember every detail, but it proved impossible. There were too many unrehearsed surprises: Mida dropped the ring while passing it to Ofelia. It fell onto the floor and rolled down the steps before Devon rescued it. Everyone laughed. It grew quiet again when they exchanged their vows, but in the middle Osvaldo's dog barked. Osvaldo had refused to be the flower boy unless he could bring the dog with him. Father Jordan performed the service in both Spanish and English, alternating between the two. The Spanish version, romantic with long flowery phrases, detailed the responsibilities of married life in a way Eric found peculiar. A husband doesn't beat his wife. He sets a good example for the children. He avoids sin and supports his family. He honors his wife. A wife supports and loves her husband, lets him take the lead, does not embarrass him in front of his friends. The English version was short and to the point, without the details. It was so obviously edited that it made the guests laugh.

A mile away across town, in a meadow still echoing the merry bells and birdsongs, the laughs and the cries of occasions long past, butchers and pastry chefs, cooks and bartenders, delivery trucks and waiters prepared for the evening to come.

> Somewhere in the thick foliage surrounding the meadow, a strange creature stared out at the staff. They were too involved in their preparations to notice. Days of searching left the creature poised and ready to leap, but the opportunity did not present. Not yet. Faster than the wind the bizarre beast scurried away with a horrible screech. One of the waiters heard a loud noise and dropped a whole tray of champagne glasses.

An hour set aside for photographs followed the marriage service. Everyone got their turn: Ofelia with her parents, with her grandmother, her father, her mother, the bridesmaids, the groomsmen, Eric, Osvaldo and his dog, Eric's mother and grandmother, Devon, Karen, and special friends.

After submitting to the photographer's endless arrangements and rearrangements, Eric and Ofelia were whisked away in a black limousine. Eric tried to remember the day he had his first glimpse of Tijuana.

His head reeled with all the events of the past few months. And now he was with Ofelia, married.

Arriving at the reception intimidated him. Eric expected a mob, but the crowd was even bigger than he let himself imagine. He hadn't seen so many people since he graduated from USC when he sat like a blackbird in a row of identical blackbirds. He'd nodded his head and listened to the speeches and made his way at last to the front to receive a piece of paper that verified he'd won the battle with bonehead English. Now, after all his sorrow and pain, here he was, confronting a new life. Mida once told him, "*Cuando se inicia una vida, otro se termina"* (when one life starts, another ends). Maybe it was self-indulgence, but Eric believed there was more to come. Intuition is good for everyday life, but not for understanding what's at the core. Mexico had changed his mind, enlarged it. He still had to sort it out. He needed time alone with Ofelia, but he had to wait. He shook hands and spoke with friends, acquaintances, and total strangers until the reception line disappeared.

The mariachi music was in full sway. Eric was concerned when Devon disappeared with the prettiest bridesmaid. He didn't want Devon to do something stupid that might compromise everything. Devon and the girl returned shortly with new musicians who'd been hired to keep the younger crowd happy. Soon the guitars blared and the young guests danced. The older ones shook their heads in amazement and laughed while they enjoyed the food and drink.

Manny stood by the bar speaking with the bartender.

"Si, hombre, *that* is tequila."

Manny choked on his first sip.

"Awp!" "It... has a very sharp taste, doesn't it?" Manny hiccupped after downing the shot.

"Mehican whiky, señor." The bartender's white teeth shone under his black mustache when he smiled.

"Having a good time, Manny?"

"Absolutely, Eric! Congratulations. Ofelia is beautiful. You're a lucky guy." Manny's chest burned. He burped. "Awp!"

"It's the tequila! Be careful, Doc. Lucky? No, I'm entitled, don't you know? I've worked hard for this. Got to go. I'll try to catch you later."

Manny was still bewildered. He made a mental note to meet with Doctor Doggett on his way home.

Waiters in white shirts and black ties brought out the main courses.

Eric reached the table where his mother and grandmother had been seated with Rogelio and Amelia and Ofelia's grandmother. His mother was caught in a daydream, looking around at the other guests when he arrived. "What do you think of it all, Mom?"

She wondered why women yawn when they're jealous and curious. She'd noticed it hundreds of times. One of her favorite pastimes was to watch the people in crowds, people who didn't know they were being watched. She liked to guess their history and predict their future. Sometimes she got it right, which confirmed to her that she was a good judge of character. From the photos Eric sent of Ofelia and her family, she knew things were going to be okay.

"Oh, Eric, it's you. How do you feel, honey?" She straightened the hat on her head, unaware that she was doing it. She folded her hands together on her lap, then moved them to her knees, then folded them together again.

Eric was worried when he saw she was nervous. "I'm great, Mom. Are you having a good time?"

She wanted wealth. Her pulse quickened in the presence of such opulence as she saw today. She hoped her agitation wasn't evident to everyone as she longed for everything here, though she knew in her heart it was out of reach.

"Oh, yes! Rogelio and Amelia are perfect hosts." His mother smiled at Rogelio. Eric could sense that Ofelia's parents were pleased. They wanted everything to be perfect, and it was.

Adjusting to the life of a single woman had been hard for Eric's mother, but she'd accepted her fate. Today was a rare chance for her to enjoy life as she wished it. Eric was grateful that he could give her this day.

She thought silently how tiresome life was without an income. What little she got from Devon's father hardly lasted the month, and after he'd remarried, Eric's father gave her nothing. She had to go into her savings to get her dress for the wedding. Often a desire to wear something lovely seized hold of her, but she resisted it for the vanity it was.

"How about you, Gram?"

Eric's grandmother was short and plump and had very strong opinions on everything. She cleaned her teeth with her tongue, and made little clicks when she spoke.

"I'm enjoying my talk with Rogelio's mother. We're like two old turkeys gobbling about, aren't we Mariana?"

"Yes, Edie." Mariana smiled at Eric. "Your grandmother tells me you make sugar from beets instead of the sugar cane we use, and that at home you have apricots bigger than Rogelio's nose!"

"Not when you include my mustache," laughed Rogelio.

"No! Not then, my son," laughed Mariana. "You're quite right."

"We do have lovely vegetables and fruits and nuts at home, but I would drive down here once a week just for the shrimp," said Edie. Her tongue no longer clicked and clacked.

"I'm happy everyone's getting along so well. Now it's time for me to join Ofelia."

"She has you on a leash, eh, hijo?" Rogelio's eyes twinkled as he spoke. It pleased Eric that Rogelio called him son.

No one was aware that Ofelia was pregnant. Eric knew how excited his mother would be, but for now it would remain a secret between Ofelia and Eric. The band started to play again. They went over the chords to *Black Magic Woman*. Eric wondered, *If I listen to a song often enough in life, will I hear it when I'm dead?* Everything seemed like a grand illusion, a ploy by forces beyond his control to confuse his senses. He had changed, changed for the better, but how would he know if he hadn't? How would he know if everything that had happened in these past few months was nothing but a dream?

Eric looked at Devon when he heard the chiming of wineglasses. It was time for the speeches. His stomach was queasy but he wasn't in pain. Rogelio rose and walked to the stage.

"Thank you all for coming out for Eric and Ofelia. We especially thank those of you who traveled all the way from Mexico City and California." He stopped to clear his throat. "We have known Eric for only a few months." Rogelio looked at Eric. "Yes, only a few months. During much of that time, Eric has been in a fierce battle, not only to recover his health, a battle he has won, but the even more difficult battle to take the hand of my daughter from the grasp of her stubborn father. You see, our children are a gift from God. Amelia and I have been blessed with three, Osvaldo, Orvaline, and Ofelia. We've watched them grow, and we've tried to teach them how to live as God intended." As he spoke Rogelio glanced at Father Jordan and Father Gomez. "We have given them what we could to help them make their way in this sometimes cruel but always beautiful world of God's design."

Rogelio choked up when he looked at Ofelia. "A vigilant father protects his daughter. She is the flower of his eye and seems so fragile and vulnerable that he knows he would do anything in his power to keep her safe and happy, but a good father must be more than vigilant. It's a difficult job. As the Prophet Micah told us, a man must love kindness and walk humbly with his God. Even the best father cannot control the lives of his children. He must learn when to let them go their own way. My pride and my fear slowed me in my understanding of this, but in the end I found my way." He looked at Eric. "I welcome another son into our family today. As our two families join into one, may nothing ever come between them."

Everyone clapped and shouted their approval.

Orvaline was at first too shy to speak. He stood slowly, and shook a little as he mumbled his words. "I remember getting off to a bad start, Eric, but I also recall telling you that you would get your chance with our family. Well, now that you have it, don't let down your guard for a minute, 'mano! Devon and I will be watching you very closely. Take good care of my sister, or else!"

Orvaline exhaled a breath of relief and collapsed, nearly falling into his chair. Everyone laughed.

Devon got up next. "Okay, I'm younger, but I've had some experience with this sort of thing. Ofelia, I hope you know what you're getting into. Let me give you a few pointers. First: Sunday morning. My advice? Leave him alone. He can be really nasty before he reads the newspaper and eats his breakfast." The guests chuckled and sipped their drinks. Devon continued, "If he goes off on one of his rampages on vocabulary or punctuation, don't argue with him. Just let him go on until he gets it out of his system. Try to stop him from chewing the hair off his arms. We've tried but failed, and we all worry his stomach is filling up with fur balls. That's all the advice I can give. Most of the time, he'll be lost in his head, but don't worry if he seems a bit distant. He always comes back in time for dinner."

People clapped and yelled. The band was tuned and ready to go.

"And, to you Eric, you lucky... oops, I can't say that here. For you, Eric, I hope you have some idea how lucky you are. You're here in the most beautiful place in the world with the most beautiful girl beside you and with all these wonderful people who have no idea what a real... oops, can't say that either. So, congratulations to you, condolences to Ofelia and her family, and now for the toast." Devon raised his glass. "May you both live happily together and give my two girls many cousins."

Everyone clapped again. Eric and Ofelia cut the cake. Mida caught Ofelia's bouquet, and Osvaldo grabbed the garter when Orvaline missed it. The band struck up a throbbing dance beat. People were on their feet. This party would last into the wee hours of the morning.

Father Jordan and Ana Luisa's grief for Danny had receded, but it would never disappear. They laughed and clapped with all the others, but they were brokenhearted. Their friend, Louie Frieze, was not there to console them. They'd heard that Hector Hernandez had been seen in San Kuuchamaa. This was bad news indeed. Hector was a vulture that feasted on the carcasses of the weak. Whatever he was doing there, he was up to no good. They feared for the safety of Itandehui and Mr. Penalt. Ana Luisa had been unable to get in touch with Carlos, but she would keep trying. She wanted him to warn Itandehui in case Hector had evil on his mind.

Eric and Ofelia found themselves alone at last, exhilarated and exhausted after the party was over. They talked and made love and talked and finally went to sleep.

Eric woke in a cold sweat. He felt a strange presence in the room. It was quiet and dark. Ofelia slept calmly next to him. The only sound was her gentle breathing. A distinctive, gamey animal odor drifted through the air, something that reminded him of his time in the hospital at Stanford. He lay on his back, motionless and silent, while he listened. Several minutes passed. Nothing. He drifted back to sleep.

Eric tossed and turned.

"You mustn't *try* to do what the doctor says, you must *do it!*"

He choked. He couldn't breathe. A terrible pressure built in his chest. He dreamt he was battling Nurse Marta and the doctors. He awoke exhausted, then fell right back to sleep as streaks of sunlight peeked into the room when the morning dawned.

A man came into the room.

"Why did you tell my sister-cousin about the ZamZam water? Why? She made them take it away and now, now I'm going to die."

"What? Who?"

"Why, sir? Why did you tell her?"

He'd become so lean, so gaunt, his eyes so hollow in his head. At first Eric didn't recognize him. He looked awful. So this was what it came to in the end. This was the hell where he was headed.

"I didn't tell her. I didn't tell anyone."

"Light gone, light gone, light gone, light gone! Who's out there? I get no lift."

61.

The Reconciliation

Tomás was counting on the Senate hearings to give the green light for them to move ahead with the Laetrile business. When he heard what happened, how Napier and his group had become the laughing stock of cartoons and TV shows, he turned white with rage. Rafael tried to exert some control, but Tomás went on a rampage. He threw a bottle of whiskey across the bar and broke two shelves of glasses. The girls scrambled to avoid the flying shards. An old dog in the corner awoke from its slumber and barked.

"We invested a fortune in property, in supplies, in permits, and those bribes—those worthless bribes! I am going to kill that stupid gringo!"

"Settle down, Tomás. You are going to cost us a fortune in bar supplies."

"I told you, Rafael, we were crazy to get mixed up with him. He's a stupid hijo de puta! Do you hear me?"

Tomás threw another bottle. It shattered the mirror. The bartender turned white. Blood streamed down his forehead from a sliver of glass that had impaled itself above his eyebrow.

"I hear you. I hear you. Now, settle down."

Rafael nodded to one of the girls. She cautiously approached Tomás and started to run her fingers through his hair. He jumped off his stool and slapped her face, knocking her to the floor.

"Get out of the way, you worthless puta bitch! Rafael, we're going to see Napier. Right now! Where's the fucking driver?"

Rafael wiped the sweat from his face. There were only a few customers at that time of day. They all ran out of the bar. The girls, huddled in a corner, shook and cried in fear.

"He's in the car, Tomás. The driver's in the car."

Napier was waiting for them when Tomás and Rafael barged into his office. He had his sources. He'd been warned. He'd made his peace with Zacco, who was standing by for a phone conversation.

"How could things go to hell in Washington? Tell me, *cabrón,* before I drive this knife through your worthless heart."

"Settle down, Tomás. There's plenty of blame to go around. We had Frieze, remember? We reached an agreement, but you let him get away. He was the key to our success at the hearings. Look, I'm as disappointed as you are, but we haven't lost yet. We made some points in the meeting. We got some good press out of it. Some of the states have already passed laws legalizing Laetrile. We'll win the next time, I'm sure of it. Doctor Milagro's clinics are operating at full capacity. The demand for our Laetrile products is booming. Profits will come as more and more people from the States come down here to escape the restrictions they've put on us up north. Zacco's on the phone. He wants to say something."

"Hello, Tomás, Rafael. Yes, things are a mess at the moment, but Napier is right. I blame Congressman Shipley. He was supposed to prepare the way for us. He failed. He's caught up in some big political thing right now. If he succeeds, it could be good for us. He's worried about his past catching up with him. I've got the goods on him and he knows it. He hired some weasel to spy on me, and I don't like it. He has no idea how to operate in our world. I'm going to use his idiot spy, Drago Nuncio, to teach the congressman a lesson. He'll pay more attention to us after that."

Zacco had put two of his best men, Dominic and Finnigan, on Nuncio's case. Shipley would get the message.

Rafael was his usual schizophrenic self. He pranced around Napier's office, occasionally bumping into a chair or a table. His hand shook as he held the phone to his ear. Tomás had settled down.

"Napier's green and hazel eyes looked hard as granite. Sit down, Rafael. Relax. We're going to carry on, okay? Just like before. We've all had setbacks, right? You just go on. The turtle wins the race. Has there been any word about Frieze yet?"

Bringing up Frieze enraged Tomás all over again. "If you'd let me follow my instincts on this, Frieze would still be with us."

"Maybe, or he might be dead," said Napier.

Tomás gave a fierce look at the insinuation.

Rafael sat in a chair by the window. He spoke for the first time. "Hector continues to search, but we don't have much hope. We've cut back Hector's responsibilities in the organization. Tomás says he's gotten too powerful."

Zacco, who'd warned Tomás about Hector, was pleased to hear this. It gave him a little more confidence in his Mexican partners.

"We have no choice. We have to move forward without Frieze. I'll keep the pressure on Krump to come up with a better formula. In the meantime, even with Frieze gone, there must be some of his Laetrile out there. He was producing it before he went missing. It has to be somewhere. He couldn't have taken everything with him."

Napier had confidence things would come around. He knew that Tomás and Zacco could pull the plug on him at any moment. He wouldn't go down without a fight, but he was no fool. Before they came after him, he'd get out. He already had a plan.

"All right," said Zacco. "We can't accomplish much more today. I'll hang on for now, but if things get worse, I'm out. This Laetrile business is peanuts, Tomás. We'll find another way to launder our money. We can't let the relationship fall apart because of this. We need some results fast, Napier. You got that?"

"Yea, Joey. I'm on it."

62.

Fateful Decision

Hector knew there was some of Frieze's Laetrile in San Kuuchamaa. He'd contacted a man at the village to find out where it was stored. It was late in the day when he arrived. He drove his truck as close to the mountain trail as possible. He hired two young boys. One stayed with the truck while the other helped Hector move a large wooden cart up the trail. The cart had siderails and four sturdy wheels to navigate the rocky path.

Along the way, he ran into a snag. The cart wouldn't fit through the narrowest part of the trail. The boy told Hector about a shortcut that might work. It required negotiating a tricky section on the edge of a steep cliff, but Hector was determined, Choosing the shortcut was a good decision. There was no one else on the trail at that time of year, and they arrived at Itandehui's storage shed ahead of schedule. Hector was delighted.

The shed wasn't locked. Everyone at the village knew where Itandehui kept her remedies. No one thought to tamper with them. They all depended on her skills when sickness came, and they knew better than to interfere in the world of the spirits. The boys who helped Hector were of a different generation: corrupted by easy money, they cared nothing about the spirits.

Inside, Hector quickly found the jugs of Laetrile. He got every single one of them, and filled the cart. It was bulging, but he was sure they could guide it back down the same way they'd come up.

Dusk arrived, but there was still plenty of light. The birds came out of their cool resting places at this time of day. If Hector hadn't been in such a hurry, he might have taken the time to watch and listen to them like Itandehui did when she sat by the pool in the early mornings. As a young boy, Hector had learned the ways of the birds and animals, and the knowledge helped him avoid many missteps, but he'd become too busy in his new life to bother with such things anymore. Had he listened, he might have heard an ominous sound, shrill like a flute or trumpet, mixed among the bird calls. He might have been more careful.

The boy saw the leaves shuffle slightly in the jungle foliage nearby, but was afraid to say anything. He tried not to look at Hector's face, which frightened him, so he focused on the wheels of the cart and watched them churn through the sandy soil. Hector pulled the cart from the front and the boy pushed it from the back.

They reached the dangerous part of the trail where it skirted the cliffside. The cart's wheels were nearly off the edge, and the heavy load made it difficult to steer. Hector pulled it too close to the side, and one of the wheels jammed on a partially buried rock.

"¡Puta!" Hector yelled at the cart. He used all of his strength to pull harder. "Push! Push, you skinny little rabbit," he yelled to the boy, who gave a mighty shove. The wheels buckled. The cart bounced off the side of the cliff as the wheels snapped free, and everything flew into the air, including Hector.

"¡Ay-eee! Dios Mio! D—i—o—s!"

A series of echoes were the last words the boy heard as everything fell in a jumble down the mountainside into the canyon below. He watched the jugs of Laetrile explode on the sharp rocks, watched the cart fall behind them like a bird with broken wings. Hector sailed after it. Everything was smashed to pieces at the bottom. The boy's heart pounded in the silence. He could barely make out Hector's crumpled form below, but he knew Hector was dead. Eyes wide with fear, the boy raced back to the trail's entrance and told his friend. They went straight to Itandehui's house to confess what they'd done.

They shook uncontrollably and both spoke at once. She took them inside and made them a bitter-tasting tea, then lit a foul-smelling cigar and blew the smoke all over them. It made them choke and cough. She told them to say not a word about what had happened, to never discuss it with each other or with anyone else, not even their parents.

"You've been consumed by a sickness that you cannot see or touch. Only the angels can heal you."

The boys looked up to the sky. The boy who'd pushed the cart cried and said, "I don't see the angels."

"No, child. Only the healer can see the angels." She gave each of them another cup of tea. "You must drink these herbs so the angels can smell you and know where to meet you with their healing power. They know to help you. They look for you, and they will find you if you do as I say."

Itandehui blew more smoke on them and chanted. When she had finished, she said they could leave. She told them she would take care of Hector's truck, his things, and him. She told them to go home, and to never again go up the mountain. They did exactly as they were told.

Inside, alone in the darkness, Itandehui sat with her eyes closed until she felt the presence of the spirits. She asked them for a favor, but they did not answer. She sat, patiently waiting. The night came. The black jaguar moved in circles outside her house, only its two golden eyes visible. Itandehui could smell blood—the jaguar had come to be healed.

63.

Penalt's Return

Itandehui was at the back of the house tending her flowers. Penalt waited for her to acknowledge his presence. He sat on a rough wooden bench that looked as if it had grown up with the garden like some deformed squash. A snake slithered through the grass. Penalt hated snakes. He'd been bitten once as a young boy. The fear of it was still with him. Itandehui had told him never to kill a snake.

"Trying to kill a snake makes it angry. The snake's spirit will harm a friend or a relative. Killing one snake will bring more. You can kill a snake if it bites you, but not the others."

Penalt picked up a rock and threw it at the snake. He missed, and it slithered away into the shadows.

Itandehui didn't turn to face him when she spoke. "Look, touch, and listen. Knowledge comes slowly—listen, watch and be patient."

She once told Penalt that when a person is born and his soul formed, so too is a soul double, a nagual, among the animals, a companion and a shadow. Paths diverge and come together again. Above the overgrown garden outside Itandehui's house, above the tree line, a red-tailed hawk circled round and round. If he had a nagual, Penalt pictured it on one of those elliptical paths the hawk took, paths traced by its shadow on the ground, paths taken through the air displaced by its wings. There were an infinite number of elliptical paths. He listened. He thought he could hear his nagual beckoning: *I'm here. Follow me.*

An old woman turned toward him and laughed. He saw the missing teeth, the wrinkled face. He saw her hair, gray and wild, flowing in the wind. He was sure he had lost his mind.

"Every action produces a result."

Penalt tried to make sense of her words.

"The sick person's intentions, conscious or not, can determine the course of events. A healer must hold a vision of a healthy future for that person. To be healed, a person must be convinced he is well after he comes to the healer believing he is not. The healer interferes with fate. That's very dangerous. Sometimes a chain of events is set into motion that no one has control over. The spirits gather and decide. Like birth, healing is messy and confusing; there is commotion and disorder. Before you can become a healer, you must make friends with chaos."

Itandehui walked into the front room where Penalt had put down the supplies from the market. He followed. Working together in silence, they unpacked and stored everything in its place. He towered above her and could reach the upper shelves without standing on the ladder as she had to do. He followed her around, doing what seemed obvious. When they finished, he went outside, sat on a stool, and looked up at the mountain.

Above the tree line, thin streaks of clouds crossed like white lines on blue paper. The lingering rays of the sun played with the treetops. A solitary bird chirped in the shadows. A spider toiled at web-making in the corner of the porch where Penalt sat. He tried not to think. Itandehui told him that if he found words for his thoughts, the thoughts would die. Thoughts were strange, too strange to be spoken. They were organic, alive like his skin and blood and bones and flesh.

When Penalt looked back, Itandehui was there behind him.

"I saw something in town... at the games... something going on inside Eric."

The sweet aromas from the herbs and plants stored in the cottage drifted out the door and awakened Penalt' senses. He waited. A curandera doesn't give away her secrets. They emerge on their own when one is ready to receive them.

"You had a vision."

"I suppose you could say that. I think it had something to do with the noise of the Jai Alai games. It sounded like the clacking of a rattle, or a drumbeat that reverberated in my ears, not melodic but haunting and monotonous."

"It put you into a trance."

"Well, maybe. I'm sure I saw something odd inside Eric. I could see right through him. There was a battle going on. When he turned and caught me looking, the vision stopped. He told me about his cancer. Was that what I saw, the cancer? Is that possible?"

Slow to answer, Itandehui said, "Don't be in such a hurry. I can't tell you what you saw. What do *you* think you saw?"

"If I knew, I wouldn't ask you."

"Ha, ha! Now you make friends with chaos. You have ventured outside the borders, Roger. You must find the meaning yourself. Then you will know what to do for your friend."

"You treated him. He's better. I know you gave him Laetrile. I saw him take a jug with him the day I arrived. I want to test it. I want to see how it works."

"You want to explain away the magic with your science, but science will tell you nothing about how to start the process of healing. To heal, to be healed, we need to believe in the possibility of healing, in a greater world, in higher powers than our own."

"I know. I want to understand all that, I really do, but another part of me says I must test the Laetrile. I must test it to satisfy myself."

"The Laetrile is gone. There is none left to test. I don't know anything about how it works. If you want to work with me, it will have to be with the medicines I know, not those I don't know."

"There isn't any left, none at all?"

"None."

"What happened? I know you had some stored here before I left."

"What happened is not your concern."

"Where did it come from?"

"Jordan had a friend who made the Laetrile."

"Then I'll ask Jordan."

"It won't do any good. His friend is gone, and all the Laetrile is gone with him."

"How was Eric cured? Tell me. Was it the Laetrile or did you cure him with your healing powers? How did it happen?"

"You will have to ask Eric."

"I may never see him again."

"You will see him. He will come to the village."

A knock at the door interrupted the conversation. Itandehui had been tending to a man with a chronic ulcer on his leg. He'd come for another treatment. She bathed the ulcer in *melón* tea made that morning by boiling the entire plant. The cause of the ulcer was poor circulation. It had originally been the size of the man's hand and an inch and a half deep, exposing three inches of shinbone. Itandehui had been treating him with the tea for over a month, and the gaping cavity had now filled with healthy pink flesh. The man recovered the use of his leg even though the lesion had no covering of skin.

One of the first things Penalt learned from Itandehui was the disinfectant and healing characteristics of plants that grew around San Kuuchamaa. On his first day with her, a man arrived whose hand had been smashed between two boulders. Itandehui told Penalt to cut a piece of *cardón* cactus from one of the plants in the back garden. She had him peel off the spines and bark and cut a hand-sized rectangle of the tough, white pulp. Next she had him slice two thin wafers from the rectangle and wrap them around the man's hand. They finished by bandaging them to the hand with gauze and tape. The pulp of the cardón not only has a built-in painkiller but also contains a disinfectant and a powerful healing agent. In a week the man's hand was completely normal and pain-free.

The chemical qualities of some plants healed physical wounds. That was easy for Penalt to accept. What he didn't understand was how Itandehui could cure Eric's cancer with a strange hocus-pocus of leaves and cigars and bizarre ceremonies. He'd come a long way. He'd seen and felt things he would never have imagined. Still, he was not Itandehui. The Laetrile was easier for him to understand. He was convinced it was the reason for Eric's recovery, but he needed more proof.

64.

The Honeymoon

Colorful birds chirped and jumped around in the palm trees as Devon walked to the chapel to meet with Jordan. A maid swept the walkways around the chairs and tables; she didn't look up as he passed the room where he'd stayed with Eric on his first visit. A woodpecker worked on a dead tree in the lot across from the clinic, and rapped out a persistent drumbeat of hollow notes A silent airplane sailed above, through clouds that were tightly clumped like giant heads of white cauliflower spread out on a pale blue blanket.

Devon learned to pay more attention in Mexico. He learned about awareness. He knew nothing about Buddhism, but he'd heard about the idea of mindfulness. It seemed to him that awareness was a unique feature of all life forms. Even the simplest cell had a primitive form of the five senses. As he walked up the hill he caught himself paying close attention to everything. The birds, the maid, the woodpecker, the airplane, even the clouds, became more than they were, more than they'd been before. Devon was changed by what he saw, and what he saw was changed by him. There was a give and take to all forms of awareness.

An old man walked slowly on the other side of the courtyard, leaning on his crooked oak walking stick, his white mustache overgrown, his untamed hair refusing to gather into any kind of order. Life's entropic comedy. Devon imagined what faded memories hid behind the man's crazed eyes.

The life of a young boy astounded at the world around
him, the life of a young man passionate with curiosity
wanting everything at once. Memories ravaged by the cold
black winds, covered thick with the velvety pollen of angry
pine trees, blew through the courtyard with the man as he
trudged along.

A breeze off the ocean rushed over the hill to shake Devon from
his daydream. The man was gone. Robins pecked at worms in the
tall grass.

Consciousness, the feeling and the knowing, that was the real
magic. We, in all our loving and trying, even if we fail, are what
matters. Devon might never get it straight, but he sensed something
at that moment, some kind of truth that tried to get through. He
wanted to meet with Jordan to do something for Eric, to make up for
his earlier narrowmindedness.

Devon found Jordan playing a soulful piece on the harp. "I'm
not sure where to start, Jordan. I'm so sorry about Danny. I didn't
meet him, but I sense what a wonderful human being he was. I wish
I could do something to help. I've tried to pray, but I'm not very good
at it. Eric thinks the world of you. I hope you know that."

Jordan sat back from the harp. His white hair curled over his
head. Eric was right about *The Canterbury Tales*—Jordan was from
a different century.

"He could sing a good song and he could tell a good story, my
Danny. His mind was razor sharp. He remembered everything he
saw. His heart was made of pure gold. He helped anyone who asked.
There wasn't a wicked bone in my boy's body. By all that's right and
just, for the love of God, there was no reason for him to die. I'm sorry,
Devon. The pain doesn't go away. It just doesn't."

Devon noticed the quivering in Jordan's lips, the rise of his voice
at the end. He reflexively wiped away the tears that formed in his
eyes. Jordan spent his life comforting others, but now, when the time
came, there was no one to comfort him. It didn't seem fair.

"I'll move on, lad. I'll move on. God will not suffer us to be
burdened beyond that which we are able. He'll give us a way to escape
so we can bear it." Jordan turned to hide his grief. "We have to trust

that God made the world orderly and reasonable. Some questions have no answers. It's best not to dwell on them."

"You have the memories, Jordan. That might seem small right now, but it's something to hold on to. Danny accomplished much in his short life. He lived fully and intensely. He made a difference."

"He could have accomplished even more, I'm sure, but you're right, he gave it his all. I'm thankful for that."

Jordan knew Devon had other matters on his mind. "Come, now, why are you here?"

"I want to ask you to help me do something for Eric."

"For Eric? Why, of course I'll help. What must be done?"

"I know Eric isn't up to a typical honeymoon. What he and Ofelia need is time to enjoy each other. I want them to be somewhere Eric can continue to get the help he needs. Everything changed for him after San Kuuchamaa. Is it possible for them to return there after the wedding? Would Itandehui see him again?"

Jordan's eyes brightened. "What a grand idea. I'm sure we can arrange it. I'll contact my friends in the village. I can fly them to San Kuuchamaa myself when they're ready."

Devon was elated. "I want this to be my wedding present to them."

Jordan smiled. "If I had a brother, I'd want him to be as thoughtful you, Devon. The good Lord knows how much you love Eric. You and I know how difficult he finds it to share his feelings, God be with him, but he jolly well loves you. We both know that, don't we?"

"Yes, I know it. Thank you, Jordan, for everything."

The two shook hands, and Devon left.

Eric was a gambler, and gamblers have their superstitions. Thinking too hard can ruin everything. The best athletes get into the groove and let instinct take over. Eric had thrown the dice and won. It was impossible to know how. Maybe it was pure luck. Devon was not going to play the little jinx. He wouldn't dwell on it. Trying, that's the key to success. If all you try to do is avoid mistakes then you won't try, but then you never beat the odds.

A silhouette moved across the courtyard. A woman in a flowing gown walked, her hands out at the sides for balance. Stop and go. Stop and go. She was deep in thought. She turned. Devon was shocked. Her eyes were sunk into the sockets. Dull white teeth hid behind slightly parted lips. Some question seemed to puzzle her. She hesitated as if she'd forgotten her destination. The furrows of her wrinkled face demonstrated how the consciousness of death draws such lines on us. Ahead, in the dark beyond the shining exit gate, a shadow stood waiting.

The clouds turned dark gray against a pink sunset. They traveled across the sky like a herd of massive turtles, necks straining forward while the bodies lagged behind.

Had he just had a vision? Devon had no idea. He'd seen something. Was it real? What did it mean? He walked to the bottom of the hill totally confused.

The day after the reception, Jordan arrived in his blue van. His eyes opened wide when he saw how much they'd packed to take on the journey.

"I hope you've no objection to shrinking down to one wee suitcase. We're limited in how much weight we can carry in the plane."

The corners of Ofelia's mouth turned down.

"Don't worry, Ofelia," Eric said. I can leave most of my things here. I won't need much."

Jordan smiled. "I see you've adjusted to married life," he quipped. He still had his gift of making everyone around him feel good. His sense of humor was back.

"The bees are stirring—birds are on the wing," recited Jordan with a twinkle in his blue eyes. "Coleridge."

Ofelia blushed red.

"Look out," said Eric, "for that Aztec priest standing next to you, Ofelia. He might cut your heart out."

Jordan had a master's in theology and a great interest in colonial history. He'd spent hours rummaging like a detective in the dusty tomes of the national library in Mexico City. With his knowledge of Spanish and local Indian dialects, he'd resurrected many original documents.

"The Aztecs had a fascinating history, lad. One marvels at what they knew so long ago. Of course, their religion had a brutal side. Most religions do."

Eric always worried that his odd sense of humor would be misunderstood. "I meant it as a joke."

Jordan rolled the cigar around in his mouth, with that mischievous grin on his face.

"So did I, lad. So did I, but you're right. I chose my poet poorly. Coleridge is too dark for this wonderful day. Let's get on with it."

Once inside the plane, Ofelia sat in the back while Eric sat alongside Jordan. They flew a leisurely route, and Jordan pointed out some of the provincial towns, ranchos, farms, and hamlets he had visited over the years.

"You certainly know your way around Baja, Jordan."

"That I do, far and wide. In my Flying Anchor I've journeyed as far as Sinaloa, Nayarit, and Jalisco, but these small villages in the mountains of Baja are my favorite spots. The people here seldom see outsiders. Most o' the time they're easy and friendly, but they can be very protective of their local communities. Things can turn ugly if they think you're intruding too much into their lives."

"What do you mean?"

"Well, look yonder at that small village on the left." Jordan turned the plane and tilted the wing to bring the village into view. "An American visited there some years back. He fell in love with the place, you see, and decided he wanted to buy a piece of paradise. He flashed around some dollars, and a couple of unscrupulous locals sold him a house. These communities have a rule against selling to outsiders. When the man arrived to take possession, the village rose up against him and disputed the ownership. He took them to court in Tijuana and won the case, but enforcement o' the law in these solitary parts is another matter. One evening while he and his wife were enjoying the view from their deck, a group of men wearing masks rushed in and beat him badly."

"That's horrible. What happened next?"

"The police leave the locals to take care of themselves. Wisely, the man left after that—paradise lost. He was never seen again. In these isolated areas, the ancient beliefs hold sway. The people are fiercely independent. We dream about a golden time long ago and a place where everyone lived peacefully and life was easy. I dunno why, but God put a worm at the core of human nature. No such place exists on this Earth."

Jordan lifted the plane and they moved quickly along toward San Kuuchamaa. As they flew over the mountain, Jordan offered up some more history: "The mountain at San Kuuchamaa has always been used for acquiring healing power. In each generation the most powerful shaman has lived there. In some mystical way, the spirit of their God stays there, calling the shamans to the mountain. Healing rituals and special herbal knowledge is taught in dreams by the spirit gods. For sure, I know these local stories sound strange to you. They sounded strange to me too, at first. Medicine people use the stories like mirrors, to catch an image of our hearts so that our minds won't stifle our spirits."

"Mi abuela told me about the spirit helpers," said Ofelia. "The three helpers during the daylight hours are the eagle, the red-tailed hawk, and the raven. They fly over the Earth and constantly watch everything that goes on below. The fourth helper is the owl, who flies and watches over everything at night."

Eric assumed that such tales were passed down between the generations like the nursery rhymes his mother had read to him long ago. There were moral points to be made, but he wasn't to take the stories literally. His life had become so much more complicated after his illness that he didn't know what to believe.

"These are just myths, Jordan, right?"

Jordan didn't respond. Ofelia reached from the rear of the plane and put her hands on Eric's shoulders. "A people's myths are not what's false, but what's most true, Eric. You should know that by now."

He didn't know what he knew anymore. Cracks had developed in his brittle scientific view of the world. Strange, undecipherable thoughts were leaking through that disturbed him.

"I guess I see that now."

He thought back to the young boy he'd seen guide the elderly man with the cane on the trip back to the palapa with Orvaline. It was after one of Eric's treatments at the clinic. What he saw that afternoon was the beginning of the changes. He was like the man who heard thunder but could see no lightning, but the lightning now revealed itself whether he was ready or not. The arc of his life had changed. His path through space hit a curve. He was in two worlds at once, and he had to make a choice.

Eric jerked erratically in his sleep. Nelson pulled the sheets over his legs and tucked them in tightly in an attempt to calm him. Outside the window the hospital service workers picketed. They hadn't called a strike yet, but it was inevitable. He hoped he'd have time to see Eric through to the end.

"You gotta watch yourself around here," he said to himself. "They're always looking to take advantage. Don't tell 'em what you do unless you got an angle."

He looked down at Eric. "I'm not s'posed to be here, Jack. Just sneaked in while the bitch was busy."

"Nelson... Nelson... where are you?" Eric's voice was weak.

"Settle down. I gotta go. Things are heatin' up outside."

"You *must* see it," said Ofelia, "if you are to get well, Eric. Healing can't happen if you don't believe in healing. It's what you believe that counts. If you believe in molecules and drugs, they will be your truth. If you believe in the power of the spirits, they will have the power to heal you. Speak to the spirits. Don't be embarrassed by it. You have to become another person. Don't intellectualize it. Wonder has its own reality. You told me once about your favorite philosopher, Lao Tzu. Remember? *Those who say do not know, those who know do not say.* You know how to do it, Eric. We all do. It might be easier if you talked less."

The goosebumps rose on Eric's arms. An odd sensation arose in his chest. Lao Tzu? When had he told Ofelia about Lao Tzu?

He was jolted as Jordan guided the plane onto the grassy runway. A stranger was waiting in the Jeep. This time Jordan didn't put on his priestly vestments. Eric asked about Carlos. Jordan said Carlos's cough had developed into something worse. He was too ill to drive. The new driver took them directly to the *hacienda.* They arrived unnoticed by the townsfolk. Only two guests had been told of the visit, Penalt and Itandehui.

65.

San Kuuchamaa

It was cool and fresh in the mountain village. Tijuana—the oppressive heat, the dust and grime, the teeming crowds—that vulgar scene was replaced by a lightness of spirit that heartened Eric. Two black-chinned hummingbirds hovered nervously above some red trumpet vines while a yellow spider dozed in the safety of its web. Sun and shade played hide-and-seek in the treetops while in the understory silent dramas unfolded. Time destroys, turns all the ups and downs of lives into rubbish. The only thing for sure is the present moment. It felt good to be back in the mountains. Everything had changed for Eric the last time he was here. He experienced his first real optimism. Doctor Doggett's diagnosis confirmed what he felt. He built on that. How he built on it! He knew how lucky he was, and was exhilarated to be back in San Kuuchamaa.

Penalt took Eric aside when they met. "Look, Eric. I don't want to pry into your life. We hardly know each other, but I feel a certain camaraderie. I know you took some of Itandehui's Laetrile back with you that first day we met here in San Kuuchamaa. How much do you have? That man Hector who works for Dos Negros came here to steal what was left. He almost got away with it."

"What do you mean?"

"There was an accident. Hector and all the Laetrile crashed into the canyon as he tried to bring it down the mountain. Hector was killed, and all the Laetrile was completely destroyed. I'm sorry."

"All of it?"

"Yes, I'm afraid so."

Dread lit on Eric's shoulder. There was only one gallon of Laetrile left, the one Ana Luisa had found, and no way to know how much more he would need to beat the cancer.

Like Penalt, Eric was sure it was Frieze's formula that had turned things around. Doctor Doggett told him there was no other explanation. A total disappearance of cancer was unheard of for someone in an advanced state like Eric, but what if they were wrong? What if Itandehui was the reason? Everything changed after she worked on him. If she did it once, she could do it again.

It was as if a tectonic plate had shifted and Laetrile no longer mattered. Eric was ready to take the plunge into the curandera's strange world, with or without the serum. He was grateful for the time alone with Ofelia. He wouldn't let anything ruin it. He had never felt so strongly that luck was with him. One setback wasn't going to change his path to recovery. Itandehui could finish the cure. He'd watched her pull the illness out of his body in the darkness of her hut. Unbelievable as it was, he saw what he saw. He wasn't going to second guess his sanity—not after he'd been granted so much.

"Look, Penalt, I'll get by. Let's not tell Ofelia. I don't want this to ruin our honeymoon. I'll tell her when I'm ready."

He would carry the burden alone. Itandehui would finish what she started. Everything would work out.

Jordan rented a beautiful hacienda for them, which had been built for the mining company bosses when they were shipping gold and silver back to Spain. A local man had recently renovated it after it lay in ruins for years. Wealthy Mexicans used it for weddings and parties and romantic trysts.

Eric and Ofelia were the only guests, the only people there except for the cook and the maid who left them alone to enjoy each other and to explore. The rooms were massive—the walls painted in soft colors and adorned with handwoven textiles and oil paintings in the style of famous Mexican murals. All the conveniences were provided, a rarity in such a remote place—tiled bathrooms, ceramic sinks, porcelain toilets in colors that accented the tiles. It was like living in an art museum.

Devon paid for everything. Eric told him it wasn't necessary, that it was foolish to spend his small savings.

"I want to do it, Eric. Don't argue with me about this." Devon pointed his finger at Eric and feigned a scowl. "Whoever shall say to his brother, Thou fool, shall be in danger of hell fire."

At this, they both laughed. When they were kids, they had traded biblical phrases back and forth after Eric became an altar boy. Each tried to outdo the other. They were so proficient at this that the priest at their church pointed to them as an example of how to read the Bible. Little did he know they made comedy and tragedy out of every phrase. They read the Bible the way they read Shakespeare, with a double meaning.

The hacienda was remarkable in other ways as well. There were artifacts and historical documents, ledgers, books and letters from the old mining company, everyday tools and utensils used at the time, jewelry made from the local silver, oil paintings by the Spaniards who'd once ruled the town—all this and more was kept in a small museum on the property.

"Oh, if only I could paint!" cried Ofelia, ecstatic as she admired the trompe-l'oeil that covered the walls. "Art is the true language of the emotions. I cannot imagine how people indifferent to art spend their time. How they live is a mystery to me. An artist leaves part of herself everywhere she goes."

"What I like about art," said Eric, "is that it reminds me that there are some truths that can never be known, a terrifying idea to those of us who want to know everything."

Ofelia's brown eyes shone. "It's amazing how we understand our own experiences in terms of the artist's creation. We each interpret a painting in our own unique way. The only one who can interpret a painting is the one who sees it. It's the same with stories or dreams. The artist's intention may be completely different from the effect it produces, don't you think?"

Eric had so many reasons to be happy, but the fragility of his health, the inability to know anything about his future, and the fear that he might be going mad made him feel as though he could fall through the ice at any moment.

"It's all just an illusion, a diversion to make life bearable. Art sustains our imagination, but we mortals trudge along in the murky swamp. If you look too closely, think too carefully, reality eats you alive."

"Eric, don't ruin this moment. We've been given so much. Let's enjoy it."

"I wish I knew what to hope for, Ofelia, what I *could* hope for."

"Let's hope for a good week."

The hacienda was a massive structure with foot-thick walls and great wooden shutters and doors. The rooms surrounded a large open courtyard. Eric closed his eyes and saw children run and play among the fruit trees and between the vines in the vegetable garden while their parents roasted savory meats on the barbecue, cold drinks in hand. He had to stop the gloom before it devoured the precious minutes of their time here. He could not know what was to come, but he did have some control over the present moment. The future laughs at the past while the present surveys the course of destiny and gropes its way in the dark.

"Oh, I'm sorry, Ofelia. Here I go again with these gloomy thoughts. I *am* thankful to be alive, to be here, to be with you."

"Remember Eric, there are no accidents. Everything has a cause, happens for a reason, usually a very personal one. Good is more powerful than evil. Trust in the spirits. They are all over here, in the walls, in the garden, and throughout this town. If you can bring yourself to do that, you'll be fine."

How to trust? How to love? That had been the struggle all his life.

Father Jordan left the next day. He promised to return later to take Eric and Ofelia back to Tijuana.

A trail wound into town from the hacienda. Eric looked forward to the walk they took each day. He recovered a bit of his physical strength. He loved walking early in the mornings and late afternoons, savoring the clean, crisp air of the *Sierra Juárez*. He thought back to that Sunday morning with Manny when everything changed. Manny had saved his life. He had a chance now, a small chance, but a reason to hope. Borges wrote that we are one of very few creatures who know they are going to die; most animals need not grapple with that thought because they think they are eternally alive. Thoreau, even in the midst of all the beauty at Walden, remarked that we live lives of quiet desperation. To go on, that's what matters, whether we live in reality or in a dream—if in reality, then for the joy of it, if in a dream, then for something to remember when we awake.

Penalt sat in a café on the corner of the square. Two old men smoked at a table speaking *rápidamente en Español* and reading the newspaper. A young boy selling fresh pastries strolled by the table.

"I would appreciate it to you, señor. You want buy?"

Penalt ignored him. The boy stared at him patiently, painfully. Guilt finally won, and Penalt made a small purchase. Tiny Indian women sat in a row along a stone wall surrounding the square. Clasping their colorful shopping bags, all filled to the brim, they laughed and spoke in a soft Indian dialect, their black hair tumbling down in braids or gathered neatly into chignons on the tops of their heads. Their grandfathers, wraiths floating in the air, trudged along on their way to the silver mines, whispering in muted tones of the sorrows of yesterday, today, tomorrow. Across the square a few women walked out of the church, rosaries hung on their shoulders and arms. Men waited for them in the shade of an ancient laurel tree.

Eric and Ofelia entered the café. Ofelia went to explore the shops around the square while Eric sat and talked with Penalt. "Do you really think you'll stay here, Roger?"

"Yes, I want to. I came to do a job. The events with Frieze and the tragedy with Hector have made that impossible. I'll have to quit the company that pays my expenses. It'll make it harder to stay, but also easier in some ways. I've found something totally unexpected that draws me in and surprises me with its power. What about you? What are you going to do now that you're married?"

As they spoke, Ofelia ambled along the perimeter of the square. Eric watched her from a distance, thinking how much had changed.

Just months ago he faced death. Now he had the possibility of life—life with the woman he loved, the woman who carried their child. Karen had warned him, so had Devon. They felt his decision to marry was too hasty. Like Rogelio, they thought the illness made marriage impossible. Eric had followed his own instincts. He'd gambled against the odds and was rewarded with a new life. He wasn't going to let it slip away.

"I feel like a feather falling through space. The path is unpredictable but the descent is inevitable. Of course I want to live long enough to enjoy life with Ofelia. The best moments are like a sunrise. When it's at its very best you want to say, oh, if it would just stay like that forever, but if it did, you'd never know what noon was like, or midnight."

"That's an interesting way to put it, Eric."

Roger had to tell Eric about the vision he'd had at the Jai Alai games. He was nervous but needed to get it off his chest. "You know, I saw something, Eric. I guess you could say it was a vision. That night at the Jai Alai games I looked right into you. I don't know how to explain it. I feel silly talking about this, but I have to tell you. The vision was dim, everything was indistinct. There was a struggle going on inside your body. That one vision has been followed by a series of doubts, but I can't shake it. I know what I saw."

Eric smiled awkwardly. He knew what Roger spoke of. "My God, Roger, you've gone completely off the deep end."

"Yeah, I thought so too at the time. I jettisoned all that supernatural stuff a long time ago. Now I'm confronted by it again. It's weird. Science was something I could count on, but there are certain extraordinary experiences—things that our minds can only grasp vaguely. Everyone has these, I'm sure, if they just pay attention. I've had them before, but working with Itandehui has opened my mind. That vision unnerved me. I've tried to understand it. Itandehui isn't any help. She says I need to figure it out for myself."

"We're all vulnerable, Roger. Look at the market for organic foods, supplements, magic cures, and even Laetrile. Hell, I think about it all the time. I know one thing for sure: I feel better. That's what I know. I don't want to worry about it too much. I don't want to undo the spell."

"You do look better, Eric. I'm happy for you, but Frieze and his Laetrile are gone. What're you going to do now?"

"Here comes Ofelia. Let's not talk about this in front of her. I have one more gallon of Laetrile. I'm here to see Itandehui. That will be enough. It *has* to be."

Ofelia carried a small package. She looked like a little girl with a surprise.

"I found this framed picture of San Kuuchamaa. I thought it would be a nice memento to pull out someday to show our son."

Penalt nearly fell out of his chair. "You're having a baby, a son?"

Eric laughed. "Yes, we're having a baby. I didn't know it was going to be a son. Maybe Ofelia has that second sense women have?"

Ofelia put her hands to her stomach. She was not showing at all but pretended her stomach was big as a pumpkin. Her brown eyes sparkled in the sunlight. "*¡Dios mio!* I can tell. It's a son."

"Okay, then. I suppose we should start thinking about names."

Penalt was dumbfounded. He looked at Ofelia, and suddenly jerked back his head, afraid to look. It had happened again, just like what he'd seen inside Eric, but different. This was crazy. It had to be an overactive imagination. He looked again. No, it was there, a tiny light pulsing inside her. He saw it.

An Indian woman sitting next to them moved her head nervously from side to side. There was nothing on the table in front of her, but she wiped it off again and again.

Penalt turned back to Ofelia. The light was gone—no, wait—it was there. Was it the heartbeat that pulsed? The blood rushed through Penalt's brain and made him dizzy.

"How about calling him Roger?" suggested Eric.

"For God's sake, don't name the kid after me," Penalt blurted, his voice shaky. "I'm a wreck. I don't understand the world anymore. Everything I thought was solid has turned into thin air."

"You're a little late, Roger. The physicists stumbled onto that idea years ago. Atoms are mostly empty space, don't you remember?"

Penalt turned pale.

"Are you ok, Roger?"

"Uh, yeah... fine."

Eric turned to Ofelia. "So what do you think we should name our son, if not Roger?"

"I'd like to name him Daniel, Daniel Cabrera Martin. Jordan would be pleased. I think it's a beautiful name, don't you? Roger can be the godfather."

"I accept," said Roger enthusiastically, still bowled over by what had just happened. "I'm not religious, but I'll take on the job if that's what you want. Maybe the kid will teach me something."

"We would be pleased," said Ofelia.

"It's set then," said Eric."

The soft bells of the church rang out over the square. Penalt stood. "I have to go. Itandehui wants to take me herb gathering today. I'll see you both this afternoon. Congratulations!"

"Thanks, Roger. See you then."

"The aromas coming from the kitchen are making me hungry," said Eric.

"Look through the open door," said Ofelia. "They're roasting chilis and garlic and tomatoes on a large *comal*. We shouldn't eat, though. I've asked the cook at the hacienda to make us something special." Ofelia looked forward to surprising Eric with a favorite family recipe she'd brought from home.

As he walked outside with Ofelia, Eric noticed the little apples forming on a tree behind the café. The sun beat down. He had a vision of a scene from his childhood. Outside his grandmother's house he saw the same apple tree, the same apples, the same sun. Could it be that in life we sometimes have intimations of an afterlife, of another life? The more we focus on absolute reality, the more we discover that nothing is absolute or real. We bite off reality in chunks and imagine we've got the whole hog. There simply isn't any fixed point of view, no absolute reference point from which to view anything. Stories are written when they're read. Life becomes real when it's lived.

Ofelia walked ahead of Eric. He realized that everything that mattered was right here, right now.

"How many miracles do we have in a lifetime, Nelson?"

"At the outset of life God gives you a certain number of angels, man. They float over you, protect your ass from danger, but if you cross the line too many times, they get the hell away. Just accept what comes. Don't ask so many questions."

"It's all new. Each day is full of new experiences. It's like my life is starting all over again."

"That's right. You finally gettin' it. You learnin' to live from the beginnin', like a newborn babe."

"She's here, isn't she, Nurse Marta?"

"Don't worry 'bout that ol' bitch. I'll take care of her."

Nelson knew it was an impossible job. He couldn't take care of Eric forever.

"Thanks, Nelson. I'm depending on you."

Ofelia jumped. Eric heard her scream, "Ow! Help, I've been bit!" Ofelia grabbed at her leg and shrieked. *"¡Ay! Me mordió una serpiente!"*

Eric ran to her. A big rattlesnake slithered off into the brush.

"¡Dios, duele tanto! It hurts so bad Eric. Help me, please."

Eric had to think fast. They weren't far from town, but he didn't know anyone there who could help. Better to go off the trail through the thick brush to Itandehui's house.

They made their way through the jungle as fast as possible. Going too quickly would spread the poison faster, but if they went too slow, it might be too late. Eric was mad with worry. Ofelia was sick to her stomach. She nearly lost consciousness, but Eric held her up and kept them moving. They ignored the scratches from the sharp bushes and gave no thought to the other dangers that lurked in the dark. They arrived just in time to catch Itandehui and Penalt before they left on the trail up the mountain. By now Ofelia was in bad shape, and Eric was not much better. Roger saw the scratches from the thorny vines and the rips in Eric's shirt.

"What the hell is happening? Is someone chasing you?"

"Thank God you're still here. We need your help. Ofelia's been bitten by a rattlesnake."

Itandehui knew what happened even before a word was spoken. She ran inside to gather what she needed.

Eric and Ofelia were a mess. Soaked in sweat, they struggled to suck in enough air after the wild race through the jungle. Penalt was amazed they'd been able to make it. Eric did his best to hold Ofelia while Roger used all his strength to steady her leg. Itandehui wrapped a band around the leg just above the bite.

"*¡Ay! Creo que voy a estar enfermo.* Ay, duele! It hurts, Eric!"

Ofelia swooned into Eric's arms.

"Hold on, Ofelia. Things will be better soon."

Itandehui took a small knife and made an X-shaped gash at the wound to start the flow of blood to flush out the venom. Ofelia let out a cry. "¡Ay! Duele."

Itandehui sucked the wound and spat out the venom until she was satisfied it was all gone. Penalt went inside to boil some water and fetch a jar of ground-up *yerba de la vibora.*

The waiting made Ofelia frantic. "I don't want to die! Oh, God, I think I'm passing out. Don't leave me, Eric, please."

"I'm right here."

Eric was stunned. Was this a bad joke? Was God going to take Ofelia away just as they began their life together? Never had he loved like this. He couldn't let it happen. He'd die with her if that's what it took. And what about the baby? Could the rattler's poison harm an unborn child?

Penalt returned with the yerba de la vibora and hot water. Itandehui put some of the herb into a cup of hot water to make tea. She put another batch into a small ceramic bowl and made a thick paste that she applied to the wound, then undid the band around Ofelia's leg and dressed the wound with a bandage.

"Relax, Eric. She'll be all right. The shock and terror of a snakebite is worse than the bite." Roger laughed to lighten things up. Eric looked worse than Ofelia. Penalt saw the dirt and scratches on Eric's face and the dried blood around a hole in his shirt, but far worse, he was astonished at what he saw inside Eric. Vague splotches of gray and black intermixed with faint red clouds. As he looked more carefully, he saw the splotches were formed by tiny points of light similar to the works of pointillist painters. Looking more closely still, the points mysteriously coalesced into what looked to Penalt like a chess set of gargoyles and monsters warring with each other. What he saw shocked him. He looked away. When he looked at Eric again, the bizarre scene was gone. Roger hoped it was just an illusion, but by now he knew otherwise. He had this new peculiar ability; it scared him but he also found it fascinating.

Ofelia was coming back around. The color had returned to her face and her eyes were clear.

"Oh, God, I feel so foolish. How stupid of me. I've been acting like a child. Look at what I've done to you, Eric."

"I'm more worried about you, Ofelia, and about the baby. Could the snake's venom kill our child?" Eric looked at Itandehui.

"*Bebé está bien, no te preocupes.*"

Roger knew she was right. He saw the light inside Ofelia pulsing steadily, unperturbed. Penalt knew from his scientific studies that our brains are tricked by what we see. What we think we see depends on the subjective conclusions we draw. Even knowing this, the images he saw inside Eric, and now Ofelia, were too unusual. He couldn't entirely dismiss them.

"Just a bit of bad luck," Roger said. He tried to appear calm. The baby did seem fine, if that was in fact what he'd seen, but what he saw inside Eric, that was not good. There was something seriously wrong. "Get some rest and take this jar of herbs with you to make tea. Drink it regularly for the next day or two. If you get sick to the stomach, come on back. Otherwise you're good to go. You should have some of the tea too, Eric. It'll calm you down."

His panic subsiding, Eric laughed. Ofelia, too, looked relieved. "You sound like a professional, Roger," said Eric.

Itandehui put everything away and waited for Penalt.

"I have to go," he said. "Can you make it back to the hacienda on your own?"

Ofelia nodded. "Yes, thank you both so much."

"Come back tomorrow, Eric. Itandehui will give you another treatment." Penalt couldn't get the strange visions out of his mind. He looked at Itandehui. The impassive look on her face told him nothing.

"Thank God you were both here. I don't know what we'd have done if you'd been gone."

"You need to get the poison out quickly," explained Penalt. "Most of the time it's not as bad as it seems. The snake doesn't always successfully inject the venom, but it's never wise to take a chance. Now, Mr. Martin, you go back and take a shower and then a long nap."

For Eric, the thought of a snake stealing everything he'd been given was unthinkable, like the Garden of Eden playing out all over again. Eric and Ofelia made their way back to the hacienda. They did their best to resume the idyll, but both were deeply shaken. Life, they were reminded, was unpredictable and fragile. A snake could slither into the garden whenever it pleased and take away all their dreams.

The next morning, Eric went to see Itandehui. Penalt was gone. A few chickens free-ranged outside the cottage door while a goat loafed at its stake. A banana tree overloaded with little fruits bunched among its big leaves drooped low. He had to stoop to walk under it.

Itandehui knew how to release the spirits. She didn't know *how* they worked. She accepted that they worked. "Healthy body... you need not know how make... spirits make... must know how bring spirits... trust spirits."

She looked so small and fragile, yet she was so strong. She gestured for Eric to lie down as before, and gave him some bitter leaves to chew. She positioned herself at his side and began to shout hot, crisp words while she clapped and chanted—a full-bodied canticle, a sacred and ancient summoning of the spirits.

To think too much about it would be a mistake. What mattered were the warm callused fingers placed on his chest, the salty, acrid taste of the leaves, the haunting sounds that came from deep inside the old woman's body. Eric soon underwent a strange but familiar experience.

The walls of the hut dissolved. Eric rose, floating in space, a disembodied eye, looking down at the room like an owl, looking at Itandehui, at himself. It all seemed quite normal. He tried to speak but no words came out. He tried to move, but he was rooted in the ground like a tree. There was a moment when he thought he saw a giant woman dancing in the corners of the room. Then there was a shower of stars. His mind went blank.

When Eric woke, he smelled the copal incense and the tobacco smoke. He continued to lie flat. Both his mind and his body were relaxed. Itandehui brought him a bitter tea. It didn't have the same taste as before. He drank it, then rested. Sometime later he rose and went out through the kitchen to the toilet. Itandehui was sweeping cornhusks off the floor. She didn't look up when he walked past. When he was finished, she met him and walked him around to the side of the house. He recognized the pirul tree. She picked a branch and swept it around him and sang softly. He stood completely still. It was finished. She had done all she knew how to do. She pointed to town. It was time to go. As Eric left, Itandehui disappeared into the house.

Later that night, Eric had an odd dream: A group of shamans assembled at the top of the mountain, and danced on a large rock. They danced so long they wore a series of marks into the rock. Their skin and flesh fell away, and they transformed into dancing skeletons. They all faced him Eric, and he saw holes where once there'd been eyes and mouths. The skeletons fell apart, but the bones danced until they faded away. Eric climbed to where they had been. He strained to look at the rock where the dancing had taken place. The white dust of the bones lay on the rock and formed a series of marks.

When he awoke the next morning, Eric remembered the dream in great detail. He could even remember the faces of some of the shamans. When he and Ofelia met Penalt for their morning coffee, Eric told Penalt all about it. Penalt got very excited. He told Eric and Ofelia to come at once with him to see Itandehui, who listened to Eric's story, then asked Penalt to explain what Eric said and to ask him to describe the shamans he'd seen in his dream and what he could remember of the dance. She asked him to draw as carefully as he could the marks he saw worn into the rock.

"We go to spring." Itandehui's eyes glowed bright. She was clearly excited by what Eric told her. Never before had Penalt seen such an expression on her face.

"This is a very good thing," said Roger. "On the southwest side of the mountain, there's a spring that drips over a rock. The locals call it God's Tears. The spring can only be approached if one is summoned in a dream, one like your dream. I've never seen this part of the mountain. Itandehui told me she's only been there a few times herself. You must go, Eric. This is a big deal."

Eric hesitated, feeling unready for another march through the jungle. "What happens there?"

"It's a special place for healing. Sometimes those too ill to walk are dragged there on beds stretched across poles by their families. After the healing, they're able to walk back out. It's extraordinary that you've had this dream. I've heard about this, but have never witnessed it."

Itandehui gathered the materials she would need, and they set out. It was a long hike, and Eric needed to rest along the way. They heard the sound of water in the distance long before they arrived. At last they came to a pool fed by a waterfall from high in the mountains. Lacy green ferns and large gray rocks surrounded the pool. From a place that had been worn flat where people had visited in the past, Eric gazed deep into the pool. It was clear but so deep he couldn't see to the bottom. On the opposite side the overflow ran down the other side of the mountain.

Itandehui lit a cigar. Eric sat in front of her on the edge of the pool, so close to the waterfall he could feel the spray. Soon he was engulfed in a cloud of smoke. He hated cigarettes, but the smoke from the cigar was strangely pleasant. He thought back to the earlier treatments. Despite the smoke, the world around him was light and airy. Itandehui asked Penalt to help her hold Eric under the spring. The cool water dripped onto his head and all over his face. They put him under the water several times.

Eric laughed. "It's like being baptized, Penalt."

"Shh. Don't talk. You'll disturb the spirit healers." It was remarkable. Penalt watched as the points of light once again lined up inside Eric's body. There were definitely two different forces at work. It seemed as if hideous gargoyles and monsters were jumping over each other in an attempt to avoid the white rays of an intense light that had the power to destroy them. Penalt couldn't believe it. He'd never seen anything like this, and had no idea what to make of it. Itandehui chanted and rattled a string of gourds. Soon, Penalt himself fell into a trance.

When the healing ceremony ended and Roger came back around, he helped Itandehui pull Eric out from under the waterfall.

"Don't wipe away the spring water," Roger said. "Let it dry on its own."

They walked back down to the village, Eric dripping while Roger rambled on excitedly. Eric was stunned. Normally he would have dismissed the whole thing as a pile of baloney. Something inside forced him to take it seriously. They went to the little café to eat while Ofelia went to the hacienda to pack. Both men were flabbergasted. One thing was certain: neither had ever experienced anything like this before.

"How does it work, Roger? Do you know?"

"All I know is that the healing treatments can be dangerous if not done exactly as they've been passed down from one healer to another. When I first came to the village, before I started working with Itandehui, I met a different healer. She claimed to be able to teach me, but she wanted money first. I was suspicious. While I was curious to see the process, I didn't trust this woman. I found out later that Itandehui never asks anyone to pay. She accepts whatever they give.

"The herbs and plants can be dangerous if not used with great care. Navigating the ways of the healers may seem tedious but it can be treacherous if you lack the proper knowledge. Each healing is unique."

"I don't understand, Roger. Either the plants work or they don't. What's so complicated about that?"

"It's not like that. This other curandera, Juana was her name, treated a young girl who was pregnant. The girl had been involved with a ranch hand. He passed through town and she made a mistake. She didn't want the baby. Juana told her she could "cure" her with a plant called damiana."

"You mean, induce an abortion?"

"Damiana is a very dangerous plant that's sometimes used to treat disorders in women. Few of the men will discuss when and how it's used, and the women just hold up their hands and say, "*No sabe.*" They all know, but they don't want to talk about it. This poor girl, she was only eighteen, perfectly healthy, pregnant. Juana injected a brew made from damiana into the girl's womb. The girl died. It was horrible. I nearly left after that. Itandehui assured me that with the right skills and the proper ceremonies, the cures are safe and they work. I know now she was right. I keep having visions like the one I had at the Jai Alai arena. I've asked Itandehui to explain them, but she says I must interpret the visions on my own. So far I haven't been able to do that. I hope someday I'll be able to."

"I don't know what to believe—secret Laetrile, mysterious visions, bizarre healings. I've lost my bearings, Roger. The other day I freaked when I thought Ofelia was going to die. I worry every day that *I'm* going to die. We all die. To complain is useless, but I'm happier now than I've ever been. It's a crazy way to live."

"Let me tell you, Eric, I don't know anything about the Laetrile. I was sent down here to get a sample of Frieze's serum, but it was all gone before I could get it. The company sent me down because they thought it worked. I'm a scientist. I believe in matter and energy, not ethereal spirits, but what goes on inside our bodies is complicated. We understand only a small part. Itandehui can go deeper. I don't know how she does it, but I think there's something to it."

Penalt could see that Eric's disease had progressed. Whether or not what he saw inside Eric was more than his imagination, anyone who looked closely at Eric could see the progression had slowed but not stopped. The peculiar magic of Itandehui's cure was all Eric had left. As yet, science had no cure, no hope. Would it ever?

"Ofelia and I go back tomorrow. Jordan will pick us up in his plane. I'll miss our morning talks, Roger."

"So will I, Eric. Tell Ofelia goodbye for me. I want to see my godson when he arrives. I know we'll see each other again."

That night Ofelia woke suddenly when Eric bumped against her leg, thrashing in the midst of a nightmare.

"Whas a matter for you, black man? My looking for you. Why you ah run way?"

Nelson knew he was in trouble. He saw it in the bloodshot eyes. He should've run, but he didn't. Two Mexican men were after him and they had knives.

"How much a money you got, hey?"

Nelson pulled out his wallet. "I got nothin' in this here world worth takin' 'cept my wallet. Here."

Oh, God, why you sendin' me more trouble? Don't Eric and me have burden enough?

Nurse Marta had rushed on ahead of him. For once he wished they'd stayed together.

"What for you want look at us Mehican, hey? Why you come here?"

The two men took the money and threw the wallet on the ground.

"My friend, he ah want know your name. *Cómo se llama?*"

"My name's Nelson, man. I gave ya all I got. There ain't no more." He tried to smile, nervous as he was.

The two men spoke together quietly. Nelson was frantically looking for a way out. "They got plenty bad hearts down here, and two of them right in front of me."

"We want ah, find out. You got gold tooth?"

Oh, Jesus, no, thought Nelson. He stood there afraid to open his mouth.

"American goddamn hijo de puta! You try cheat us Mehican? You got gold tooth!"

The larger of the two men lunged forward and put a knife through Nelson's heart. Nelson opened his mouth and tried to speak, but all he could say was "Why?"

"Let's ah get that gold tooth, hey?"

The shorter man knocked out Nelson's tooth with the butt of his knife. The two men laughed and ran away.

"Eric! Eric! Wake up, you're having a nightmare."
He rose up and reached out.
"No! No! No!"
"Eric," Ofelia shook him hard. "It's just a dream, Eric. Everything's okay."
But he wasn't okay. They stayed awake and talked until the sun came up. Eric explained about Nelson, what a comfort he'd been at Stanford, and how there were moments when he felt like Nelson spoke to him, even now.
"It was just a dream, Eric, just a dream," said Ofelia.
"Sure. He's okay. Wherever he is, he's okay. You're right. It's just a stupid dream, that's all."

66.

Calhoun's

A Bar in New Jersey

Dominic and Finnigan met at Calhoun's on the way to do the job for Zacco.

"That guy at the bar put his finger to my chest. Can you believe it? If he does it again I'm gonna break his fuckin' finger off, Dom, right at the goddamn root."

"Let's not forget why we're here, Finn."

"I don't want to think about it. That pishhead in the corner, he's lookin' at us."

"I don't give a fuck about any bloke in the corner, Finn."

"He's got his fuckin' eyes on us, I tell you."

"I don't care about no pishhead's eyes. I gotta go and take a wee bit of a pish."

"Hell, Dom, once you break the seal, you'll be pishing all day."

"Hey, there goes Mr. Finger on his way to the pisher. I'll introduce that fuckin' guy to Mr. Porcelain for ya."

"Want me to do it?"

"I'll do it myself. Pay the bill. We're outta here. It's time to go to work."

"Say, why we doing this Nuncio guy? Who is he?"

"I got no idea. Some messenger, I think. Calm down. We got a job to do. That's all I know."

"Maybe this Drago Nuncio guy ain't so bad. Do we have to do him?"

"We do not get paid to be fucking philosophers, Finn. Just pay the fuckin' bill. I'll be right back."

"Okay. I'll meet ya at the door."

67.

Grief

When they came to tell his mother, Marcos was in the back room. They didn't think he heard them, but he listened. Mrs. Martinez came, and even the old witch Lucy Alameda. At first his mother let out a shriek, then a howling moan, and then she fell to the floor. Marcos peeked through a crack in the door as they got her back into a chair. Mrs. Martinez ran to the kitchen and fetched his mother a glass of water.

"She needs a drink of whiskey," said Lucy.

"Don't mention that in this house," replied Mrs. Martinez with a scowl.

Marcos took his accordion and slipped out the back. He walked all the way into town and he played. He played all the day and into the night, but Hector didn't come. That's when he knew what the women said was true.

The next day Marcos went to climb the tree. He hadn't been back since the day he locked El Diablo in the pit. The Frenchman's yard was overgrown with weeds, and the house had been ransacked. Marcos listened to the angels flying in and out of the tree around him. He had never tried to speak to them, but today he had to tell them—he had to tell someone—about Hector. He spoke, not words, but using his mind, and they listened. They shone and glittered and danced in circles. They filled the tree with all the colors of the universe.

The tree uprooted and flew into the sky, and the angels held Marcos so that he wouldn't fall. They told him to look up above the tree. The sunlight was blinding, then everything became clear, and he saw Hector smile down on him. The grimace was gone. Hector looked like the pictures Marcos kept in his room from before the accident. It was the Hector he saw at the top of the stairs before everything changed. Hector sang in the language of the rainbow-winged angels and they listened. Marcos understood everything then—what life was, how it tricked you into little corners where you could get stuck, and how love and only love could get you out. Marcos wished everyone could hear his brother sing.

Marcos stayed there sleeping for a long time. When he awoke, the sun was low in the sky, the tree was back in the ground, and the angels were gone. Marcos climbed down and walked home. His mother sat at the kitchen table, her head in her hands.

"I miss him too, Mama," Marcos said, and he hugged her gently with both arms.

She kissed Marcos on the head.

He pulled slowly away and looked at her with his soft brown eyes. "Mama," he asked, "what will happen to Hector's red car?"

68.

Reactions

When Rafael heard the news about Hector, a series of thoughts ran through his brain: Concern for the business, disappointment over the Laetrile, and worries about how Zacco would react. There was even sorrow about Hector and remorse over the suffering of his family.

Tomás thought only about the business. Their lieutenant was gone. They needed another. Tomás sent two men to the site of the accident to search for any Laetrile that might have survived. He redoubled the effort to find Frieze.

When Roger Penalt heard that the Dos Negros men had left the mountain empty-handed, he thought of looking for some of Frieze's Laetrile at the other mountain villages. He asked one of the local men to act as his guide, and told Itandehui he might be gone for a week or two. Time meant nothing to Itandehui. She turned away without a word.

Father Jordan and Ana Luisa discussed Hector's sad fate over their morning coffee in the garden where they'd had so many Saturday lunches with Louis Frieze.

"Perhaps Hector's in a better place, Jordan. His unfortunate life was filled with little but sorrow. What about Frieze, have you heard any more?"

"God be with him, Ana. With all my heart I hope he is alive, but I think he's dead. Hector would not have gone to San Kuuchamaa if Dos Negros had abducted Frieze. I am ignorant, but I daresay they don't know where he is either. Indeed, his disappearance is a complete mystery."

"As much as we liked him, you must admit Frieze was a sad and bitter man. Maybe he'd had enough of life, Jordan. The last few weeks have been unbearable. I'm not sure how much more I can take. I think often of those words of Jeremiah—"Cursed be the day on which I was born." Frieze told us the same thing at our last lunch. I hope he's in peace, dead or alive. Somehow I know we'll never see him again."

"Old Frieze was full o' fun, but he did have a bit of the curmudgeon inside. For the love of God, I just can't believe he's gone. I thought I was getting through with all my pleas to let us help him. His work meant so much to him, you'd think he'd have left something behind. They say they found none of his Laetrile anywhere in the house."

"He was a true artist, Jordan. For an artist, to do your best is enough."

Jordan and Anna Luisa sat in silence.

"Shall I make lunch?" she asked.

"No, Ana. It wouldn't feel right without Louie. Let's just go out today... I'll pray for my old friend. I know he wasn't a God-fearin' man, but I don't think he'd have an objection, and the Lord is merciful."

Ana walked into the kitchen with a tear in her eye. They'd had so many setbacks. Their beautiful son, then Frieze, and now Hector, all these precious lives gone forever. Life was nothing but tragedies. She was loath to admit it to herself, but everything seemed futile. We have high hopes. We watch them shatter like broken glass. There are no answers before we die. Yes, we develop wonderful ideas but these just explain life in different ways. We never get to the big things, the real things. How could we? Only a true healer like Itandehui can speak to the Nameless One, talk to him, maybe understand him. It's very delicate. He doesn't like strangers. Mostly we just move along. We watch patiently over the lives of men, over the blades of grass and the animals that feed on the land, try to be kind to others, and hope to last long enough to find the good life, but no one finds it. Not even Itandehui can find it. Anna began to think that Frieze was right. We wander in time and space, our existence pointless. Everything we hold holy, everything we love and pray for, even ourselves—pointless. She couldn't tell Jordan. Even after Danny, when Jordan nearly lost his faith, the God she'd lost so long ago gave Jordan back his faith and optimism. Jordan told her he had too many people counting on him to throw in the towel now. Ana didn't dare admit the despair she felt, not even to herself, except in those moments of great loss that punctuated her life with merciless arrows.

69.

Unraveling the Mystery

Manny had too many tequilas at the wedding. In his drunken stupor he spoke with Russell Napier and Doctor Milagro and was not impressed. Eric's recovery was a puzzle he couldn't ignore. With Eric's permission, he made an appointment to meet with Doctor Doggett on the way back to Sacramento. Eric had won the lottery, and Manny wanted to know how it happened. It was good news but also quite inexplicable. He'd never heard of such a thing, and wanted some answers.

He walked into Doctor Doggett's office with a head full of questions.

Doggett said, "It's a pleasure to meet you in the flesh, Doctor Marx. I've heard about your work in Sacramento. Everyone has. As you know, I've referred a few patients over the years. Thank you for your work. But that's not why you're here."

"No. Thank you, Doctor Doggett, for your kind words, but I'm here to get your assessment of Eric Martin. I looked over his chart and spoke with Doctor Rice before Eric went to the Mexican clinic. I believed at the time he was under a death sentence. I'm trying to comprehend what's happened in the last few months to cause this remarkable change in his health. Am I reading your diagnosis correctly?"

Doctor Doggett stood up as he spoke. "We both know that spontaneous tumor remissions are among the rarest and most mysterious events in medicine, with only a few hundred well-documented cases in the literature. Remissions have most often been reported in melanoma and kidney cancer, but the phenomenon may, in fact, be considerably more common than previously thought. There's been evidence for quite some time that in certain cases the patient's own immune system can play a critical role in combating cancer. How this happens we still don't know. One of the first scientists who tried to trigger the immune system into attacking cancer was the New York surgeon William Coley back in the 1890s."

"I remember reading something about Coley's work," said Manny. "My recollection is that it was never accepted."

"You're right, Doctor. Over the years, there have been numerous trials of anti-cancer vaccines designed to train the immune system to recognize and destroy cancer, but the results have been lackluster. None of the new vaccines has been approved in the United States, though several have been approved in other countries. There are even some countries where the original Coley toxin is still in use. In every trial there were some successes, enough to encourage a few doctors to use these vaccines with patients."

"Did Eric get this kind of treatment at the Mexican clinic?"

"No, and that is what baffles me," answered Doctor Doggett. "He's only been taking Laetrile with various other so-called metabolic treatments. Rigorous tests have shown Laetrile to be ineffective. He told me, however, that he had access to a strain of Laetrile that's not widely available to the general public. It was made by an old French chemist who seems to have gone missing. As unlikely as it seems, my guess is that this chemist, whoever he is, somehow mixed in one of the anti-cancer vaccines with the Laetrile to create a more effective serum. In any case, it seems to have worked for Eric."

"You must know, Doctor, how fantastical this sounds." Manny was still skeptical.

"Well, either Eric is the beneficiary of divine intervention or there is some rational explanation."

"Have you been able to track down any of this mysterious serum?" asked Manny.

"I'm afraid not. Eric tells me that he's run out of his supply. The man who came up with the idea has disappeared into thin air. Sadly, I have some bad news to report. While the growth of Eric's cancer has been arrested and the visible signs of the tumors have disappeared, the cancer has not been eradicated. It remains in his system. There could be a recurrence at any time."

"Does Eric know this?"

"Yes, Doctor Marx, we had a frank discussion about his health."

"This is all very interesting. Thank you, Doctor Doggett."

"Eric has authorized me to keep you informed. I will do that as circumstances warrant. I'm not treating him at this time, but he might return to me if his condition changes. I will let you know if he does."

70.

Jig's Up

Napier's luck soon soured. When he heard about Zacco taking out one of Congressman Shipley's stool pigeons, he realized the situation was more dangerous than he thought. He decided it would be best to cut his losses. Another setback occurred shortly after the hearings. Elvin Krump died of a heart attack. Krump had been humiliated and embarrassed at the hearings. Combined with his poor health, the stress was enough to push him over the edge. Napier had no hope of finding Frieze or his secret recipe. The options had run out for legalization in the United States. The research reports were unanimous in their negative findings.

> The Commission has collected information concerning 44 patients treated with Laetrile, all of whom either have active disease or are dead of their disease, with one exception. Of those alive with disease, no patient has been found with objective evidence of control of cancer under treatment with Laetrile alone. Nine patients dying from cancer after treatment with Laetrile have been autopsied, and histological studies done for the Commission by five different pathologists have shown no evidence of any chemotherapeutic effect.

In two independent studies by experienced research workers, Laetrile has been completely ineffective when used in large doses on cancer in laboratory animals, in lesions which are readily influenced in useful chemotherapy.

From the data obtained, Laetrile cannot be considered as a palliative in cancer therapy on the basis of the biological rationale advanced by the manufacturer.

The Food and Drug Administration has seen no competent scientific evidence that Laetrile is effective in the treatment of cancer. There is no acceptable evidence of therapeutic effect to justify clinical trials.

When BioPharm stock became worthless, Napier panicked. Ever the entrepreneur, he contacted a group of businessmen from Las Vegas, the Mormon mafia wing of the Howard Hughes organization, a group he'd dealt with in the past. Over the years, Hughes had spent millions buying up mining claims all over the world, especially in Pan America. Some of Hughes' associates were unhappy that these claims were just sitting there gathering dust. They told Napier they'd gone to Hughes and struck a deal whereby they would develop the claims in their own corporation and split the profits with Hughes. The rub was that they could not get the corporation through the U.S. Securities and Exchange Commission.

Napier offered to use his contacts in Canada to get the Pan American Mines Company approved on the Canadian stock exchange. It sounded like a sweet deal in which everyone, especially Napier with his large commission payable in stock, could make a fortune quickly. This would enable him to repay Zacco and Dos Negros so he wouldn't have to worry that they might come after him.

At first, everything moved along nicely, but then the rug was pulled out from under Napier. After the stock had been sold to the public, it turned out that the people who sold it hadn't paid for the mining properties. They were expecting to use the money raised in the stock offering to pay. When the news got out, the share price dropped from $11 to 11 cents, and everyone connected with the deal went broke.

Napier was convicted of stock fraud and sentenced to a year in jail and a $25,000 fine. That was the end. The Dos Negros severed their relationship with him and took over all the operations of BioPharm. Business continued, though it slowly dwindled over time as the relentless campaign against Laetrile by U.S. authorities gathered strength. With Louie Frieze gone, rumors about a secret strain of Laetrile died down and eventually disappeared altogether. Doctor Milagro's clinics continued to operate despite all the setbacks. Remarkably, they thrived. Whenever an older treatment crashed and burned, a new one rose out of the ashes like a phoenix. The con artists continued to survive, supported by the true believers, but the industry shrank to insignificance.

71.

Reality

The weeks went by. Eric vacillated between the extremes of bliss and despair. He was overjoyed with Ofelia and the prospect of their soon-to-be-born son, but the cancer continued to grow. He hated everything about his disease—the hyperactive cells that grew inside him like a demonic pregnancy, the perverted twin that grew faster and adapted better and thwarted his every advance toward normalcy. Now, at the very worst time, he was running out of hope. He was down to the last vial from the philosopher's stone, the substance created by Louie Frieze to transmute apricot seeds into the gift of life.

One night alone while Ofelia slept, Eric lifted up his final cup of magical tea and praised the vanished Frenchman. "To you, Louie Frieze, the Mangy Parrot, the great man I never met, the solitary saint and noble explorer who like Dante dared to forge a trail through hell."

It was an emotional moment after which Eric collapsed in his chair.

The initial descent was slow. Eric was able to hide his bitter disappointment and even his pain from Ofelia. In some grateful moments, he even hid it from himself. He wanted to survive, to see the birth of his son. He also wanted to prevent his curse from being passed on to the single offspring he'd created. He thought to save a bit of Frieze's formula for his Daniel but dismissed the idea as a hopeless fantasy.

At night he stayed up alone to ruminate on the absurdities of his past and present life. One night he noticed the monkey. It sat quietly in the corner and observed his every move. He sensed something else, something evil, watching him as well. Nelson disappeared after the nightmare at the hacienda. Eric had been afraid since then that he was now in the battle alone, terribly alone.

As time inexorably moved onward, it became harder to hide the illness. Ofelia knew, but kept it to herself. There were a few wonderful weeks when both Ofelia and Eric thought only of each other and the baby, but the bliss did not last.

Eric carried on with the Laetrile from the clinic. He tried to fool Ofelia, but she knew he now used the inferior serum. Ofelia was so happy with their life that she managed to forget the inevitable. By now she was showing, and she looked forward to the baby. They told all the parents, and when a healthy baby finally arrived, Karen and Devon and everyone they knew expressed happiness at their good fortune. Penalt came to visit and was more excited than all the others.

It surprised Eric how he continued to hold up. Though he began to lose weight and at times found it hard to breathe, he was able to hide the effects by wearing loose clothing. He kept up his appearance, something he'd never before given much attention. He didn't go back to Doctor Doggett. He didn't want to hear any news that might tempt him away from whatever optimism he had left.

One night, he awoke with severe pain in his abdomen. He limped out to the front room and sat in his chair as Daniel slept soundly beside Ofelia in the bedroom. The monkey sat in the corner impassively. The wind blew open the shutters, and an eerie chill filled the room. The frightened monkey jumped onto Eric's lap. It was the first time Eric and the monkey had touched. Eric was shocked at the reality. He could feel the hair on the monkey's body and smell its sweaty fur. He looked into the monkey's eyes, and though he could not decipher the thoughts behind them, he realized then that his long, odd journey had ended.

The next morning Ofelia found Eric asleep in his chair. Asleep, unshaven, unkempt—she could no longer deny it. He was near death. She refused to rob him of any last hope. She filled a pot with warm water and gathered the implements to clean and shave him as she had done that long-ago morning at the clinic. He woke and smiled as she brought him back to life, brought him back as she always did. They kissed when she was done, and the day went on as usual, then another day and yet another. One day, quite unexpectedly, when Eric held their newborn son in his arms, Ofelia saw the time had come. Like the storm you've been waiting for, it arrived suddenly and with deadly force.

Ofelia took Daniel to her parent's house. It was a short drive.

"We need a few days," she said. She didn't want to alarm them with the truth, but they too had seen the changes in Eric. They all knew, but no one dared speak about it. Back home that afternoon life seemed almost normal.

They sat on the deck of the small house they had rented. Eric told her everything. They both knew what was coming. He told Ofelia about the monkey, his nagual. She didn't know what to say. He said the monkey was there now in the corner. Of course Ofelia saw nothing. Eric explained that the monkey had chased him through the streets and in the markets when he went to town. He spoke of the meetings in the courtyard behind the locked door where he had gone in his dreams. She listened to everything, patiently, attentively, holding back her tears.

Suddenly Eric's face contorted into a series of abnormal shapes.

"Look," he cried and pointed with his finger. Ofelia looked but saw only the hummingbirds, their rainbow wings glittering in the last rays of the sun.

Eric jumped up despite his weakened state, and yelled at the top of his lungs, "Go away! Leave me alone! I won't go! I won't. I refuse, refuse..."

He flailed about, waved his arms, and stomped his feet. Ofelia was terrified.

The beast ran out of the corner, pounced on him like a lion, and tore at him with her rows of sharp teeth. Her tail swung around to strike him, but the monkey jumped up onto her mane and began biting her ears.

"Get off me, you foul ape! Get off!" the beast cried.

Ofelia watched Eric jump around, lurch, and fall. Unable to see what he saw, she feared he had lost his mind.

The beast's poisonous spines shot out everywhere, but they missed their target. It bellowed like a trumpet, turned with wild eyes, and grabbed Eric by the neck, but the persistent monkey would not let go of its ears.

The beast had him at last. Eric knew there was no escape. He was lifted on high by her bat wings. His face drew close to hers. He could see the pores on her nose and the thick dark hairs growing on her upper lip. Her face was all out of proportion, skewed to the right while her piercing blue eyes strained to pull away from her enormous mouth. She was hideous. Her eyes were wild, stretched and distorted, distant and near at the same time. She bellowed and roared like a lion.

The monkey lost his grip on the beast's ears and screamed. The beast's tail whipped around like a snake but the poisonous spines still could not find their target. It was an epic battle, Eric and his nagual against the furious manticore.

The beast suddenly opened and encircled them with its ugly webbed wings. Her head came down on them like a hammer. The stench as she opened her mouth paralyzed him. Her three rows of teeth, wickedly sharp and powerful, impaled Eric and the monkey and devoured them both in one massive crunch. The manticore roared the loudest of roars: "I am the way and the truth and the law around here, Mr. Martin. No one gets anywhere except through me... through me... through me!"

Nurse Marta had been watching him while he dreamed pleasant dreams with a smile on his face. She was enraged to think he could escape this world without the full experience of the pain and suffering he deserved—he who had caused her so much grief. There was no one else in the room. She reached up and turned off the flow valve for the morphine. She backed out of the room with a cruel smile as Eric's body began to twist and shake in agony.

His eyes snapped open. A tide of pain ripped through his body. His quiet world was abruptly disturbed. He strained to see. He'd been brought back out of the soul's weird mine where he slept silently like a rock amidst forests made of mist. The torments of life did not follow him there where he had a glimpse of what was to come. Now the ancient strings pulled and tugged. His arms and legs flapped about and he struggled to find his way.

Part IV

72.

Stanford Hospital

May 1972

The hospital walls came slowly into focus. His head pounded, he was nauseated, bright lights blinded him. The worst part was the pain. It came at him like a huge hammer beating him everywhere at once. In the distance he heard a little popping noise like a needle falling onto a record, then the words of a song.

Crazy...
For thinking that my love could hold you
I'm crazy for trying
And crazy for crying
And I'm crazy for loving you.

He looked up and saw Nelson readjust the morphine drip.

"I seen what she did. This'll make everything okay again. I gonna fix the pain, okay? You gonna see the other side soon. You ready? You all good?"

Eric relaxed into Nelson's wide smile. Nelson turned away to hide his tears. Eric's burnt-out heart would not have to wait much longer. A promise was in the air. It blew at him through lips he couldn't see or know. The air grew strange and pure inside the room, then turned icy cold and everything went black.

The light of consciousness flickers on and off for but a brief moment. It lasts just long enough for the dream to finish, the dream itself merely the dream of a dream. It ends, as it must, with one simple understanding. All the drive, love, pride, anger, hope, and anxiety of this life achieves only this—that the cycle will perpetuate.

73.

The Stanford Medical Center Riot

When Nurse Marta discovered that Nelson had tampered with Eric's morphine drip, it was the last straw. She'd had quite enough of Nelson's interference. She turned over all the rigorous notes she'd made of Nelson's unauthorized dealings with patients. She categorized the numerous times he'd refused to carry out the orders of the medical professionals, and accused him of willful negligence on the job. She produced evidence that he was the leader of a group that was trying to organize the non-medical staff to petition for higher wages and better working conditions. He'd gone so far, she claimed, as to discuss the merits of Black Power with hospital employees. In short, she claimed he was a troublemaker and had to go.

Nelson sat on the bench with his back against the wall in the janitor's room. He was guilty of everything Nurse Marta claimed, except for the negligence. He was good at his job—the best. Nobody, especially that old bitch nurse, was going to ruin his reputation. He'd sue their asses if it came to that. The bastards had fired him because he helped the patients when no one else would. They fired him because he stuck up for his rights and the rights of others, trying to get the bosses to treat the hospital employees fairly. Now he'd become the catalyst for this crazy demonstration. He wanted no part of it. He rose from the bench and walked out to his car. He heard the demonstrators on the other side of the building, but he didn't look back. He got into his car and drove away.

Nurse Marta sat brooding in her secret room. Things were getting dangerous. Students and civil rights groups had organized a rally to protest what they saw as inequities at Stanford Medical Center. The personnel department was looking into all employee dismissals. If they discovered how she'd tampered with employee and patient records to get revenge against her enemies, she would not only lose her job but might face lawsuits. It was time to box up the mementos she'd collected from patients and get rid of all the other evidence against her.

When she hauled the boxes to her car, she saw the protestors, hundreds of students and wild-eyed troublemakers were marching to the office of the hospital director, carrying signs and shouting demands. Nurse Marta quickly stashed the boxes in the trunk of her car and returned to the ward to clear out the rest of the incriminating files.

She watched the bizarre spectacle through a window.

It's all the fault of these damn protestors. If they would just leave well enough alone! Nelson had left quietly. In a couple of days, everything would die down and things would be back to normal.

The protest came to a stop outside the director's office. Someone announced over a bullhorn that the director was out to lunch. At first Nurse Marta got her hopes up that this ridiculous mess would collapse under its own weight. Several of the protestors decided to leave. They broke up into groups and slouched back to campus, into classrooms and into the student union, dragging their signs with them. A few dozen diehards decided to stage an overnight sit-in by occupying administration offices.

The first response was to let this radicalized group stew in its juices overnight on the assumption that they'd grow weary and leave like the others, but these protestors held firm. It soon became clear they weren't going to leave peacefully.

Nurse Marta finished cleaning up the records to make sure she was in the clear. Her shift was over and it was time to go home. She left the hospital expecting things to be back to normal in the morning.

Nelson sat in front of the TV watching the news about the protest while his wife fixed dinner.

"Oh, Lord! I don't need this. They gonna lay a world a hurt on me if I stick around this damn place."

"What'd you say, honey?"

"I say we leavin', mama. We gettin' in that car tomorrow and drivin' north."

"Where we going, honey?"

"I don't know yet. Just away. Far, far away."

Things got out of control the next day when Stanford officials called in the police after negotiations failed. Palo Alto cops arrived in riot gear along with a squadron of sheriff's deputies. The protestors used desks, chairs, filing cabinets, tabletops, and other furniture to barricade both sets of reinforced plate-glass doors to the director's office.

Nurse Marta watched it all unfold from a balcony outside the ward, and said to the young nurse beside her, "I blame Nelson. They never should have hired that freak. He was trouble from the beginning. They should have stopped him before it ever came to this."

She heard the acting president of the university blaring over the loudspeaker. "There will be no further negotiations while the occupation continues. Our first obligation is to the sick people who depend on this hospital for their care."

He gave the protestors five minutes to leave without facing arrest. They didn't budge.

"You're not going to leave, then?" His words rang out loud and clear.

"Right on!" yelled the protestors who still occupied the building.

"Jesus!" said Nurse Marta to the petrified young nurse. "They're going in!"

The police used a six-foot battering ram to attack one of the reinforced glass doors. After several attempts, one pane was smashed, and police sprayed Mace at the demonstrators, who used a fire hose to fight back. They repelled both the charging cops and their irritant. One policeman hit by a flying stapler collapsed, bleeding from a head wound.

The Mace blew back on the police, reporters, faculty observers, and onlookers. Outside, the crowd, held back by a double line of riot-equipped police, shouted encouragement to occupiers and obscenities at the officers.

"Them white folks acting like us niggers," Nelson said to his wife as they listened to the events live over the radio.

"They smarter than us, honey," she replied. "They already *at* the hospital. Ain't no wait for an ambulance that never comes."

The young nurse said to Marta, "I've never seen anything like this in my life!"

"Neither have I. They're all crazy. We better go inside and notify the emergency crews to stand by."

Below, a woman in the crowd yelled at the police: "It takes a lot of nerve to hold those clubs against unarmed people!"

The crowd was chanting, "Power to the people."

The police captain and his officers pushed back the onlookers and the press. The cops repeatedly assaulted the barricaded doors, but were repelled three times by the fire hose and assorted missiles, including telephones. In desperation, they loosened one door with a crowbar and a pair of bolt cutters, and finally, using a rope, succeeded in pulling the twisted door out of the way.

The police stormed in with shouts: "Let's get 'em!" The protestors opened a door at the other end where only a few policemen were stationed. They were quickly overwhelmed and most of the protesters escaped. Demonstrators armed with clubs beat a few policemen to the ground. Others climbed through smashed windows and shimmied to the ground on a fire hose. Most escaped without being arrested, but a small cadre remained to face off with the police, who won this last battle. Enraged by the way the demonstrators had treated them, they penned this radical group inside the corridor and beat them brutally before making the arrests. With the building finally secure, injured police and demonstrators were treated by hospital personnel. Nurse Marta was commended for her presence of mind in organizing the quick response.

The next day the police ransacked the offices of the *Stanford Daily* newspaper in an attempt to identify and find all those involved in what became the bloodiest riot in Stanford history. The *Daily* sued and the case went all the way to the U.S. Supreme Court where, several months later, the student newspaper won.

74.

Out of the Depths of Darkness

"Nelson? Nelson? Where are you?"

Nelson was confused. His mind was playing tricks on him.

"Hey, man! I thought you were gone. What you doin'?"

"It's so dark. I can't see. Where am I?"

"Course you can't see. You a real nigger now, black as the ace of spades. Ha! You right inside my head, boy. You right here inside my head."

"Right inside your head? What does that mean?"

"You a memory, kid. That's what happens when you die. You died. We all do sooner or later. Now you a memory inside my head."

"I don't want to be a memory. I want to be a real person. I want to feel like a real person. I want to be alive. I don't want to be dead."

"Well, you are dead, but you real too. Look, you're smilin', ain't that right, brother?"

Eric considered this. "I guess."

"Sure you are. You smilin'. I see you. You can't be dead. You breathe when I breathe. You laugh when I laugh. You part of me now, man, so you real."

Nelson snapped his fingers as he drove the car. His wife was asleep in her seat. Things were silent for a while.

"Nelson, are you still there?"

"Look, Jack, you gotta find another place to hang out, okay? Take your shit and go. You're knockin' stuff all around inside my head, messin' things up, fuckin' with my brain. You gotta get by on your own now, brother. My wife, she ain't gonna like this, so, vamoose!"

It took a while to get used to being a memory. Eric popped up in strange places. He could go forward and backward in time, even go outside of time, but he hadn't learned to control these new powers, and everything was chaos at first.

"What the fuck you doin'? I ain't gonna keep this up no more, see?"

"Sorry, Nelson. I'm just trying to get used to this memory thing. I died in the dream, right?"

"You died in the goddamn hospital, man. You're dead. I ain't gonna sugarcoat it. You need to know. You caused me enough trouble already, now leave me alone."

Nelson changed lanes to pass a big truck. He was heading north. He didn't know yet how he'd make it but he figured he could get a job in another hospital since he'd had no part in the riot. Surely no one could blame him for that.

Eric felt dizzy. He swirled around in a fog. He was a cloud of particles in Brownian motion, banging against each other like miniature pool balls. Thump, thump, thump. The collisions produced little flickers of light that ricocheted off bits of dust circulating in the mist.

"Ouch!"

"What did you say this time?"

Eric tried to pull himself together. He remembered parts of the dream.

"Ofelia! What happened to Ofelia? What happened to Daniel... to Jordan... to all the rest?"

"Jesus Christ! That was your dream, Jack. You gotta tell *me* about it. How'm I s'posed to know what you were dreaming?"

"You mean... none of it was real... it was all just a dream? Ofelia, Daniel, and all the rest?"

"You still don't get it, do you?"

"Get what?"

"Look, white boy, you said they were all real. How could you forget that? I wrote everything down. A dream is a story, you said, or somethin' like that. All stories are real in some way, just like you said. Or was that Ofelia? Christ, I can't remember now who said it."

"I want to know what was real and what wasn't."

"You're pissin' me off. I'm tryin' to get away from all that shit. You're driving me nuts! I'm gonna blow my brains out if this keeps up."

"No! Don't do that, Nelson. I'll figure it out. I'll find a way to set you free."

Eric had no eyes to close, no mind to think with. The only thing he had for sure was Nelson's memory, and Nelson didn't like that. This put Eric at a disadvantage. Then, the dream continued on its own.

On Danny's first birthday they all gathered at the beach—Ana and Jordan, Roger, Ofelia, Orvaline, and Devon. Danny was there too, but he was too young to remember. Orvaline arranged for the boat. They rowed out with Eric's ashes to the place where the two countries divide. A Coast Guard boat trolled toward them from the north as Ofelia threw Eric's ashes into the wind.

They heard the loudspeaker, but no one paid attention.

"Ofelia, the boat's leaking," cried Orvaline. "Quick, give me the urn."

Orvaline used it to bail out the boat while the rest of them rowed quickly back toward shore. Everyone was in such a fright as they struggled to keep the boat from sinking. It was hard to tell what happened next. Ofelia thought she saw something swimming away from them over the waves toward the horizon. She wondered if monkeys could swim, but kept that thought to herself.

"That's cool, that urn thing. You still got it even though you're dead, man."

"Thanks, Nelson."

They all met downtown at El Azteca for breakfast. It was the last time they were together.

They were seated at a large table. Ofelia fed Daniel while Devon spoke. "Before Eric came to Mexico," said Devon, "I tried to talk him out of it. I was wrong. He got the time he needed to live his dream. I know he rests in peace, Ofelia, thanks to you and Daniel. That means everything to me. What will you do now, Ofelia?"

"I've set up a fund for Daniel with Eric's money. My parents have agreed to send us to London. I need to get out of Mexico." Daniel fell asleep as he sucked on his bottle.

Devon laughed at his new little nephew. "Do you think babies dream, Ofelia?"

"I'm sure they do. They create real thoughts inside their little heads."

"God bless you," said Father Jordan with a sad smile. Ana Luisa put her hand on Jordan's knee.

"Jordan and I have agreed that it's time for him to step down. The Church has tried to get rid of him ever since our marriage became public. He's been too stubborn to walk away, but now we are both ready. We're going to relocate near Mexico City where Jordan can pursue his studies on the history of Mexico. We'll miss all of you. Endings are sad, but sometimes they lead to new adventures."

"Eric once told me," said Ofelia, "that new beginnings are often disguised as painful endings. It was a quote from Lao Tzu."

"Well, I'm staying here," Orvaline said.

A gloomy mood at the table led to a few minutes' silence. Everyone sat quietly, each lost in his own thoughts.

Roger broke the silence. "I'm leaving, but I'm coming back. I don't know if I'm cut out to be a healer, but I have to find out. Before meeting Itandehui, I was stuck inside an office. I had no idea whether I'd enjoy working with real people, making them well, seeing the chemistry come alive that seemed so dead and useless in my lab. Eric's example taught me that conventional medicine lacks one critical insight: Real healing cannot take place unless the patient and the healer are willing to change their lives. Eric was healed because his life changed in an important way before his body died. That's what I think, anyway. I'm going home to settle my affairs. Then I'll come back to work with Itandehui. Whether or not I ever become a healer on my own, I plan to spend my life understanding and cataloguing the plants and herbs the curanderas use and the methods they pursue. Most of my friends think I'm crazy. I can't help that. When you know what you want to do, you do it. I learned that from Eric."

"I'm happy to hear it, Roger," Devon said enthusiastically. "Eric would be proud to know he played some part in this. I wish he'd known."

"He does know, Devon. We talked about it the last time he was in San Kuuchamaa."

Breakfast ended. They all went their own ways, knowing that part of the dream was over.

"You still there, Nelson? There's one more thing."

"You back again? Now what?"

"Roger. He's in the dream, but he was a real person. I knew him when I was alive. He's somewhere out there with you too, isn't he?"

"Shit happens in dreams. Manny's real. Devon's real. It's time to get over it. A dream's a story. That's all you need to know. Now buzz off, Jack. You're gonna wake up my wife and she'll be grumpy."

"Okay, okay. I'm sorry. I'll have to figure out the rest for myself."

75.

Penalt

Penalt sat in his Sacramento apartment and stared out the window. He felt like a character in a play, as if he'd been dreaming or acting out a role in someone else's story, but it was real. He'd gone to Mexico, witnessed healing, life, and death in a world completely different from the ordinary world he'd worked in all his life. He had met and worked with Itandehui. Back in his customary surroundings these experiences might well seem like a dream, but they weren't a dream. He would never be the same.

Alex dropped by to see him. "What about the fish, Roger? Do you want him back?"

"You keep him, Alex. You've earned the right."

Alex grinned in delight.

Penalt reached into his duffle bag. "Here, I brought you something. I hope you like it. It's a necklace made of red-tailed hawk talons. The red-tailed hawk is an important bird for the Indian healers in Mexico. It flies high in the sky and watches over the world. The necklace came from a famous healer outside Tijuana."

Alex's eyes opened wide. "Wow! I love it."

He grabbed the necklace and ran out to find his mother. "Mom! Look! Look what Roger brought."

Penalt smiled later as he sat in his office thinking of how he'd been at Alex's age. The phone rang. It was his friend from Yawnix.

"Hey, Roger, how's the desk job?"

Penalt could hear the suspenders snapping in the background. "I'm sorting it all out, thanks."

"So, tell me the truth. What did you find down there?"

"You mean the secret formula you sent me to collect?"

"Of course, what else?"

"I didn't find any."

"None at all?"

"Not a drop. I don't know if it even exists."

"Gee whiz. My sources must have been wrong. Those guys set me up all the time for these impossible tasks. Oh, well, thanks for trying. You certainly stayed down there a long time. How long was it?"

"Maybe a year, I guess."

"Well, let me know when you want another adventure. We owe you that."

"Not right now. I'm going back."

"What? Why?"

"I discovered something about myself there, something I want to pursue."

"Well, you've always been a little goofy. I guess this is goodbye, then."

"Yea, goodbye for now. Hang in there with Yawnix. Someday you'll hit the jackpot and retire rich and maybe even happy."

"God, I hope so. The new wife spends money like water. I always seem to make the same mistake. I'm still paying off debts from the last wife."

Roger hung up, then picked up the pack he'd taken to Mexico and shook it out. A small card fell onto the floor. He reached down to get it. "AT LARGE" was all it said, along with a phone number. On the back, scribbled in smudged ink, he could barely read "San Kuuchamaa." He smiled, turned it around and around in his hand, and threw it away. Yes, he was going back to work with Itandehui. He knew now what that entailed, and he was ready.

"Nelson, how did you know about my dream? I was asleep."

"Okay, look, Jack, this is the last question, right?"

"I promise. Just tell me, how did you know about the dream?"

"You were a blabbering monkey while you were sick, talkin' up a storm, delirious, talkin' in other people's voices too. I wrote everything down, pages and pages. Had nothin' else to do but sit on my ass."

"Where are they, all the pages? What are you going to do with them?"

"I keep 'em in a box. Right now they're in the back of the car. I'd love to get rid of 'em, but I can't seem to let 'em go."

Eric thought carefully. "Okay, this will be the last thing I ask. I promise."

"Glory hallelujah!"

"I want you to give the notes to Devon. I want him to have them."

Nelson breathed a sigh of relief. He was done with the hospital, with that bitch Nurse Marta, and with those "Black that," "Black this" fools who got mixed up with the rich Stanford kids and got arrested. He wasn't going to let them make him a pawn in their game. A few sick-ins and employee strikes at the hospital wouldn't bring any change at all. He knew that. He got out with his nuts intact. That's all he cared about.

"Look, man, I want you to know this. I did my job, did everything I could to help you and to keep that bitch and those goons away. Doctors! They got the gall to call themselves doctors. Shit, man, they were like that Mengele cat you talked about in your dream. I looked him up. He was one crazy fuck, using all them poor folks as guinea pigs. I kept you on the pain meds even though they said not to. I knew what you were goin' through. I'd walk the walk and talk the talk when they watched me, you dig? But I did what I knew was right when they weren't lookin'. They couldn't pay me enough to follow their stupid orders. That got me into some deep shit, but I don't give a fuck. I faked what they said to do, and did what I knowed was best. None of them people scared me. What scared me was knowin' that one day my son would ask: "Hey, what did you do, Daddy, when the shit was goin' down?" "I did the right thing, son." That's what I'm gonna tell him. I did the right thing!"

A minute or two passed.

"You gone, jack? You there? I guess he's gone."

Nelson was crossing the Bay Bridge.

"What was it I was supposed to do for him anyway? Sometimes I can't remember shit."

76.

Devon

Berkeley, California

The fire trucks arrived at the apartment across the street, sirens blaring, bells ringing. Devon's two girls ran up, and Margot jumped into his arms. Leon, Eric's black cat, jumped onto the windowsill to have a look.

"What is it, Daddy? What does it do?"

"It's a fire truck, Shawna. The firemen are here to put out a fire."

But there was no fire. It was a false alarm. The men in yellow suits ran around in circles, then regrouped by the truck, rolled up their hoses, and left. The excitement was over and it was as if nothing had happened, nothing at all.

The doorbell rang, and Devon's wife, Mia, yelled from the back room, "Devon, would you please answer that?"

"Sure. Got it."

When he opened the door, Devon saw a black man smiling and holding a box.

"Hello, Devon. Remember me?"

"Well... yes. You're the man who took care of Eric before he died. Nelson, isn't it?"

"Sure is. You got a good memory, kid, better than your brother. Hey, man, Eric wanted you to have these. They're notes I made of the

540

stuff he said, dream-talk and the like, at the end. I forgot all about them when everything got crazy down there, but here they are at last."

When Nelson handed Devon the box, it was like a heavy weight falling from his shoulders.

"'Goodnight, sweet prince,'" Nelson murmured, "'and flights of angels sing thee to thy rest.'"

Devon looked startled. Nelson gave him a look. "Niggers read too, y'know?" Nelson laughed, and his gold tooth glared in the sun. "Sweets to the sweet."

Devon was puzzled, but he let it pass. "Thanks for going to all the trouble to bring these to me. Anything I can do for you? Do you wanna come in?"

"No trouble at all, man. I should've remembered a long time ago. I can't come in. My wife's waitin' in the car. We're off to start up a new life. I guess you know I got fired from the hospital. I gotta go somewhere where the grass is greener, you dig? You take care now. You had a fine brother, Devon, a real cool cat. He was proud of you, too. He told me so, many times."

"That's very kind of you to say, Nelson. I read about the riots and demonstrations. Sounds like they really screwed you. I'm sorry. You know, when I sent Eric to Stanford, I thought it was the best thing to do. He had this crazy idea to go to Mexico for some quack treatment with Laetrile. His stepmother almost talked him into it. I wonder now if I made the right decision. I'm glad he met you, though. You made his last days comfortable. I appreciate everything you did. Good luck, Nelson!"

They shook hands. Nelson left. Devon went inside to put the box on the kitchen table, leaving the door ajar.

"Who was it, Devon?" Mia asked as she walked into the room.

"It was the man who took care of Eric at the end. He brought a box of notes he made of Eric's ramblings when he was delirious. He thought I might want them."

"What kind of notes?"

"I don't know, I haven't read them. In those last days Eric went on and on about a lot of things."

"What are you going to do with them, the notes?"

"I don't know. Right now I'll just store them away somewhere. Maybe I won't do anything with them. Look, I have to go to a class. I'll leave them in the box for now, and put them away when I get back."

"You should edit those notes and make them into a story. Our girls could read it someday and learn something about their uncle Eric."

Leon jumped onto the kitchen table and began purring and sniffing at the box as if it were full of catnip. He tried to nuzzle the box open with his nose but the top was held tight. Then something extraordinary happened. Leon jumped off the table, ran out the door, and disappeared into a flash of bright sunlight.

77.

A Few Months Later

Yawnix Headquarters

"He got arrested? That friend of yours, what's-his-name?"

"Penalt, Roger Penalt."

"Sonofabitch! Do we have any liability in this?"

"I don't think so, sir. I mean, no, of course not."

"We sent him down there, didn't we?"

"Yes, but he went back later on his own."

"He and that healer lady, Indira or something. They got busted for practicing medicine without a license?"

"Something like that."

"I don't want this to come back and bite us, you hear me? Your job depends on it."

"Yessir. You can count on me, sir."

"Shred everything! I don't want a single record of this anywhere, understand?"

"I understand, sir."

"Next thing you know, those people... those people down there... they're gonna..."

"Don't say anything else, sir. I'm on it. I've got your back. Don't give it another thought.

Whew! That was close. Poor Roger. I wish I could do something to help him, but he's on his own now. What an idiot. What a fucking idiot!

78.

Four Walls Do Not A Prison Make

It took some time for Penalt to find his way around inside La Mesa Penitenciaria. The first day he was placed in a communal cell with a dozen other prisoners, all Mexican. That night he slept on the cement floor where he had to fight off mice, bedbugs, lice, and other bloodsucking bugs he had no names for. He choked on the stench of vomit, urine, and shit that permeated the cell. There was no electricity, no running water or toilet. The prisoners did their business on the floor—and not always in the corner of the room. In the middle of the night, three Mexicans assaulted him, stripped him naked, and tried to force themselves on him. He screamed and fought back, flailed around, scratched and kicked like a wildcat. Luckily for Penalt, he was in the first ward nearest to the guards. A fat, sleepy one stumbled up to the cell, grumbling about the noise. He watched with amusement for a few minutes while Penalt fought desperately to protect his manhood. The guard then banged on the bars with what looked like a cattle prod. Penalt found out later it was an electroshock weapon. The Mexicans retreated to the back of the cell. Penalt pulled up his pants. His shirt and shoes were missing.

The guard extended his chubby hand. "*Propina*." He wanted a tip. Penalt checked his pockets but they were empty.

"*No tengo*." (I don't have any.) "I'll pay tomorrow."

The guard kept him in suspense for a few minutes, then waved the wand at the Mexicans at the back of the cell. Penalt didn't sleep a wink the rest of the night.

The next day he met *El Oyo* (The Eye), who was the "boss" of Ward 1. The name referred to the empty socket filled with mangled red flesh where his right eye should have been. El Oyo had lost the eye in a fight. The prisoners said the eye lived in the walls and floors of La Mesa. Consequently, El Oyo saw everything, knew everything. No one messed with him. He'd lost an eye but he'd killed his opponent, knocked the man down and kicked him to death.

Itandehui was held in the women's section, on the other side of the prison. There were only a few dozen women at La Mesa. They were less violent than the men, but their section was no rose garden. There were prostitutes, drug addicts, and thieves, some of whom were accused of murder. One woman, Paola, with a snaggle tooth and a body like a man's, was the unchallenged boss of the ward.

Because of her age, Itandehui was excused from the daily chores of cooking and washing, sweeping, and cleaning the latrines. When she first arrived and spoke only in her unintelligible Indian dialect, the other women thought she was a *bruja* (witch) until Maite, one of the younger women who knew about her from the outside explained: "No, not a witch, she is a curandera from San Kuuchamaa in the mountains."

"Yeah," growled Paola, "she's here for selling drugs."

"Not drugs," said Maite, speaking softly so as not to rile Paola. "Mushrooms, the ones that make you dream."

On the men's side in La Mesa, fighting happened all the time. The place was a tinderbox, the prisoners always ready to explode. Being surrounded by people they hated, living with them, seeing their faces every day, hearing their voices, smelling their stinking bodies, made fights inevitable, not only between prisoners but also with the guards. The guards and prisoners were always at odds. There is no capital punishment in Mexico, but the guards can kill a prisoner who tries to escape. Any prisoner who crosses a guard will eventually be "caught escaping" and get the *darlos la madre* (the shit beat out of them) or worse.

El Oyo focused his one eye ominously at Penalt. "You be here long time, amigo. You have bad time here. You need protection. You pay me, I protect you."

Penalt walked to the other side of the courtyard where some other American prisoners were standing in a group. Most of them were young and looked more like college students than prisoners. Americans are big business in Mexican jails. The prison had arranged for Western Union to wire money directly there, but the money had to be sent in the name of the "bosses" who ran the wards. Everybody got a cut, from the gang leaders to the ward bosses all the way up to *El Colonel* who ran the prison with an iron fist. The Colonel's job was a political plum paid for with money from extortion, drug dealing, and the free labor of the prisoners.

Penalt had the money to pay the propinas and other bribes, but he knew that paying would make him look weak. He also knew his money wouldn't last forever. Americans in Mexican jails are eventually abandoned, their business partners always the first to bolt. Penalt hadn't received a word from his friend at Yawnix despite the letters he'd sent. It's difficult enough to mail a letter from a Mexican prison, but tougher still to receive one. The American Embassy in Mexico City was no help at all. Under Nixon, the American government wanted only stability from their Latin American neighbors. Ever since Cuba, the fear that communism would take over had caused the Americans to intervene in their neighbors' political affairs only to support the dictators, regardless of the absence of democratic values and human rights. There was no way Nixon and his cronies would risk pissing off the Mexican government for the benefit of a few jailed Americans, especially under the dubious circumstances that had landed them there in the first place.

Most of the women in La Mesa were unfairly incarcerated. They'd been tricked into fraud, had kidnapped their own children, or were victims of witnesses or judges who'd been bribed or coerced. There were a few political prisoners, but most of those were in Mexico City. One woman was pregnant. Many of the imprisoned women were sexually abused by the guards or by male prisoners who bribed the guards to set them up. Itandehui gained the trust of the women prisoners because she treated them when they were injured or sick. This news about her curing abilities reached the Colonel. He sent for Penalt.

"You, gringo. *¿Conoces la curandera?*"

The Colonel spoke only Spanish. He was tall for a Mexican, impeccably dressed and groomed, but beneath the façade, Penalt saw the evil inside the Colonel that had propelled him into his position of importance. Penalt knew instinctively that the Colonel was capable of anything. He would kill on a whim if he were crossed.

"*Si, jefe.* I know Itandehui."

"La Mesa need you, gringo. You and the curandera help us, we help you."

The Colonel's wicked smile and a handshake sealed the deal. This was how Penalt's new life started. He and Itandehui were instructed to work together to care for the prisoners who were sick or the victims of prison violence. At first Penalt didn't understand. It seemed out of character that the Colonel would want to help the prisoners in this way. After some reflection, it made perfect sense: The prison hospital was a dead-weight expense. That cost was reduced by letting Penalt and Itandehui provide medical services to the inmates. The extra money went straight into the Colonel's pocket.

For Penalt it meant a private cell and a few conveniences that he was able to assemble over time. He was not required to participate in the brutal *fajinas* (work details). He had access to a private shower rather than being forced into the *baños* where the prisoners were sprayed down as a group with hot steam followed by freezing-cold water. Some of the Mexican prisoners had never seen a hot shower.

Even on the women's side there were crazies and real criminals. Whenever Paola felt threatened by a new prisoner, she would set one of the crazies on the new girl to see how tough she was. Suspicious of Itandehui because of her "magical powers," Paola thought about killing Itandehui, but with the Colonel's new arrangement, Itandehui was protected. Paola's hands were tied.

The pact between the Colonel and the healers gave Penalt a unique opportunity to learn all of Itandehui's methods. The prison was a war zone, and these poor prisoners had every ailment in the book: torn ligaments, dislocations, brain contusions, welts and bruises, broken bones, staph infections, knife and "suicide" injuries, lost teeth, gouged eyes. One dark, dank cell housed the poorest prisoners, the unfortunates who were like rejects from a freak show. They never saw the sun. They had missing eyes, club feet, deformed limbs, twisted backbones, growths all over their bodies, dry leprosy. It was impossible to heal everyone, but there was plenty to learn from both the successes and the failures. Penalt had no idea how extensive were the cures and medicines Itandehui had at her disposal until he saw her put them into practice.

The Colonel agreed to bring in anything Itandehui needed. This allowed Penalt access to every type of herb or plant or substance Itandehui used over a lifetime of healings. It was a remarkable opportunity, and Penalt spent all his free time cataloguing and describing. While there were strict rules and searches for anything coming into the prison, there were no rules about taking things out, so Penalt sent all his notes and manuscripts to a friend in California who held them for safekeeping. In this way, week by week, Penalt created the first comprehensive guide ever assembled of natural medications and alternative healing techniques.

There is no bail in Mexico. People remain in prison until their innocence is proven or until they've done their time. Penalt and Itandehui had become an important source of income for the Colonel, who was insistent on keeping them in jail full-term. As long as Penalt was learning new things, he wasn't really anxious to leave. Even if the circumstances were a bit strange, he followed his dream in a way he'd never thought possible. There came a time, however, when he wanted to leave La Mesa and publish his work.

It was Ofelia's parents who came to the rescue. In a strange turn of events, they had rehired Hector's father as their gardener after having forgiven him for what he'd done to the family. From his time at La Mesa, Hector's father had witnessed serious abuses of power that put the Colonel at risk. Rogelio met with the Colonel and explained he would take this information to the governor if Penalt and Itandehui were not released.

Not long after that meeting, Penalt was back in California, working on the book he hoped would change the course of medicine forever.

Back in San Kuuchamaa, Itandehui knew her days were numbered. One night she saw Maayhaay, The Great One, and he beckoned her to the mountain. She climbed the trail in the moonlight, and stopped when she reached the pool where she had received the tailfeather of the red-tailed hawk. She soon realized she was not alone. Slowly, out of the darkness, the black jaguar appeared. It sat beside her and nuzzled against her, purring like a kitten.

Later, when the villagers found her, there was nothing left but a few bones scattered around the pond. They buried the bones where they found them. The villagers say that some have seen the bones unearthed, dancing around the pond, but only in their dreams.

79.

After Berkeley

Devon was too busy in the months and then the years after Nelson had given him the notes. He forgot all about them. More years raced by, and with them his life raced by too. Suddenly he was an old man with a bald patch on his head, his daughters married, leaving him alone with nothing to do.

He began to reflect. Why hadn't he put it all down? It would have been fun to fool around with the facts. He could have given Eric a new life with a wife and a child and a whole bunch of crazy experiences. It would've taken hardly any effort at all, but it would all have come to tears, to the bitter moment when he realized he'd been letting his imagination rip. There he would be, sweating and suffering with his heroes, shivers running down his spine, and then it would dawn on him that he'd made it all up, like waking from a dream with sleepers in his eyes and a fuzzy head, then getting hit with the hard, cold facts of another day. He couldn't go with that, not at all.

The last thing Eric saw was Daniel running ahead of Ofelia, the boy's small thin legs pounding up and down like pistons. He lurched to the left, then to the right, then turned and ran back in front of his mother and then behind her. He ran circles around her. Suddenly he stopped, ran up to her, and asked in a breathless voice, "Can you hear my heart? Listen to my heart." And he stood there beside her and waited and waited and waited for her answer.

Epilogue

Eric's story is an imaginary tale about my brother, Errol Miller, who died of cancer in May 1972 at age thirty-three. He planned to go to Mexico for treatment with Laetrile, a substance that we know today is of no medical value. In those days, Laetrile was all the rage among many who had lost faith in the ability of conventional medicine to cure them. The actual letter below from Errol to a friend was the germ that led to the story.

May 1972

Dear P,

"I am home and somewhat happy. I walked out of the hospital one day early—I checked out but refused to stay another day.

"In one of my last tests (air up the rear end and into the intestine) the pain was so bad I actually screamed. I'm telling you this because it is the last time it will happen to me. This is probably the last of the unpleasant letters. I never intended to keep this form of correspondence up anyway—too heavy for you.

"I'm not going through radiation and I'm not going to take drugs that thin my hair out. I'm going to Mexico for therapy. My stepmother, C, had all kinds of information on this when I got home, and almost insisted that I not let any doctor touch me with drugs.

"My appointment in Mexico (clinic just outside Tijuana) is May sixteenth.

"Given my outlook, I have no doubt that I am making the right decision. Under conventional therapy on internal spread the chance of survival according to one source is 1/10,000. On mere logic alone that's enough to give Mexico a chance.

"The information that I have would make you cry if you read it. They do not claim cure and yet, P, they bring some hopeless ones all the way back. Some of the shit that some poor people went through before they got down there is horrible—old people, teenagers, and a pregnant twenty-four-year-old girl—what sad stories.

"The suppression of information by the AMA and the failure of the FDA and Natl Cancer Inst to test this thing is criminal.

"I will soon embark on the greatest adventure I have ever taken in my life. It is imaginative and I like it and besides, I will be with warm people that I have always loved—Mexicans (God bless 'em).

"I will be on the beach a lot and will try to learn Mexican. How long I will be there I do not know. What will happen to me I do not know. Without being too corny, I know I am going to find my destiny and I am not frightened."

Love,

E